GW00469534

BOOKS
AND
BONE

VEO CORVA

First published in 2019 by Witch Key Fiction
Copyright © 2019 Veo Corva

All rights reserved.
This book or any portion thereof may not be reproduced or used
in any manner whatsoever without the express written
permission of the publisher except for the use of brief quotations
in a book review.

*All characters and events in this publication are fictitious and
any resemblance to any real persons, living or dead, is purely
coincidental.*

ISBN: 978-1-9161009-5-4

Veo Corva
Website: https://veocorva.xyz

Witch Key Fiction
Website: https://witchkeyfiction.xyz

Cover art by Anna Pazyniuk (AnnDR)
Website: https://www.deviantart.com/anndr/gallery/

Many thanks to the supporters of the
BOOKS & BONE Kickstarter campaign.

Joh – for saying 'why not necromancers?'

CONTENTS

CONTENTS (continued)

Drawn by rumours of bounteous dead and macabre knowledge, seven necromancers from all across Ard came to the lost crypt of many kings. At the heart of the crypt, they prepared to battle, each intending to claim it for themselves. But a priestess, Arthura, walked among them.

As they gathered their power, a pillar of red spirits screamed down to consume her, and when it cleared, there was a hole straight through her head, as if the goddess of undeath herself stood before them. 'Don't be fools,' she said in the yawning voice of Morrin the Undying. 'This is my city, and I won't have you ruining it. Play nice.'

The necromancers were awed, so when the goddess left her human vessel whole and unharmed, they only battled a little. Thus was Tombtown first settled.

~from *A History of Tombtown* by Emberlon the Disloyal

CHAPTER ONE

THE BOY IN THE CRYPT

There was a boy in the crypt, and he wasn't dead. Ree gripped the doorframe, transfixed by the sight of him as he crouched and muttered to himself. Not an adventurer come to plunder, or an acolyte seeking to disturb the dead, but a boy — curly haired, sepia-skinned, and shockingly, hypnotically alive.

'Rats and rotten luck!' The boy touched the shards of the ceramic jar at his feet. The sound of it shattering had drawn Ree here. He tsked and tutted, sifting through the remnants. 'Oh it's all broken — and over there, look. Drat! It'll take an age to reassemble this.'

Ree had never heard someone with such scattered speech. It made her want to smile — or grimace.

He was in one of the old embalming rooms. Narrow and cold, with rusted tools and dusty jars scattered among the many shelves. A gnarl-legged table stood in the centre, and beneath the grime and moss, Ree could still make out the dark stains of the grisly work it had once seen.

The boy was lit by a flickering torch he'd propped into one of the sconces. Orange light, shifting and angry, made a monster of his shadow. Nobody Ree knew had need of torchlight. Like Ree, they could see in even pitch black — a ritual her father had done for her when she was first born. One of many small magics required to live among the dusty dead, far away from sun and sky.

He shouldn't be here. The thought was intrusive, pushing to the fore of her mind again and again. *He shouldn't be here.* Upworlders only came in two kinds: those that would kill her people, and those that would be killed by them. She had no idea which kind he was.

She ought to run. Let the crypt kill him, before he had a chance to kill her. But though her pulse ran fast, her legs wouldn't move. He looked so different to anyone she'd ever known, so bright and vibrant. Utterly misplaced among the crumbling stone and heavy dust.

Someone leaned over Ree's shoulder, drooling and moaning. 'Not now, Larry!' Ree swatted at the undead man trying to gnaw at her shoulder. Some of his flesh flaked off as he backed up, his yellowed eyes rolling in his head. He didn't groan, which was a mercy, but she couldn't completely repress the spike of guilt as he shook his head in confusion, slack jaw lolling.

Inside the room, the boy was still thinking aloud. 'Come now,' he said. 'You're the foremost burial scholar in the Grand University — surely you can identify a few gooey remains without the accompanying script.' His accent was strong and strange to Ree — full of the nasal twang of the upworlder upper class, much like old Emberlon's, the town archivist and her teacher.

He shouldn't be here; she shouldn't be here. But Ree's curiosity had always been terrible. She eased into the room on soft-soled boots, the split skirt of her dusty robes swishing around her legs. She had a better look at him now — bespectacled, in a plain, fine-clothed shirt and trousers, a much-mauled leather satchel hanging from his shoulder. He might be eighteen or nineteen, only a few years older than her.

He didn't *look* dangerous. Odd, maybe — but then, what was odd to a necromancer's daughter?

He poked gingerly at the jellified organ mulch at his feet. 'Brain!' he said confidently. He drew a journal and pen from his pack and began to scribble.

Ree wrinkled her nose and made a decision. 'That's clearly liver,' she said. The boy yelped and scrambled back along the floor, knocking into the embalming table. A rusty hook fell from the surface and bounced from his shoulder to ping across the stone bricks. The torchlight glittered against his glasses.

The boy rummaged in his pack. 'Stay back, undead creature!' He drew a solid iron sarakat from his pack and held it out as if to ward her off. It was the twisting, tree-shaped religious symbol of some upworlder life god or other. Hard to imagine what protection he hoped to gain from it.

Probably not dangerous. The boy, nor the sarakat.

Ree raised her eyebrows.

The boy lowered the sarakat slightly. 'Pardon me, but … you are an undead creature, aren't you?'

'I'm Ree,' said Ree, because she didn't know how to respond to 'you're an undead creature'.

It was also completely unfair. In a town full of necromancers, she looked the *least* undead. Long exposure to death from life in the crypts had made her skin a bit ashen, and maybe there were dark smudges around her eyes, but as she wasn't a practitioner, the changes were minor. She noted again his flushed cheeks and bright eyes. Maybe not minor compared to *him.*

Larry stumbled through the doorway.

'Ah!' The boy raised his sarakat again. Larry shuffled toward him, arms outstretched. 'Ah! Get back, you fiend!'

'*That's* an undead creature.' Ree straightened as the boy cowered away. She gave Larry a shove; he toppled, gargling as he went.

The boy scrambled to his feet and sidled to the opposite side of the room, keeping the wall at his back. As if Larry was a ghoul or a sentinel, or any kind of greater undead, instead of a mindless, masterless minion.

The boy's eyes flicked to Ree. 'You *pushed* him.' Larry groaned and flailed, drawing the boy's gaze once more. 'Is he alright, do you think?'

Ree's eyebrows twitched. 'Barely a breath ago, you called him a fiend.'

'Yes. Well.' He cleared his throat. 'Will he get up again?'

Ree watched Larry kicking his legs like a turtle flipped on its back. 'Eventually.' She glanced at the boy; his wide-eyed terror was softening into confusion.

'Aren't undead creatures meant to be dangerous?'

Ree shrugged. 'Most are. Larry isn't.'

'Larry?'

Ree crossed her arms, beginning to regret her curiosity. She wasn't used to this much conversation. And certainly not with a stranger. She darkened her expression, hoping to make her discomfort look like power, as her father would. 'Do you have a name?' She asked it as imperiously as she could.

'Uh … yes, of course. Terribly rude of me — I'm Chandrian Smythe, Third Rank Historian at the Grand University and the foremost burial scholar in the southern reaches.' This formality seemed to have brought him back to himself; he puffed up his chest.

Ree wasn't certain he ought to be proud. She'd not met many scholars before — certainly not those who didn't practice the Craft — but it was hard to be impressed by someone who couldn't tell a jellified brain from a jellified liver. After all, this was a third era embalming room — third era culture ate the brains of their dead to preserve their souls, and embalmed the bodies to preserve the spirit. She'd played with enough embalming jars in her childhood to know there wouldn't be any brains in this sector of crypts.

Ree smoothed her robes and sat down on a heavy urn in the corner. 'What are you doing here?'

The boy, Smythe, blustered a moment. 'I — well, I'm a historian! I'm doing some very important excavation work. I have plenty of reason to be here. The real question is what are *you* doing here?'

He asked it as if he were speaking to another upworlder. Ree's cheeks heated. 'I live here.' She nearly mumbled the words, relieved that her grey-tinged skin wouldn't show her blush.

Larry managed to roll onto his side. He started to gnaw the table leg.

'You shouldn't do that, Larry, you'll ruin what's left of your teeth.'

'Live *here,*' said Smythe.

'Or hereabouts.'

Smythe took out his journal again. 'How did you end up here? You must be terribly lonely.'

Ree frowned. 'Not especially.' She didn't completely understand the concept. There had always been plenty of people around, even if they tended to ignore each other. And there were always the dead. Honestly, she spent a large portion of her time travelling so she could get *away* from all of them.

'Did you run away from home? Or get lost from a — a merchant caravan, perhaps. Festering rats —' he looked like something awful had just occurred to him, '— you weren't abandoned here, were you?'

'No, of course not.' Ree glared. She didn't like the way he was looking at her — like she was equal parts pitiable and fascinating — not unlike the reaction children had to Wandering Larry. Her parents had been among the first settlers of the crypt, and she was proud of her heritage. 'I was born here.'

There was a moment of silence and indrawn breath broken only by the sound of Larry howling as he chipped a tooth.

Ree sighed and stood up. 'Look, you really shouldn't be here. Even if the undead don't kill you, an adventurer won't think twice before running you through, and we do seem to get a lot of them. That's what I came to tell you — that you should leave, and that you won't find any brains in a third era embalming room. That's just common sense.'

That, and she'd so badly wanted to see the boy — a living upworlder boy who wouldn't stab her as soon as look at her. Her cheeks heated again, and before Smythe could ask any more questions, she fled into the musty corridor.

'Wait! Where are you going?'

Ree skipped up onto a crate and hauled herself onto a thick wooden crossbeam just as Smythe skidded into the corridor, torch in hand. She crouched above, holding her breath as he looked each way and scratched his head. He picked a direction and started to jog, running beneath her crossbeam and down the corridor, torchlight surrounding him in a flickering orange globe.

Ree put her back to cold stone, breathing deeply. She'd done more than anyone would ask of her. She'd given him a solid warning, and once he realised she was gone, he would surely pack up his things and head back upworld. Given his reaction to Larry, she didn't think he'd have a taste for the night horrors and guardians that wandered the crypts, so it shouldn't take him long to come to his senses.

She swung herself down from the crossbeam and landed lightly on the stone floor. She cringed as she landed, imagining how much better it would be if she were as light as a cat or as graceful as a cave spider. She tracked back down the other side of the corridor and squeezed through a damaged bit of wall that let her into one of the resting rooms, stacked with corpses on stone shelves like children in bunk beds. As she passed, a pale hand reached for her. 'None of that,' she said absently.

She took a pinch of herbs from the pouch at her belt and threw it in the creature's face. The corpse withdrew its hand and stilled. Though she had never desired to learn the Craft and had no power over the dead, she'd learned some priestess tricks from her mother — such as using the herbs, fluids, and sometimes incense used to prepare corpses to calm lesser undead.

If she'd had the Craft, like her father, she could turn them with an exertion of will. If she'd been a healer, like her mother, she could destroy them in a pulse of warm light. But she'd not chosen either of her parents' fields, and without magic, the best she could do was trick them into sleep with prayers and plants — and when that failed, flee.

Her thoughts turned again to the upworlder. Smythe had been a bit rude, calling her an undead creature. Not that she didn't get mistaken for one from time to time, but she'd never been called one by someone her own age. By someone who wasn't trying to kill her. She flushed at the thought — that he'd looked at her and mistaken her for a corpse. It was true that denizens tended to look a little greyer and more hollow-eyed than upworlders, but she'd always thought she looked very normal, for a denizen. She was stockier and stronger than anyone she knew — physical fitness being a necessity for life in the crypts without magic. That was a *healthy* look, surely.

'I'm seventeen,' she said to one of the corpses. 'Do I look old and rotten to you?'

It gazed lifelessly at the stone above it. Ree sighed and rubbed her eyes.

It didn't matter what some random boy thought she looked like. Certainly not one so stupid as Smythe. 'Right.' She shook herself and drew a long breath. Smythe was almost certainly gone by now. It was time to collect Larry and head back into the eastern archives, where she'd been sorting books before Smythe had drawn her out. 'Rest well,' she advised the room of corpses. Her father would point out that her words meant nothing to the dead; her mother would remind her that she owed the dead her respect.

Her eyes lingered on those faces, slack with death, wrapped lovingly centuries before in treated bandages to preserve their physical forms. For those above, the sight of them would elicit fear or disgust, but for Ree there was only a sense of warm familiarity edged with caution. She was not a necromancer like her father and nearly everyone she had ever known. But there was no-one who loved the crypt as she did. None who had explored it as deeply, nor plumbed as many of its secrets. There was no-one who had a stronger claim on it.

And she knew that there was no place here for someone like Chandrian Smythe.

She eased back through the crack in the wall into the previous corridor, smoothed the creases from her robes, and followed the slow, shuffling sound of dragged feet. It wasn't long before she caught sight of the shambling creature, with his cobweb hair and green-tinged skin. 'Larry,' she called. She snapped her fingers.

Larry turned ponderously, arms swinging like pendulums, and shuffled toward Ree, drool pooling at the corners of his lolling mouth.

They called him Wandering Larry, though who had first named him, Ree didn't know. He was an anomaly, a minion without a master, but he was a harmless one. He'd been here before the town was founded, bumbling after this person or that, pathetically failing in his attempts to eat people. As the first child born in the crypt, Ree had grown up with him. She was equal parts fond of him and frustrated by him, like an old, smelly, family dog.

Now that he'd caught her scent again, he would reliably follow her back to town. She set off down the corridor, up a spindly staircase and up a crumbling stone wall, trailed by the putrescent Larry. It felt good to be moving again; it loosened something in her brain, as if her thoughts had been lodged by a hard rock and could now flow freely.

At times like this, she usually thought about her personal research. This place in her mind — and in her journal, tucked safely in her pack — was solely for her. It was as much a promise as a comfort. One day, when her research was complete, everyone would be forced to acknowledge her power. They would be more polite when they asked her to fetch books *then.*

And yet the river of her thoughts kept winding back over and over to the moment she revealed herself. *'Pardon me, but ... you are an undead creature, aren't you?'*

Ree gritted her teeth. She dropped from a ledge into a shallow pit, old bones crunching under her feet. She stepped aside just as Larry landed on his face, flailing among the bones. Ree sighed and flicked a knucklebone from her collar. 'It's more than a little insulting,' she murmured. While Larry struggled, she pulled herself up on the other side.

She tried to think of herself as other people saw her. Stocky build, sickly skin, shadowed brown eyes, and with dark hair pinned and trapped beneath her hood. Unremarkable among the denizens. Maybe unremarkable anywhere.

She'd never put much thought into her appearance. It wasn't like people spent a lot of time *looking* at her. And on the rare occasion she attracted a snide comment, it had slipped from her mind without care. But it was different this time. She would grit her teeth and force her mind to other things, and yet it still kept circling back. The look of horror on his face ...

They carried on their journey upwards, across a rattling bridge and along the side of a steep black ravine. 'Think about it, Larry. It's not like I march into people's homes and compare them to monsters or goblins. I bet when you were alive, you wouldn't have put up with that.'

Larry gargled at her and tried to bite her arm. She shook him off with an admonishing tap on his forehead. 'It doesn't matter.' Ree turned the corner. 'I don't care —'

Ree froze midstep, panic seizing her muscles as surely as a healer's spell. Cold pierced her like an arctic wind. Her gaze locked with white marble eyes in a translucent-skinned face, mere feet from her own. Horror clung to Ree like sweat.

She reached for her father's training, for the mental wards that would protect her, but she couldn't tear her eyes away from its pale gaze and already she could feel herself disappearing into it as if caught in a blizzard.

The Lich leaned closer. It was a pale, man-like thing that hovered an inch above the ground, robes swirling like tentacles. Its breath rattled through peeled-back lips and its long-nailed fingers reached for her, slowly.

There was only one being in the crypt with such tangible, arresting power. It had been a necromancer, once. So old and so far-gone into the Craft that it had forgotten how to be human. It was the biggest monster of the crypts, but also its most powerful protector — so long as nobody crossed its path.

Ree's chest squeezed. She leaned away from the Lich, torn between the danger of getting caught and the danger of running. A lifetime of her parents' warnings drummed in her mind, a constant litany of *'Don't get caught. Don't let it see. Do not disturb the dead.'*

And now, just as they'd always warned, she could feel the air grow heavy with tiredness as its magic pooled around her. Her eyelids drooped, her body sagged.

It spread its arms wide. *'Imaz kwizzat?'* it whispered, with magic as dry as parchment. *'Kwizzat erd vizzin?'*

Its power pressed on her, leeching energy from body and mind. She felt exhausted by it all; by her life in the catacombs, by her fear of the Lich, the constant twitchy thoughts of whether to run or hide. It would be so much easier to give in …

'Don't close your eyes. Don't fall asleep. Don't forget you're alive.'

Its arms started to close around her, a cold embrace with the overpowering smell of dust. She heard it chanting the words of binding even as its magic drained the life from her and let it bleed into the stone. It was just so very hard to care …

'I say, Ree, is that a friend of yours?'

Smythe's cultured, upworlder accent shocked Ree out of her stupor. She reeled back, even as the Lich whirled and glided toward this new intruder, death magic trailing it like red mist.

'Run!' Ree shouted, but her tongue was thick and sluggish.

'Wha —?' Smythe froze as the Lich rose up in front of him, the tatters of its robes swirling about it in slow motion as if underwater.

Adrenaline surged; Ree leapt for Smythe, but the Lich was already sliding one withered hand under his chin.

Smythe stared into its marble eyes. 'I — I beg your —'

'*Erd.*' The word curled in the air. Smythe's eyes rolled up into his head and he collapsed to the floor.

The Lich started chanting; Ree snatched at Smythe's hands, steeling her mind to the Lich's cloying necromancy. The Lich reached for her and its magic pressed down on her, a suffocating force. As lethargy set in, she savagely bit her lip; pain seared as hot blood poured down her chin, reminding her she was alive.

She tried to drag Smythe away but he was heavy, made all the more so with the Lich's eyes on them. She just needed a moment, just to get Smythe out of its sight ...

Larry shambled in, groaning forlornly. The Lich's back straightened; its nostrils flared. It turned slowly on the spot to face Larry.

Its magic faded along with its attention. Ree seized her moment. She grabbed Smythe, cursing him for his considerable weight even as she fought the tail of the Lich's lethargy. She dragged him behind a stack of crates, her pulse pounding in her throat. Escape routes flashed through her mind: the drainage tunnel at the back, the trap door beneath the southern wall, but she could take advantage of none of these without abandoning Smythe, who was even now rapidly paling, his skin growing as clammy as a corpse.

She ought to leave him. What was he to her, really, this boy from the world above?

This boy who had saved her life.

When the Lich turned back from Larry to find his quarries missing, Ree held her breath. His white marble eyes swept the room, and Ree pressed further back behind the crate. Then, the energy in the room eased; the Lich folded its magic back into itself. It hunched in, and the light in its eyes died. It crooked a finger at Larry, almost an invitation, but the minion only gawped at it. Its arm dropped; it glided from the room as if nothing had ever happened.

Ree peered out from behind the box, her entire body tensed to flee. Larry spotted her, gargled what might have been delight, and tottered toward her. Ree slumped in relief.

Larry bumped into her shoulder and she patted his leg fondly. 'You did well, Larry.'

He tried to nibble her hair, and she swatted him away.

Though the immediate danger had passed, it was hard to let the tension from her body. They had come so close to a fate worse than death; to be a minion of an immortal Lich, forever enslaved.

She had lived under the threat of the Lich for as long as she could remember. How many times had she watched it from afar as it searched through the archives or chanted its rituals? It had always seemed to her some kind of sinister automaton, but its danger had felt contained, its threat unreal. It lived its life on rails, unaware of anything that didn't directly interrupt it. She'd been taught its schedule, where to avoid and when. It had become familiar. She had almost felt fond of it.

Now, she trembled from the memory of its magic. Larry touched her head with his clammy hands, groaning piteously. Bizarre to think that if he'd been following anyone else today, Ree would now be dead — or undead.

Her gaze fell on Smythe. His chest barely rose and all colour had drained from his face. 'And what am I supposed to do with you?' Ree murmured. Larry leaned around her, drool dangling from his open mouth. 'Okay, Larry, I need you to — no, don't chew on him! Just hold still ...'

The denizens of Tombtown were loathe to chain themselves with rules and regulations. In those early days, they agreed on only one: no outsiders, unless they were fellow necromancers. They had all been ill-used by those of the world above, and intended the crypt to be their sanctuary. But six years after founding, that law would be put to the test when a healer of considerable power descended into the crypt.

After disintegrating the defending minions with a single fell blast of magic like sunlight, she put her lone hand on her hip. 'I'm building a house. Don't bother me.'

The necromancers were awed, so when the healer settled in their town, they only bothered her a little. The law was given a very small addendum: no outsiders, unless they were fellow necromancers — or otherwise too powerful to chase out.

If there is one thing all necromancers can be trusted to respect, it is power.

~from *A History of Tombtown* by Emberlon the Disloyal

CHAPTER TWO

THE TOWN HEALERS

Girl and minion dragged Smythe's limp body through dusty tunnels and crumbling halls, right into the heart of the town: the central mausoleum. There, winding between tombhomes and with a worried eye over her shoulder, Ree smuggled Smythe into her house without catching the attention of curious necromancers. She panted from the effort, her hair plastered to her forehead.

Now, she stood before the tall, wan form of one of the only other non-practitioners in town, not quite meeting her eyes.

'You've brought home a dying man? Such a dutiful daughter.' Ree's mother's lips quirked, the iciness in her eyes melting minutely. She stalked around the body sprawled across her kitchen table, darting gaze taking in the colour in his skin, the healthy fullness of his cheeks. Her fur cloak flared as she walked; her cassock scritched along the floor.

They stood in the family tombhome, a repurposed small stone tomb that her family had lived in since the town had first been settled some nineteen years earlier. With exposed stone-brick walls, scratched marble floors, and aged furniture padded with limp cushions, it had a certain 'small-town cemetery' charm — and gravemould smell. The uncluttered serenity of home.

Ree squared her shoulders, trying to push away the discomfort she always felt when her mother went into priestess-mode. While her father was on the town council and so deep into the Craft that he barely looked human anymore, he was a steady and predictable force in her life — if not always a positive one. Her mother, though, with her brittle mane of ash blonde hair, the eyes of a fanatic, and a manner that shifted between eerie priestess and hard-hearted huntress, was something else entirely. Ree trusted her mother, but she never knew quite what to expect from her. Such was the trouble of a mother who was also the Priestess of Morrin the Undying.

Ree took a deep breath while her mother peeled Smythe's eyelids back and peered into his rolled-back eyes. 'Mother, I need —'

'What twist of fate led you to an upworlder boy? No — nevermind. I know better than to question what Morrin provides. You can help me with the burial rights — the goddess prefers them with a little life left.' She pinched Smythe's wrist to take his pulse, then let it fall again. Smythe's lips moved, mumbling unintelligibly.

Ree's stomach lurched with something between hope and dismay. 'He's not for sacrifice, he's —'

Ree's mother cupped her cheek, the rough cloth of her cassock sleeve scratching her skin. Ree jumped at her touch; an unexpected show of affection. 'We'll have to move quickly if we're to get him to the Altar of Many Gods before your father returns.'

Smythe moaned something that sounded a little like 'fascinating', his head turning.

'*Mother.*' Ree mimicked her father's tone of command, wishing she could imitate the crack of power that went with it. She couldn't quite suppress a sigh when her mother stopped, her head tilting to one side. She was so tired of being spoken over, even within her own family. 'I intend to save him,' she said.

Her mother's eyebrows lifted. 'Save *him,*' she repeated. The disbelief in her voice encompassed a hundred questions.

'I owe him.' Ree rubbed her eyes. 'Look, it's … sort of a long story.' And if she revealed the Lich's part in it, she would be in a world of trouble. The town council forbade interacting with the Lich, for fear that it might follow someone back to the town. 'Can you heal him?'

Her mother clasped her hands in front of her. 'There's no shame or dishonour in letting the dead pass, Reanima.' Her voice was gentle, reassuring, but Ree wouldn't meet her eyes. 'It is the natural order of the world. The living die, and their souls pass into the keeping of the gods. The bodies are exalted and put to service of the living. You may not practice, like your father, but you know it's true.'

She wanted to snap at her mother that she could make up her own mind. That Smythe wasn't dead yet, and Morrin was welcome to him when he was. But an argument would get her no closer to saving him, so she stored it away in the black pit in her chest where she kept all her resentments. 'Can you heal him?' she repeated as evenly as she could.

Ree's mother pursed her lips. 'Possibly. But the town council will be furious if they hear. Did anyone see you bring him?'

Ree shook her head. She'd used all her knowledge of secret pathways to get him into town unnoticed.

Ree's mother shrugged off her patchy fur cloak and rolled up the voluminous sleeves of her brown cassock. She hovered her hands over him, closing her eyes; white light shone through her skin and limned Smythe where he lay. Warmth pulsed from her in a heartbeat rhythm.

Even under a death curse, Smythe looked out of place in Ree's home. The old stone walls of what had once been a small tomb were cold and dull, the marble floor carpeted not in fabric but in straw and moss and hardy cave mushrooms. Bricks had been pulled from the walls in places, and filled with pottery and urns taken from the surrounding tombs. Once great treasures or works of art, now they held food or trinkets, the odds and ends of daily life. The furniture, largely made of reclaimed crate wood or scavenged from embalming rooms, was old and rickety, and frequently scattered with knuckle bones or femurs, such as Ree's father required for his Craft.

Amongst the grey and green, and the flickering light cast by the tallow candles, Smythe looked altogether too alive, jarringly vibrant amongst the gloom.

Ree's mother's eyebrows pinched together. 'This is no normal curse. It's knit deep into him, hooked into his bones. Do you know what cursed him?'

Ree crossed her arms. She didn't want to tell her mother about the encounter with the Lich if she could possibly avoid it. The town council would be nothing compared to the fear and anger of her worried parents. That she had been so foolish as to walk directly into his path was bad enough; that she had dragged this buffoon with her was beyond careless.

Her mother took her silence for uncertainty. 'It must have been a greater dead, at least. Maybe even a greywraith.' Her lips pursed. She'd named a minion so powerful that few could summon one — a creature of rags and grey flesh, only half-corporeal. The essence of a body, pure and dangerous, with none of the physical drawbacks of a minion like Larry. But nothing compared to the Lich.

The trouble Ree would be in if her parents found out she'd crossed the Lich didn't bear thinking about. They'd try to force her into learning the Craft, and that didn't suit Ree at all. Once you started using a school of magic — necromancy or healing — you were locked in. And Ree had other plans.

Her thoughts flickered uneasily, torn between the boy she owed and her determination to continue her study at all costs.

Ree's mother turned from Smythe and considered her daughter. 'How much do you like this boy?'

Ree shuffled her feet. She didn't like where this was going. 'I just met him.'

The light faded from Ree's mother, gradually returning her to her wan, haggard self. Her eyes were solemn as she considered her daughter. 'I haven't the skill to save him. He'll die on this table before the day is out. We could take him to Andomerys ...' She trailed off, but Ree knew where the sentence ended.

They could take him to Andomerys, but then the whole town would know. And that was dangerous in an entirely different way.

If Andomerys even agreed to save him.

Ree's mother wasn't concerned about the danger to Smythe. She was only thinking of the trouble it would mean for Ree. Ree would have to face the wrath of the town council, and she'd always gone out of her way to avoid their ire.

There were very few rules that a town full of necromancers would agree on, but Ree had broken the only one that mattered: no outsiders allowed. If the upworlders found out about Tombtown, it would bring disaster (or worse, *priests)* down on all their heads.

It would be a blow for her. Another reason for her parents to claim she was helpless and the council to call her clueless, an outsider in her own town. They might finally force her to learn the Craft, as they had been threatening for years, as if being a practitioner would somehow give her better judgement.

And, of course, they would kill Smythe.

She looked at Smythe, greying and shallow-breathed. He might not even live. What did it matter that he'd taken a curse meant for her? It would be a mercy to die quietly now, before the council got their claws into him.

Ree scowled and scrubbed at her face. 'We'll use the back stairs,' she said.

Her mother canted her head to one side, as if Ree had surprised her. Ree shrugged off her scrutiny.

Smythe was all arms and legs as they bundled him out the door and dragged him up the back stairs, no doubt adding several back-bruises to whatever lumps and bumps he'd received when Ree and Larry first hauled him into town.

'Morrin's teeth! He's gangly as a spider.' Ree's mother puffed with the effort of carrying him.

Smythe's back hit another step; he grunted, and mumbled, 'foremost burial scholar at the biggest ...' He trailed off into incoherence.

Ree's mother wrinkled her nose. 'Urgh. There's no shame in letting him pass beyond, Ree. He'll be welcomed into Her court.'

'*Mother.*'

Her mother made a snorting sound that Ree interpreted as 'you can stop using that tone on me', but they eventually heaved him up the final flight of moss-strewn steps and laid him in front of the door of a crumbling wooden shack — the only true 'house' in the whole town.

There was a story behind its construction. There was a story for almost every house in the town, of course, and Ree had been present for most of them. But though this wooden shack was an intimidating replica of upworld society, Ree was much more interested in the woman who had built it.

Ree scanned the town behind them, stretching below in a honeycomb of repurposed tombs and altars. Robed figures milled about the town square, and a cabal oversaw a small horde of minions at the northern passage, but there was nobody close enough to question why Ree and her mother were dragging around a body that was still breathing.

'Andomerys!' Ree's mother rapped on the door. 'My daughter requires your assistance. Perhaps for once, you will not shirk your sacred calling!'

Ree nudged her mother. 'Maybe don't antagonise her, since we're asking her for help?'

'The Goddess asks us to live as honestly in life as we will in death.' Ree's mother sniffed.

Andomerys yanked the door open. Her rosy cheeks glowed with health, her skin a warm brown. Her thickly curled hair made a dark halo about her head. One arm ended at the elbow. She wore robes of ocean blue, and though Ree had known her since she was a small child, it never stopped being shocking how vital and bright she appeared. Her scowl, however, was plenty dark. 'Arthura. Ree.' She looked down. 'A body.' She nodded, as if confirming something to herself, and slammed the door in their faces.

Ree's mother immediately banged on the door again. 'You *dare* slam a door in the face of Morrin's chosen?'

A muffled bark of laughter was her only answer.

'Mother —'

'Morrin as my witness, you *will* show me respect —'

'Mother!' Ree tugged sharply at her mother's sleeve.

The priestess stopped and blinked at her, the red rage fading from her eyes. Healers rarely looked as necromantic as Ree's mother — but then, few were also priestesses of undeath.

'I can handle this,' said Ree. 'Go home.'

Her mother's gaze shifted from her, to Andomerys' door, then back again. Her lips parted as if to argue, but she only inclined her head and swept away.

Leaving Ree on Andomerys' doorstep with a dying man at her feet and no clue how to gain the healer's help.

Andomerys was the most powerful healer Ree had ever heard of, with reserves of magic so deep that she had passed into legend. But thirteen years ago, she'd fled the surface and made it clear that she was leaving healing behind.

Townsfolk came to her with everything from cursed hearts to broken limbs, but she turned almost everyone away.

Ree did not consider herself a persuasive person, but the stakes were high. She liked Andomerys; maybe Andomerys liked her too. She could only hope it would be enough.

She leaned against the door. 'Andomerys?'

No answer.

'It's just me. I sent mother away.' She paused a moment, then continued, 'You're probably at least a *little* curious as to how I came across an upworlder.'

Footsteps. The door creaked open. 'You finally went to the surface on your own?'

Andomerys had encouraged her, over the years, to seek companionship in the upworld. *'There's a world of opportunity up there, for a smart girl with her wits about her,'* she'd said. *'You wouldn't have to be the bottom of the heap then.'*

'I won't always be the bottom.' Ree's tone had been conspiratorial. *'There are other kinds of power —'*

'Ugh.'

'Well, it's not like you liked it up there either.'

Andomerys' eyes had grown distant. *'I liked it plenty. Nobody chooses to hide away, Ree. Not even necromancers.'*

Now, Ree grimaced at the healer. 'Of course I didn't. But I did talk to him a little. He seems ... different.'

Andomerys' expression didn't flicker. 'Different.'

Ree shifted her weight. '... Nice.' She paused. 'He saved my life. Please, Andomerys.'

'I won't heal him.'

'Will you at least look at him?' She looked down at Smythe, muttering at her feet. The curse was slowly leeching the colour from his skin. He looked faded, like a painting left too long in the sun. It was an effect she'd found fascinating on her excursions to the surface with her father for supplies, but it was disconcerting on a human. 'I don't even know whether he *could* be saved.'

'Ree ...' They locked gazes, cold brown eyes meeting warm. Andomerys made a sound like a cat guarding its dinner. 'I'll look, all right? Just look.'

Hope bloomed in Ree, strong enough to choke. 'Thank you.'

'I don't need your thanks.' Andomerys looked away. 'I doubt I'll do anything to deserve it.'

The seven founding necromancers set themselves up as a town council to settle disputes among the denizens and to intimidate unruly necromancers into obedience. As necromancers naturally form into cabals under more powerful practitioners, this shape of governance worked with little rebellion.

As of the time of writing, only three of the seven founding council members have been executed for treason and mutiny.

This success is much celebrated, and at solstices, the tortured souls of the offending council members are summoned to warn young denizens of the dangers of trying to grab too much power. It is a delightful tradition and a favourite of children.

~from *A History of Tombtown* by Emberlon the Disloyal

CHAPTER THREE

STRONG-WILLED INDEED

Andomerys' house was like the woman herself: full of bright draperies and busy carpets, an explosion of colour that Ree found eye-watering but wonderful. Cushions and blankets were cast about, each crafted from old but expensive fabric that was soft to the skin and gleamed in the candlelight. Clear relics from her life on the surface.

Now, that same woman hustled Ree, begrudgingly, through her house.

'Through the back, through the back — and try not to drop him!' The healer used her hand and arm to help manoeuvre Smythe around her armchair.

Ree had seen the back room a few times before that she could remember — once, when she had crushed her leg when the floor in one of the towers collapsed, and once when she'd accidentally awakened a slumbering knight and he'd cut her across the middle. Andomerys had broken her no-healing rule to save a child. It looked just as it had then — white stone walls and a meticulously clean steel table, with a cabinet of cruel-looking tools to one side. Ree wondered what it said about Andomerys that she had come here to give up healing but had built a healer's room and filled it with equipment.

'Not a delicately built fellow, is he?' said Andomerys.

'Very important discoveries,' Smythe mumbled. 'You must take me serious-largh ...'

Ree narrowed her eyes at him. Somehow, he couldn't stop talking even when unconscious. 'Humble, too.'

They hustled Smythe onto the healer's table. His head lolled at the movement. Andomerys looked him over, hovering her hand and her short arm over the patient. Now, a golden light suffused her, just as it had Ree's mother, but Andomerys' light was brighter, warmer, transforming the sterile stone cube into a sunroom. Ree gritted her teeth against the force of it. The heat was slick and humid against her skin.

'A powerful curse.' Andomerys' gaze flicked up to Ree, as if she knew Ree had had something to do with it. 'If it had been completed, I doubt he'd have lasted this long.'

'But?'

The light around Andomerys pulsed, then faded. 'He's resisting. He must have a strong will indeed.'

Smythe's head whipped to the other side. 'I demand to speak to your superior,' he mumbled.

Andomerys raised her eyebrows. 'Or maybe just a strong ego.'

Ree's eyes widened and she looked at Smythe uncertainly. 'Strong-willed' seemed a poor description of the bumbling scholar. Perhaps he had hidden depths. She bit her lip. Very hidden.

'So.' Andomerys leaned against the healing table. 'You tangled with the Lich.'

Ree's mouth dried. If the healer told Ree's parents or the town council, it would mean more trouble for Ree than just an upworlder could bring. Bringing an upworlder home would make her look foolish. Angering the Lich would make her a liability — and necromancers tended to kill those pretty quickly. With effort, she nodded, her thoughts racing for an explanation.

Andomerys cursed and rubbed her eyes. 'Don't look at me like I'm your executioner, young Ree. I won't tell if I don't have to, but I know the Lich's work when I see it. You understand?'

Ree nodded. Andomerys would only tell if Ree had upset the balance — if encountering the Lich had somehow woken it up and drawn it back to the town.

Do not disturb the dead, her parents always told her. It was her one true rule, a mantra never to be forgotten. It was why she kept a pouch of herbs on her belt, her mother's prayers on her lips, and an amulet full of her father's magic against her heart. All the denizens of Tombtown put together couldn't hope to stand against the Lich if it woke up the entire crypt and brought judgement down upon them. This was their home, but it belonged first and last to the dead. She must never forget that.

If she'd started learning the Craft at sixteen, as the other teenage denizens did, and as her father urged, she might not have to be so wary. But her sixteenth birthday had come and gone, and then her seventeenth, and now her father could barely look at her, and her mother thought her odd.

But there were other kinds of power. Forgotten magics so old that they'd passed into myth. She thought of her research journal, hidden away where nobody would ever find it, and drew some strength from it.

But if she'd learned the Craft like her parents wanted, she might have been able to protect Smythe, at least a little ...

Andomerys narrowed her eyes. 'Take that hangdog look outside. I need a moment to study him properly — so I can send you in the right direction, if there's help to be had. *Not to heal him myself.*' She waved Ree away, crushing the spike of hope her words had created.

So Ree sat on the crumbling step in front of Andomerys' house and rested her chin in her hands. Her mind was on Smythe, crouching over shattered ceramics, lying cold and grey on Andomerys' table. She thought about his shock on meeting her, about him following her into the Lich's path, about Andomerys' words: *'He must have a strong will indeed.'*

How strong-willed did you have to be to resist a curse from something more powerful than all the denizens put together?

Down below, a group of young acolytes about her age had dragged in a wolf carcass and were setting up a ritual to raise it. Across from them, Mazerin the Bold, a weedy little necromancer, had set up his weekly Bone Market stall and was trying to coax the acolytes into buying some of his fresh scry-bones. It all looked so normal, such a sleepy, small-town scene, that it might have sent Ree off into the deepest, unexplored levels of the crypt just to bring some excitement into her life. But right now, Ree didn't feel normal. Bees buzzed in her head and anxiety pecked at her belly like angry birds.

She'd never had much cause to worry about other people. Larry was already dead, her parents were as dangerous as anything else in the crypts, and Emberlon was as careful as she was. In truth, she'd always lived in a world where people were worried for *her.*

In Smythe's case, she couldn't decide whether she was worried for him, or worried what he might cause. But for better or worse, she'd brought an upworlder into the town. Now, all she could do was wait.

She fished in her pack for something to occupy her twitchy hands. First, a piece of rat jerky, salty and hard between her teeth. Then her research journal, which she dared not get out in plain sight, full of animal sketches and half-drawn spell diagrams. Instead, she pulled out book she'd been collecting for Uzma Plaguebringer, a denizen with a special interest in animal minions. She leafed through it, liking the feel of the heavy parchment between her fingers. Most of it was written in old Antherian, a language dead to any but necromancers, who used it in their Craft. Ree was fluent enough, but all the talk of necromancy made her eyes roll back in her head. She returned it to her pack just as the door behind her creaked open.

She leapt to her feet. 'Andomerys!'

The healer frowned. She looked more worn than Ree had ever seen her, though her skin almost glowed, as if she were still casting now. Healing magic kept its practitioners young; Ree wondered again how old Andomerys really was. 'It doesn't look good.'

Ree swallowed, her mouth suddenly dry.

'I can stop the curse spreading, and stop it killing his body, but it's wrapped around his soul as well, and I know very little about that. The soul is traditionally the concern of necromancers, not healers.' Her eyes were hard, as if steeling herself against her own words. 'He's not conscious, and not likely to become it. If I remove my magic from him, he'll die.'

Ree nodded, but the situation called for words. She cleared her throat and said quietly, 'He saved my life.' She'd meant to say that she understood, but the words had come pushing out. It was at the front of her mind — that he'd come *looking* for her, that if he hadn't, she would have been cursed and probably dead.

'I'm sorry,' said Andomerys. 'There *were* healers who could heal souls. Or so history tells us. But I haven't the knowledge.' She paused. 'Would you like to say goodbye?'

Ree nodded but something in the healer's words had caught in her mind. 'Or so history tells us ...' she murmured, halfway through the door. She stopped with her hand on the doorframe.

'Ree?'

Ree's eyes lifted to meet hers. Shadowed versus bright. 'Could you learn it from a book?'

Andomerys frowned. 'If there was such a book.'

Ree nodded to herself. Several of the libraries had healing books in their magic collections — some of them very, very old. 'Keep him alive for a few days,' said Ree. 'If there is such a book, I know how to find it.'

'Ree —'

Ree hurried down the steps.

Andomerys grunted in frustration. 'I didn't come to this crypt to be a healer!' she shouted.

No. But she was *still* a healer.

'I'll be back soon! A few days, at most!' Ree called.

'Days?!'

Ree ran down another flight of stairs and into the complex of tombhomes. She wound past lumbering minions carrying boxes and tools for their masters, leapt over the wolf the young acolytes had just got twitching, and shouldered past Etherea Eversworn in her high brocade collar and lace veil, who threatened to curse her shoes. She skidded to a halt in a small alley to knock loudly on a salvage-wood door. It creaked open.

'Emberlon.' Ree looked at her mentor and ducked her head in a reflexive bow that she never seemed to be able to shake. 'I need your help.'

Emberlon drew the door wider. 'Best come inside.'

I wore a bear today. It felt wrong to me: large and cumbersome, and I rattled around inside it. I will always prefer my hawkskin — perhaps it is true what they say, and no shape ever feels as right as your first.

I did enjoy the power of it, though. I went to the village on the plains outside and roared at their hunters. One of them soiled himself — oh, I shall be laughing about that for days! I didn't eat him, of course. Just the other, cleaner one.

But the importance of the first shape. I must remember to put it in my book, if the King ever gives me leave to write it.

~from the journal of Wylandriah Witch-feather

CHAPTER FOUR

LATE RETURNS

It was with the awful sense that she was about to be found out that Ree walked through her mentor's door. She lifted herself up onto the stone sarcophagus at the centre, letting her legs swing. She kept her head bowed and folded her hands in her lap, steeling herself to the weight of the archivist's gaze.

Emberlon closed the door and turned to face her, his hands clasped in front of him. He was always grave like this: something about his manner made the air heavy. He was an older man, well into his fifties, with a mass of curly white hair and a close-trimmed grey beard. His eyes were an ice-chip blue that stood out against the near-black of his skin. His clothes were little better than rags, but he wore them with straight-backed poise as if they were the richest finery. An ebony chain disappeared under his sackcloth shirt.

'I need to find a book, a healing book,' said Ree. She didn't dare meet his eyes. She felt like her guilt was written all over her — that if he looked at her closely enough, he would gasp and condemn her for breaking town law.

It was like that with Emberlon.

Emberlon only inclined his head in acknowledgement, but there was a question in his eyes. 'Finding books is what you do.'

Of course he would wonder. 'It's important,' she said. She locked her hands behind her back to hide their fidgeting. 'It's to help Andomerys.'

She didn't want to waste any time searching for the right book, and she didn't want to risk Smythe's life by telling everyone about his presence. Emberlon knew the archive and libraries even better than she did. She was certain she would find what she needed, and quickly, with his help.

Emberlon had never been one much for asking — or answering — questions. If he was curious about something, he would wait to see if there was anything you wanted to say. The trouble was, it was difficult to let Emberlon down — and not just for Ree. She'd heard others comment on how it was almost like a compulsion to tell him what he wanted to hear — like the bow Ree couldn't stop herself making. Emberlon had a power that had nothing to do with necromancy.

Ree steeled herself to it, clenching her fists at her sides.

There was a long silence while he considered her and Ree stared into her lap. At length, he said, 'I can help you.' He rubbed his chin. 'Which book are you looking for?'

The sudden change of tone set her off-balance. She leapt to her feet while her mind spun over the question. 'A healing book,' she said. 'Healing and curses ... and souls, maybe.'

She watched him carefully for his reaction, but he only looked thoughtful. 'I can't recall any books of that topic. We'll have to check the records.'

'Of — of course!' Ree slid off the sarcophagus. It no longer seemed strange to her that Emberlon had refused to have the sarcophagus relocated when he moved into the tomb. *'There's room enough for both of us,'* he'd said, and he'd been true to his word. Emberlon's tombhome was more tomb than home; scant possessions or furniture beyond a chair, a change of clothes, and a straw bedroll laid across a stone shelf in the antechamber. There were a lot of mysteries about Emberlon — where he'd come from, why he'd left — but whatever life he'd had before, he had taken none of it with him.

Nothing except his weighty gaze and powerful manner. Emberlon had arrived ten years ago surrounded by rumours — rumours only exacerbated by his decision to go by the name Emberlon the Disloyal. Ree watched him sidelong as they walked. She still wasn't sure whether she believed them.

As they crossed the town square, some of the acolytes called to Ree. 'Come help — we've got it twitching! One more practitioner and we'll have it dancing next!' A cloth-wrapped corpse lay at their feet.

But Ree only pulled her hood higher and shook her head, scurrying to keep up with Emberlon's long-legged stride. Their magic fizzed at the edges of her senses, cold and faint. She glanced at Emberlon, who quickly looked away.

Everyone wanted Ree to learn the Craft. Everyone except Andomerys and Emberlon, at least, which was one of many reasons she preferred their company. Emberlon was a necromancer himself, but more of a dabbler than anything.

39

Ree suspected he only kept up the practice to ensure his place in the town.

It didn't take them long to get to the archives. When they got to the stone doors, Ree drew the heavy iron key from around her neck and unlocked it with a twist. Together, she and Emberlon shouldered the door open and then heaved it closed behind them.

What must once have been a storage room had been repurposed, and now every drab stone wall was lined with filing cabinets and stacks of books were scattered about, waiting to be processed and returned by Emberlon or Ree.

Emberlon strode over to the first cabinet and started flicking through index cards. 'You're being meek.'

Ree dragged a step ladder to the far end of the room. 'I'm always quiet.'

'Quiet, yes. Meek?' Emberlon shook his head.

Ree's gaze flicked to him and then away. She didn't want to talk about her refusal to learn the Craft, or the pressure the young acolytes put on her. Sometimes, they would invite her to join them, knowing she would refuse. Other times, they would harass her, laughing, as she came into or out of town.

But there were more important things to think about. She slid a drawer open and started flicking through the records. 'I have a lot on my mind.'

Emberlon withdrew an index card and flipped it to examine the back. 'Far be it from me to pry into another's secrets. Just … take care, Ree. Some secrets can eat you up inside.'

His voice had taken on the dull tone it always did when he considered his past, but Ree knew better than to try to comfort him. She merely nodded and kept searching the records.

She found a lot of records for healing books. Most of them seemed to be in the small Iyadi library near the surface, but there were plenty scattered across the other libraries of the crypt. References to curses or souls were harder to find when crossed with healing. She kept coming across necromantic texts, but they would be no use to Andomerys.

It might take her hours to find the record if she carried on like this. She needed a way to narrow down her search. Andomerys had said that soul healing was ancient magic. Maybe, if Ree only searched records for books published pre-third era ...

She searched in an ever-tightening spiral of specificity, telling herself that such books *had* to exist — she simply wasn't searching correctly. She tried not to think that there was a fine line between history and myth. That maybe the kind of healing she was looking for had never existed. And all the while, time was rolling on like the iris of a suneye. How long would Andomerys keep Smythe alive without Ree to vouch for him?

She also tried not to think about all the libraries they had yet to index. Any one of them might hold the book she needed. And every denizen knew that the Lich had its own library, and had taken its pick of the other libraries when creating it.

'Ree?' Emberlon held a card of yellowing parchment aloft. 'I think I've found your book.'

Ree accepted the index card. *'Astaravinarad,'* she read. She bit her lip. *'The Book of Body of Light?'*

'A good translation,' Emberlon said approvingly. 'I read it as *The Book of the Lightness in Body*. If you look at its categories and description, it's a healing book and not a necromantic text, but it's concerned with spirit and soul, which are normally necromantic domains.' He paused. 'It's written in *iyad-anar*, which I know you aren't as familiar with, but Andomerys undoubtedly will be. Most healing texts come from Iyad.' He named the nomadic culture from the Long Plains. Necromancers from that part of the upworld tended to keep (even more) to themselves.

She turned over the card in her hands, searching its location. She frowned. 'It's been overdue for six months.'

Emberlon inclined his head. 'To Veritas.'

Ree bit her lip and moved to the borrower records. It wasn't uncommon for denizens to push their luck with the archivists, and a lot of Ree's work involved tracking down distant necromancers and convincing them to give their books back.

She slid a drawer open and withdrew a stack of index cards that crackled under her touch, then turned and sat on the footstool to consider them.

Varric ... Vectora ... Veritas. His name was inscribed in Emberlon's tidy hand, the writing compact, as if he feared taking up too much space. 'Astorfell Tower, northern tunnels,' Ree murmured. Veritas had chosen a home as far from the central mausoleum as it was possible to get. She had a vague memory of the necromancer; stoop-shouldered but proud, and laden with hand-spelled talismans and rings.

She checked his borrowing history, and sure enough, *Astaravinarad* was his most recent book, and it didn't contain a return date.

It wasn't impossible that he'd lost the book. A crypt was not a safe place even for a necromancer, and sometimes things got left behind or trampled by a horde or gnawed by Larry. But three years of working in the archives with Emberlon had taught Ree that it was far more likely that Veritas simply didn't want to return it. Necromancers were greedy by nature and were more than willing to try their luck at keeping a useful title to themselves.

It would be a long and dangerous journey, and she had no guarantee that this book would contain the magic Andomerys needed. She ought to stay here or track down a less promising book closer to home. There had to be limits on how far you were willing to go to help someone — especially someone you didn't know.

And yet ...

She thought of his awkward introduction, of his appearance when the Lich had her mind-snared. She thought about whether she wanted to be the kind of person who let kind people die.

Ree took a map from the rack on the right-hand wall and tucked it into her belt. 'If I'm not back by the end of the week, scry for me.'

Emberlon fixed her in a solemn gaze. 'I always do.'

Ree drew a shuddering breath. She checked her hood was properly pinned to her hair, hefted her herb pouch to make sure she had enough for a couple days, and squeezed back through the door and out into the town.

She'd made it to the northern passage before a slim, dark figure stepped into her path. 'And I suppose you're off on some grand adventure again?' the girl drawled. Her short black hair was slicked back against her head, making her long forehead all the more pronounced. Her eyes were almost colourless, stark against her dark skin, and her cheeks were sharp and hollow.

'Usther,' Ree greeted her warily, taking a half-step back. Usther was a few years older than Ree and was more impressive than beautiful, all sharp angles and sharper words.

Ree could rarely decide whether she was happy to see Usther or not, but she certainly didn't want to see her while she was harbouring an upworlder with Andomerys. If Usther could be counted on for anything, it was to look out for herself. And turning in Smythe could get her the council's favour.

'There's no need to be *defensive,* I'm just saying hello. Is that so terrible?'

Ree decided it was better not to answer. Usther clucked her tongue and put her head to one side, bird-like. 'Where are you going?'

'I'm collecting a late return.'

'Which book?'

Ree shifted her weight from foot to foot, then said, '*Astaravinarad.'*

Usther's eyes widened. 'That sounds like it's in *iyad-anar.* Thinking of learning healing, are you? Oh, your daddy will be *so* disappointed.'

Ree made a show of adjusting her satchel on her shoulder and brushed past the older girl. 'Well, it's a long trip, so if you don't mind —'

Usther fell into step beside her. '*Healing* magic.' The word rolled from her mouth, loose with disdain. 'I knew you had to dispense with this "magicless" nonsense soon and make a choice, I just thought you'd make the only *reasonable* choice and learn the Craft.'

Ree gritted her teeth. She didn't want to have to lie about what she needed an ancient healing text for — and it would be a very bad idea to tell Usther the truth. Likely, she assumed Ree was getting it for her mother or Andomerys and was just taunting Ree for her own amusement.

But oh, how Ree *burned* to tell her the magic she was *really* studying. Every time Usther spoke down to her, she could feel a retort hot on her tongue. But nobody could know until she had proven it was possible. Until she could show them all what she was capable of.

She didn't think she could bear to have Usther ridicule her dreams.

'Ghosts and gods, you'd have to *touch* people. Can you imagine anything more *foul?'* Usther, who was regularly up to her elbows in entrails, shuddered at her own words. She glanced at Ree, who kept her face carefully blank.

'Honestly,' she continued, 'I'd always thought you were more likely to learn *therianthropy* than healing.' She laughed. 'Gods, that's just the kind of thing you would do. Poring over dusty books trying to learn how to turn into a *rat* or something. Chasing after fairytales rather than learning good, *practical* Craft.' She snorted.

Ree looked away very deliberately. Inside, she went cold. For one frozen moment, her thoughts fixated on her research journal, tucked lovingly into her pack.

But Usther didn't *know.*

'Look.' Ree cut her eyes at the older girl, not quite trusting herself to give a full glare. 'I have quite a lot of travel to do, so if you don't mind —'

Usther grabbed Ree's wrist with a bird-claw hand. 'You're hiding something.'

So many things that it was starting to feel crowded in her head.

Ree wrenched free. 'Everyone here is hiding something.'

'Not you.' Her pale eyes burned into Ree's. 'Never you. If I can count on you for anything, it's to be utterly unremarkable. And you won't even *look* at me right now. So what *exactly* is this all about?'

Unremarkable. She hated the word, the way it dropped in her stomach like a stone in a still pool. That word was every dismissive gaze, every shun and every disregard.

People thought that she was something less. But she knew, with a bitterness that burned her throat and set fire to her chest, that she would be more than they could ever imagine.

Ree turned her back on Usther. 'You don't know anything about me.'

But Usther was not to be left behind.

'What are you doing?'

'I'm coming with you. We are *friends* after all.'

'Only in the sense that we dislike each other less than we dislike the others,' said Ree. The two were united in their unwillingness to join the teen cabal with the other acolytes — Ree because she had no desire to practice the Craft, Usther because she had no desire to share her power with others.

Usther shrugged a bony shoulder. 'Isn't that what true friendship is?'

Ree didn't have any idea what true friendship was. Her relationship with Usther was largely based on Usther lounging around insulting Ree while Ree carried out study, or demanding that Ree dropped whatever she was doing to track down a book Usther required. Friendship seemed a strong word for that.

Lack of response left Usther undeterred. 'Don't be *rude*. If I'm to come with you anyway, don't you think you might as well tell me where you're going?'

Ree continued to ignore her, but Usther walked with her, keeping up with the ease of a long stride. Ree ran through problems in her head. If Usther found out about Smythe, she would be quick to turn him in to the council — or even kill him herself. Usther was nothing if not ambitious, and killing Smythe would earn her favour with the most powerful necromancers in town.

But right now, Ree just needed to collect the book. With a practitioner with her, she could travel more directly, as she wouldn't have to avoid the more powerful undead. And Usther might be useful in negotiating the return of the book. Necromancers were not usually keen on sharing ...

'I'm going to Astorfell Tower,' she said at length. She watched Usther sidelong as they climbed a flight of stairs.

Usther raised an eyebrow. 'Astorfell ... let me think ... that's not old Uzumir, is it? I thought he gave up and died.'

'No, he just retired to research immortality. It's Veritas.'

'Veritas.' Usther tapped her lips thoughtfully, but whatever she thought about the necromancer, she didn't say.

Usther didn't have many friends among the denizens — just Ree, really, and that was more of a tenuous tolerance than anything. But she kept close tabs on the other necromancers and their studies — all the better to swoop in and claim it for her own if it proved useful. Maybe it was that urge to spy on her fellow practitioners that kept her following Ree, rather than turn back when faced with a long journey, as Ree had expected her to.

The journey with Usther was unpleasant but safer than Ree was used to. Though Usther complained constantly and never missed an opportunity to mock Ree if she tripped or let an undead get a grip on her, she was a competent necromancer and there was very little they encountered that Usther couldn't turn aside with a sneer and an exertion of will.

'So how far *is* Astorfell, exactly?' She followed Ree up onto a narrow stone path that skirted one of the bone pits where the remains of slaves were dumped. There was a malevolent energy about the place, and few of the necromancers chose to harvest there. *'There are some evils that linger after death,'* her father had warned her once. *'You must respect their afterlife, and be wary of treading too close to them. They are not friendly minions, like Larry or the town servants.'*

The crypt was full of places like this. Places where people had died in their masses, and their bodies had been tossed aside. No embalming or burial rites for them; no special tombs or coffins or shelves, no treasures or silks or ceremonies. Though Tombtown was a sprawling hodgepodge of tombs and catacombs built by many different cultures spanning hundreds of years, there were enough places like this bone pit to make it clear that it had rarely been built by willing hands.

Ree didn't mind living among the restless dead. It was the memory of those tortured living that gave her pause.

She looked down in the pit, her stomach clenching. All was still below, just a mess of bones and debris, but it radiated a sickening energy that she would be glad to leave behind.

The path was too narrow to tread normally. Ree put her back to the wall and sidestepped along; her toes slightly overlapped the edge of the path, over-hanging the pit below. 'It'll take us the rest of the day to get there, and maybe half the next. I don't know the northern tunnels very well.'

'That's what maps are for.'

Ree clamped down on her irritation; it was enough work focusing on traversing this ridiculous path. 'I have a map. I *make* the maps —'

The stone beneath her foot gave out and she lurched sickeningly downward. Her hands scrabbled for purchase on the wall, but she'd lost her balance and was leaning ever outward.

'Morrin's teeth!' Usther seized Ree's arm and yanked her back onto the path. Ree gulped down air and clutched the older girl. The fall might not have killed her, but the idea of being trapped in a bone pit, hours from home ...

And if there really was something in there — a greater dead, roused by the memory of violence, or a skeleton hidden among the bones — her mother's death herbs would not protect her. Only a necromancer could fight such restless beings, and Ree was not a necromancer.

'Ree.' Usther turned Ree's head, meeting Ree's eyes with her colourless ones. 'You're fine. It was only a stumble. Right? You're fine.'

Ree stared at her for a moment, then nodded. Her mouth was dry; she cleared her throat. 'I'm fine.' The words sounded dubious to her own ears.

They shuffled the rest of the way, Ree's breath balling painfully in her chest. Usther kept close, pale eyes darting to Ree and away again.

Safe on the other side, the tension in Ree's chest eased in a sickly trickle. Usther's mouth was pinched; Ree's eyes were on the floor.

'Thank you.' Ree spoke past a lump in her throat. She thought again of the bone pit, of the way it seemed to pulse with rage and bitterness.

Usther shrugged. 'You're more useful alive. You'd make a very poor minion.'

Another few moments passed with just the sound of Ree panting and Usther tapping her foot. At length, Usther said, 'Since we're having a moment, and I saved you from a torturous undeath ... I don't suppose you'd consider "lending" me a copy of *A Blackfort Affair,* you know ... off the record?'

Ree glared at her.

Usther sniffed and smoothed her dark hair. 'Some people are born ungrateful.'

But that wasn't the case at all. Ree reflected uneasily that she owed her life now to two people in as many days. Her thoughts brushed against Smythe, lying still and cursed on Andomerys' table, and she squared her shoulders. She would repay Smythe in kind; Usther, she would deal with later.

The rest of the journey passed mercifully without incident. Usther raised a few minions to shamble after them as soon as she found some likely corpses. Their eyes were white and empty in their withered faces. Ree took extra care whenever they crossed a bridge or scaled a wall.

Finally, they came to a wide stone chamber lined with pillars carved to resemble long-dead kings with their heads bowed benevolently, their faces crumbling under the pressures of time. Ree felt very small, surrounded by that echoing expanse. She glanced at Usther, standing with shoulders back and chin raised. Usther looked at those ancient kings as if they were unruly dogs she would bring to heel. Behind them, Usther's minions milled, arms hanging loosely at their sides. She'd raised them as soon as she found some likely corpses. Unlike Wandering Larry, these minions were controlled. They did not groan much, though their limbs did creak as they moved.

'Astorfell?'

Ree pointed to the other side of the chamber. 'Entrance should be over there. See the windows?'

'A tower inside a wall. How dull.'

Ree rubbed her eyes. 'This is only where it starts. I've been to Astorfell; it actually comes up out of the mountain and you can see around outside. When the sun hits it, it's quite beautiful.' She remembered a soft sky and a bleeding sun, and a warmth like she'd never experienced before.

Her mother had asked her, once, whether she would prefer to live in the upworld, after a rare visit to an upworld town. *'I pass no judgement if you do,'* she'd said. They'd been sitting in the Altar of Many Gods, playing scrolls and skulls on a finger-drawn grid on the dusty floor. It was a strategy game much loved by necromancers, about positioning undead forces. *'But unlike many here, there is nothing tying you to the crypt. You could make a life for yourself up there, in the sunshine, among the green trees and the sweet yellow fields. There are more people than you can imagine. The world is much bigger than you know.'*

Ree had been stricken to find that even her mother thought she didn't belong. As if she would trade darksight for sunshine, or the grand crumbling arches of the amphitheatre for some poxy trees, or the still sway of a horde of minions for the push and press of a sweaty city crowd.

She *did* belong here. There was more than one way to be a denizen.

Usther wrinkled her nose. 'Sunlight?' Her sneer brought Ree back to the present. 'How can Veritas get *any* serious work done in broad daylight?'

Undead generally grew weaker the longer they were exposed to direct sunlight, but Ree wasn't terribly interested in how Veritas made it work. He was an experimental necromancer — everything he did seemed strange. 'Come on,' she said. 'We'll get the book, stay overnight with Veritas if he'll let us, and head back. You should release your minions.'

'I will not.' Usther flicked a piece of rubble from her shoulder. 'A true necromancer never enters another's territory unguarded.'

'As well that you're only an acolyte, then.' Ree pulled her hood more snuggly about her hair and headed for the door. Usther and her handful of shamblers followed.

Ree glanced over her shoulder and bit back a warning. While it wasn't polite, attempts to recover late books didn't always go smoothly. Normally that resulted in a heart-pounding chase for Ree. She might be glad to have a necromancer on her side, and antagonising Usther seemed a bad way to go about it.

As she came upon the door she wondered, again, what to expect from Veritas. He lived so very far from the other denizens and was so rarely seen or heard from.

She reached for the handle, unease growing in her belly.

'Wait — don't touch that!'

Ree jerked back from the handle, but not before her fingertips brushed the cool iron. A spark of magic unfurled from the metal to wrap around her throat, a shadow rope with the feel of gut.

'Us — us-ther ...' Her fingers scrabbled at the rope as it crushed her throat. Her breath came in thin gasps.

'*Krizhott!*' Usther pointed at Ree's throat and voiced a deep, gravelly incantation; the shadow shrivelled away and the rope came loose, leaving what looked like a withered intestine to slither from Ree's shoulders.

Usther's eyes sunk deeper into her face with the expenditure of magic. Her nose wrinkled and her lip curled in a snarl. 'That is *very poor manners,*' she hissed. Behind her, her minions seemed to grow and flex, their shadows lengthening.

Ree rubbed her throat. The skin was cracked and bleeding where the shadow rope had squeezed. Her eyes drifted to the door.

It was never easy with the late returns. And this time, a life hung in the balance.

Tales of witches in sealskin cloaks luring sailors to their deaths and stories of lionesses demanding riddles of trespassers in their caves: this is the legacy of therianthropy — fables and fairytales of brave heroes defeating evil shapeshifters. Not much of a foundation on which to base the existence of an entire school of magic.

So-called 'scholars' of the dead-or-mythical magic claim that therianthropy was an oral tradition passed on only by word of mouth. Why then was the infamous Wylandriah so willing to put her experiences to paper?

No. More likely the magic is myth and the apocryphal witch Wylandriah was mad or given to penning fiction. Only the romantic and the foolish vaunt her journals as proof of an otherwise entirely vanished magic.

~from *The Shapeshifter Obsession* by Delian Wan

CHAPTER FIVE

STITCHWORK MONSTER

Ree massaged her throat. Each breath was painful. She wondered wildly whether her windpipe was crushed. Did she need healing?

Usther stalked ahead of her and kicked open the door to Astorfell. Her minions crowded in behind her, made larger and fiercer by the angry pulse of her magic. 'Veritas!' she called. Her amplified voice rasped with a death echo, a mark of her active magic. 'Come and greet your guests, Veritas!'

Ree rubbed her throat again. Panic still fluttered in her ribcage like a trapped bird, but she hadn't suffocated yet and that gave her a little strength. She followed Usther inside, her shoulders hunched and her hood drawn as she tucked herself into the corner by the door.

'Veritas!' Usther called again. Her minions started to shift and moan, picking up on her temper. 'It's rude to leave people waiting!'

But though Usther's minions stomped and groaned, Veritas did not appear.

Ree gradually got her nerves under control. She withdrew from the shadows to peer past Usther to the staircase. 'Perhaps he's not in?' She took a few steps up the stairs. 'Veritas?' There was no answer. She turned to Usther. 'I'm going to take a look around.'

Honestly, given the traps on his doorstep, she'd rather not run into him.

Usther glared at her. 'On your own? Hardly.'

'Well, I'll struggle to do it quietly trailed by your pack of angry dead men.'

'They're not *angry,* they're righteous.' Usther pinched the bridge of her nose between her fingers, then turned to her minions. 'Wait here. Defend yourselves. Warn us.' She flicked the command at them with a small sting of necromancy, then turned to Ree. 'After you.'

Ree started up the stairs, Usther on her heels. She gritted her teeth at Usther's clicking steps — the older girl wasn't even trying to sneak.

Usther herself seemed to be softening. The hollow darkness that her full magic brought on was fading along with her temper. She looked more like the bird-like, irritable girl Ree knew than the angry death goddess her magic turned her into.

'Surely he must have heard us?' Usther murmured as they crested the first floor.

'If he's in the middle of a particularly complicated ritual, he might not acknowledge us even if he did hear us.' She glanced at Usther. 'At least, that's how it is when Pa is deep into the Craft.'

'And exactly which rituals has dear old dad been doing? No, don't look at me like that.' Usther made a face. 'You can hardly blame me for trying.'

They crept further up the crumbling staircase, and the further they went, the more concerned Ree grew for Veritas' mental state. Wild diagrams and gruesome anatomical art were nailed to the walls. Dried blood caked the steps, and red handprints lined the stairs. Ree kept her hand to the pouch on her belt, while Usther travelled with her arms crossed and a thoroughly annoyed expression.

They got to the first floor and paused. It was a study; the room was scattered with bones and smeared in ugly brown stains. The smell of gore and rotting flesh was almost overpowering. Ree was unused to a smell so fresh and bloody. Most of the corpses she encountered were both ancient and preserved by oils and chemicals, or wrapped in special scented cloths. Ree gagged at the stench, but Usther only wrinkled her nose.

'Do you sense that?' she asked.

Ree hesitated, reaching out with her senses. She wasn't a practitioner of the Craft, so her affinity for death magic would never be as strong as Usther's, but you couldn't grow up in a city of the dead without it rubbing off on you.

She could sense something. A magic that was not only chill but ... slimy. She looked to Usther. 'A ritual?'

Usther nodded. 'Old magic. Really old. Perhaps even older than the third era.' Her nose wrinkled further and she bared her teeth in a snarl. 'Nasty stuff, whatever it is. Leaves a foul taste in my mouth.'

There was a door at the other side of the room. Usther headed toward it, but Ree motioned for her to stop.

'One moment,' said Ree. Her eyes were on the desk at the side of the room, and the several blood-splattered books that lay open on it.

'Seriously? Just books?'

'It's what we're here for,' Ree replied sharply.

Usther kicked a femur. 'It's what *you're* here for,' she muttered as it skittered across the floor.

Ree studied the books, fingertips brushing the crisp pages. Her eyebrows pinched as her gaze swept across the text. 'It's not here.'

'What isn't here?'

'*Astaravinarad.*' But it wasn't looking good. Each of the books had blood brushed like paint across their open pages, forming the outside of a spell diagram — the heart of which was missing in a book-shaped gap.

Why did they ever lend more than one book to any practitioner? Necromancers were always finding new and dangerous ways of defacing their texts in the name of some long-lost ritual or other ...

'Usther ... what does this mean?'

Her eyes lingered on the blood diagram. What if these defaced pages were key to Smythe's recovery? She could barely make out the words beneath the blood ...

Usther strode over. 'I hope you're not about to admit that you don't know how to read?' She studied the tableau of defaced books. Her eyebrows sprang up. 'Oh *interesting*. He's attempted a binding *on the books.* I wouldn't have thought it possible.'

Ree rubbed her eyes. 'Please explain, for the non-practitioner in the room?'

'I've always said I'd be happy to teach you, so whose fault is that? Bindings are advanced rituals for spirit summoners.

To properly harness the strength of a spirit, you need to bind it to a physical body. These books have been bound together in the same way — like he's trying to bind the spirits of the books.' She crossed her arms and lit her pale eyes on Ree's face. 'Do books have spirits?'

'You're the necromancer — you tell me,' Ree replied. As far as she knew, only living things had souls. It was perhaps a glib answer — in her two years apprenticing to Emberlon as town archivist, she'd seen too many strange things and left too many mysteries unsolved to question whether there was more to books than leather, ink and paper, but she didn't need to tell Usther that.

'Well, he almost certainly has *Astaravinarad* at the heart of the ritual. I'm eager to hear how he's faring with it, just as soon as I express my *displeasure* with his security measures.'

Ree's hand went to her throat, touching the raw abrasions there. 'We're just here for the book.'

Usther sniffed.

Ree considered the remaining books. They weren't overdue, but there was no way she was going to let him keep them if this was how he treated them. Binding rituals aside, all this blood was going to make it very difficult for anyone else to read them. She was pretty sure Emberlon knew a few complicated incantations to get the blood out, but nonetheless ...

She scooped up the remaining books, bound them in twine, and held them out to Usther. 'Could you have one of your minions carry these?'

Usther rolled her eyes. 'Oh, so *now* you want my minions.'

Ree shrugged. 'Since they're here ...'

Magic pulsed from Usther, and Ree heard shuffling footsteps on the stairs. 'Just leave them on the desk.'

Ree carefully set down the bundle of books and wiped the dried blood off on her robes. This was the main reason she wore traditional black robes; all the better for hiding the kind of gory stains you picked up in a town full of necromancers. 'Well, let's go see what he's up to, then.' She said the words lightly, as if her chest didn't pinch at the thought.

Usther bared her teeth. 'Gladly.'

As one of Usther's servant corpses fumbled with the books on the desk, Ree and Usther passed through the doorway, which led to a short stone antechamber streaked with yet more blood.

Ree lifted her robes as she stepped gingerly through the gore, errant bits of viscera squelching under her boots. Usther looked around dispassionately. 'If he's attempting blood magic, he's doing a very poor job of it. So much *waste.*' She pushed through the next door and froze.

Ree peered over her shoulder, throat tightening. Anything that could give Usther pause was something she needed to steel herself to see. The door looked out over a vast chamber, and the smell of gore was so much that Ree turned and retched into the corner. Usther seized her wrist and dragged her back. Her grip was far too tight, her bones cutting into Ree's hand. 'Look at what he's doing,' she hissed.

Ree wiped spittle from her mouth and held her herb pouch under her nose in an attempt to mask the fetid stench. Usther dragged her further into the room.

They stood on the landing of a staircase overlooking a wide marble chamber, a tableau of kings and wars etched into the walls. But that history was near masked in blood and obscured by body parts; a necromancer stood amidst a pile of broken limbs, stitching pieces to a great red beast with a broad body, long arms, and a small, fleshy head.

Ree shook Usther off and headed down the stairs. The necromancer seemed unaware of their presence, so absorbed was he in his bloody work. His black robes glistened with a thick coat of blood, and he wore a mask over his nose and mouth and goggles over his eyes. Even his scrubby white beard was tucked into cover of a scarf. His hands, though, were bare, as practitioners' usually were: the better to feel and direct the magic they channelled. Thick leather gloves poked from his pocket.

'Veritas.' Ree called the name warily.

The necromancer stiffened, and didn't turn. She could feel him gathering his magic about him in a sucking wind, but he only said, 'Who's there? I'm a bit busy at the moment.' His voice was high and nasal, muffled through his mask.

'It's the archivist,' said Ree. Many of the more absorbed practitioners had no memory for names or faces, so it seemed easier to identify herself this way. 'You have a book that is long overdue. We've come to collect.'

At her side, Usther stiffened. Her lip curled, as if she were viewing the antics of a particularly naughty child. 'I wouldn't try it, if I were you,' she said in a low voice.

'I don't know what you — aha!' He cursed into the air in a voice that echoed with magic, a dart of black shadow flying toward them. Usther stepped in front of Ree and knocked it aside with a wave of her hand and an exertion of will. And now her hair and robes were starting to rise; darkness clustered around her, and distantly, her minions began to scream in rage.

'Usther!' Ree grabbed her shoulder. 'We're not here to fight!'

'He seems quite intent on making it one.' But she let her gathered magic leak away; the screams of her minions died out and she crossed her arms in the picture of necromancerly disapproval. 'I am more than willing to test my power against yours, Veritas. Especially as your poxy security system nearly *strangled* the archivist.'

'The book, Veritas.' Ree fixed the necromancer in a level look she had learned from Emberlon, trying to exude authority.

Veritas took off his goggles and slid down his mask. He was a middle-aged necromancer, so he could only have come to the Craft later in life, as it tended to slow down or even stop ageing. His eyes were wild and his bald head had a crust of old blood. 'I'm not finished!' he said. He picked up the book from the among the gore and clutched it to his chest. Ree pushed down a spike of anger at how carelessly he treated such an ancient tome. '*Astaravinarad* is *essential* to my work! I cannot part with it.' He sneered at Ree. 'I don't expect a plebian crypt-crawler like you to understand the complexities of the Craft, or any magic.'

Ree fought down a retort, clenching her teeth. She knew more about magic than this man could possibly realise.

'What exactly *is* your work?' asked Usther.

Veritas' eyes bugged. 'Generation! Creation! *Birth!*' He swept his hand in a flourish toward his grisly statue. 'I have uncovered a formula to create life from unlife. This "construct", as you might call it, will have twice the power of an ordinary minion and strength such as even a greywraith cannot equal.'

He didn't seem likely to attack them now, at least. Ree kept her eyes on the book he clutched in his bloody hands.

'Flesh constructs are a myth,' Usther replied testily. 'No practitioner of any worth wastes their time trying to build one.'

'Ah, but no other practitioner has ever combined the knowledge and souls of the working texts of the different eras, as I have!'

'Books don't have souls.' Usther glanced at Ree for confirmation, but Ree shrugged.

'That is where you are wrong! You are just as closed-minded as any *upworlder*, just as lacking in vision as you are in meaningful power.'

Usther raised her eyebrows. 'I'm sure that would cut me deeply, were you any more impressive than a child making a "man" out of mud and sticks.'

Thus the argument continued between them. Ree, forgotten in the heat of their disagreement, walked over to study the patchwork gore monster. It was entirely red and yellow, as if it were a creature that had been turned inside-out. It had no skin, and no complete parts — where she might have expected to see a limb from one body here and from another there, there were only slivers of muscle, painstakingly stitched together with gut and twine. It had no eyes, only empty holes in its lump-jawed face. Unlike the normal dead, it was hard to imagine this fleshy statue alive. It did not look like anything that had ever lived.

While Veritas got ever more shrill in defending his genius, Ree waited for her moment. She reached under his arm and snatched the book from him. Veritas made to grab it, but Ree skittered back, holding the book aloft. 'It *has* to return to the Archive. If you try to stop me, it will go to the town council, and you know how that will end.'

'I'm not afraid of a bunch of talentless busy-bodies —'

'Talentless!' The air around Usther flexed.

'— and my construct will crush any who dare oppose me!'

Ree looked again at the stitchwork monster. 'It works, then?'

Veritas hesitated, his expression turning sheepish. He steepled his fingers. 'Not ... as such.'

Ree and Usther exchanged a look. Usther's nostrils flared; no doubt, she was still infuriated over his 'talentless' comment. Ree tucked the book into her pack. 'We're taking the book —'

'No!' He grasped toward her, but she edged out of reach. 'I *need* it for my work!'

'So what ... will you attack us then? Kill us for the book?'

Veritas pursed his lips. 'Well ... noooo.' He seemed to be turning the problem around in his mind. 'I suppose your father wouldn't like it if I killed you.'

Ree barely blinked at the suggestion that her father was the only reason Veritas wouldn't attack her outright. Necromancers respected nothing so much as power, and her father had a lot of it.

It was an empty threat, anyway. The council tried to crack down on murder. If one person got away with it, it would give the others ideas.

'And the door curse?' said Usther.

Veritas kicked at a lump of gore. 'Was meant to keep nosy adventurers out.'

Ree headed for the door. 'Thank you for the book, Veritas!' she called over her shoulder. 'If you'd like to borrow it again, you'll have to petition Emberlon.'

'What? Noo, he'll *never* let me have another book after this!'

He sounded like he meant to pursue, but Ree was quick and used to evading far quicker beasts than he. She hurried back into the main room and ducked under his desk, pulling the chair snuggly in front of her. When he finally came puffing into the room, he found it empty of both girl and books.

'Festering rats! How can she already be gone?' He hurried to the door, wringing his hands.

'Ree's good at that. Quick. Sneaky.' Usther crossed her arms and leaned against the doorframe. 'I suppose she needs *something* to make up for her complete lack of ability in the Craft.'

Veritas cast her a worried look. 'She's really gone?'

Usther shrugged and examined her blackened fingernails.

Veritas shuffled back into his gore chamber. 'Well, I suppose I could alter the ritual somewhat. Perhaps if I elide the transmographic elements of Talthir's Summons, I can —'

Usther swung the door shut behind him.

'What a tedious little worm.' She looked around the room. 'You're in here somewhere, I assume?'

Ree pushed the chair out of the way and crawled out from the under the desk.

'How resourceful.' Usther paused. 'Like a cockroach.'

'Yes, that's how I prefer to think of it.'

'No need to get *snippy,* I just gave you a *compliment.*'

Ree supposed she even thought that was true.

They made their way downstairs and through Usther's pack of drooling minions.

'So that's the job, then,' Usther said. She wrinkled her nose. 'Not the most pleasant work I can imagine.'

Ree resisted the urge to roll her eyes. 'You spend most of your days up to your elbows in blood and dead bodies.'

'Dreamy, isn't it?' Her eyes went soft. 'The power coursing through your body, the touch of death, the spark of unlife, the comforting smell of decomposition —'

'Lovely.' Ree managed to keep a straight face, though Usther shot her a narrow-eyed look regardless. 'But that's not really the job. It's usually Emberlon who takes on the recoveries. For me, it's mostly mapping the crypt and collecting and returning stock from the various libraries.'

'That sounds even more tedious. So are you going to tell me why you *really* want a dusty old healing book?'

Ree ran her fingers done the spine of the book, the leather split and cracked from decades of hard use. 'No.'

'But I just covered for you with Veritas! Hey! Where are you going?'

Ree didn't break her stride and said nothing in response.

She had it. She had the book. If she could just put it into Andomerys' hands ...

Usther growled and chased after her. 'I *knew* you had a secret!' Her minions lolloped at her heels.

Smythe. He might be dead now. Or dead soon, if the town found out about him and she wasn't there to speak on his behalf. She thought of him, lying cold and grey on Andomerys' healing table, all the vibrant colour she had seen in him in the embalming room leeched away by the Lich's dark magic.

No. Andomerys was the most powerful healer Ree had ever heard of, and if Ree put *Astaravinarad* in her hands, who knew what she might be able to do?

The other denizens believed in blood and bones, but Ree believed in books.

For a society built around the study of ancient texts, there is a notable disregard for books and those who tend them. Practitioners see books as a means to an end, and one they prefer to bypass. They hate to be reliant on the knowledge of others.

One wonders what might happen, were one to rise who was both a committed necromancer AND a consummate scholar. They would surely be a strange and craven creature. But more, I worry at the power such a one might possess. With all the knowledge of centuries and civilisations at their disposal, their ascent would surely be swift and deadly.

~from *A History of Tombtown* by Emberlon the Disloyal

CHAPTER SIX

ASTARAVINARAD

As soon as they set foot in town, Usther shed the comfortable silence they'd fallen into on the journey home. 'Where are you going in such a hurry? What can *you* possibly need that book for?' Usther kept pace with her easily, her long stride taking two of Ree's steps for every one of her own.

Ree dodged Ursula the Under Queen, a wizened practitioner who'd come to the Craft late in life. Ursula dropped her cane in surprise and shook her fist at Ree. 'I'll add you to the list, young Ree!'

'Sorry!' Ree called over her shoulder without breaking stride. She wasn't terribly concerned about being added to Ursula's kill list — she was already on there multiple times and she was fairly certain Ursula had never met someone she didn't want to take revenge on. Ree made for the outer stairs, Usther still dogging her steps.

'Ree. Ree! Are you even *listening* to me?'

'As a rule? No.'

Usther's dramatic gasp left Ree fairly sure she wasn't about to be cursed for her rudeness. It was when Usther went silent that you had to worry.

'We're passing your house — we're — where are we going?'

Ree didn't bother to respond. As she climbed the final steps to the healer's shack, Usther hesitated for the first time.

'But what would *she* even want with a magic book? Everyone knows she hates healing. Didn't she come here to *die* or something?'

Ree shrugged and knocked on the door. It was a rumour she'd heard before. The act of healing kept people young — but Andomerys had gone to the one place in the world where she would rarely, if ever, be asked to heal, and didn't have to feel bad about saying no.

The door creaked open. Ree heard Usther hold her breath.

Andomerys scowled down at them. 'The book?'

'Here.' Ree took it from her pack and handed it to the healer.

Andomerys turned her dark gaze on Usther. 'What are you doing here?'

Usther puffed up. 'What am *I* —?' her outrage was cut short by Andomerys' glare. 'Nothing. I was just leaving.' She threw Ree a dirty look as she retreated down the stairs.

Andomerys went back inside but left the door open behind her, so Ree followed her in.

Andomerys sat down on her cushioned chair, the book open in her lap. Lacking another chair, Ree hovered beside her.

'I can't read this,' said Andomerys. She flicked through the pages then looked up at Ree. 'Is there a translation?'

Ree bit her lip. 'I could translate it, I think. You don't read *iyad-anar?*'

'I read modern *iyadi.*'

Ree's mind spun, trying to think her way around the problem. Translating the whole book would take ... well, weeks. Andomerys was keeping Smythe alive with her own magic, something she'd come to the town to specifically to avoid. She'd already saddled her with that responsibility for a few days. How much more could Ree ask of her before Andomerys refused?

They didn't even know whether *Astaravinarad* had the information Andomerys needed ...

'May I?' She gestured at the book and Andomerys handed it over with a grunt. She studied the table of contents. 'Do you have any paper? Quill and ink?'

Andomerys pointed at a drawer to one side of her colourfully appointed room. 'Help yourself.'

Ree opened the book to what she was sure was the table of contents and set about translating it, as best as she could given the situation. She wasn't very keen on translation work — it taxed her in a way that exploring the crypt never did — but she'd put a lot of time into learning the old languages and there was unlikely to be a more important use for it than now. She had one hand on her forehead while she worked. Her brain felt squeezed, her thoughts stuttering every time she came across a word she didn't immediately recognise.

It took a long time. She wasn't fluent in *iyad-anar* the way she was in Old Antherian. Once she had the table mostly translated, Andomerys picked out a likely chapter to translate in full.

Ree stopped to pace often, and had to leave and find a syllabary and translation guide (which mercifully were in one of the local libraries). She worked into the night, not needing candlelight, as Andomerys did, and thus could carry on without disturbing the healer.

A toe in her side nudged her awake. Ree got wearily up from the floor, her back and sides aching from a night with only a thin rug between her and hard stone. She groaned, taking in her surroundings. Paper and books dripped from the table and encircled her on the floor. She must have wanted more space at some point, but she had no memory of moving from table to floor — nor of falling asleep.

'Well?' Andomerys put her hand on her hip.

Ree shook her head. 'Give me a minute —' She sorted through the papers around her, looking for the most recent translation. She scanned a page thick with text, then thrust it up at Andomerys. 'I think this — I think maybe —' She found it hard to say the words aloud, as if voicing it would make it hurt more when she failed.

Andomerys glared Ree into silence — Ree had never known her to tolerate stammering — and studied Ree's cramped translation. Ree stretched her sore back while she waited for a response, wincing at every ache and twinge. She could remember, now, feverishly translating the chapters Andomerys had requested. She'd been crazed, fuelled by sleep deprivation and desperation in equal measure.

Now, in the harsh light cast by Andomerys' candles, with an actual trained healer standing before her, she was increasingly uncertain. She wasn't that fluent in *iyad-anar,* and she knew very little about healing magic.

Emberlon would tell her that it wasn't an archivist's job to *know* all the information, but to know how to *find* it. And she had done an archivist's job, searching for the most likely books from the records that she held, and then going to retrieve them, and translating them as best as she could. But this wasn't for a necromancer's fancy as to whether undead fish would decompose in water, or tracing the genealogy of a young acolyte who wanted to claim hereditary greatness. A man's life hung in the balance, and she didn't think Andomerys would suspend his life indefinitely while Ree tracked down better sources for a magic that might not even exist.

'This.' Andomerys tapped the paper, stirring Ree from her panic. 'I can use this.' There was a hard glint in her eyes that Ree recognised as scholarly fervour, something she'd never expected to see from Andomerys. The healer picked up the rest of the translation, turned in a whirl of brightly-patterned robes, and strode into her healer's room. Ree scrambled after her.

Smythe lay stretched on the table, his skin ashen and his eyes closed, his arms straight at his sides. As Ree's eyes swept his face, she noticed the faint glimmer of Andomerys' magic, an oily sheen across his skin.

Ree pressed a hand to her chest. He looked like he was already dead. How many times had she seen her mother lay out a recently deceased body for cleansing and vigil? There was a stillness to a corpse that couldn't be replicated.

And he might be one for real, soon. If the magic failed or worsened his condition. She wondered what exactly the Lich had done to him. For the first time, she had time to worry. What would Smythe become if Andomerys couldn't save him?

Andomerys read through Ree's notes again, mouthing the words. Then she took her hand and put it on his heart, and rested her short arm on his forehead.

Ree hovered just inside the door. She could feel power building in the room, warm and humid like a summer's day. Andomerys' hair stirred, as if caught in a breeze, though there was not even the faintest draft in the small, stark room.

The glow around Smythe flickered and flared, growing in strength and turning from gold to white.

Then Andomerys began to chant, but rather than the death echo of necromancy, her words became the pure notes of chiming bells. She was saturated with power, her skin growing translucent, as if her body was only a thin shell to hold in a being of pure light. For the first time since Ree had met Andomerys, she remembered that healing was the opposite and counterweight of necromancy, that a powerful healer could destroy undead and unravel all the magic a necromancer had wrought. That a healer was every bit as dangerous as a necromancer.

She was humbled and awed by the magic she was witnessing — a power greater than she'd ever seen, and a magic so old as to have passed from memory.

Smythe's shoulders jerked. Something black and fluid bubbled at his mouth, then snaked into the air above him. Andomerys took her hand from his chest and crushed it in her hand; it burned up in flash of white light.

The magic drained from the room; the chill of the underworld returned. Ree took a step forward, her eyes shifting uncertainly between healer and patient. 'Is it … done?'

The light was leaking away, until Smythe was once again beneath a pale sheen of golden magic.

Andomerys shook her head. Sweat slicked her hair and skin, and soaked the collar of her robes. 'The first of many treatments.' She must have seen Ree's concern, because she added, 'It's a start.' She walked unsteadily toward the door. 'I need to rest. Come back tomorrow, if you must.'

Ree kept to her room that night, not wanting to discuss Smythe's condition with her mother and certainly not with her father. She stretched out on the padded stone shelf that had once held a cadaver and flicked through her journal, reading and re-reading the results of her own study.

Today she had witnessed a magic thought long-dead. 'It's possible,' she whispered. 'Anything is possible.' She ran her fingers over the much-repeated word in her notes, sprawling in her own script: *Wylandriah.*

Another thing to thank Smythe for. If he survived, anyway. The thought made her chest tighten.

She tucked her journal under her pillow, closed her eyes, and willed morning to come.

She left through the back door as soon as the suneye in her pocket flashed hot. She pulled it out — a hardened, treated human eyeball. The eye had grown warm; the iris looked at the sun in the sky — or where it would be, were there not layers of rock, tomb, and subterranean city between it and the surface. She'd bought it from Mazerin the Bold many years before, and as long as she kept it polished and had her father charge it every full moon, it was usually accurate.

When Andomerys opened the door to her, she brushed past into the healer's room. 'That's fine!' Andomerys called after her, a growl in her voice. 'Barge in whenever you like!'

Smythe lay still and unmoving on the bed. Ree's breath caught. 'Is he —?'

His eyes flickered open. 'Hello again.' His voice was cracked. A nascent smile grew on his lips. 'Terribly sorry about all this. I hear you saved my life.'

Little is known about the Lich of Tombtown. It was here before the first settlers arrived and appears to be many centuries deep into practicing the Craft. They tried to kill it, of course. It is said that the entire crypt frosted over in the chill wind of its power, and that the earth shook with the sound of hundreds of corpses standing up at once.

It is also said that all seven founders banded together and with their combined might put the Lich into a deep sleep that even now still clings to it. This is untrue, as further investigation reveals that the founders barricaded themselves into a tomb and hid until the Lich passed.

As for the Lich's trance-like state, it is unclear whether this is a side-effect of its advanced age, or merely boredom.

~from *A History of Tombtown* by Emberlon the Disloyal

CHAPTER SEVEN

CONVALESCENT CONVERSATIONALIST

Ree tried to make her mouth move, but somehow couldn't. Smythe was alive — alive and *talking*, and though the curse still marked him in subtle ways, there was a wry twist to his mouth and an embarrassed flush in his cheeks.

She glanced at Andomerys for help, but the healer was sitting in the corner of the main room with an embroidery circle in her lap and didn't so much as look up.

Smythe didn't seem put-out by her inability to articulate. 'I think Andomerys also mentioned something about getting ceremonially lynched by the town. So that's two reasons to thank you. Well — three, I suppose, as you did identify those remains rather brilliantly —'

She got control of her mouth and managed to say: 'They hardly ever do that. The lynching, I mean.' Although that was largely because no upworlders ever came to town. Adventurers were usually killed by the Lich, if not by the various undead, and new practitioners were told the rules and sent to turn a tomb into a tombhome. Smythe was the first upworlder she'd heard of that wasn't here either to kill them or to join them.

She couldn't quite believe the situation. It was all so surreal — standing in Andomerys' house, talking to an upworlder as politely as if she were shopping at the Bone Market.

But he didn't *belong* here. Even after the lengths she'd gone to, to save his life, she'd never really thought about what would happen after. And now there was a boy on a padded pallet on Andomerys' healing table and it was *all her fault*.

Her chest tightened. She'd never been responsible for another *person* before. Nor had she ever done anything more controversial than delaying her education in the Craft.

This was a big deal.

This could be a problem.

Smythe sat up, wincing. 'Even so, the possibility, you know.' He shrugged, as if to say 'I'm just not too keen on ceremonial lynchings', but he didn't look all that concerned. His brows pinched together, suddenly, and he said, 'Are you … quite all right? You've got some dust —' he started to point on his own face, hesitated and said, 'Well … everywhere, really.'

Ree's cheeks heated. She was profoundly glad that the dust would hide it. 'I'm fine. I've just been travelling. Not a lot of opportunity to —' she cut herself off as she considered what she must look like to him. Coated in tomb grime, dust and cobwebs, unwashed and sticky-haired from a night sleeping rough in one of the lesser tombs while Usther's minions kept watch. Then she'd spent the night with parchment and ink on Andomerys' floor, and she hadn't bothered to bathe at home.

She would *definitely* do that now ...

Her mouth dried as she cast about for something normal to say. Whatever she might look like, she definitely didn't want to discuss her hygiene habits with him. She turned to Andomerys instead. 'The healing went well, then?'

'Going.'

'What?'

Andomerys rolled her eyes. 'The healing is *going* well. Don't get up,' she added without lifting her head.

'I beg your pard-*aahhh!* Smythe's knees gave out and he slithered to the floor, desperately clinging to the healer's table. His skin greyed, his eyes hollowing.

Ree hesitated, hands twitching at her sides, uncertain of whether she should help or stay out of the way. Andomerys stepped past her and braced Smythe, helping him back onto the bed.

'You know he's alive,' said Andomerys, once he was settled. Her magic glowed faintly around him as his eyes closed. 'You should come back in a few days. He needs to rest.'

Smythe's eyes cracked open. 'You *will* come back, won't you?'

Ree tucked a stray hair behind her ear. She found the earnestness of his gaze unnerving, but couldn't quite look away. 'I'll come back,' she promised.

The next few days were a misery of worry. She stopped her mother every time she came through the door. 'Do the council know about —?'

'No. Nobody knows. Morrin, in her wisdom, is shielding him.'

Personally, she thought it was more to do with Andomerys shielding him than anything, but she held her tongue. She didn't want her mother — or Morrin — to catch her blaspheming.

Emberlon gave her archive work closer to the town, and never asked any questions about the mysterious emergency book request. She couldn't shake the feeling that he *knew*, though. Something about the measuring look in his eyes ... she was probably being paranoid.

The additional benefit of the work was that it kept her away from Usther, who seemed determined to track her down. Ree wasn't sure what it was that had made her so suspicious, but she had no intention of giving away Smythe.

When she finally stood again on Andomerys' doorstep, she wore her best robe (which rather than black was just a *really* dark red) and her hair was carefully pinned. She'd washed that morning in a fresh trough of river water and she still couldn't feel her toes.

Andomerys opened the door and walked away without so much as a greeting. Ree followed her in, hating the way her heart clenched and her pulse jangled. She wasn't used to this desire to impress, and she didn't much like it.

Smythe sat at the spindly table, with a ceramic mug steaming in his hands. He looked brighter, fresher, the warm colour returned to his skin. As she walked in, he fumbled the mug to the table and lurched to his feet.

'Ree!'

Ree wasn't sure what expression she was meant to wear. She flushed as he beamed at her.

'I'm so pleased you came back! I realise you said you would, but even so you must be very busy, necromancing and what not —'

Andomerys cleared her throat and Smythe faltered. 'Oh. Um. Anyway, I'm all better now.'

Ree looked to Andomerys. The healer was embroidering again, what looked like tiny suns on the sleeves of her robes. 'He's really better?'

'Yes.' Andomerys carefully pulled the needle through the silk and pulled the thread to its extent.

'No complications?'

'No.'

Ree glanced at Smythe, who was staring at his lap. 'I may have slightly ... somewhat ... overstayed my welcome.'

Andomerys's eyes flicked up, then back to her work. 'You talk a lot,' was all she said. There was an air of long-suffering and barely contained temper about her.

Smythe looked at Ree and shrugged. Now *he* was blushing, his face positively glowing with embarrassment. Nobody in Tombtown blushed like that. None of the necromancers or their children *could*, and though Andomerys' healing magic fended off the effects of the nearness to death, Ree doubted Andomerys was capable of embarrassment.

Ree twisted her skirts in her hands. 'Well ... as you're better, I suppose I'd better take you back to the surface.'

Smythe eyes widened.

Andomerys sighed. 'Please do.'

'Please *don't!*' Smythe leapt to his feet and took Ree's hands in supplication — Ree flinched out of his grasp. 'Oh — sorry.' He looked sheepish a moment, but then his hands curled at his sides. 'Madam, I have gone to some considerable effort to get here and — well, I'm not ready to go back.' His jaw set in a firm line. 'I've spent my life in pursuit of history, a history that you *live* among every day. I don't know how you could — I mean, I've *seen* it! I've seen the tombs and — and the tunnels! I could spend the rest of my life here exploring and studying and never waste a day in boredom.'

'And there's the libraries,' said Ree, almost without thinking.

He smiled tentatively. 'Libraries?'

'Several of them.' She didn't know why she felt the need to sell him on her home when he would be leaving as soon as he was physically able, but she couldn't seem to resist. Maybe it was the memory of his shock and pity at learning she had been born here. 'I'm actually one of the town archivists — there are books here that are hundreds of years old, from many different cultures.'

'Fascinating!' His eyes glowed with enthusiasm. 'And where might one find these librar —'

Andomerys cleared her throat.

'Oh, um. I beg your pardon.' Smythe ran a hand through his hair. 'I didn't mean — I just get a little over-enthusiastic sometimes and ...' he trailed off.

Ree hesitated, teetering on the edge of a bad idea. Looking at him now, so keen to explore the world she loved, it was hard to imagine sending him away. But if he didn't go, and go quickly, she would have saved his life for nothing. She knew her neighbours: they would kill him if they got the chance. They would do it out of fear for themselves, and of the danger of Smythe telling others of their secret home, but they would do it nonetheless.

'You need to leave.' The words came out gentle. 'The necromancers here ... they'll kill you. And the town council will back them up if they do. You have to leave before they know you're here.'

She'd thought her words would elicit shock, or concern. Or perhaps dithering, as he seemed a dithery sort of person. But instead, his mouth firmed into a hard line. 'I have only just arrived.' He raised his chin. 'I have barely scraped the surface of this place, and already I know this is a site of historical significance unlike any other. I know — look, I realise you must think me a bit strange as I didn't grow up with bones under my feet, but I'm *not* weak. I'm very — I'm determined. I didn't survive the ridicule and constant sabotage of my peers at the University just to run away from a fight.' His gaze was flinty for a moment. He coughed, then smiled at her hopefully. 'So, uh, who do I speak to about staying here? Is there some sort of permit I can get? And somewhere to stay — an inn, perhaps?'

Ree wrung her skirts between her hands, torn between frustration and shock. 'Did you not hear me say that they'll kill you?'

'I heard you, but I must respectfully disagree.'

Andomerys watched Smythe with raised eyebrows. 'They might not kill him. They didn't kill me.'

'They *couldn't* kill you!' Ree felt close to tearing out her hair. 'Pa says all seven founders hit you with a curse and you shook it off and threatened to break their minions with your magic!'

'Ah!' said Smythe, while Andomerys shrugged. 'So they *can* be reasoned with!'

Ree pressed her fingertips to her temples. 'I wouldn't call that reason.'

'Look,' said Smythe. He clasped his hands in front of him and gave her a look so earnest that it made her uncomfortable. 'I do hear you. You *know* this place. You're — you're so knowledgeable. So competent. And you casually rediscovered a lost art of healing to help me. But I *can't* leave. I couldn't if you dragged me away.' His eyes were bright. 'This discovery is my *life's work*. I must see it through.'

The words pierced her. She knew too well the irresistible pull of passionate study. The sense of destiny around every breakthrough.

She feared for him. But she couldn't make him leave, and now she knew that she couldn't convince him to.

'Well,' she said, wondering if she was dooming him with these words. 'My father is on the town council. I'll help you make your case to him.'

Smythe's eyes widened. 'Really? Oh, that would just be jolly of you!' He seized her hand and pumped it up and down. 'Just excellent, thank you!'

Ree was torn between shock and nerves. She wasn't used to being touched by strangers, and only rarely by her parents. Was it always this warm? Did it always tingle? Her breath came short and her face flushed even hotter. Carefully, she extracted her hand.

Worse was the feeling that he was thanking her for delivering him to his executioners.

'It's no problem, really,' she said. She also couldn't decide if she was relieved or disappointed not to be touching any more. She clasped her hands behind her back so that it wouldn't happen again. There was too much going on right now for her to sort through. 'Um ... come with me, I guess?'

She looked at Andomerys, but the healer had gone back to ignoring them.

'Excellent!' Smythe started fussing around the table, shoving sheafs of paper and various writing implements into his worn leather satchel. 'Andomerys, is it alright if I borrow —?'

'Just go.'

Smythe raised the book he'd been reading, grinning cheerfully. 'I'm inexpressibly grateful.'

Ree paused in the doorway on her way out. 'Thank you,' she said quietly.

Andomerys inclined her head. Then, as she closed the door, she caught the faint advice: 'Try not to let him die.'

A task that was looking more difficult by the minute.

Ree led Smythe down from Andomery's hut, sneaking guilty glances at him. He was so strange and out of place, and after a week spent worrying about whether he'd live or die, she couldn't shake the feeling that he might vanish at any moment.

Fortunately, Smythe was too preoccupied to notice her furtive study of him. 'Gosh, it's dark out here, isn't it? I hadn't realised.'

It wasn't dark to Ree, but she let it pass. She would have to find him a torch or something if they were to explore, but a small amount of light filtered through the cracks in the domed ceiling of the town where it touched the surface.

'So this entire town is built inside an enormous tomb?'

Ree nodded and looked away from him, twisting her skirts between her hands. 'We call it the central mausoleum. It's a collection of smaller tombs connected to a much larger one.'

'A king?'

Ree nodded. 'We call him the Old King. We aren't sure which one.'

Smythe stopped and turned to face her, his eyes alight. 'I accept!'

Ree blinked. 'What?'

Smythe grinned at her, one cheek dimpling. 'Of *course* I'll put my research skills to the task of finding out which King is in your grand tomb —'

'I mean, we don't really call it that —'

'— I *am* the youngest Third Rank historian in over two hundred years, you know, and the foremost burial scholar in the southern reaches —'

Ree didn't like where this was going. '— Smythe —'

'— Let's see, I'll need some tools and two assistants with steady hands —'

'Smythe.' Ree fixed him with her father's 'if you interrupt me again, so help me, I'll feed you to the greywraiths' look.

Smythe stopped mid-sentence, his hands in the air. He lowered them and cleared his throat. 'Uhm. That is … quite the stare. I can't quite remember my train of thought.'

'It doesn't matter which king it was,' Ree said firmly. She would need to watch him carefully, she realised. Not because he meant any harm, but because he was so headstrong and enthusiastic that he would plunge into danger with a wave and a grin.

She had never been like that herself. Her parents worried that she was defenceless without the Craft, but she was ever cautious. She crept and climbed and bided her time. She balanced the risks and always erred on the side of safety.

All except once.

Smythe was still frowning at her. He looked quite pale. 'How did you do that ... thing ... with your eyes?' He pointed at her face with a trembling hand.

Her eyes did something? Interesting. She'd have to try the look in a mirror sometime, if she could find one that wasn't cursed ...

She exhaled through her nose. 'Smythe. Focus.'

'Right. Sorry. You were saying ... it doesn't matter which king it was.' He deflated as he said the words. 'I'm ever so sorry, madam, I know I can be a real wretch sometimes when I get excited.'

He stared at the floor, shoulders hunched and jaw clenched. He looked so forlorn that Ree relented. 'Look, you'll get to see it soon anyway.'

Smythe straightened. 'Really?'

Wandering Larry, who had caught Ree's scent on her way up, stumbled up toward them. He leaned in to bite Ree's shoulder. She gave his shoulder a shove, sending him tumbling back downstairs.

'At the town meeting to decide your fate.' She gestured for Smythe to follow her. Not many people climbed these stairs unless they needed Andomerys for something, but the longer they spent outside, the more likely it was that Smythe would be spotted.

She wished there was another way, but she couldn't see it. She couldn't hide Smythe from her father, or from anyone else if he was so determined to remain. She'd just have to approach the council and plead Smythe's case — get them onside before the rest of the town weighed in. It would be so much *easier* if he was a practitioner, but it took no more than a quick glance to tell that he'd never cast a necromantic spell in his life. He just looked so *healthy*. In an upworlder way, anyway.

'At the town meeting!' He repeated, delighted. His eyebrows pinched. 'At the town meeting?'

A better reaction would be fear, or the growing sense that he'd made a terrible mistake, as Ree had. If they couldn't get the town on Smythe's side, they would kill him to preserve their secrets.

But threats to his life didn't seem to dissuade him much, so Ree only said: 'We use the tomb as a town hall.'

'Splendid!' he said, though he looked more puzzled than pleased.

It wasn't long before he seized on something else to query. Ree somehow towed Smythe downstairs amidst cries of 'What's that limping fellow doing over there?' (it was a minion, watering Zamia's fungi garden) and 'Why does everyone wear black?' (it was traditional and hid bloodstains a treat) and 'Is that little girl's dog missing half a jaw?' (obviously). Larry lolloped after them, gargling happily. Ree gritted her teeth through all of it.

When she finally shunted Smythe through the back door of her family's tombhome, shooed Larry away and slammed the door closed behind them, she could hardly bear it when Smythe opened his mouth to ask another question.

'Who —?'

'Smythe. Please.' Ree rested her back against the door. It juddered as Larry pounded on it. 'I'm struggling to remember a time when you weren't talking.' Her legs still ached from two days of hard travel and all she wanted was to stagger into her bedroom and fall asleep on her nice comfy stone shelf. 'Would it be alright if you just read your book while I sort out a place for you?'

Smythe froze. 'I — yes. Of course. Jolly rude of me, to pester you with questions. I was just going to ask — nevermind.' He hunched his shoulders, leaving Ree with the unpleasant sensation of having scolded a puppy.

It wasn't that she *disliked* his chatter. She just didn't feel equipped to cope with it.

But she'd agreed to help Smythe. She owed him her life.

And he was a scholar. He appreciated learning on its own merits, not just in pursuit of power. There were precious few of those in her life.

'Thank you,' she said, relenting. She lit a candle and handed it to him. 'I appreciate it. Now — ack!' She stopped as she was about to turn into the main room.

Usther sat at the table, legs crossed and head cocked. 'Who's this?'

Ice formed in the pit of Ree's stomach.

An archer loosed at me today — the arrow tore my hawkskin and I fell tumbling from the sky, hitting tree branch after tree branch in my cumbersome human shape. I ripped my best blue robe, and lost quite a bit of my actual skin.

The limitations of the therianskin are well-warned in the stories my masters sang to me as a child. But I cannot help but feel frustrated at the vulnerability. I think: what is the point of wearing this skin if a pinprick can expel me from it? Why become a bear, or a wolf, if I cannot crush my enemies beneath my paws and crunch their skulls between my teeth?

I feel the necromancers could help me with this. Their magic is all about holding broken things together, after all, and its scent is akin to the scent of therianthropy. But I have no allies in this community. They are too cold, too ambitious, too self-absorbed for friendship.

I could ask the King to step in and send me an advisor, for if my power grows, so does his. But it may be wiser not to. I do not trust a necromancer not to smile while she stabs me in the back.

~from the journal of Wylandriah Witch-feather

CHAPTER EIGHT
SPECTRE-PUNCHED

Ree had spent a lot of time, energy, and social currency saving Smythe, and now he was striding toward an executioner with his hand outstretched.

'Chandrian Smythe, Third Rank —'

Ree stepped in front of Smythe, cutting him off. 'It doesn't matter. What are you doing in my house?' She masked herself in cold annoyance, hoping it would hide the fear clambering up her throat. If anyone found out about Smythe before she could get the council on her side, he would be killed. 'Don't you have anything better to do than break into my house? Spy on other practitioners? Insult passers-by?'

But Usther's gaze was fixed just above Ree's shoulder. Her colourless eyes were bright. 'So *this* is your secret,' she said, getting to her feet. 'This is why you were running around in such a hurry.' She bared her teeth at Smythe and said, 'Oh, Ree. You are in so. Much. *Trouble.*'

Ree tried to remain calm, though her pulse slammed in her veins. 'Don't be so dramatic,' she said coldly. Behind her, Smythe shifted nervously.

'You brought an *upworlder* home.' Usther nearly purred the words. 'Oh, this will be *very* good.'

'Sorry — good?' Smythe said. His voice cracked a little at the end.

Usther smiled in a way that made Smythe duck back behind Ree.

Ree scrubbed at her face. She needed to shut Usther up until she could talk to the council. Which meant talking to her father, first in a long list of things she didn't want to do. She *wanted* a book, she wanted to *think,* she wanted ten minutes where Smythe wasn't talking ...

Something howled and pounded on the door.

'Shush, Larry!'

Ree breathed out through her nose, thinking fast. She looked between the two of them, Smythe looking properly afraid for the first time since he'd mistaken her for a minion, Usther looking like a cat presented with a live mouse. There was a terrible feeling of inevitability about all this, but Ree pushed it back.

'There's nothing to be gained here,' Ree said, crossing her arms. She rolled her eyes, giving Usther every drop of bored disdain she could muster. 'I've already spoken with the council. They know he's here. We're waiting for the verdict.'

Silently, she prayed to Morrin and any gods who might be listening that Usther was gullible today.

Usther's eyes narrowed. 'You've already spoken to the council,' she repeatedly flatly.

Ree shrugged.

'And they're just letting you wander around with a potential witchkiller?' She referenced the many different factions in the upworld who took it upon themselves to kill people just because they might have dug up a few bodies or dabbled in black magic.

That was all of their greatest fear, of course. Adventurers killed them because they were between them and their coveted 'treasure'. Witchkillers killed them on principle, and went out of their way to do it.

Smythe peered over Ree's shoulder. 'I'm a historian, actually, quite a well-known —'

'*Do* shut up.' Usther stood up and brushed down her robes. She was wearing a very impressive robe with trailing spider lace cuffs. Her eyes were sunken into her face, shadowed and hard to read, but they were fixed not on Smythe, but on Ree.

Ree could see her lie growing smaller in Usther's eyes. It seemed vanishingly likely that the ruse would work, but to admit her lie would only spur Usther on. 'Are you finished posturing?'

'When you have power like mine, who needs to posture?'

Under other circumstances, Ree might have smiled at that, but her gaze was still locked with Usther's and there was nothing funny about her expression.

'You know ...' Usther began. 'I don't think you *did* tell the council.' Her shadow twitched in the candlelight, seeming to pulse larger and larger. 'Don't you think someone should?'

Ree took a step back, one hand on the table behind her. 'Smythe, go into my room.'

'Uh — which room is that?'

'Any room!'

Usther's eyes filled with shadow. 'Handing in an upworlder will put the council in my debt. Show them I'm a responsible and *civic-minded* denizen. It's only *practical.*' Her voice had the hint of a deep death echo as her power gathered.

Ree bumped into Smythe. 'You need to *leave.*'

Smythe's hands caught her shoulders, so warm she startled at the touch. 'I don't think I should.'

'Gods' weep, just *go* —'

Usther lifted her hand. Ree acted on instinct, diving aside.

Usther blew gently across her palm. Dust stirred and coalesced into a faded creature of tattered flesh and rags, gliding at Ree. Ree snatched at her herb pouch, but too late. The spectre collided with her, pinning her to the wall as if by a strong wind.

Usther smirked and lowered her hands. 'No hard feelings, I hope.'

Spectres were only the weak cousins of greywraiths. The summoned essence of a body pulled from gravedust, weaker even than a lesser minion like Larry. To use one against her was a slap in the face, and yet ...

Ree gasped for breath. Her fingers twitched toward her pouch, but the spectre had transfixed her. 'Us-ther ...' Her lungs squeezed, devoid of air.

Smythe got up from the floor, where Ree had knocked him. 'Now see here, you can't just —'

'Effet.' Usther waved a hand at him; another spectre smashed him into a chair, then disappeared in an explosion of dust. She didn't spend the magic to keep him pinned; she barely spared him a look. To Ree, she said, 'He's only an *upworlder*. And the council will be *so very pleased* that I've exposed him.' She walked to the door. 'If you stopped to think about it, you'd realise what an excellent plan it is. I'll be back soon with the council.'

The door slammed shut. Ree struggled against the spectre, but it only breathed in her face. All she could smell was mould and old cloth. It fixed her with a milky-eyed gaze.

If she was a necromancer, like her father, she would dispel this creature with a snap of her fingers. If she was a healer, like her mother, she would burn it away in a blast of radiant light.

But she was only Ree, and her dreams of a magic more powerful than either were still only dreams. The spectre continued to pin her, snatching her breath in its phantasmal wind.

'Ree!' Smythe scrambled to his feet. There was a purpling bruise under one eye, and his glasses were askew. He skidded to a stop in front of where the spectre pinned her, hands opening and closing. 'What do I do?'

Ree tried to draw breath, but the spectre pressed her further into the wall. ' ... Pouch.'

'Pouch. Pouch? Pouch!' Smythe's eyes lit on her belt, where her hands still twitched helplessly. 'Can I just ... ahh ... right.' He reached through the spectre's ghostly rags to fish in Ree's pouch. 'Ahh ... terribly sorry about this, old chap,' he told the spectre. He withdrew the herbs, hesitated, then threw them. The herb clouded around the spectre. It drew slightly back.

'Be at peace,' Ree wheezed. The spectre's eyes closed; it faded into nothing. Only a pile of grave mould on the floor marked its passing.

Ree staggered; Smythe caught her by the arms, bracing her. 'We did it! Rather impressive stuff, I should say. Would you mind if I took notes on — what are you doing?'

Ree shunted him back and into her bedroom. 'Stay in here. Shut the door. Don't make any noise.'

'Wait. What? Why? Ree! Where are you going?' His brown eyes were round with alarm.

She felt the pull of it. The desire to sit down and explain everything. To try to make sense of the mad world of necromancers he'd bumbled into when he first had the bright idea of excavating the crypt. To spend one day not running around trying to put everything right.

His gaze sharpened. 'Why are you helping me?'

She wished she knew. What did she really owe him, now? He'd saved her life; she'd saved his. She was foolish to even try. She tore her eyes from his and snatched up her father's spare staff from the corner. She pulled up her hood and ran for the door. 'I'm going to convince the council to let you live,' she told him, not trusting herself to meet his eyes. 'Before Usther gets them to kill you.' She slammed the door behind her and ran out into Tombtown's dusty streets, praying to Morrin and the slumbering dead that she wasn't too late.

Tombtown is very welcoming of strangers. Normal-ers, less so. As nearly all denizens immigrated from the upworld — often with angry villagers or righteous priests on their heels — there is a tolerance for the odd and the outcast which is rarely seen in settlements of its size. Necromancers are accepted yes, but so are the cursed, the ugly, the poor — if they can find their way here and survive the journey.

On one famous occasion, the town agreed to let an ex-dancing bear take up residence. Its chains were removed and it was given a tomb not far from the central mausoleum as a den, and food was left for it periodically.

It is not empathy the denizens lack: it is forgiveness.

And any who wander the long halls of the crypt had better not resemble those upworlders that hounded the denizens into hiding.

~from *A History of Tombtown* by Emberlon the Disloyal

CHAPTER NINE

THE BONE AND BREW

Ree made it about three feet before she collided with a wall of cold flesh and greenish skin. 'Larry!'

Larry flopped on the floor like a beached fish. Ree grabbed his arm, dragged him to his feet, and raced off after Usther with her father's staff still in-hand. How many minutes had she lost, pinned to the wall by Usther's spectre? Five minutes? Fifteen? How long would it take Usther to turn the council against her?

Ree had meant to do this carefully. She'd have spoken to all the council members individually, starting with her father. She'd have introduced them all to Smythe, because who could believe such a goofy imbecile was any more dangerous to the town than Larrry was. She'd have explained that she owed him, but would avoid the encounter with the Lich ...

She skidded around the corner, narrowly avoiding a necromancer in heavily singed robes. 'Watch it!'

'Sorry!'

She ran on. She could hear Larry crash into the necromancer but couldn't stop to survey the damage. At this time of day, most of the council would surely be at Mortana's tavern. She saw the sign of the skull and flagon and burst through the door.

Mortana looked up from a bar strewn with ingredients and alchemical equipment. She was a pallid-skinned necromancer with wild ocean-spray hair and eyes with a vicious red tint. She was also a wyrdling, the only one Ree had ever met, with two small horns peeking through her hair and a heavy, copper-scaled tail that dragged behind her. 'Everyone's tearing around today. Can't I get ten minutes of peace?'

Ree didn't point out that Mortana ran a tavern, and that people were necessarily a part of that. She was fairly certain that the tavern keeper's only reason for doing so was to spy on the customers.

'The council —'

Mortana groaned and rolled her eyes. '*The council this! The council that!* That snooty acolyte was after them as well. When I told her to pipe down, she knocked over the spiders' eyes I was brewing, and they were nearly potion-ready!'

Ree could see the tavern keeper was building up to a rant. She could hear her tail sweeping the floor behind her. 'Mortana, I just need —'

'No.' She put her hands on the bar and leaned forward. 'I never wanted the council in here in the first place. If you're here to buy something, stay. If not, get out.'

A hundred options flashed through Ree's mind. Her hands clenched and unclenched; she gritted her teeth. She considered suggesting Mortana's access to the alchemy books be curbed, or reminding Mortana of all the council notes that had mysteriously turned up in books Mortana returned. Smythe's life was hanging in the balance, and her nerves burned that Mortana dared obstruct her.

But she was also not keen on conflict and very short on time. She hesitated; her eyes flitted to the double doors that led to the back rooms of *The Bone & Brew*.

Mortana's eyes narrowed. She started to gather power. 'Ree. Don't you —!'

Ree darted around the bar, just barely whipping out of reach of Mortana's clawed hands. She barrelled through the doors, tripped down the step, and tumbled into a low-ceilinged room with a large, pitted table at the centre, and four surprised necromancers sitting around it. Her father's staff flew from her grasp to skitter across the floor and fetch up against a familiar pair of muddy black boots.

'Reanima.' Ree's father plucked the staff from the floor and laid it on the table. His charcoal hair was tied in a neat tail at his neck. His robes were pressed and wrinkle-free; his eyes were black and without whites. Years of the Craft had kept him young, but had also traded much of his life with unlife. His skin was the colour of a rain-soaked sky, and veined with ink. 'How nice of you to join us.'

'I *told* you she would.' Usther perched on a barrel in the corner, legs and arms crossed. 'She'll do anything to protect him. A rather pathetic defender, I must say.'

Ree swallowed heavily. She pushed herself to her knees, then to her feet. She bowed low to the dark-haired man. 'Pa. This isn't what it looks like.'

'And what, exactly, does it look like, Reanima?' He lowered himself back into his seat while the other council members murmured. Ree winced at the use of her full name, as if pricked by a thorn. While her mother only used it when she was annoyed, her father refused to shorten it. Each time he spoke to her, he brandished it like a whip: a reminder of what a disappointment she was, of the dreams she'd betrayed.

They weren't my dreams, she wanted to say. *That isn't me.*

'I found a boy,' said Ree.

Usther snorted. 'He looked plenty grown up to me.'

'In a Third Era embalming room. He was just studying.' She couldn't quite bring herself to meet her father's eyes, so she looked at each of the other council members in turn. 'We talked. He didn't attack me. Didn't even want to. He wasn't hurting anyone.' Ree said it as firmly as she could. Kylath, one of the younger council members, pursed her black lips. Bahamet the Eternal, who was nearly a Lich himself, only twitched slightly in his seat.

'You should have made him leave,' said Kylath. Her mouth twisted. 'We have no need of *upworlders* coming here and disturbing our dead.'

'Better yet, you could have killed him.' This from Tarantur, with brown-grey skin, a rat-like dart to his eyes, and spell diagrams tattooed across his face. He was far from the most powerful necromancer in town, but was close to the most knowledgeable. People whispered that he'd once marched an undead army on the capital of Assur in the northern valleys.

Kylath made a face at him, but Tarantur only shook his head. 'Without secrecy, we are nothing. If those out there knew about us, they'd send their armies in after us to dig us out of the tombs and burn the bodies.'

'Adventurers find out all the time,' Ree said impatiently. 'We're still here.'

'No, that's not the same at all. You see — you see, adventurers are greedy. They think "I have found this tomb, and I can keep its treasure for myself." Governments are greedy too, but they need not be secretive about it. They think "I own everything in this country anyway. If the people find treasure, I will just take it from them." It's not worth the risk.'

'That's not what Smythe is like.'

'And you know him well, do you?' Kylath narrowed her eyes. 'After just meeting him, you trust him with our town, our way of life?'

'No, I didn't say that —'

'You should never have brought him here,' said Tarantur.

'He knows too much,' said Kylath.

Ree looked from Kylath to Tarantur to Bahamet, seeking sympathy, patience, the tiniest *hint* of support, but she found none. At last, she turned to her father. 'He saved my life.'

The words hung in the air a moment. Even Bahamet stirred, turning shadow-pit eyes to focus on her.

Ree's father's face clouded. He leaned forward. 'Explain.'

'There was a greater dead,' Ree said. She tensed as Usther slithered from the barrel, but refocused on the council. 'I was unprepared. I was caught in a mind snare. If he hadn't arrived, I'd be dead now.'

She saw the effect her words had on her father; the way he closed his eyes, the way his jaw tightened. 'A mind snare,' he said quietly, and she could almost taste the scorn on the air, bitter and cold.

'A shame you never learned the Craft.' Usther started to pace the room. She had all the presence of a cobra. 'You might not have needed rescue from an interfering upworlder if that were so.'

Ree's eyes flitted to her father, then away. Her chest tightened at the shame writ so clearly across his face. *It was the Lich!* she wanted to say. *Not one necromancer in ten could resist a mind snare that powerful, and I* still *got away!* But if they found out that Smythe had disturbed the Lich — let alone Ree — then he would certainly be killed, if only to appease it.

She pressed her lips together and looked at her feet. 'He isn't a danger to us.'

'That remains to be seen,' said Kylath.

'It's not worth the risk,' said Tarantur.

'Usther was telling us about this upworlder.' Her father's tone was flat. 'He's a greater danger than you're letting on. Speaks unguardedly, knows nothing about our ways, and he's well-known in the world above.'

'A historian,' said Usther. She stopped next to Ree and made to lean on her shoulder; Ree elbowed her in the ribs. 'He intends to write about us for his disgusting establishment.' She flapped a dismissive hand. 'I'm sure it would make him a name among his peers: the man who found a community of freaks and delinquents, living in a city of the dead. Quite the headline.'

'That's a terrible headline,' said Ree. 'And he's not like that at all. He just wants to learn, and explore. He's not — not dangerous! He's just curious. Like —'

'Like you?' Usther raised an eyebrow. Ree's stomach twisted and heat rose to her face. There had been many times in her life when Ree had thought she hated Usther, but just then she would have struck her across the face if the council weren't there to watch.

'A decision must be made,' said Tarantur. 'And in light of this information —'

'Excuse me, but — don't I get a say?'

Ree went cold. The door creaked open. Smythe nodded and smiled as he entered, missed a step, and staggered into Ree. She steadied him as he straightened his glasses. Larry lumbered in behind him.

For a moment, the room was silent but for the sound of Larry gently whining.

Smythe, for his part, looked almost undead as he considered the room of necromancers before him. She had never seen him look so ashen, or so shocked. 'I'm terribly sorry,' he said into the silence. 'The tavern keeper kindly pointed me this way. I hope I'm not intruding.' He gave Larry a reassuring pat on the shoulder. 'There there, it's not so bad, old chap — argh!' He barely managed to snatch his hand away as Larry's teeth clicked shut.

'Smythe.' Ree's voice was barely more than a shrill whisper. Her throat was tight; her heart thumped painfully against her ribs. 'I thought I told you to stay in my room.'

'I know, but I wanted to help —'

Pressure built up in the room. The temperature chilled. The air thinned. Ree could see Smythe's breath clouding in the air. Her eyes flicked to the assembled council members, all standing, and acted on instinct. She stepped between Smythe and the necromancers, throwing her arms wide and backing him into the wall. 'You are *not* going to hurt him!'

she said, throwing up every mental ward her parents had ever taught her. Her eyes met her father's. 'Pa, please!'

His nostrils flared. The pressure in the room continued to build, but no spells were cast. Ree held her breath, praying that she hadn't angered the other council members enough for them to risk going through her to get to Smythe.

'Fine!' Her father snatched his staff from the table and slammed it down onto the ground. Shadowy tendrils swirled around him. His voice boomed, shaking dust from the ceiling and echoing around the tomb: '*All denizens to the town hall. Now!*'

The magic faded. He jabbed a finger at Ree. 'Don't you let him out of your sight for a *second.*'

'This is a bad idea, Igneus,' said Tarantur. 'We ought to deal with him ourselves.'

'She says she owes him her life —' said her father.

'You do?' Smythe whispered.

'— it's out of our hands.'

The council members filed out of the room, until it was just Ree, Smythe, Usther, and Larry.

'*Excellent* work, Ree.' Usther cocked her head to one side. 'Really, some truly *bronze-level* ideas there. Now he'll be killed by a mob instead of a council; *much* more entertaining.'

'Shut up.'

'I have to ask why you are putting so much *effort* into trying to preserve a man who is clearly destined for lesser minion-hood. Why must you insist on saving him?'

'Because I like him!' Ree stalked up to Usther, meeting her gaze for gaze. 'Because we shouldn't kill people just because they're different.'

'And why not?' Usther sneered down at her. 'That's what *his kind* would do to us, isn't it?' Then, sharply: 'You don't understand. You don't know what it's like up there.'

That's what it always came back to. All the other denizens had been driven here. This was Ree's home town, but it was Usther's only refuge. If Ree really wanted, she could live up there. She wasn't a practitioner; there was nothing about her for the upworlders to detest.

But she knew, in her gut, that she *belonged* here. More than being born here; more than her mother and father being part of the fabric of the town. Her destiny was here, and it was waiting for her to find it.

Usther was still staring at her, all scorn and indignation. Ree shook her head and spun away from her. She tore her hands through her hair, scattering pins across the floor. 'If the only people allowed to live here are necromancers, then what does that mean about me?'

The sneer faded from Usther's face. Her lips pressed together; the spark left her eyes. She brushed past Ree. 'Come on. We shouldn't be late for the council.' She left the room without looking back.

'Ree?' Smythe looked at her. His colour had returned with a vengeance; he was red-faced, and wide-eyed, and trembling. 'Are, um — are they really going to kill me?'

'I don't know.' Ree kicked aside a chair and sank to the floor, robes pooling around her. She looked at him; so alive, so confused. She shook her head. 'I should never have revealed myself to you. You might never have come across another denizen; you'd be safe now.' She opened her hands and stared at her grey palms. She'd just been so *curious*. She'd never seen an upworlder her own age, never heard one talking about the things *she* was interested in. She'd been charmed by his constant chatter. She'd wanted to know him.

And now he was going to die.

'I don't know about all that,' he said. He knelt beside her, staring at his lap. 'Maybe it wouldn't be necromancers, but I suppose that very old chap might've done for me —'

'The Lich,' Ree murmured.

'—yes, that's the one. Or any number of undead creatures.' He pulled his iron sarakat from around his neck and considered it. 'I don't suppose this would have been as much help as I first thought.'

Ree's lips quirked in spite of herself. 'None at all.'

Smythe scooted tentatively closer. 'And I wouldn't have met you, or Larry, or seen this *incredible* town —' He stopped, and took a shuddering breath. Hand quivering, he touched his fingertips lightly to her hand — warm, tingling, and utterly strange.

Ree startled. Her eyes leapt to his.

'What I'm saying is: I'm glad you corrected me in the embalming room.' He hesitated. 'And ... I'd rather not die.'

Larry made a gargling sound and leaned over Smythe's shoulder. Smythe gave him a friendly pat. 'No offense, old chap.'

Blood sacrifice. The first recorded instance was three years after founding, when a witch hunter tracked a young acolyte, Namura, into the crypt. He burned her alive. The murderer was captured, and the council voted that his blood would be used in defense of the town, in Namura's memory.

Though the blood sacrifice has dark roots, its tradition has become a festive one. Those who mean the town harm are sacrificed for the good of its denizens, and everyone sings along with the ritual spell and shares a hot cider afterwards.

Namura's ward, from a necromantic perspective, protects the town from scrying and amplifies the powers of those who practice within its bounds. But far more importantly, from a sociological standpoint, it is a beloved bonding experience between denizens that usually live and work in isolation.

~from *A History of Tombtown* by Emberlon the Disloyal

CHAPTER TEN

IT TAKES A VILLAGE

'I suddenly feel quite unwell.'

'Smythe ...' Ree wanted to reach out to him, but though her fingers twitched in sympathy, her hands remained at her sides.

They stood outside the tall black iron doors of the town hall. Everyone she knew was already inside. Waiting.

She took in the sweat beading on Smythe's forehead, the tremble in his chin, his wavering eyes. Again, he seemed fragile to her. He was bright and lively and unsuited to her world.

But she'd dragged him into it anyway.

She didn't really know what to say. She had no comfort to offer. If the town voted to kill him, she would hardly be able to stop them. 'Are you ready?' Her voice was small; it seemed a woefully inadequate response to his fear.

He nodded, then nodded again. 'Yes. I ... yes. I'm ready. Of course I'm ready.' He took a shuddering breath.

Ree leaned on one of the tall black doors. It swung slowly open under her weight.

She flashed him a sad smile, hoping it was less than half-grimace. 'Welcome to the Old King's Tomb.'

They were bathed in golden light as the door opened, reflected from the treasure piles mounting the walls and falling through the cracks in the artworked ceiling. The room itself was largely built of an austere black marble, a low hall climbing up to a raised dais on which the Old King's sarcophagus rested. The council stood at the sarcophagus, as if at a wide lectern, talking among themselves. It was a room at once too grand and too fine for its current use, eclipsing the rows of rickety seats regimented below the dais.

Ree's father stamped his staff on the marble floor; a boom rebounded from the marble walls. He pointed his staff at Ree and Smythe. 'The upworlder arrives.'

The chamber erupted. Denizens leapt to their feet, shouting and arguing, their words incomprehensible in the chaos. Beside her, Smythe blanched and stepped back. Ree grabbed his sleeve and pulled him onward. 'It's okay,' she said, leaning in close. Her eyes skipped over the angry faces; she needed to be strong for Smythe, 'You're with me, you can —'

Someone yanked him from her grasp.

'Uh — Ree! Ree, what's happening —'

Ree spun; two minions had him by the arms and were shuffling him toward the dais. Ree looked up at the council. Tarantur waved a lazy hand, conducting his minions from above.

She gritted her teeth. If she were powerful, like her father, no-one would dare insult her this way. But Ree was always a safe person to snub, the person even the acolytes could look down on. She could no more put Smythe under her protection than she could put the council under a spell. Nevermind that Smythe had done nothing wrong; nevermind that Ree had vouched for him — Ree, who created their maps and provided their books; Ree, who was more at home here than anyone.

She clenched her fists at her sides. 'It'll be okay!' she called to him, trying to believe her own words. 'Don't struggle!'

It wouldn't always be this way.

'Hey, now.' Emberlon appeared at her side, tall and grim-faced. He took her by the shoulders, easing her into a seat. 'Don't let them eat at you. Nothing will be done until a ruling is reached.'

She realised she was trembling, literally shaking as her veins filled with hot flame.

'There's no need!' She almost spat the words. She raised a quivering hand to point at the council. 'They have no reason to manhandle him like that. He's terrified!'

Emberlon sat beside her, folding his hands in his lap. 'Don't let your anger stop you from paying attention.'

Ree bit back a retort. How could she possibly look away from this? But Emberlon's expression was pointed beneath his usual melancholy, and he'd never steered her wrong before.

Ree gripped the edges of her seat and glared at her father, standing dark and stoic behind the sarcophagus. The minions ascended the steps, dragging Smythe between them.

Mazerin the Bold, a weedy necromancer with thin white hair and shadowed eyes, sat on Ree's other side. He elbowed Ree in the ribs. 'Look at that, eh? A live upworlder! How long's it been since we had a proper ritual sacrifice? Three years? Five? Normally they get eaten up by the ghouls in the lower levels before we get hold of them!'

'We're not sacrificing him, Maz,' she said. She shied away from him, scooting closer to Emberlon. Mazerin wasn't very powerful, but he was one of the more temperamental necromancers. She'd once seen him literally curse a child for knocking over his bone stall.

The parents had extracted their vengeance from him in blood, of course, but it still made her nervous.

Mazerin's grin dropped. 'Aren't we? Why?' He looked Ree up and down. 'You didn't have something to do with this, did you?'

Ree's chest tightened. She kept her eyes fixed on the dais.

Mazerin leaned closer to her. She could feel his breath on her cheek. 'Did you —'

Ree's father banged his staff again. Mazerin straightened in his seat. All eyes snapped to the dais as the echoes died out.

Kylath placed her hands on the sarcophagus and leaned forward, red eyes sparking. 'We're here to deal with this intruder, an upworlder named Chandrian Smythe, found wandering the eastern tunnels.'

One of the acolytes, a girl Ree's age called Symphona, yelled, 'Blood sacrifice!'

A cheer went up.

Ree seethed in her seat, crossing her arms so tightly that her chest ached.

Tarantur waved the crowd quiet. 'In due time.' He smiled to one side.

Kylath continued, 'He was dutifully brought to our attention by Usther the acolyte, whose concern for —'

'Is that true?' Emberlon murmured to Ree, looking askance as Usther stood up a few rows ahead and took a bow. She received no applause, and Ree could imagine her secret fury at being referred to as an acolyte rather than a full-blown practitioner.

Ree inclined her head. 'I think she's planning a power grab.' Her eyes were not on Usther, but on Smythe.

Emberlon stroked his chin. 'Aren't they all?'

'I'm not,' said Ree while Tarantur stepped forward to list all the reasons it would be better to kill Smythe. 'You're not.'

Emberlon's eyes took on a faraway look. His mouth tightened. 'Some of us have already had more than enough of power grabs.'

Ree looked at him sidelong, blindsided by the rare nugget of personal information. She remembered the rumours about Emberlon, and about the missing king of the upworlder kingdom of Sirennia, and wondered again exactly how much she should believe.

If only all the rumours were true. Perhaps the denizens would listen to an actual king — provided that king was also a necromancer.

'— so I think that about covers it,' said Tarantur. His fingers were steepled and he wore a punchable smirk. 'Now all that remains is to decide the *method* of punishment —'

'Blood sacrifice!' Symphona yelled again, to more cheers. Ree's eyes went to Smythe, still dangling between two large minions. He looked very small, and his eyes were very wide.

Ree considered replacing Symphona's map with a very *special* map full of 'surprises'. She'd never liked the older acolyte, who seemed to think Ree was some kind of servant, and she liked her flippant calls for Smythe's death even less.

Ree's father stepped forward. 'Not yet. Is there anyone here to speak in defence of the upworlder?'

Ree stood up, twisting her skirts between her hands. Her anger was lost among the churning in her gut. She stared resolutely up at the dais, ignoring the feeling of eyes crawling over her. She'd never made a spectacle of herself like this; she'd always kept her head down, always been in the background. '*Better not to draw attention to yourself,*' her mother had warned her once. '*Until you practice the Craft, you will have no respect from them.*'

'*You don't practice the Craft,*' said Ree. She'd been sulking in her room; her father had forbidden her to come with him on a journey into the sealed sectors of the crypt. '*Andomerys doesn't. Nobody cares.*'

'*I am a priestess of our Lady of Unlife,*' said Ree's mother. '*The nectar of her power is like water to me, and to anger me is to risk her displeasure. And Andomerys is a very powerful healer. When someone's ritual explodes in their face, they're glad to have her to stitch it back on again. You have no magic and no place. You need to avoid drawing attention to yourself.*'

It had been strange to be told she had to fear the people she'd grown up with. The neighbours who'd given her knuckle bones to play with while they babysat her, the elders who'd pinched her cheeks and told her she'd be a fearsome dark wizard one day. But she had a place now. She was apprentice archivist, the keeper of their most valuable knowledge. And she would have to risk raising her head if she wanted Smythe to have any chance at all.

Several rows ahead and to her left, Andomerys stood as well. Ree sucked in a breath. Her eyes searched for her mother, wondering if Arthura, Priestess of Morrin, might also stand up for her daughter's cause, but wherever her mother was, she didn't stand up.

It was exactly what she expected from her parents, yet she was still torn between disappointment and bitterness. They weren't going to spend their social currency for a boy they didn't know, not even if Ree asked them to.

Andomerys didn't wait to be called on. 'I healed that boy when he was suffering from a heavy death curse. He was brought to my house. He was polite. I don't think he's in danger of anything but boring people to death.' She nodded at the council and sat down.

'You healed an upworlder?' someone yelled.

'You slammed the door in my face last week when that ghoul bite got infected!'

Andomerys crossed her arms and leaned back in her chair. 'I don't owe you healing, Ungoth.'

There was a muttered, 'But it hurt!', nearly lost among the susurrus moving through the crowd.

Ree took a deep breath. 'We can't kill Smythe,' she said. Again, that feeling of eyes crawling over her. She wanted to yank up her hood and hide under a chair, but she gripped her skirts with white fingers and set her jaw. 'He saved my life.'

Tarantur rolled his eyes. 'From a mind snare, we know. We can hardly take that into account when you have the means to learn to defend yourself.'

'Why not?' This was from Yngrid, who'd taught Ree skeleton blind spots as a child. Her curly hair was the colour of crusted blood, and her once warm brown skin was dusted slate grey from using the Craft. 'She's one of us, isn't she?'

'*Is* she?' Symphona again. She threw Ree a narrow-eyed look. 'All she does is scurry around the tunnels like a rat. She doesn't respect the Craft.'

Necromancy wasn't the only magic. Ree swallowed hard, her cheeks burning, fighting a sting in the corners of her eyes. And a person's value ought to be more than their knowledge of the Craft.

She wanted badly to flee. Her knees shook; she locked them. She said, 'I've never betrayed you. Neither will Smythe. If you're worried about him telling people about us, just don't let him leave. He's already expressed a desire to stay.' Her eyes found Smythe; his hair was rumpled, his glasses askew. Sweat drenched his shirt. His eyes filled with pleading. 'If he becomes a denizen, we have nothing to worry about.'

'Sounds reasonable,' called Yngrid.

'But ... the blood sacrifice,' said Symphona.

Ree's shoulders raised. She held her breath as the argument continued. She felt Emberlon's eyes on her, weighing. She prayed to her mother's goddess that he would speak up for her and Smythe even as she knew that he never would. Emberlon shied away from politics like a horse from snakes.

And all the while Smythe was looking at her, suspended between two minions, while the town argued his fate.

'It's not practical,' said Tarantur. 'Who will make sure he doesn't leave? Young Ree? We can barely stop *her* from wandering. And the rest of us are too busy with our research.'

Ree locked her hands behind her back to hide their shaking and tried to school her expression to stillness, worried everyone would see the rage burning in her eyes. What gave him the right to speak about her as if she were some wayward child? She did important work for this town that *he* had benefited from nearly every week. And *still* her father was silent beside him.

'Enough of this,' said Kylath. 'Let's put it to a vote. Should the upworlder be used in a blood sacrifice, yea or nay? Yea?'

A thunderous shout went up.

'And the nays?'

Ree faltered with the word, as paltry others shouted with her. It was feeble, worthless. Her eyes flicked to Tarantur; he didn't bother to hide his delight.

'The yeas have it,' said Kylath. 'We'll sacrifice him at sundown. Now, onto our next order of business. Someone has been digging up the graves near Volturo's tomb, and it's making the dead there restless. We also need to discuss acceptable garden plants, the knotweed is getting out of hand —'

Ree stood there, stunned, as the town meeting moved on without her. There was pressure on her arm as Emberlon eased her back down into her seat. 'He didn't do anything wrong,' she said in a low voice, struggling to keep her volume in check. In the background, two necromancers got into a shouting match over who had precedence in one of the newly discovered tombs. 'He's harmless.'

Emberlon nodded. 'They're doing what they think is right. They're scared. The world out there isn't kind to necromancers.'

'They're cowards,' said Ree. She gripped her chair, tension making her entire body ache. 'They're cowards and they're greedy. They don't really think Smythe is dangerous, they just want another blood sacrifice.'

Emberlon shook his head. 'This is the way the world works, Ree. You've lived here all your life — longer than me, longer than all but the first settlers. You must have known that this would happen.'

But she hadn't, not really. She'd been worried, but she *knew* these people. She'd had a plan. If Usther hadn't — but Usther *had.* Ree burned at the memory of the smug look on her face.

At the end of the meeting, the denizens gradually filtered back out of the Old King's Tomb, away from the golden light and sparkling marble and back to the damp and gloom of everyday life. Smythe was still imprisoned on the dais. Ree ascended the steps and approached the council, fists clenched at her sides. 'I want to say goodbye.' Her voice was hoarse with repressed anger.

Tarantur waved at Smythe. 'As you please. He's right there.'

'Pa.' Ree looked to her father.

He gazed back, expressionless.

'Pa, please.'

He sighed and rubbed his face. 'Let him loose, Tarantur. It's not like he can get far.'

Tarantur barked a word in the old language, and his minions dropped Smythe and stepped aside. Ree pulled him to his feet. 'I'm so sorry, Smythe.'

This wasn't right.

Smythe tried to smile, but his mouth wobbled back into a frown. 'Serves me right, I suppose, wandering into the crypt alone. It just seemed like such an opportunity, and I — well, never mind.' He shook his head. 'Ree, I just wanted to say —' But he looked at the council and the words died on his lips.

This wasn't right.

Ree's chest ached. Her stomach churned. She felt like at any moment, she might retch.

Smythe looked at the floor. 'Will you be there for me? When — well, you know.' He stopped and cleared his throat. 'I would appreciate a friendly face, as it were.'

She had to make this right. 'Of course I will.' The words were thick in her throat. Her hand moved toward the belt on her pouch.

'Um. Ree?'

She spun and threw herbs in the faces of Tarantur's minions. Their eyes closed; they crumpled where they stood. Tarantur shouted; power gathered behind her like the first rumblings of an avalanche. She grabbed Smythe and lunged down the dais, heading not for the double doors but the back of the tomb.

'Ree, what's —'

'REANIMA!' Her father's voice thundered after her. A curse smashed an urn to her left; another exploded on the step just behind her. She kept her grip on Smythe's hand, pulling him after her.

'Keep close!' she gasped.

Behind her, Tarantur shouted, 'They're getting away! Igneus —' His voice cut off in a gasp.

'If you try to curse my daughter ever again, there will be nothing left of you to bring back,' her father said in a low voice.

Ree didn't look back, she plunged down a narrow walkway, little more than a snake-trail of clear footing. Smythe waded after her, scattering coins. 'Where are we going?'

'Morrin forgive me,' she muttered, 'I hope it's really here.'

They came to the wall, to an elaborate mural of Death standing over the Old King. It looked like a dead end, but she was the archivist's apprentice and Tombtown's only cartographer. She knew more of the crypt's secrets and pathways than anyone else in town. Her hands scrabbled down the lacquered marble. 'Find the sarakat, find the —'

'Is this —?'

More shouting. The pressure in the room was building. She looked over her shoulder; the town hall was flooding with necromancers, their minions stumbling through the chairs. A few spectres breezed past them, their red eyes fixed on Smythe.

Ree nudged Smythe aside and dug her fingers into the sarakat, finding a groove around the arch of it. She tugged. A small doorway swung open, just the height of the image of the Old King. 'Come on!' She shoved Smythe through, then kicked the door closed behind her.

I've been remembering the masters today. The colours they wore on their faces, the music they played. I remembered my choosing, deep in the Wilds, far from the village that birthed me. I remember the animals closing in around me: a wolf, a bear, and a stag with gore-tipped antlers.

They could see the wildness in me. So they put a knife in my hand and sang me the ancient teachings and led me to my first kill and my first skin.

They were rare even then. There are no masters now. Perhaps there are no therianthropes at all. Certainly, I have met no others since the witchkillers purged the Wilds.

I enjoy being special. It affords me stature in the King's underkingdom that I would otherwise not enjoy. But I do not wish to be the last, and I have not managed to find an apprentice, nor anyone worthy of the teaching songs.

I am not so foolish as the necromancers — my magic might extend my life, but nobody lives forever.

Tomorrow, whether the King wills it or not, I will write my book. And one day, someone with wildness in their heart will read it and therianthropy will live beyond me.

~from the journal of Wylandriah Witch-feather

CHAPTER ELEVEN

CAST OUT AND CURSED AT

They ran until the cries and curses and hammering on the marble wall faded into a distant whisper. Ree stopped and hunched over, panting. Smythe crashed into her.

'Ow! Do you mind?'

'Terribly sorry.' He was panting as well. 'I'm not used to running for my life through the dark. It's ... sort of thrilling, isn't it? The excitement, the danger, the not-being-dead. Heady stuff.' He smiled at her. His smile froze on his face. '... Ree?'

'We should keep moving.' Ree straightened. 'There are five or six intersections within this passage. Between them, they might know at least a few of them.' She frowned; Smythe was still staring at her, his smile slipping into something like horror. 'What?'

'It's nothing, nevermind.' He straightened as well, then opened his mouth as if to say something. He shook his head and started to walk off, stopped, and said, 'I'm terribly sorry, but ... your eyes.'

Ree rubbed her eyes and blinked a few times. 'What? Is there something wrong with them?' She wondered fretfully if one of the curses had landed without her noticing. She'd been so focused on *running* she'd barely given a thought to her mental shields.

'They're *glowing,'* said Smythe.

'Yeah, well, it's dark in here,' replied Ree, whose parents had performed a darksight ritual for her when she was five years old. 'You can hardly expect me to blunder around blindly just because I couldn't bring a torch.'

'That's exactly what I expected,' Smythe whispered, half in fear, half in awe. 'Could you do that to me? So I could see in the dark?'

'We don't have time. And I'm not a necromancer.' She nudged him with her boot. 'If you can't see the way ahead, just stay close to me.'

She jogged off. After a moment's hesitation, Smythe followed.

Even with darksight, Ree wished she had a torch. The tunnels were painted hazy blue to her, with darkness tucked into corners and cracks, and every flash of light was like staring into a solar flare. It was also silent but for the patter of their feet on dirt and stone, and the occasional, 'Oops! I am *terribly* sorry about that,' as Smythe bumped into her in the dark.

Ree was no stranger to darkness, or silence, or wandering the lonely, forgotten passages of the crypt. But it was a very different experience when straining for the sound of muttered incantations and shuffling feet, and squinting ahead for the telltale shadow of black magic.

What was she doing here? What had possessed her, that she'd decided to grab Smythe and run? Tarantur's curse had been aimed at *her*. She'd marked herself as the outsider she'd always sworn she wasn't.

She didn't *make* reckless decisions. She was cautious, considered. She had survived for seventeen years in this crypt without magic. She had built a place for herself and earned her way. And she was risking it all for ... what? A man she hardly knew. A debt she'd already paid.

'Ree?'

'This way,' she said. She took his wrist and guided him around the corner.

They would let her back. Necromancers had a terrible rage but were easily distracted, and none of them really wanted her dead. They knew her, they'd watched her grow up. But in the heat of the moment, filled with bloodlust and righteous power, they would curse first, think later.

But she had some advantages. In her mind, she was envisioning the maps she'd found and annotated or drawn herself, assembling a collage in her mind, a multi-level diagram of where they'd come from and where they needed to go.

If they turned left at the next junction, she could take him across the shallow stone bridge into the eastern levels. If they spent the night in the tower there, she could take him to the surface in the morning without passing any of the denizens' usual territories.

There were sometimes ghouls in that part of the crypt, and ghouls were far more troubling than any lesser dead or minor minion, but if they took care to ward one of the upper rooms, she was confident they could —

'What was that?' she held out her arm, stopping Smythe in his tracks.

'What was —?'

'Shh!' She could hear it now. Low voices, nearly inaudible, echoing down the narrow walls of the tunnel.

There was no guarantee they would be able to outrun them. It could even be a trap — scare them into running on, and chase them right into the arms of another group. Necromancers usually hated working in groups, but they were crafty and had minions at their beck and call.

She looked frantically about. What did she know about the construction in these parts? Were there any secret doors, were there high ceilings, any crumbling walls she could take advantage of?

They needed to hide. Needed a tomb or a tunnel or — yes!

These tunnels were often flooded, having been built beneath a lake. Most tunnels in these parts had large drainage systems. If she just looked down —

She seized Smythe's wrist. The voices were getting louder.

'What's happening? Should —'

'They've found us.' She dragged him back and to the wall. Yes, there was the drainage trench, and a little further along — 'Down here, Smythe.' She crouched beside a narrow tunnel that only came up to about knee height. 'You crawl in first.'

Smythe scrambled over to the tunnel, ducked his head, then dithered. 'I don't think I'll fit!'

'Then get lower!' She hissed. She shoved him in and crawled in after him.

'Eurgh, disgusting! It's all wet!'

'Shh!'

When she got in, she grabbed his ankle. 'Wait a minute.'

'And on my good adventuring trousers, too,' he whispered.

Ree decided the best bet to get him to quieten would be to ignore him. She crawled into the crossway of the tunnel, ignoring the freezing damp climbing up her robes. She turned, crept closer to the entrance, and waited.

Footsteps on the cold stone floor. Torchlight, flickering and warm, announced their presence. There was a splash. 'Eurgh!'

'Ungoth! Shh!' That sounded like Symphona, one of the acolytes Ree's age.

'I think I stepped in a puddle. It's probably ruined my shoes.'

'Shh! They could be nearby.'

There was a pause. 'Where?'

There was a thumping sound. Ree was fairly certain Symphona had hit Ungoth.

'I'm sure they were here a moment ago.' The footsteps grew closer. Ree held her breath as Symphona's legs stopped in front of Ree's hiding place. 'I swear I could hear that drippy upworlder whining.'

Ree thanked the gods that Smythe managed to hold in whatever indignant bluster she was sure that mark elicited.

It made her uncomfortable that Symphona was hunting them. The older girl might only be an acolyte, but she was cruel and ruthless. It had made her the unofficial leader of the younger necromancers — all but Usther, who reacted poorly to being given orders. If Symphona was out looking for them, *all* of the acolytes would be.

'They must have run on, got away from us.'

'No, not possible. I have a spectre up there waiting to report.' She started tapping her foot.

'Then what? Do we double back?'

Ree's knees began to ache and the cold soaked all the way up to her belly. *Just leave,* she willed them. *Keep walking.*

Symphona was silent, thoughtful. Ree continued to will her to leave with all her might, wishing she could mindpush, like in the old stories of psychomages and telepaths.

Symphona turned.

Leave, leave ...

A pause. Symphona's face filled the tunnel entrance, her curly pink hair stark against her dark skin. 'There's my little sacrifice.' She smiled. The air thickened as she drew power. She started to mouth a spell.

Ree flung a handful of water and grit into her face. She spluttered and reeled back.

'Go!' Ree roared at Smythe.

'Right, right, going!'

Ree crawled out of the other end of the tunnel and Smythe pulled her to her feet. They were in a parallel passage, much like the one they'd just left.

Smythe danced where he stood, wringing his hands. 'Which way, which way?'

A curse zipped out of the drainage tunnel to smash against the wall.

'Ree!'

'I'm thinking! Give me a moment!'

Distant shouting: more necromancers ran toward them from the left.

'Okay, this way!' Ree fled down the other end of the passage, Smythe close behind.

She led them on a winding chase, but they couldn't keep this up forever. At every crossroads, there were more necromancers, or minions, or a spectre waiting to swoop down on them. She was losing track of where they were, how long they were running. Her lungs burned; Smythe gasped for breath.

'Stop!' She threw out her arm, catching Smythe in the chest. They were in a widened out passage lined with corpses, resting in recessed stone shelves. It was obvious this was one of the less-travelled passages; everything was blanketed in dust and curtained with cobwebs.

She looked for an empty shelf and shoved Smythe toward it. 'Quickly, climb in and lie down.'

Smythe blinked at her. 'Are you quite certain? I really don't think —'

Shouts from behind them, drawing nearer. She glared at Smythe. He squeaked and slid in.

'Close your eyes and don't move until I tell you, okay?' She pounded on the ceiling of the recess; dust dropped and carpeted him in grey. She ran across the room and did the same, trusting to the horribly thick dust coating her face that she was well and truly hidden.

A cabal of necromancers came running in, their fast steps mingled with the shuffling of their minions. They shouted and argued and ran on, never stopping to check what were clearly long-undisturbed corpses.

Ree let five minutes pass, then ten. When the sounds of their frantic search had long passed, she climbed out of the shelf, coughing and wiping dust from her face. 'Smythe?'

'Here!' He half-fell from the shelf, as grey and pasty as any minion. He rubbed the dust on his sleeve, revealing his usual colour, then wiped his glasses on his shirt. 'That was most resourceful! How do you come up with things like that?'

Ree shrugged and tucked her dust-coated hair behind her ears. 'You have to do a lot of running when you're a denizen without the Craft.'

Smythe looked around. His eyes fixed on one of the bodies. 'Is that a scythe he's buried with? Why would a farmer be entombed here —'

'Smythe.' She rubbed her temples. 'Later.'

'— right.'

She tried to think through the adrenaline fogging her brain and her heart beating in her ears. Her original plan didn't seem likely to work now. Travelling any distance from here on would be fraught with pursuit. They needed to hide for the night, settle down. Necromancers were easily distracted. She doubted their hunt would be half as strong in a day's time.

Somewhere to hide. Somewhere close. Somewhere nobody else could find.

She nodded to herself and turned to Smythe. 'I know where to go.'

'Top notch,' said Smythe. He grinned at her through dust and weariness, and for a fleeting moment, Ree felt warm inside.

She led Smythe for another three hours, down stairs and through grand empty chambers, in an extended game of hide-and-seek with the denizens, but wherever they were chased, she would always guide them back. At last, they came to a steel door.

Smythe rattled the handle. 'Festering rats!' He pounded on the door. 'I just want to sit down!'

Ree tapped him on the shoulder. She raised a key and her eyebrows.

Smythe reddened. 'Terribly sorry. It's all this "running for our lives" business. Makes it dreadfully hard to think straight.'

Once the door was safely locked behind them, Smythe froze, mouth agape. Ree tucked away a tired smile. 'It is impressive, isn't it?' she said. She looked around at the small library, as if seeing it for the first time. It had a small reading room down a set of stairs to the side, and it was lined on all sides with heavy oak shelves and thick tomes in several languages. 'There are several libraries in the crypt, some from the kings and bureaucrats, some built by some long-ago denizens, before the town was settled. This is one of the smaller ones.'

Smythe walked up to a shelf and ran his hand down the spine of a book. 'This must be a hundred years old,' he said. His eyes shone as if he'd just fallen in love.

'I think that one's ... maybe a hundred and twenty? This isn't the oldest of the libraries, but it's cosy.'

She watched Smythe scan the books, his eyes wide with awe, his curls falling across his eyes. Something in her loosened, something that had been winding ever tighter since Usther had run off to warn the council.

She touched his elbow and gently guided him toward the stairs. 'It's not safe here. They might make Emberlon hand over his keys. Come on.'

'But — all right.' Smythe took the book he'd been eyeing, then paused to take a couple more. Ree frowned, but Smythe shook his head. 'I'll bring them back, I promise! I know better than to cross a librarian. I *am* an experienced scholar, you know.'

'I've been made aware of the fact,' said Ree, but she didn't make him return the books.

The reading room was small; one large round table, scattered with books, and a couple lecterns between the bookshelves on the walls. The floor was mossy stone, as was most of this part of the tombs, but there were four large gems on the floor, cornering the table.

Ree stopped Smythe in the doorway, then took four books from the reading table, and placed them on the gems. Each one lowered with a click. Then she reached under a lectern and pulled a small hidden lever. The wall behind the lectern recessed, then slid aside with the grating of stone on stone.

This was a secret that was hers alone. Even Emberlon hadn't found this passage, and she hadn't marked it on any of the public maps. Like her father, like Usther, like any denizen of Tombtown, she didn't share *all* of her knowledge.

'Quickly.' She waved Smythe over.

He scurried toward her, arms laden with books. 'What would have happened if you'd pulled the lever without placing the books?'

She pointed over his head, to a small hole above the doorframe. 'I'd have been thoroughly impaled by flying spikes.'

Smythe blanched. 'Oh.'

She pulled a lever on the other side of the door and the wall slid back into place. Now they were in a third reading room, a secret reading room. A bedroll — Ree's — was tucked up against the far wall.

'A secret library inside a secret library,' Smythe said. He straightened his glasses as he turned to Ree. 'You really are quite incredible. I'm not sure I would believe you were real if I didn't actually know you.'

Ree ducked her head, her cheeks heating. She didn't know whether he meant it as a compliment, but it pleased her all the same.

They settled there for the night, Smythe reading the books he'd brought with him, Ree taking notes from the books she'd left there. There wasn't much to eat; only the meagre provisions of jerked meat and dried fruit that Ree had hidden there in the past. They didn't hear anyone come or go from the main library. Those denizens still searching into the night did not come near them.

At length, Ree stretched out on her bedroll while Smythe made himself comfortable on a lavish but stiff chaise longue. The candles they'd lit were dwindling, and exhaustion was coming fast for Ree. She closed her eyes.

'Ree.' Smythe's voice was a whisper, though there was nobody to wake but her.

She opened her eyes. He was propped up on one elbow, gazing at her quite anxiously. 'Mm?'

'Thank you for saving me. I — I know I can't completely understand, but — it must have cost you a great deal to go against your town for me. I hope you know I take that debt seriously.'

Ree said, 'I didn't do it so that you'd be indebted to me.' As she said it, she wondered why she'd done it. What it was about Chandrian Smythe that led her to such terrible decisions.

'No — no of course not. That's not what I — no. Sorry.'

Silence. Ree closed her eyes.

Then: 'Ree? Why aren't you a necromancer? That's what they were saying, wasn't it? Usther and the council. That you don't practice necromancy.'

She was looking at him properly now. This moment felt very still, here alone in the darkness, knowing they were being hunted and yet so far from danger. She wasn't used to people asking about her. She wasn't used to *people.*

Smythe blinked and looked away. 'My apologies, I didn't mean to pry, I just —'

'I never wanted it,' said Ree. Smythe immediately shut up. He watched her with fierce attentiveness, as if what she was saying was important, as if it *mattered* what Ree did or didn't want. She took a steadying breath. 'It's all my parents ever wanted for me, and everyone I know practices the Craft. I just wanted to ... I don't know. To explore. To discover. First with books, and then with maps. It just seemed like ... like if I was going to learn magic, I wanted it to be something more. Like *I* wanted to be something more. More than the name my parents gave me.'

'Reanima,' said Smythe.

'Reanima,' Ree agreed. 'Necromancy changes people. The more you use it, the less alive you are. Eventually, necromancers become like the Lich — not really human anymore, just power inside a withered body, going through the motions. I wanted something more.'

'It all seems rather phenomenal to me,' he said. 'That this kind of power exists in the world. But it must all seem rather dull to you.'

'Never dull,' said Ree, with a wry smile.

Smythe rolled onto his back. Their conversation seemed to have eased him, somehow, though Ree didn't know what he had taken from it. 'What were you making notes about?'

She hugged her journal to her chest.

For a moment, she considered telling him. The real reason she didn't learn the Craft. The rest of the reason. The books hidden in her room, in various stashes and secret libraries across the crypt. The rituals attempted and failed. He was so strange, and they had been through so much.

Instead, she hugged her journal to her chest and rolled over. 'It doesn't matter,' she said. 'Goodnight.'

'Goodnight.'

Ree closed her eyes, but sleep wouldn't come. Her thoughts hummed angrily like an over-turned beehive. She thought about Smythe. About how he was a historian who had travelled to a dangerous and unknown place in service to his study. He literally studied the past, had devoted his life to it. If anyone would understand what she was trying to do ... surely he would.

And tomorrow, he would leave.

She relaxed her death-grip on her journal and half-turned toward Smythe. His eyes were closed, but a frown pinched his brow, as if some heavy problem occupied him.

It took her a moment to find her voice again. Perhaps she'd been closer to sleep than she'd realised; the words rasped from her throat. 'Smythe? Are you awake?'

The frown deepened. His eyelids fluttered, then opened. 'Is everything alright?' His eyes were glazed in the dark; likely, he couldn't make her out.

It would be so easy to just roll over again and say nothing more about it. So easy, and yet ...

Her heart clenched. She wanted to share this secret.

She got to her knees and lit the stout candle in the shuttered lantern in the middle of the room. It flared and flickered as she shook out the match. Smythe sat up, shading his eyes against the sudden glare.

She offered her journal to him. He took it, a question quivering on his brow. As he flicked through the pages, her fingers twitched in a barely suppressed urge to snatch it from him.

'This is your research?' He looked up, but Ree avoided his eyes.

She ducked her head in assent.

He rescanned the page, as if checking the evidence of his own eyes. 'This is —'

'Therianthropy.' A shiver rippled down her spine. Even to name it aloud felt like a spell. She'd spent years keeping this secret — hiding her research, evading questions about her future. Her eyes met Smythe's, expecting him to jump in with more, but he only waited.

Ree ran her hand through her hair, wondering how to explain. 'I found a book when I was fourteen. I was with Emberlon on a collection. We were trying to find a book for — well, it doesn't matter.' She drew a shuddering breath. 'It was a necromantic grimoire, but it referenced "lycanthropes, the creations of therianthropes" making superior minions, and advised obtaining the services of a therianthrope. That was my first encounter with therianthropy as a real discipline, and not a folktale.'

Smythe looked down at the journal laying open in his hands. 'So this journal represents —'

'Three years of my life.' Ree stared at the familiar journal, with its many loose pages and notes thrust into it. How frustrating — how humiliating — that three years of research had not even been fruitful enough to fill one journal, however thickly bound.

When she looked at Smythe, she could see the surprise on his face — the lifted eyebrows, the lips parted in sympathy. He quickly smoothed his reaction away, but Ree still felt the bite of it.

'What is — if you'll excuse me — what is the limiting factor?'

A gentle way to ask her why three years of her life fit so comfortably in one book. Ree's shoulders lifted and her jaw clenched. 'Lack of resources. There are a lot of references to therianthropy and some first-hand accounts, but no useful guides or studies.' She shook her head. 'Therianthropy is old — very old. It predates bound books, and many of the scrolls on it were destroyed by witchkillers in an attempt to purge the art itself centuries ago. Even when I get my hands on a promising text, it's often too archaic to understand, or in a language I can't translate. But there are precious few even of them.'

Smythe nodded. His brow pinched as he considered the problem. 'Historians speculate that therianthropy was largely an oral tradition anyway. It's part of the mysticism around it, and why many cultures considered it barbaric, or so I hear.'

Ree snorted at the word. '*Barbaric.* As if there could be anything more sophisticated than changing your shape using only the skin of an animal. The spell work is meant to be extremely intricate.'

'Therianthropy uses *skin?*' He couldn't quite manage to hide the revulsion in his voice, but this time Ree's lips twitched in a scant smile.

'Is that your only protest?' She studied him closely, looking for signs of pity or disdain. 'Just that it's practically unpleasant?'

Smythe's eyes widened. 'I — well, yes? It's not really for me to judge another's course of study. "Cast not the eggs from your nest, lest you find it empty", and all that.' He looked a bit sheepish. 'But ... honestly? I think there's no more noble pursuit than to revive lost history. And I know I haven't known you very long but — well.' He straightened his glasses, eyes bright. 'You're quite, um — ah. You seem more than capable of doing anything you set your mind to.' His cheeks flushed. 'Why settle for the ordinary?'

It was like he'd dropped a stone into a still pool. Ree could feel the ripples of it moving through her. She wanted to say something back, but unlike Smythe, she couldn't find the words.

Smythe returned her journal, and Ree again rolled over on her thin bedroll, hugging her journal to her chest and replaying their conversation in her mind.

It had been worth it to save him just for that. Just that small moment of someone *seeing* her. Seeing what she wanted to become, not what she had failed to be.

She turned slightly, looking at the curled shape of him in the dark. She wanted to ask him ... but this wasn't going to be a friendship. He was a man misplaced. He didn't belong here.

Tomorrow, she would take him to the surface, and this whole strange episode would be over. For the first time, the thought brought her no comfort.

There is a madness in necromancy. Not in the decision to practice it: necromancy can be a beautiful and helpful magic which does not inherently harm anyone living.

But in the throes of the magic itself, there is a sense of godhood. Of otherness to the world around the practitioner. Perhaps it is the nature of a magic that walks so neatly between the world of the living and the spiritual realms; it cannot help but set its practitioners apart.

Does this mean that it should be avoided, or used sparingly? I have returned to this question again and again in my studies. But ultimately, my feeling is this: a necromancer can only go mad in isolation.

And in Tombtown, there is little chance of that. The denizens are always interested in each other's business.

~from *A History of Tombtown* by Emberlon the Disloyal

CHAPTER TWELVE

THE CRAFT

Ree was first aware of her frozen cheek. She pushed herself off the cold stone and onto her bedroll; she must have rolled off it in the night. Blearily, she sat up, rubbing her eyes. 'Did you say something?'

Smythe hovered anxiously at the door, palms flat against the cool stone. 'I think there's someone out there.' He flashed Ree a worried look but seemed unwilling to look away from the door for too long.

Ree stretched and got to her feet, wincing at the ache in her back and hips. Sleep was rarely comfortable, but a night on the unblanketed stone floor had certainly not made it better.

Smythe pressed his ear to the wall with an expression of intense concentration.

Ree sighed. 'You don't need to worry.' She stooped and collected escapee hairpins from the floor. She tried to wrestle her hair into obedience, wincing whenever she jabbed herself with a pin. 'They don't know we're here, they can't hear us, and they have no way of finding us. Whoever is out there will leave soon enough.'

Smythe hesitated. 'Far be it from me to gainsay you. I believe it's been made abundantly clear that your expertise is worth far more than mine. Only ... I can hear some sort of undead creature in there. It's been there for some time.'

Ree started to pack books into her satchel. 'We can wait it out. No-one's going to maintain a minion in some forgotten library for long when they have no reason to believe we're here.'

Smythe still looked tense, however.

What must it be like, to have come into these ruins full of hope for his future, and to be chased out under threat of death? Ree was reasonably certain she could convince the townspeople to spare *her* once he was gone, but for Smythe, meeting anyone in this crypt other than Ree would mean certain death.

And he was so ... *nice.* It wasn't a descriptor she'd ever thought to apply to anyone. It wasn't even something she'd felt was lacking in her life. But there was something about Smythe and his chatty amiability that made her want to be nice, too.

Certainly, he didn't deserve death by blood sacrifice.

She pointed into the corner. 'If you're worried, there's actually a peephole over there. It looks through one of the bookcases.

'Bookcases?' Smythe hurried to follow her point and pressed his eye through the peephole.. His shoulders drooped; his entire posture relaxed. 'Oh, it's only Larry!' He went to pull the lever to release the secret door.

'Wait!'

The lever thunked home just as Smythe started to turn. Ree's breath seized in her chest. The door ground slowly open.

'Hide!' she hissed. Smythe feinted left then right in a futile search for an adequate hiding place, before diving under a table.

Ree walked up to the slowly opening door. She breathed in, shoulders rising. She pulled up her hood and patted it into place, and smoothed the creases from the front of her robes. Her fingers dug into the pouch on her belt, though it would do her little good if a necromancer went straight for a curse.

Then she strode through the gap, frantically assembling a plan in her mind.

Larry was in the reading room, walking repeatedly into a bookcase. Every time he bounced off it, another book fell to the ground. Ree stifled a sigh; only a buffoon would let Larry into a library where, given enough time, he would doubtlessly gnaw through priceless texts. As she approached, he stiffened and swung around, arms swinging like pendulums. He groaned, yellow eyes rolling back into his head.

'Hello Larry,' she said. He shuffled toward her, but she ignored him, scanning the corners of the room while the door rolled closed behind her.

Larry was not a minion, or at least, not in the truest sense. Whoever had animated him centuries before was long since gone, though somehow their power lingered and kept him whole. No magic guided him, so on base instinct, he was drawn to the living.

Larry would not have left the town unless he was following someone.

Larry bumped into her shoulder, gargling; Ree shushed him and walked on, peering into the main library. No-one.

Ree's heart thumped painfully in her chest, but she walked sedately to the door, as if nothing were amiss. She didn't want to abandon Smythe, but she'd have to if she were to lure away whoever hunted them.

She approached the steel door, now ajar, and swallowed hard. She stepped through the door, drew her key, and made to close the door behind her.

Usther seized the door from the other side. 'Fancy meeting you here.' She bared her teeth.

Ree spun, but Usther seized her by the back of her collar and yanked her back, sending her sprawling across the floor.

Ree scrambled to her knees, but Usther slammed the door and leaned against it. She gazed at Ree dispassionately. 'I suppose you're hiding him in that secret room of yours?'

Ree got up into a half-crouch, ready to sprint free at the earliest opportunity. 'How do you know about that?'

Usther sighed and examined her nails. 'I follow you, sometimes, you know. I've seen you disappear into this room more than once, and then I hear that terrible grinding noise. I set a watch, and sometimes you are in there an abominably long time. Even *you* surely can't be sustained by only books. I knew you were going *somewhere*. Now. The upworlder.' She curled her lip at the word.

'I got him to the surface,' Ree said. She willed her expression to smoothness. She refused to give anything away. 'I got him most of the way, set him on the path, and led the pursuit away from him. He's long gone by now.'

Usther stood up and flexed her spidery fingers. 'Now Ree,' she said. She tapped her foot. 'You don't expect me to believe you let that clumsy fool find his own way to the surface, after everything you've done to protect him? The man's utterly ridiculous. He'd be ghoul-food by sunrise.'

'Believe what you like,' Ree said. Her mouth was dry; she cleared her throat. 'But he's gone. So unless you intend to capture *me,* I suggest you get out of my way.'

Larry bumped into Ree's shoulder, knocking her forward. She scolded him and nudged him out of the way, keeping her eyes on Usther.

Usther snorted. 'Or what? You'll *look* me to death? Or cower until I submit? No.' Usther straightened and in two long strides, she was in Ree's face. 'You know what I think? I think I *could* bring you in right now, and there's not a thing you could do about it. The council would thank me; the town is in uproar.' Her pale-eyes bored into Ree, stark against her dark skin, almost a mindsnare all on their own. 'Everyone's wondering what to do about the wayward daughter of Igneus and Arthura, the girl who refuses to obey our laws or lifestyles, and who also refuses the courtesy of just getting the hell out and joining the world above.'

'I don't belong in the world above.' Ree matched Usther's glare with her own. She put all her anger into it, all her resentment at being forced to live as an outsider, at her motives being questioned at every turn. That they dared to try and curse her, when she was more a part of this place than any of them. She'd been the first child ever born in the crypt. She mapped its paths, travelled farther than any other denizen. She knew its heart and its rhythm better than any necromancer.

Usther bared her teeth. 'And I suppose you think you belong *here*? Not. Without. The Craft.'

Ree started to retort, but Usther swept back to the door, crossing her arms and leaning against it. 'But as luck would have it, I'm not here to capture you, or the upworlder, or even to suffer through dull conversation with you. I'm here to help you get your fool to the surface.'

Ree froze. She struggled to draw air into her suddenly thin lungs.

Usther rolled her eyes. 'Don't gawp at me like a minion, Ree. A thank you will suffice.'

There was no way that she could trust this. Usther was standing just to the side of the door now; if Ree was quick, she might be able to escape and draw Usther off. 'Well, that's very generous of you,' she replied with more than a bite of sarcasm. 'But he's gone, and I don't much fancy your company.' She subtly shifted her stance, trying to judge the best path through the door.

Usther pressed a hand to her heart. 'You don't trust me.' Her tone was wounded.

Ree resisted the urge to roll her eyes. 'Well, as my mother would say: nightshade is nightshade. Don't drink it in tea just because it blooms prettily.'

'How ... trite.'

Ree shrugged and inched to one side, letting Larry amble past to pester Usther. The moment was coming, she could feel it.

'Look.' Usther crossed her arms. 'I can see that you're still upset with me for some reason, but you're not thinking this through. I have the approval of the council, the town is in chaos — I have everything I want. Do you know how many people's sanctums I raided today? Three! Three sanctums, and one of them even had a half-decent ritual going. Nobody is about to guard them. By the end of the week, I'll know what everyone in this town is up to *and* the council will owe me a favour.'

Ree stopped her slow edge toward the door. Usther's words were making sense — Usther never wanted anything so much as to spy on the other denizens and steal their secrets — but Ree couldn't see why she wouldn't still want the prestige of catching the runaway upworlder. 'So what, Usther?'

'So? So I've got everything I want. So I want my friend back now. If I help you save your upworlder, you'll drop whatever ludicrous grudge you're building and the whole "betrayed you to the council" thing will just be water under the bridge. So you should just get Smith out from your secret room and we can get started. Face it: you'll struggle to make it to the surface safely without necromantic intervention.' She took a deep breath. 'But I'll leave if you want me to. Begging is unbecoming of a woman of my power.'

Ree was stunned. That Usther could think what she'd done was a small matter she could easily patch up. That she considered helping Smythe a necessary inconvenience in the name of maintaining Ree as a useful contact. That Usther could possibly think Ree would surrender Smythe to her after all she'd done.

But as she studied her, her disgust diminished. Usther was trying to act nonchalant, but her shoulders were tense and her eyes were worried. Her eyes weren't shadowed with magic but baggy from lack of sleep. She looked like she was trying, with every fibre of her being, to pretend that she didn't care whether Ree accepted her help.

Ree blinked at her. A hundred responses crowded on her tongue, waiting to be spoken, but what Ree actually said was: 'It's Smythe, not Smith.'

Usther shrugged. 'I'm not hearing a difference.' Her crossed arms didn't look so much casual as like she was hugging herself.

'I want my friend back now,' she'd said. Maybe she meant it.

Ree went back into the reading room. She walked up to one of the bookcases and peered through the hole in the back of it. A bright brown eye blinked back at her, then, with a click, the door depressed and slid open.

Smythe emerged, wringing his hands. 'Are they gone?' His eyes moved to Usther. '... Oh.'

Ree placed herself so that she could jump between Smythe and Usther if she had to. 'Usther's going to help get you to the surface.'

Smythe's eyebrows raised. 'Oh?'

Usther glared at him.

'Oh.'

Ree elbowed him in the ribs.

He jumped. 'Right. Sorry. Erm ... pardon me for asking, but I don't suppose you happen to have any food?'

Usther fished in her pack and produced three withered apples, some cheese, and a loaf of bread. 'Good enough.'

'Hmm,' said Smythe. Ree nudged him again; he looked not unlike Larry when he was about to bite.

They took Usther back into the secret room and closed the door behind them. While Smythe read and Larry tried to bite him, Ree and Usther argued about the best path to take Smythe on. While Ree knew the tunnels and passageways of the crypt better than most, Usther knew the dead and their habits better than Ree — and claimed to know the minds of the other denizens.

'If we take him past Rictus Eij's tomb, he'll certainly be caught,' Usther said hotly. 'It's a prime ritual spot and the dead there are very tame — you could leave a toddler there unattended. It's far too popular.'

Ree gritted her teeth. 'First, only a complete monster would leave a toddler in Rictus' tomb. Second: it's the most direct way into the eastern catacombs. So what if there's one location of danger — there's hardly going to be someone there all day!'

Usther pointed a long finger at Ree. 'You will waste no time blaming me when he gets scooped up the moment we set foot through Eij's wards. If you weren't so *prideful* of your little map-making hobby, you'd realise that I'm giving you useful advice and —'

'Ree?'

Usther and Ree both looked around. 'WHAT?' they snapped.

Smythe blinked. 'Terribly sorry, I didn't mean to interrupt. I'll just stay quiet, shall I? Right. Sorry.' He clasped his hands and stared into his lap. His cheeks were flushed with embarrassment.

Usther turned to Ree. 'As I was saying —'

Ree waved her silent. She hated snapping at Smythe. Somehow, making him feel small made her feel even smaller. 'Go ahead, Smythe,' she said, as gently as she could.

Smythe glanced up at her, then back into his lap. He spun his thumbs thoughtfully. 'It's only that I've been thinking,' he started.

'Dire state of affairs,' Usther muttered, but silenced at Ree's glare.

Smythe took a deep breath. 'I don't think I want to go to the surface,' he said. 'But — now hold on a moment! I know I can't go back to town either. At least, not as things stand. Andomerys seemed jolly enough, and Usther, you seem, er, *amiable* —'

Ree seized Usther's wrist before the older girl could curse him and nodded for him to continue.

'It's just — perhaps, maybe — I want to learn the Craft.'

Ree could only stare as the sound of Usther's laughter filled the reading room.

They say that necromancy is a sister to my art, but today I cannot see it. They are all so petty and competitive, spying and sabotaging and plotting against one another. Even the King, though I hesitate to write it, sees me as a tool to get the edge over his rivals.

Is it a prerequisite for learning their Craft? Or does the magic itself do this to them, the way wearing a skin for too long makes it hard to remember a human shape?

I have no answers. I only know I long for the masters and the tribe that taught me. There, we were a true pack — not pretenders, like these.

But I cannot find my tribe, and I hear I am the last.

I do not want my magic to end with me, but even less do I like the burden of the end of my culture.

~from the journal of Wylandriah Witch-feather

CHAPTER THIRTEEN

MORE CURSE THAN CRAFT

'No.' Ree shook her head then shook it again. 'No, no.' The thought of Smythe trying to hide out in the crypt was bad enough. The idea of him learning the Craft was beyond ridiculous. It was incongruous. Smythe was a cheerful, somewhat bumbling upworlder. His world was one of lecture halls and academic papers. He had no concept of the dangers of necromancy, or the toll it would take from him.

Usther had stopped laughing now. She wiped the tears from her eyes. 'Oh, *yes.*' She started to circle Smythe, who stood ramrod straight, as if he expected her to leap at him with claws drawn at any moment. She looked at Ree. 'Oh, can you imagine it? This chatty fool elbow deep in intestines as he completely *butchers* the learner rituals?'

'In — intestines?' Smythe visibly gulped. 'And that's quite necessary, is it?'

'It's *necromancy*.' Usther reached into her belt pouch and held out a palmful of bloody teeth. As Smythe recoiled, she rolled her eyes. 'You can hardly expect it to be daisies and sun rituals. We deal with the dead. It's a *higher calling*.'

'Forgive me, I just ... is there something less, um, *smelly* to start with?'

Usther sneered. 'Shall we all just sit around over a cup of tea and discuss the *theory* of it? Don't be pathetic. If you can't get your hands dirty, then you don't have what it takes.'

Smythe sat down at the little research table, his shoulders hunched and his gaze low.

Ree came and took the other seat. 'Smythe.' She reached out to take his hand, then withdrew at the last moment. The movement caught his eye; he looked up, startled, his cheeks aflame. 'Why do you even want to learn the Craft? You already have your calling. Third Rank Historian at the Grand University, the youngest to ever achieve that rank.' She tried to smile encouragingly, though the expression felt strange on her face. 'You already have a place in the world. You don't need to hide away in ruins.'

Smythe's eyes wavered; he glanced at Usther then dropped his gaze. 'Perhaps that's why I want to learn. What historian could pass up the opportunity to learn the past from the dead themselves? Or to live among the history he studied? Direct sources are terribly hard to come by in my field — if you take my meaning.' He looked sidelong at Ree. 'I'd rather not leave, if it's all the same.' His voice was small. 'Learning this Craft of yours seems the best of all available options.'

Ree wasn't sure 'not wanting to leave the crypt' was a good enough reason for learning the Craft. This whole conversation was making her very uncomfortable, and she didn't know why. She *liked* the Craft. It was a perfectly reasonable line of work. Nearly everyone she had ever known practiced it.

But none of them were like Smythe, and she could not shake the feeling that for him, necromancy was more curse than craft.

"'Learning from the dead themselves.'" Usther ran spidery fingers over her lips. 'Sounds like you want to learn summoning.'

Ree twisted her skirts between her hands. 'So it's no good then,' she said quickly. 'You're not a summoner, so you can't teach him —'

'Oh, *please*. I can teach him the basics and he can learn the rest himself.' Usther started to pace, hands clasped behind her back. 'The gods only know, you've got enough *books* on the subject to satisfy even the most dreadful bookworm, and not many of us ever had the luxury of a teacher.'

Smythe looked between the two of them, his brow furrowing as if he were missing some essential clue. 'You must pardon me for asking, but — summoning?'

Usther flapped a hand. 'Soul summoning. You know, *talking to people from the great beyond, tethering their tortured spirits to this realm.* That sort of thing. Dull stuff, and *primitive* too, I might add. But it *is* necromancy. Perfect, given the subject.'

Smythe nodded. 'I believe I'm following but—' He frowned. 'Am *I* the dull, primitive subject?'

'Obviously.'

'Right, just checking.' He looked mildly put out, but ploughed on, 'So where would one start? You know, with this "soul summoning" business.'

Usther bared her teeth. 'Intestines.'

Her eyes invited Ree to share in the joke, but Ree's own intestines cinched tight with unease.

Ree caught Smythe's eyes. 'Necromancy changes people. Are you sure this is what you want?'

'Ugh. Don't go passing on your *irrational* bias.' Usther rolled her eyes. 'Let the man raise the dead.'

Ree studied Smythe, taking in the line of his jaw, the steadiness in his gaze.

'I'm certain.' He straightened, puffing out his chest. 'Not to sound conceited, but I'm a rather excellent burial scholar, and a good scholar uses every resource and doesn't discount new or unusual sources.' His eyes glinted. 'Think about it! Think what I could learn, directly from the mouths of those who once lived. With that kind of power, there is no knowledge in the world that could be held back from me.' He drew a shuddering breath. His next words were very low. 'And the University will be forced to take me seriously.'

'All *excellent* reasons.' Usther clapped her hands together, punctuating her approval. 'Perhaps you have the makings of a practitioner yet.'

But Ree's guts only clenched tighter as a wave of unease rolled over her. She'd been truthful when she warned Smythe that necromancy changed people, but power changed them even more. She didn't like the ugly set of Smythe's mouth when he talked about the University. She didn't like to think what might come of that bitterness when combined with the icy magic of the Craft.

'Why settle for the ordinary?' he'd said, when she revealed her long-hidden desire to learn shapeshifting magic. Who was she, to tell him that he must?

'How can I help?' she asked after a breath. Smythe's slow-growing smile warmed her but did not quite eclipse her apprehension.

Usther smoothed back her short black hair and folded onto a reading bench against the wall. 'You could get him the books he needs. You are, afterall, a fetch-and-carry minion, are you not?'

Ree almost retorted that Usther needed to raise such a minion just to carry around her inflated ego but managed to stop herself just in time. A fight with Usther when she was being hunted by every denizen in the crypt would be unwise, and Usther grew fangs whenever her pride was wounded.

It felt like she was always holding things in, holding things back. It made her feel weak and craven, the way she had to tiptoe around the other denizens, always frightened of saying the wrong thing and facing vengeance.

One day. One day, surely, they would tiptoe around her.

'Give me a list, and I'll see what I can do.' Ree locked her hands behind her back and tried to adopt a stance of detached tranquillity, like her mother. 'You'll have to teach him from memory until I get back — it might take me awhile to find anything when the town is on high alert.'

'There's no need for that, I'm sure. There are plenty of books here, and the good Usther to teach me — I'm sure we'll make do.' Smythe wrung his hands. 'I couldn't countenance you risking yourself for my sake — er, again.' He cleared his throat. 'Have I mentioned how grateful I am to you, for saving me from your neighbours? Because I am. Grateful. Uh.' He smiled sheepishly. 'Thank you.'

In spite of her discomfort, her own lips tugged in response.

'Ugh. Enough. I can't stand how *amiable* you are.' Usther wrinkled her nose. 'So distasteful. Let's get to business, shall we?'

Getting 'to business' involved searching the shelves for relevant books while Usther searched for a body to walk back for Smythe to practice on. Much of Ree's unease faded as she lost herself to the task, interrupted only by Smythe's delight at the age and rarity of many of the texts.

Ree was quite pleased with their work when they'd found three early grimoires. She sat down on one of the reading benches, and Smythe joined her, a conspicuous gap between them. 'It's amazing to think, isn't it? That all of this —' he gestured expansively, encompassing far more than the library — 'Existed beneath the mountains and nobody knew about it.'

'A few people know, or suspect,' said Ree, though his enthusiasm warmed her. 'There are a few traders who visit us, knowing we have a lot of needs and a lot of gold besides. And adventurers find us from time to time, and travellers sometimes stumble upon an entrance. How did you find out about the crypt?'

'Rigorous research and inexhaustible determination,' he said, which startled a grin from Ree. He raised his chin and puffed out his chest. 'I'm rather an excellent scholar, you know. I got hold of a text detailing the subterranean resting places of A'in Gorad and Queen Eltamere, and became interested in the similarities between the two. About thirty books later and maybe a hundred ancient maps, and I'd guessed that the location of some kind of shared tomb complex was somewhere beneath the Dead Mountains, and here we are.' He pulled a much folded piece of parchment from his pocket and offered it to her.

Ree unfolded it, enjoying the solid crispness of modern parchment, and studied the map there. It was drawn in an uncertain hand, and much scribbled over with notes, but she recognised the shape of the mountains above the crypt. Smythe had marked several possible entrances, some of which were very close to truth.

She took a much larger map from her satchel and spread it across her lap, comparing the two.

'Did you make that?' Smythe leaned in to peer at the map. 'How did you —?'

'Oh. Well, Andomerys told me you're sort of the town cartographer.' His eyes scanned the passageways and chambers Ree had painstakingly marked throughout her travels. 'This is *most excellent.* I'm rather embarrassed that you've seen my effort, to be quite honest.' In spite of his words, he seemed more impressed by her than embarrassed for himself.

She liked that about him. It surprised her to think it, but it was true. He was so open in his admiration for her skills. Nobody else really seemed to be — even Emberlon, who was a very supportive mentor, tended to keep his feelings to himself. But for Smythe, every thought just came bubbling out of his mouth, and so often his thoughts were excitable and kind.

She'd thought that he'd be gone by now. Returned to the surface world, full of bright-eyed, warm people just like him. But he was here, and it seemed he had no plans to return to the sun-soaked lands above.

The thought warmed her.

'Uh — Ree?'

She realised she'd been staring, and her cheeks flushed. 'Sorry — um, thinking.' She quickly looked away, cursing herself for her flustered response.

'Actually, I was wondering about this area here.' He pointed to a blank space at the eastern edge of the map. Some rooms and passages jutted in to it, but it was largely an empty space, her pen-strokes ending in obscurity, the passages leading there unfinished.

'I haven't been there,' Ree explained. Her hair prickled just looking at it. Beyond those trailing lines and among the shadows marked there, the Lich's wing rested. It was the only taboo her parents had ever given her that she fully respected. The Lich was dangerous — she had firsthand experience of that. The section of the crypt where it made its home was off-limits to all denizens.

'Oh? It's quite beautiful, actually. Although oddly empty.' His fingers traced the hazy shape of it.

Ree's lips parted as she tried and failed to put voice to her shock. After a moment of floundering, she managed: 'You've been there?'

'A little, yes. I actually entered the crypt around here — or more here, I suppose.' He pointed to an unmarked place near the edge of the Lich's wing. 'And then from there found my way to the embalming rooms where we met.'

Her thoughts ground over his words again and again, her eyes fixed on the empty space on the map. In the panic, she'd assumed she'd forgotten the Lich's routine and crossed its path, but if Smythe had ventured into the Lich's wing then it was more than possible that the Lich had been tracking him. If Smythe had been the cause of her near-deadly encounter with the Lich, did she owe him anything for taking that curse in her place? Or did it not really matter why the Lich had been there?

Ree watched him, eyes hazy, as she considered what had happened. Debts were important — debts held Tombtown together, all part of the web of politics and power that allowed a hundred odd necromancers to live in one place. Everyone kept tallies of them — who had helped who, and when, and what was expected in return.

Ree had no debts and no debtors — she was largely considered to be 'doing her job' when she went out of her way to find a text or map a section of the crypt. Any debts she owed were collected from her mother or father, who were considered far more valuable debtors than she. Smythe saving her life had been her first experience with debt in a real sense. She'd not expected the weight of knowing that you owed someone your life, the sense of responsibility. It had made her uncomfortable and desperate to get him out of the crypt alive and safe.

She had saved him from the council and a public and painful blood sacrifice. Surely, now, she owed him nothing. A life for a life: wasn't that how it worked?

But as she watched him poring over a grimoire with a thoughtful crease in his brow, she felt no less protective. No less worried for his future. They had shared their ambitions, alone in the dark, and now the prospect of a life without him seemed oddly bereft. Was this friendship, albeit of a different kind than she and Usther shared?

He looked up from the book open on his lap. 'Um … Ree? Are you quite all right?'

Ree frowned. 'I'm fine.'

'Oh. Good.' He cleared his throat. 'Uhm. Actually, I had a thought.'

Ree resisted the urge to raise her eyebrows. 'Is that unusual?'

'No, no — of course not.' But although he seemed flustered by her response, his eyes were bright and slightly wild.

Ree's gaze slid from him, to the book open in his lap, and back up again. 'You've found something.'

'No — well, I suppose you could say I found it "in the archives of the mind", as it were, but — look.' He leaned forward. 'I've remembered something about that blank area on your map.'

Ree waited. Something about Smythe's intensity kept her quiet.

'Not long after I arrived, I came upon a tableau in those tunnels — centuries old, quite fascinating. And quite relevant to your interests.' He reached into his pack and withdrew a leatherbound book.

'What's this?' she asked.

'*My* research journal. Well, my travel diary, at any rate.' He flicked through it and held it open to a full spread sketch.

Ree's fingers twitched toward it, but she held herself in check. 'May I?'

'Of course.'

She took it gently, careful not to rumple the pages. Her fingers hovered over the tableau reproduced there, sketched in loose lines and annotated in Smythe's scratchy handwriting.

It depicted a woman, hooded and robed, as any necromancer might be. Her hands were spread; in one, she held a cloth or rag, in the other an orb of light. A large bird with wings outstretched was behind her head, and animals of all kinds crowded in around her. Above her, a sombre king offered a blessing.

Among Smythe's notes were: 'Priestess? Animal worship?' and labelling the cloth, a note: 'Skin?'

Ree's chest tightened, and it seemed she could no longer breathe in enough air. 'Smythe, this — do you know what this is?'

A curious phenomenon in the town is the forming of cabals among the lesser necromancers, especially among the acolytes and those yet to grow into their powers. They share their knowledge and pool their power to achieve greater works of magic.

More curious still is that these cabals are allowed to exist and operate openly. The council has traditionally "disbanded" cabals to prevent a rival power growing in opposition to their own. But perhaps they realise the importance of shared knowledge, especially at that early age.

Or perhaps they wish there had been anyone to share their knowledge with, when they were young.

~from *A History of Tombtown* by Emberlon the Disloyal

CHAPTER FOURTEEN

THE LURE OF POWER

Smythe beamed at her. 'I didn't at the time, of course — just more death imagery, I thought; it's not uncommon to use animals symbolically — but after looking at your journal, I realised —'

'She's a therianthrope.' The words came out hoarse. She found she couldn't look away from his sketch. 'That thing in her hand — it's a therianskin. A hawkskin, maybe.' Her finger traced the wings behind the woman's head.

'Yes! Exactly! Look — if you want, I can give you approximate directions. I'm something of a hobbyist cartographer myself. I'm not up to your standards, of course, but considering I've had little to no training —'

'Please do.' Ree didn't want Smythe to get side-tracked by his own ego, not when she was so close to a breakthrough. She hesitated, then offered Smythe her own journal.

Smythe immediately shut up. 'Are you quite sure?' He watched her, suddenly grave.

He had been the first person to see her research journal, and he would be the first, and perhaps only, person to contribute to it. She was glad that he understood the gravity of this gesture — but then, she never would have offered it if he didn't.

She showed him where to write his directions and sketch, if he chose. He worked slowly, carefully, a marked difference from the wild scrawl of his own notes. A pathway took shape; a fork at the end of an unusually curved tunnel somewhere in the Lich's wing.

'That's it — as far as I can remember, anyway.' He set aside her quill and returned her journal to her, still open to allow the ink to dry. 'I must admit — I did get turned around a bit. Distracted by the plethora of different burial rites on show — and by the moaning, of course.' He smiled wanly. 'Must have disturbed a few of Larry's fellows at some point.'

'This is plenty, Smythe — thank you.' She surprised herself with the warmth in her voice, but nobody had ever given her such a valuable gift.

'Oh. Well, uh, think nothing of it.' His cheeks darkened and his lips pinched in a blush.

She tried to help him with his own research in return. She wasn't a practitioner, but she'd been raised by one, and grew up in a town full of them. She had a fairly solid grasp of the basic theory of necromancy and had picked up some tips and tricks by sheer osmosis over the years.

But her mind kept snapping back to Smythe's discovery in the Lich's wing, like a spirit tethered to a corpse. She'd scoured the crypt for grimoires on therianthropy, and found little more than rumours and anecdotes. She'd always been so certain that the information must be *here,* somewhere. The crypt held the accumulated knowledge of centuries from multiple civilisations.

But the Lich's wing had always been off-limits. It'd been a normal practitioner once — that's how liches came to be. And it'd obviously accumulated enormous power, or it would never have survived as long as it had. Why had she never considered that it kept all the best texts for itself? And with that tableau, it wouldn't be unreasonable to assume that there was a connection between therianthropy and whoever was buried in that part of the crypt.

The more she thought about it, the more it itched at her, until she had no choice but to jump to her feet. She went for her pack, refilling her rations and stuffing her journal and notes back inside.

'Uh … Ree?'

She didn't look up from her pack. Her hands moved with the ease of practice, tucking rations into corners and slotting her books against each other. 'I'm going to find that tableau,' she said. It would likely be a few days of travel all told, but she didn't want to concern him with that. 'Usther will look after you. Well, she'll teach you, anyway.' Ree shouldered her pack. 'She's not a very nurturing person.'

Smythe snapped his book shut and scrambled to his feet. 'I should come with you!' he said earnestly, feeling around him for his satchel. 'It'll be a jolly adventure — I've never got to work with a scholar as clever as you before. I rather think we could dazzle the world with our discoveries. And I have so many thoughts on —'

Ree raised her hands. 'No.' Her tone was clipped, firm. Smythe trailed off, eyes wide. Again, she found herself altering her tone in response; there was something about him that got under her guard. 'The whole town is looking for you, Smythe. They'll kill you if they find you. You're not a necromancer yet, and even when you are, we'll need to find a way to get the council's protection before you can safely go back to town.'

Smythe stopped, hand on satchel. 'But what about you? Aren't they looking for you, too?'

'Yes, but nobody is going to kill me or my father will kill them. It's the stalemate our town is built on — nobody will deliberately violate it. If I ever get killed by a neighbour, it'll be accidental.'

'Oh. And that's, uh — that's reassuring, is it?'

Ree sighed. *'Yes.'* She headed for the door.

'Wait! Ree.' Smythe skidded after her, putting a hand on the door.

Ree took a deep breath and then exhaled through her nose, resisting the urge to shove him aside. She liked Smythe well enough as people went, but she'd always been snappish when people told her what to do. 'Yes?'

Smythe seemed, for once, to sense her tension. He hesitated, then raised his hands in a gesture of surrender. 'I know far less about, well, any of *this* than you do.' He swept his arm to encompass the room, and perhaps the whole crypt. 'But — well, you know. You said nobody goes into that part of the crypt because of that Lich fellow, and he already almost killed me the other day, and of course you're in trouble with the town because of me, and —' He drew a shuddering breath. 'I'm — well, rather worried that if something happens to you and you go alone, there'll be nobody to help you.'

Ree paused, the key half-turned in the lock. Smythe watched her in open concern, his fingers tapping his sides.

He was worried about her. *Her,* Ree. She had been born in this place, had spent her childhood toddling though tombs with her father or helping to restore ancient shrines with her mother. Skeletons, spectres, and walking corpses held no horrors for her. Unlike Smythe, for whom this was all a new and frightening place.

Except he'd never really seemed *that* frightened. Not even when he'd been fending her off with an iron sarakat as if it held all the powers of a god inside it. He was, somehow, a creature of optimism and enthusiasm in the face of a world that wanted no part of him.

And though she could feel the tableau pulling on her like a hook in her gut, she had to admit that he was making sense. 'Okay.'

'Okay?' Smythe smiled tremulously. 'Okay. Um — okay, what?'

'I'm leaving this — in fact, you should wear it.' She reached under the collar of her robes and withdrew the amulet her father had enchanted for her — an ancient coin minted by a long-gone queen, now set with a cloudy gem. It was icy to the touch, and she felt its absence immediately — the little comforting chill that had always sat over her heart was gone.

She pulled it over her head and offered it to Smythe, who took it hesitantly. 'Goodness — very cold!'

'It's a Neverscry amulet,' said Ree. It felt strange to be handing it off. 'Usther probably has one too — it stops anyone with a bit of your hair or one of your possessions from scrying on you. There's a breakaway clasp, too — to pull it off in case of danger. It'll also help you shield your mind, before your necromancy training takes effect.' It wouldn't work as well for him as it had for her — her father had tuned it to her, especially. But it would, perhaps, help.

Smythe carefully lifted the chain over his head and settled the amulet against his chest, wincing a little from the cold sting of contact. 'So you'd like us to scry for you?'

Ree's mouth twisted to one side. 'Not really. But Usther can check on me if I'm not wearing it, so if anything goes horribly wrong, she'll know.'

She unlocked the door. 'I'll be back in a few days.'

'May Mercur roll in your favour,' said Smythe, invoking one of the upworlder gods of luck.

Touched, she smiled faintly. 'In Tombtown, we say: "Don't die".'

As the door clicked shut behind her, she heard him echo the words, sounding a little bit lost.

The only good adventurer is an undead adventurer.

~Tombtown proverb

CHAPTER FIFTEEN

AN ENCOUNTER

She set off through the dusty tunnels, pinning her hood to her hair. The journey to the Lich's wing would take a few days from here, and to get to the therianthrope tableau she would have to explore passages she had never visited before, *knowing* the Lich would kill her if it found her.

Without the chill bite of her father's magic against her heart, she felt more vulnerable than she ever had before. She knew she ought to be cautious, worried even, but for the first time in so many long years of study, she had a *lead*. Real, tangible proof that therianthropy existed, was even exalted. Her entire body hummed with anticipation at the thought.

She found a stone-carved ladder leading to a raised crawl-space and hauled herself up, her mind still spinning with possibilities. She imagined putting on a therianskin and the strange, amorphous feeling of shapeshifting. Her knee scraped a sharp rock, but she hardly noticed. Would it feel like being crushed, or would it be more fluid and gentle? Was therianthropy cold like necromancy, or warm like healing?

She travelled until her feet grew sore and then more still, fingertips trailing walls of mossy stone and cracked marble, her mind living at her destination. Every now and then she would surface enough from her excitement to check her map, but all was on course.

She managed to avoid the more dangerous chambers and passages. She passed sleepy corpses stacked on shelves and skeletal guardians that barely creaked as she went by. But as she turned the corner into a narrow brick corridor, a creature shuffled out from the shadows. Her hand went to her pouch until she recognised the familiar grey skin and lolling mouth.

'Larry,' she said gently. He gargled at her and bumped against her shoulder. 'I thought you were with Usther. Did she send you away again?' She patted his cheek. When she set off down the passage, he followed.

'I suppose I should be grateful you're coming with me. You sort of saved my life, too. With the Lich, I mean.' It was strange to hear her own voice after hours of silence, but she found she was glad to have someone to talk to. Sometimes, it could get too intense inside her own head.

Larry nodded, then nodded again, and again. Ree reached up to steady his head and his twitching stilled. They turned onto a spiral staircase. She smiled at him and helped him over a broken step.

'Where do you even come from?' It was an old question that she often asked him, as if he could answer back. An unsolved mystery that irked her, when she had time to consider it. 'I heard Kylath estimate that you're more than five hundred years old. I never heard of a necromancer older than two-fifty. How are you still going?'

Larry walked into a stone pillar. He howled, then walked into it again. Before he could start scratching at it, Ree tugged him aside so that his path was clear.

She checked her suneye, and the treated eyeball rolled on her palm until it was looking straight at the floor. 'It's getting late,' Ree said, surprised. She had been too lost in thought to keep track, but now that she knew it, all the aches of the day rushed her all at once, clamouring for attention. 'We can head for the Hall of Statues to rest, I think there's —"

Ree walked through a doorway and froze. Two men wearing hard leather stood at the centre of a lesser tomb. One had a bow on his back; the other had his boot against the chest of a lesser dead. He kicked the body away, freeing his sword.

Ree ducked to one side of the doorway, dragging Larry after her.

'*Shh!*' She put a finger to her lips.

'That all of them?' asked the archer.

The swordsman nodded. He wiped his blade on the corpse's shirt, then examined it by torchlight. 'For now. This place is crawling with undead. You get the piece?'

The archer chuckled and hefted a gleaming crown. Ree's hand went to her chest: it was from one of the sacred queens. 'Took it right from its withered old head. I was out before it noticed I was there. Made a godsawful racket as I left.'

The swordsman sheathed his sword and seized the crown, turning it over in his hands. He whistled.

'You see any necros?' asked the archer.

Ree sucked in a breath.

'None yet. Gotta be one here somewhere waking up these bloody corpses, right? I mean: the dead don't just wake themselves.'

They did. They woke themselves all the time. The presence of so much dead in one place was its own source of necromantic power — all that magic had to go somewhere, and it went right back into the bodies that formed it. Most often, they woke when someone like *them* went stomping around, stealing their things and desecrating their graves.

She was nearly delirious with relief that they hadn't found anyone: adventurers accounted for nearly every death in town. She gripped the stone doorway with white-knuckled fingers.

'This enough to head back?' He waved the crown.

She thought of the sleeping queen, woken in rage and despair as its grave was desecrated. The only sure way to put it back to sleep would be to return its crown.

That was a geas from Morrin and a teaching from her mother: to tend the dead, to respect them, and to let them rest until needed.

'Not just yet.' The archer stretched. 'I've got another day or so of looting left in me. You wanna try that weird room with all the paintings again?'

'The one with the ghosts? You're having a laugh!'

One hit the other on the shoulder and together, they left the room. Ree hovered in the doorway a moment, caught between her mother, who demanded the dead were respected, and her father, who thought Ree was too useless to put herself in danger.

But she wasn't useless, and this was her *home* they were pilfering. It would be bad for the tomb if the queen was awake and angry — many of the sacred queens had been necromancers of untold power, and their corpses still carried that magic.

If they caught her, they would kill her. She might look almost like an upworlder to the other denizens, but her first encounter with Smythe had made it very clear to her how much of a denizen she truly looked.

But she was the most careful and the most quiet of any she knew. The promise of the tableau pulled at her, but this would surely be only a few hours out of her way. Maybe her father would just kill these adventurers, or drive them out, but Ree could protect the crypt in her own way. She could put right what they set wrong.

She hesitated for one moment more, then hurried after the adventurers, keeping low and sticking to the shadows, her soft-soled boots making barely a whisper on the ground.

She followed them for two hours, seeking her moment. She watched them from around corners, peered up through gratings in the floor, and down from balconies and beams. They were disgusting, and brash, and obsessed with treasure. They talked of little but the liquor they would buy and the fame they would gain. Ree liked them less with every hour and dreaded them running into a lonely acolyte or weaker practitioner, but it seemed she was the only denizen to find them. Always, she looked out for her opportunity, but the swordsman kept the crown looped through his belt and the archer was ever watchful.

At last, in an embalming room east of the town, they settled down for the night. They shucked their packs, laid out their bedrolls, and lulled each other to sleep with lude jokes and promises of wealth.

She waited until their breathing was long and slow, and crept out from the shadows. The swordsman's belt was off, the crown resting between them as they slept. Ree edged toward it, wrinkling her nose at the stench of sweat that clung to them.

She crouched and, ever so carefully, lifted the crown from the stone floor.

'You!' A hand seized her wrist. Panic jolted Ree. The archer snarled into her face as her insides froze solid. 'I got one, Erik!' Silver flashed in his other hand.

Ree managed to gasp, 'Please! Don't—' before the knife plunged twice and pain spread like fire. The archer kicked her to the floor as hot blood soaked across her belly. She clutched it, huddling around the pain.

She watched red spread beneath her fingers. That was her, she thought numbly as the adventurers scrambled to their feet. That was her blood. She took one hand away and stared at the thick crimson coating it. She started to shake. Pain rolled over her in wave after wave. She coughed and sobbed and each movement was agony.

The swordsman moved to stab her, but the archer waved him off. 'I'll do it. You never know if these bastards have some kind of death curse hanging over them.' While Ree shivered on the floor, he strung his bow.

'Please,' Ree croaked. Her mouth was dry, the words would barely come. She tried to find some sympathy in the archer's eyes as he knocked an arrow. There was none. 'I'm not — I didn't — I only —'

The archer drew. Ree stared down the arrow. Feebly, she tried to crawl away, still huddled over her bleeding stomach.

The archer frowned and spun. 'And there's her minion.'

Ree followed his gaze. Larry ambled through the door. He saw Ree bleeding on the ground, made an excited noise, and stumbled toward her.

'Larry,' Ree gasped. Her vision swam. "Get help. Get Pa —'

The archer loosed; Larry flew back. He hit the wall and crumpled, an arrow between his eyes.

Scrying is an important part of the character and communication of Tombtown. The town itself is shielded from scrying by Namura's Ward, and scrying is the main way of family members checking in with one another across distances or for cabals to keep tabs on each other.

Due to the (largely justified) fear of scrying, most denizens wear charms or talismans that prevent scrying, removing them when they wish to communicate. Scrying is a simple ritual rarely requiring more than a bowl of water and a drop of blood.

But if I may comment, it seems strange that scrying should fall under the necromantic domain. One must wonder: why blood? And how is the connection made?

Is there something greater at work than a simple spell of communication?

But I digress.

~from *A History of Tombtown* by Emberlon the
Disloyal

CHAPTER SIXTEEN

THE GODS WAIT

'She's still alive.' A figure crouched in her vision. He smelled of blood. No. She smelled of blood. It caked her hands and leaked from her abdomen, killing her as surely as the Lich's curse.

'I'll slit her throat.'

Ree shuddered, which turned into a shiver, which turned into a spasm. She curled around her stomach, pain electrifying her nerves.

'No! Hold on. I have a better idea.' He leaned into Ree's vision.

'Don't —' It hurt to speak. 'Please —'

He pressed something to her stomach and Ree screamed and thrashed as the pain tripled. The man covered her mouth. 'You be quiet you little —'

Ree bit his hand.

'— Aargh!'

But he didn't remove his hand. She could smell the stench of him, taste his gritty sweat in her mouth. She wanted to vomit. She wanted to cry.

'Look at me.' He half-growled the words. Ree's eyes went to his loutish, dirt-stained face, then drifted past him. Larry still lay limply against the wall. She half-expected him to lurch up, gargling and howling, but he was terribly, horribly still. Ree closed her eyes.

Fingers dug into her cheeks. '*Look at me* or I kill you right now.'

Ree looked. If she'd had the energy, she'd have recoiled from the raw aggression in his eyes. But the pain was dulling; she could focus. It took her a moment to form the words, 'What do you want?'

The man, the archer, smirked. 'I want you to tell me where to find the best loot in this place. If you tell me, then this healing balm I've pressed on your wound? I'll give you more of it. I'll spare your life.' His eyes burned with greed. 'Just tell me what I want to know. And none of your necromancer's tricks.'

Ree's eyes moved down, to the potion-soaked rag he'd pressed to her abdomen. It was dulling the pain in her abdomen effectively, but there was no way it had enough power to fully heal her. One way or another, she'd die of her wounds.

But if she could keep them talking, she'd live just a little longer. 'I'm not a necromancer,' she told them.

The swordsman snorted, drawing her attention. 'Black robe. Ugly as a corpse. Sure look like a necro to me. Besides, how do you explain that?' He jerked his thumb at Larry's broken body.

Ree tried to say 'He's my friend,' but the words dried up in her mouth.

She needed to focus. She flexed her fingers; the accompanying flash brought painful clarity. If she gave them what they wanted, they would kill her. She had no doubt about that. But if she stalled them too long, they would kill her as well.

Better to die later than die now. It would have to be a calculated risk. She drew a shuddering breath. 'I'm not telling you anything.'

The archer backhanded her; spittle flew from her mouth. She thought she'd chosen wrong, that he would kill her then regardless, but the swordsman grabbed the archer's shoulder. 'Hold on, hold on! You hear that?'

The archer looked at Ree, then at the door. Groaning, shuffling feet. The sound of a pack of minions.

Hope flared.

'Shit! It's not her, is it?'

Ree gave him her best Usther-like expression, difficult with her lifeblood leaking through a hole in her abdomen. 'Do I look like I can cast spells?' she rasped.

The archer raised his knife. Ree shuddered and kept shuddering. Fear was like ice in her veins. She didn't want to die.

He lowered it again. 'Tie her up. We're taking her with us.'

She almost wished they would make up their minds. She was dizzy with adrenaline and hope and fear.

'She's not got long left. We should leave her for the corpses to chew on.'

'She's a necro. She's valuable. Now tie her up!'

The rope was coarse and abrasive on her wrists, but that was nothing to the feeling of the swordsman's shoulder digging into her belly.

As horrifying as her situation was, one thought consumed her: who?

It might be a random practitioner, out on their own business. They might never even realise she was here, but if she called out, the adventurers would certainly kill her.

Or it might be someone looking for her. Usther, or Ree's father. If so, they would follow, and Ree needed to do everything in her power to *stay alive* until they found her.

The adventurers packed up quickly and jogged away. Each step was agony for Ree, but she gritted her teeth as she bobbed against the swordsman's sweaty back. Her eyes were fixed on Larry's limp corpse as they left.

He was dead. He'd been dead for years, and yet this was suddenly and shockingly different. A lesser minion could not survive the destruction of the brain. His loss hollowed her, but she had no time to mourn. No time to remember him, as he deserved.

The world was a haze of cracked stone and mossy brick; she had no idea where she was, or how many turns they had taken.

They stopped several times — for the swordsman to complain, for the archer to put more of his potion on her wound. Ree felt like she was being stretched, like she was a thin sheet of flesh and nerves, with fire playing over the surface. But each application of the potion made her head a little clearer, even if it did little for the narrow, hateful wounds in her abdomen.

At length, the swordsman slung her into a corner like a sack of potatoes. She gasped; the stone jarred her bones and sent pain ricocheting through her body.

She thought they would interrogate her then, but their faces were pale and drawn from a day of running. They set about setting up their little camp, lighting a fire, slinging down bedrolls and tearing into their rations. The smell of bread and salted pork made Ree want to vomit, though she'd gone the whole day without a proper meal.

The archer tore into his last piece of bread and stood up. He towered over Ree, knife in hand: a casual threat. 'We carried you all day —'

'*I* carried her—'

'— and kept your worthless necro body in one piece. Used some pretty pricey potion on you, too.' He knelt and put the tip of his knife to her cheek. '*I want a return on my investment.* Tell me where to find the best treasure. Kings or better.'

Ree went very still. They'd come to it, then. If she didn't tell them something now, he would surely kill her. There was a barely controlled hatred in his eyes: he was tired after a day of running, after days more in a hostile crypt that she symbolised. He would not tolerate waiting, but if she told him where to go, he would have no reason to keep her alive.

She licked her lips: it was like sandpaper on sandpaper. They started to bleed. 'There's a tomb,' she said. 'A big one. A king so old, we can't even read the writing in his tomb.' They were both up now and staring at her intently. 'His tomb is up on a raised dais,' she said, picturing it in her mind. 'The walls, the floor, are all a gleaming black marble.'

'Get to the point.' The archer put the slightest pressure on his knife. It pricked; a bead of blood ran down her cheek.

She could see the knife now, a blur at the bottom of her vision. Cold against her skin.

'Wall to wall treasure,' she whispered. 'The whole room gleams with it. It's the most treasure I've ever seen in one place.

The swordsman whooped. 'Loot!' he cried and punched the air. 'We're gonna be rich, Jon!'

But the archer remained focused. 'The location,' he pressed.

'The central mausoleum.' Movement flickered at the corner of Ree's vision; a flash of brown cloth. 'If you follow the passages south, you can't miss it.' She was guessing now, just filling time. She had no idea where they were.

The archer stared hard at her face. 'And how do I know you're not just another lying piece of necro filth?'

The swordsman cried out and the archer leapt back. A brown robed figure stood there, his dark skin striking in the firelight. A long sword was in his hand, dull but held with practiced ease. The swordsman scrambled away from him, clutching his hand; his own sword was trapped beneath the newcomers feet.

'Emberlon.' Ree almost sighed his name, but the archivist didn't spare her a glance.

'I wouldn't try it, if I were you,' he said. He flicked the sword and it moved like a snake; he cut the knife from the archer's hand. 'I trained long and hard with a sword, under better tutors than you will have the chance to meet. But if you won't take my word for it, perhaps you'll listen to theirs.'

Minions shuffled in, packing the room behind him with flaking flesh and marble eyes. They were poorly made and weakly summoned, barely holding together.

To the adventurers, there was only one frighteningly confident man and a small army of undead. They backed up against the wall.

'Leave,' Emberlon said, his voice hard. Ree inhaled sharply; she'd never heard him use that tone before. The authority in his voice was a physical thing. The adventurers looked like they'd been whipped. 'And if this girl dies, know that the gods wait in judgement.'

The adventurers left, scrambling over each other. Emberlon's shambling minions went to block the passage behind them.

He turned to look at Ree, the strength going out of his eyes. Now he looked frightened.

'He stabbed me,' Ree said, stumbling over the words. 'He stabbed me twice, for being a necromancer.' Tears came to her eyes now. 'Emberlon, I —'

'Andomerys!' Emberlon half-roared the words with a volume that made Ree jump.

'I'm coming, I'm coming!' The silk-robed healer pushed through the pack of minions, looking harassed. She looked at Ree, and her normally rosy cheeks paled.

'He stabbed me,' Ree said. 'Andomerys, he stabbed me here —' she raised her hands, revealing the wound, and Andomerys ran to press her hand into the gap.

'Calm,' she whispered. Magic accompanied her words, a warm glow as comforting as sleep. She fixed Ree's eyes with hers. 'Calm, now.'

Ree's eyelids grew heavy as the pain faded. 'He killed Larry.'

'You can tell me later,' said the healer.

The last thing Ree saw was the healer sharing a worried look with Emberlon. She said something, but her words were muted, as if spoken underwater. Then darkness came. Ree went with it willingly.

Ree woke gradually. She was on Andomerys' healing table. There was a pressure on her stomach. 'Andomerys,' she croaked. Her voice was hoarse with sleep. 'We have to go back — I left Larry —'

Andomerys looked alarmed. She passed her hand over Ree's eyes. 'Sleep,' she ordered, and Ree did.

She flickered in and out of consciousness. She remembered seeing her father, and him calling frantically for her mother; she remembered Emberlon at her bedside, a handful of scry-bones in his palm; and then, at last, a bird-like girl with slicked-back hair.

'Usther!' Ree tried to sit up, but a flash of pain across her belly quickly put her down again.

Usther looked up from the rat skeleton in her lap. She'd been making it dance: a small, macabre puppet. 'Are you *really* awake this time?' she asked, wrinkling her nose. 'I really can't abide all this "only half-conscious" nonsense. And don't bother telling me what happened; I saw it all. *I* saved you, when you think about it. When I saw you spying on those horrible men, I sent for Emberlon. I'd no idea you'd get yourself *stabbed,* but I'm hardly surprised.' She shook her head. 'Exceedingly *boring* of you. I hope you've quite got it out of your system.'

In that moment, Ree forgot that she was furious with Usther for betraying her. Though the pain of it made her grit her teeth against a screech, she reached out and seized Usther's hand.

'*Thank you.* Really.'

Usther shrugged her pointy shoulders. 'I've always wanted a debt from you,' she said, but her disinterest was too studied. Ree studied her more closely; the shadows under her eyes were purpling, and her skin was more sickly than ashen. She'd been worried.

Perhaps, they really were friends, in whatever twisted way that might be.

Ree cleared her throat. 'So, where's Smythe?'

They were in Andomerys' back room. Even if Andomerys heard, she would be the last person to tell, but Usther still glanced around the room and leaned in close to Ree before saying, 'He's still in the library. I fed him and watered him, so he probably won't die. He's practising.'

'Alone?' Ree tried to picture Smythe, surrounded by the trappings and entrails of the Craft. Smythe, in a black robe, with shadowed eyes. She shook her head; it didn't make sense.

'Oh don't look so *tense,'* Usther rolled her eyes. 'It's just summoning — either he will, or he won't. A ghost is hardly going to eat him if he loses control. He's actually got rather a knack for it.' She screwed up her face, as if the words pained her. 'He's smarter than he looks. Or acts. Or speaks. Ugh — I *hate* him.'

'But he's learning the Craft?'

'Taking well enough to it. Better than Emberlon did, or so I hear. In a week or so, I think we can safely call him an acolyte. The absolute lowliest of acolytes.'

Ree took a steadying breath. 'Then we can take him to the council. They'll pardon him if he's a practitioner and swears not to start a blood war with us — not that he could.'

'So long as you *tell no-one* that I was involved, I don't really care.' Usther looked pained. 'Can you imagine what

Symphona would say about me if she heard I took *that fool* as an apprentice?'

Ree raised her eyebrows. This was not the first time she'd heard Usther fretting about Symphona.

Usther glared. 'Stop that. Symphona's not stupid, like the other acolytes, and she's accumulating power at an impressive rate.'

'Pretty, too,' said Ree, who thought Usther's change of heart toward this particular acolyte might have less to do with power than she was letting on.

Usther's eyes narrowed. 'Say that again and I'll sew your lips shut.'

Ree grinned. Though it hurt to laugh, she was glad to do it. Then she remembered. 'Usther. About Larry —'

'Emberlon told me.' Usther didn't meet Ree's eyes. 'He was a bizarre relic of a creature, and an utter nuisance, and I suppose we're all better off now that he's gone.' She still didn't look up. Her hands were clasped tightly in her lap. 'But — when you can walk again — we can go collect him.'

Her research, Smythe's training, all of that would have to wait. He was so much more important.

'He needs to be laid to rest,' Ree said. At least five centuries old, he'd been a fixture in her life. Larry, trying to nibble her shoulder. Larry, gargling loudly when she was trying to hide. Larry, knocking all the books from the shelves in the library. Her eyes stung. She blinked quickly to clear them, turning her head so that Usther wouldn't see. 'He deserves at least that much.'

And probably much more. Though she liked time alone, she'd have gone half-mad by now if she hadn't had Larry to chat to. The crypt would be a lonelier place without him.

Now there was an ache in her belly quite separate from her wounds.

'We'll find him and lay him to rest,' Usther said, and now she met Ree's eyes. There was no sarcastic quirk to her lips, nothing but sadness in her pale eyes. 'I swear it.'

Society, in its unending foolishness, has deemed the Craft abominable, sacrilegious, and grotesque — all without even the most basic understanding. How can it be sacrilegious when the gods still receive the soul of the deceased? The soul departs the body on death! A dead body is only a material! If it is abominable, it is only because society has decided *to view it as such.*

Take a simple minion: magic animates the body. The better conserved the body is, the less magic is required to animate it. It's a useful puppet, and one that can take a large amount of punishment before it loses use. Sudden trauma, such as destruction of the brain or heart, will sever the magic animating it. Bodies destroyed in this way cannot be salvaged. The cost to the practitioner is too high.

~from *An Upworlder's Guide to the Craft* by Nerezeth the Unyielding

CHAPTER SEVENTEEN

500 YEARS LATE TO THE FUNERAL

Ree leaned heavily on Usther as the taller girl led her to a chair in the secret reading room. She settled gingerly, wincing at the twinges and aches that movement sent shooting through her abdomen. After a week under Andomerys' care, the wounds were sealed and healing well, though two puffy red scars marked them and maybe always would.

Smythe hovered by the wall, frantically stuffing books back onto the shelves. The reading room was in complete disarray; pillars of books swayed in the centre of the room, and various other books were scattered across the floor, open and with notes in Smythe's flourished handwriting stuffed into the pages.

'That doesn't go there,' Ree said. Her tone was sharper than intended, but after everything she'd been through, she had little patience for her library looking like it had been picked clean by a swarm of hungry scholars.

Smythe froze. 'You, uh, you can tell?'

Usther perched on the edge of the other seat and crossed her arms. 'If you would let me bring some minions in here, I'd have them put everything to rights very quickly.'

An image of Larry bumping into the bookshelf flashed through her mind. 'No minions!'

Usther raised her eyebrows.

Ree pressed a hand to her abdomen and took a steadying breath. 'They can't read,' she muttered, which was probably true. 'Just ... no minions.'

Usther's lips pressed into a thin line. 'We'll give him a proper send off. There's no need to get so ...' She flapped a hand. '*Emotional* about it.'

Ree stared into her lap and said nothing.

Smythe turned. A few books tumbled from the teetering pile in his arms. 'Sorry but — you're talking about Larry, aren't you?'

Ree nodded once.

Smythe shook his head. 'I can't believe he's really gone. I mean, *gone* gone. I suppose he was already dead, just not *dead* dead.' He sat on the floor beside Ree, scattering yet more books. A frown dragged at his mouth, and Ree wasn't sure whether it was sadness or a touch of necromancy that made his skin so sickly. 'He was a really good chap, wasn't he? I mean, he was a bit uncivil, trying to bite me all the time — but he was, I don't know, good company? He sort of made all of this —' he waved a hand, as if taking in the tomb itself, '— less frightening. I remember when he —'

'I'm not here to talk about Larry.' Ree twisted her skirts with white-knuckled fingers. 'I'm here because my father has agreed to meet with you, to see if you're really an acolyte. If he's satisfied, he swears he'll get the council to give you their protection. You can join the town.'

'Oh, well — that's splendid.' He smiled, but the action lacked his usual shine. 'And he's quite nice, is he? Your father. You know — a bit like you?'

Ree thought of her father, more undead than human, with his burning eyes, and the way he seemed to wear quiet rage like a cloak. 'Reanima,' he would say, and somehow he turned her name into a judgement.

'No.' Ree smoothed her robes with trembling fingers. 'Not like me at all.'

Usther got up and stretched, each bone making a brittle clicking sound.

Ree glanced at her. 'That sounds like a skeleton trying to put itself back together.'

'Was that meant to be wit? I couldn't quite hear it over the sound of you whining.' Usther cracked each of her knuckles in turn, baring her teeth at Ree all the while. 'I'm off to get supplies for Smythe's performance.'

'You mean bodies,' said Ree.

Usther rolled her eyes. 'Well, since *one* of us is *sensitive* about the Craft, I thought I'd be politely oblique.'

Ree rubbed her face. 'Look, just meet us in the amphitheatre in a few hours.'

'And what are you going to do in the meantime? Sulk about Larry?'

Ree glared at Usther in a manner that would make Smythe squeak. 'For a start,' she said coolly. 'And I'm going to make Smythe put my library back together.'

Usther smoothed back her hair, picked up her pack and headed for the secret door. 'Sounds dull, I'm sure you'll love it. Fool,' she addressed Smythe. 'Try not to forget *everything* I've taught you while I'm gone.'

Ree breathed out through her her nose. 'What percentage would be too much? Or would you prefer I drill him in summoning rituals while you're gone?'

'I won't forget,' said Smythe. 'Did you know that I'm the youngest ever —'

'We know!' Usther and Ree said together. Then Usther was gone and the door was grinding closed behind her. Ree and Smythe were alone.

Ree could feel Smythe's eyes on her. She stared resolutely into her lap.

'Ree, um — about Larry, and the adventurers —'

'There's a system,' Ree said.

Smythe blinked. 'Pardon me, but ... a system?'

'For the books.' Ree gestured at the shelves, still avoiding Smythe's eyes. 'If you can sort them into piles by subject, I'll teach it to you.'

'Oh. Well, all right. Actually, I'm rather good at telling a book's subject at a glance. Although most of these books are in ancient languages — but I'm a scholar, of course! I won't let it deter me. I remember a time when —'

Ree let Smythe chatter, occasionally interjecting to correct his sorting. Her thoughts were ... she didn't know. They were organising the library but her brain still felt scattered and pillaged. A few weeks ago, she had been consumed by a desire for action — first for Smythe, then for therianthropy. But in the days she'd spent recuperating, she'd felt ... empty. Scoured, even.

Larry was dead. And he'd died saving her — she couldn't stop thinking it. They'd been about to kill her, before he arrived. His sacrifice had created a crucial pause in which they'd rethought the wisdom of killing her. Or killing her quickly, at least.

She tried to remind herself that he was already dead — that he was a husk, a vehicle for magic and nothing more — but no matter how many times she went over the facts, it never took. When people died, their souls departed the physical realm and went to the spirit realm. This was known — it was why necromancy had never been able to resurrect a person with all their memories and personality intact. Only program and puppet their bodies. Minions were just that — puppets.

But that image in her head, that firmly defined line between a person and a minion ... it didn't leave room for the Larry she'd known. For a creature that was clearly both a minion and a person. For a friend.

So ... with poor health and the drive to do little more than mourn, she'd let Smythe and Usther take over. Because Smythe needed to be free and safe — it was clearer now than ever that he had no intention of leaving.

Smythe had nearly put the library back into order when Ree started to worry about the time. 'Leave it for now,' she said pushing herself to her feet, one hand on her belly. In her current state, it might take them an hour to get to the amphitheatre. She walked carefully toward the door.

Smythe dropped the books he'd been carrying and rushed to Ree's side. 'Here, lean on me. I'm sure you're quite fearsome even half-stabbed, but ...' He offered her his arm.

Ree stared at him a moment. Nobody had ever called her fearsome before. If anything, people thought she was cowardly: a pathetic non-practitioner, a rat scurrying through the passages. Sometimes, she even thought of herself that way.

She lowered her eyes as she took Smythe's arm, somehow feeling warmer. They exited the library and Ree directed him toward the amphitheatre, down a passage of crumbling stone interspersed with alcoves for sleeping dead.

'Why are you so determined to stay?' she asked as he helped her up a tall step, his hands warm on her arms.

Smythe's eyes widened. He flushed and looked away, running a hand through his mess of curls. 'Well, apart from y — the historical significance of this site, you mean? I'm certain this will come as a surprise but — well, I'm not quite as well regarded at the Grand University as you might expect.' His sepia skin was splotchy with embarrassment beneath his freckles. 'They — ah. I'm sorry, this is quite hard to say — they think of me as a peculiarity. A joke. I arrived there as a boy, more intelligent than half the senior — but nevermind that.'

His lips had grown thin, and his arm was rigid beneath Ree's hand. 'Suffice it to say that none of them believed me worthy of my rank. I came here to disprove them. And as a necromancer with the power to summon lost souls, I will have more pertinent and direct historical evidence than any who came before me.' His expression became shadowed. 'They will have to respect me then.'

Ree thought of Smythe, who was learning the Craft at a ferocious rate, and yet frequently lost track of his sentences and was so hapless as to be easy prey for even Larry. She could see why the other scholars didn't respect him, but it wasn't fair on him either way.

'You must hate it, when Usther calls you a fool,' she said. 'Or — or when I tell you to shut up.'

Smythe didn't meet her eyes. 'I'm sure you don't mean anything by it,' he murmured.

Ree's throat tightened. 'You know,' she said. 'What you said — about why you want to stay — that's just why I want to learn therianthropy.'

Now Smythe did look at her. His lips quirked at one side. 'You know, I'd thought as much. Actually — I have something for you.' He stopped to pat himself down, eventually pulling a much-folded sheaf of paper from his pocket.

Ree looked a question at him as she accepted it, but he only said, 'It's not really the best time to explain, but — well, if your father doesn't kill me, I suppose we can take a moment?'

Ree tucked the papers carefully into her robes. There was something about his sudden seriousness and focus that made her shy. 'I won't let my father kill you. If we have to run, then we'll run.'

Smythe pulled a face. 'Yes, as you're in the perfect state for that.' His eyes widened as he realised what he'd said. 'Sorry, I didn't mean to be so —'

Ree squeezed his arm. 'It's fine.'

When they finally arrived at the amphitheatre, Usther and Ree's father were already there, arguing in low voices that caused incoherent anger to echo around the walls. Ree wasn't entirely sure why there was an amphitheatre in this part of the crypt. She had a theory that one of the bureaucrats buried here had been a patron of the arts and wanted to continue to enjoy them in death. Nonetheless, she appreciated the high, domed ceiling and the rows and rows of stone benches. The stone was cracked and plain but holding up well, and a wooden bridge crossed it where the high ceiling intersected with a passage on the next level. It would have made the perfect town hall, were it not so far from the central mausoleum — but that was also what made it ideal for their purposes.

'Pa,' Ree greeted her father warily.

He turned smartly from Usther, dark eyes flicking from Ree to Smythe. 'He doesn't *look* like an acolyte,' he said quietly.

Usther crossed her arms. 'He has *hidden depths.* Very, very well hidden.'

Usther had laid a withered corpse on the stage, no doubt forcing it to march itself there. Its arms were crossed on its chest and its hair was little more than cobweb fuzz. 'Your subject,' she said, crooking a finger at it. 'Maybe 150 years old, and not very *spry* for it. Go ahead with the ritual, and do *try* not to make me look bad.'

Smythe looked to Ree's father, who inclined his head, his expression impassive.

Smythe knelt beside the corpse. He pulled a long knife from his pack and started carving on the corpse's chest and hands, murmuring incantations. He chalked a spell diagram around the corpse, and dropped his own blood onto it, standing back. '*Isthet!*' he cried, throwing out his arms.

Magic like smoke threaded with red light snaked from his hands to encircle the corpse, flowing in through its eyes and mouth. Red light pulsed from its chest.

'*Isthet!*' Smythe cried again.

Ree's hand crept toward her throat. Smythe was cloaked in power, his hair flying, his eyes red behind his spectacles. Unnatural shadow played about his features. The scholar she knew was gone, replaced by a necromancer in the throes of a ritual.

She wanted him to succeed. She wanted her father to pardon him. But a small part of her was also afraid of what this would take from him. Of what it had taken from her father, and Usther, and nearly everyone they had known.

Nobody she had ever met was warm the way Smythe was. And she wasn't thinking of his body temperature.

A featureless figure of red light rose from the corpse's chest. It gasped: *'What do you want of me? Please, release me!'*

Ree shuddered. This wasn't a spectre, or even a greywraith made from the impression of a lost soul. This was the lost soul itself, ripped from the afterlife to answer its summons. It was a fate she hoped never to suffer herself.

Smythe looked at her, smiling triumphantly.

At Usther's signal, Smythe released the soul.

Ree's father's staff creaked in his grip. 'Fine. It will be done.' He walked to Ree and leaned very close to her ear. 'Even this upworld fool can learn the Craft,' he murmured. 'It's long past time that you learned it as well.'

He straightened. 'I would suggest leaving it a day or two, so that word has time to travel.'

'That's fine,' said Ree. She looked at Smythe; his hair was a little duller, his cheeks a little paler, but he was himself again. 'We have somewhere to be.'

It took them a day to find it, not helped by Ree's injuries. 'I don't see why Andomerys didn't just heal you *properly,*' Usther complained after helping Ree through a cracked wall. 'Honestly, for such a powerful healer, she's rather a disappointment.'

'She said it would be best if it healed naturally, as much as possible,' Ree said.

Usther snorted. 'Utter foolishness. Who cares whether something is *natural?'*

The room was as she'd left it. Ree could see where the adventurer's bedrolls had scuffed the dust; there was a bloodstain on the wall where she'd been stabbed.

Her blood. She pressed a hand to her abdomen, her mouth suddenly dry, as her eyes found the inevitable.

Larry's body still lay against the wall. His legs were spread at odd angles, his chin on his chest.

'Oh,' Smythe said softly.

For once, Usther had no pert remarks.

They all knelt beside him, laying him out flat on the ground. Nobody said anything as they crossed his arms on his chest.

At length, Smythe said, 'I suppose ... I suppose we should say a few words?' He cleared his throat. 'Larry was a jolly chap. I didn't know him long —'

'No.' Ree shook her head. The words were hard to say, her throat suddenly tight. She felt like her lungs were thin, like she couldn't quite draw in enough air. She looked at Smythe and Usther. 'We can't leave him like this.' She reached for the arrow.

It was crusty with blood and didn't want to move. 'Hold his head,' she said. Usther took his head and Smythe braced his shoulders as Ree gritted her teeth and pulled. The arrow slid slowly free, leaving a round black hole between his eyes.

Ree tossed the arrow aside and wiped her hands on her robes.

'Better?' Usther asked, with barely a third of her usual ire.

Ree said nothing. They all stood up, forming a circle around him.

Smythe cleared his throat again, 'Larry was —'

The corpse lurched upright, mouth gaping.

Ree skittered back, clutching her chest. 'Morrin's teeth!'

'No ...' Usther pointed at Larry, backing away herself. 'That shouldn't be happening. The brain's been damaged! He can't — he shouldn't —'

But even as she spoke, the wound between his eyes sealed.

Larry stumbled to his feet. A red light flicked on behind his eyes, monstrous, glowing in the dark. He turned toward Ree.

Ree's back hit the wall. 'Larry?'

What is there to say about Wandering Larry? Surprisingly little is known about him. Though 'he' is the oldest known minion in the crypt, none can trace a master for him, or source the magic that animates him. Despite his age, he is of little interest to the denizens. A stupid, undextrous minion of few talents and little power, at first he was more tolerated than welcomed. As far as anyone remembers, he wandered into town one day and has been wandering in and out ever since.

Over the years, as the town has grown, he has become more of a fond figure, like perhaps a town mascot, or a friendly stray dog. He is particularly popular with young children and has bonded with many a baby over a mutual love of biting.

~from *A History of Tombtown* by Emberlon the
Disloyal

CHAPTER EIGHTEEN

SECRETS AND SPELLWORK

Larry shambled toward Ree with red-lit eyes and a terrible focus. Ree shrank back against the wall. Her breath came short and sharp as Larry's mouth yawned. His teeth lengthened into cruel points.

Usther pointed at Larry, shadows swarming down her arm. '*Unnaveth. Izza Krihoth!* Morrin's teeth!' The shadows burst across Larry's chest, then scattered. She dropped her arm, breathing hard. 'Ree, get away from him!'

Ree's thoughts tumbled. This was all wrong. A corpse could not be raised without a mostly intact brain. A minion that took an arrow between the eyes was a dead one. Necromancy could preserve; it could protect. It couldn't heal. And healing didn't work on the dead.

'Come — come on now, old chap!' Smythe tugged ineffectually at Larry's shoulder.

Ree tried to dodge to one side, but pain flashed through her abdomen and she was slow, so slow. Larry's arms locked into place on either side of her.

'Larry!' she pushed at his chest, but his flesh was hard and cold as iron. *He shouldn't be so strong — he was never this strong —*

He clamped his teeth down on her shoulder and Ree screamed. 'Get *off!*' She shoved him and he budged enough for her to get her knees up. She kicked him hard in the chest. He flew back; Ree collapsed.

Ree touched trembling fingers to the fleshy wound in her shoulder. They came away wet with blood.

'You know, I really think Larry isn't quite himself,' said Smythe.

'What a helpful observation, thank you!' Ree snapped.

Usther skirted Larry where he lay on the floor. She took hold of Ree's arm; Smythe took the other. They heaved her to her feet. 'I think we should shove that arrow back where you found it,' Usther said darkly.

'That'll be difficult to do, considering *there's no wound and he's somehow incredibly strong.*' Ree shook her head. 'We need to get back to town.'

Larry was flailing on his back. He tried to get up once, twice, then eventually lurched up into a sitting position. The red in his eyes flickered, then failed. His jaw went slack. His fangs became nubs. He gargled, head lolling to one side.

Ree took two uncertain steps toward him, one hand pressed to the bite he'd inflicted. 'Larry?'

He kicked his feet as if he was already walking. Ree gently pushed his shoulder; he fell over. 'Praise Morrin,' Ree said wonderingly. She looked to Smythe and Usther. 'I think he's back to normal.'

'Yes, but *how?* This is nonsense! None of this should have happened.' Usther scowled down at Larry. 'We can't even *test* him. Whatever magic animates him has been impossible to tamper with for years.' She kicked him; he howled. 'Oh *do* shut up! You survived an *arrow through your brain,* you hideous infant.'

They waited to see if he would retaliate, but he really did seem to be the pathetic minion Ree had grown up with. After a moment, Smythe helped him to his feet. 'Jolly good to have you back.'

Ree winced as she felt the edges of the wound. 'I need to see Andomerys. This is probably infected; gods only know what he's been eating.'

'Rocks,' said Smythe.

'I saw him gnaw his own arm once.' Usther wrinkled her nose.

'The point is, we should get back to town.' Ree looked at Larry. He was as she had ever known him; gangly, loud, barely in control of his own limbs. His eyes rolled independently in his head, as if he was trying to look everywhere at once. She was so relieved to see him. He was family; as much as her parents, as much as the town she'd grown up in. It warmed her, to see him alive again.

She was also just a little bit afraid of him.

'We can't tell anyone what happened,' Ree said, fixing Usther and Smythe with her firmest stare by turn.

'Sorry, but — why?'

'Because we want to learn how he did it and use it ourselves,' Usther said, giving Larry a shrewd look.

Ree rubbed her eyes with her free hand. 'Because people might not like it.' She thought of the council wanting to punish outsiders. She thought of the acolytes, hungry to prove themselves. 'Because someone might try to take him apart to find out how he did it. Swear you won't tell anyone.' She paused, then glared at Usther. 'Promise you won't experiment on him, either.'

Smythe reached out and shook Ree's hand with both of his. 'Of course! Consider it done. Anything for this old boy. And I'm rather good at keeping secrets. I remember when Young Miss Renfield swore me to secrecy over —'

'Usther?' Ree ignored the warmth of Smythe's hands, focusing only on her friend. 'What do you think?'

Usther pursed her lips. 'I think the biggest lie you ever told me is that you're the only person in town who doesn't keep secrets.' She bared her teeth. 'Of course, I never *believed* you. I'll keep quiet about Larry.' She caught Ree's expression. 'Fine, I *swear* I won't experiment on him or give up his secret. Why must you always be so *dramatic?*'

That would have to do. She would only keep her oath for as long as it suited her purposes, but there was no need to say it aloud. Ree knew Usther thought it was implied. Betrayal was just the cost of doing business for a necromancer. Ree ignored the sting in her heart and tried not to take it personally.

Larry bumped into her shoulder, head bobbing on his neck. Ree pat his cheek. 'All right. Let's get you home.'

They returned to town, Larry lolloping behind them down the winding passages like a tall, monstrous puppy. Part of Ree flinched every time Larry lurched toward her, expecting his eyes to flare red and his teeth to grow into fangs, but whatever dark spell had reanimated him, it was buried deep. He was only Larry. And through some miracle, they had him back.

They had to travel through the night, as it was generally agreed that they shouldn't let Ree's wound fester. As they approached the town, Smythe began to twitch. 'Your, um, your father wouldn't *lie* about pardoning me, would he?' he asked Ree.

'Yes,' said Usther.

'... Yes,' Ree agreed. As Smythe paled, she hurriedly added, 'But he wasn't lying. If he didn't intend to pardon you, he'd have killed you there and then. Pa hates inefficiency.'

Smythe didn't look much reassured. Ree's stomach wrenched; she tried to think of something comforting to say. 'We're almost there, so you'll soon see either way.' She winced. 'I mean, at least you won't have to wait.'

Smythe looked faintly green.

Usther hooted. 'Oh *please* reassure him more. I want to see if Larry tries to eat his vomit.'

'Don't … mention the "V" word.' Smythe's voice was strained.

Ree hesitated, then took Smythe's hand. He stiffened; his eyes flew from their clasped hands to Ree's face. He looked, if anything, even more ill.

'We'll sneak in through the back door of my family's tombhome,' she said, as firmly as she could. Something about Smythe's expression made her feel short of breath. She carefully withdrew her hand. 'Nobody will even realise we're there.'

'Except your parents,' he said, but his voice had lost the edge of panic.

'Except my parents.'

They finally made it back to the central mausoleum. For a moment, they just stood, overlooking the cluster of converted tombhomes and the dusty market square. This place of bleak stone, luscious moss and luminous mushrooms: this was her home. Ree took a moment to draw in a long, stale breath. She always forgot how much she missed it until she was looking at it.

Usther bid them a testy farewell — her temperament was not improved by lack of sleep — and headed toward her own home. Larry ambled after her and they could hear her complaining, 'No! Go follow Ree, you useless lump!' accompanied by his happy gargling all the way into the town square.

Ree's mother was the only one home when Ree snuck Smythe in through the back door. She looked up from the candle circle she'd been sitting in and raised her eyebrows. 'Bitten?'

Ree nodded and her mother tsked. 'I thought I taught you better. Come here: let me see to it. There's no need to trouble Andomerys.'

While Ree's mother bathed Ree's neck in the warm glow of her magic, Smythe hovered in the doorway. She looked at him; his mouth opened, then closed, then opened. He seemed to be building up to something. At length, he said, 'Hello, Arthura. We haven't met while I've been conscious. Uh — hello! You must forgive me, but — could I stay here for the night? I know it's rather forward of me, but I'd prefer not to go back out given that — well — given recent events.'

Ree winced as her mother's magic knitted her skin back together again. Her magic always left more of a sting than Andomerys', as if it bruised even as it healed.

Her mother checked the wound had sealed properly, then said, 'We haven't room. You'll go to Emberlon.'

Smythe paled. 'I — but I don't —'

Ree's mother sighed as if Smythe were being very slow. 'It's all been arranged. You're one of us now: to attack you would break the sacred truce we have all sworn to our Lady to live peacefully here.'

Smythe blustered, '*Peacefully.* I'm not sure that —'

'I'll take you there now.' Ree's mother seized him by the crook of the arm and glided toward the door. 'None will bother you while you are with me.'

'Mama, I don't think —'

She had him nearly out the door.

Smythe called, 'You'll find me in the morning, will you?'

Ree nodded and then they were gone. The door slammed shut behind them.

Ree went into her room and sank onto the stone shelf she used as a bed, plumping her pillow and enjoying the plushness of her straw mattress. It seemed an age since she'd slept in a real bed. After everything that had happened — Smythe, Larry, a night without sleep — her entire body was heavy with exhaustion. She felt a call as powerful as death and shucked her dusty robes ready for bed. Something thunked against the ground along with her robes. With fumbling fingers, she searched her robes and came out with the folded sheaf of paper Smythe had given her. *'It's not really the best time to explain,'* he'd said. *'But if your father doesn't kill me, I suppose we can take a moment?'*

The door opened and slammed shut again. Ree's mother appeared in the doorway. Her expression was solemn as she glided over to kneel at Ree's bedside. 'So you found a way to guide him to the path of shadow and truth,' she said. Ree resisted the urge to roll her eyes; she hated how her mother turned each and every moment into a sermon on Morrin.

'Reanima. Watch your tone.'

Ree scrubbed at her face. 'I didn't say anything.'

'Well, your expression is speaking for you.' She sighed and relented. 'Ree. You must like him very much. But you need to be careful.'

'Of Smythe?' She thought of him begging Usther not to use the word vomit. 'I think I've made it pretty clear there's nothing to fear from him.'

'Perhaps that's true for the town, though we all bring our own dangers with us.' Her mother's gaze was steady. 'But I was referring to your heart.'

Ree snorted, but when her mother remained straight-faced, Ree shook her head. 'Mother! It's *Smythe*. It's not like that.'

'You went through some terrible things for that boy,' said her mother. 'Right from the very start, you've been bound to him.'

'Well, it's hard to let him out of my sight for more than a few minutes without something terrible happening,' Ree said, but heat was rushing to her face. She thought of that moment in the embalming room when she'd hovered in the doorway, watching him unseen.

She watched *everyone* unseen. It was just what she did.

Had she ever thought of Smythe as just 'anyone'?

'I see you understand.'

'Mother!' Ree flopped back on her bed. 'Just let me sleep?'

'Of course.' Ree's mother rose almost bonelessly from the floor and swept from the room, closing the door behind her.

Ree waited until she heard her parents' door close before unfolding the sheaf of paper. At the top of the page, written in Smythe's flourishing hand, was 'Observations on Therianthropic Practice.'

A smile spread across Ree's face. Her cheeks hurt from this new and unusual use.

She felt very, very awake. She rolled off her bed and pulled out her own research notes. Smythe had drawn from several of the same books she had but had extended some of her conclusions. One of his key notes was that the spoken spells were not just incantations, but songs. He'd even sourced a potential musical notation ...

Surely, surely ...

With no therianskin and no information on the skin-crafting rituals, she could not hope to shapeshift. But perhaps some of the lesser spells — to sharpen the senses, perhaps ...

She checked the notes, then checked them again. Then, barefoot on the cold stone of her bedroom floor, she spread her hands, closed her eyes, and very quietly sang the incantations she'd learned by heart. Her voice rose and fell in the silence, uncertain but quivering with hope. The air around her stirred and she felt something inside her core shift, ignite.

Magic shivered along her skin. *Let it be tonight,* she prayed as her lips formed the ancient words now so familiar to her.

An unexpected result of the settlement of Tombtown is the way in which it enables necromancers to experience 'normal' lives free from judgement or scrutiny. Children are born and raised in the town — the first and most famous example being the infamous Reanima, daughter of both council member Igneus the Everliving and High Priestess Arthura of Morrin.

This is a new and largely unheard-of phenomenon. Children of necromancers are being raised among other children of the same background. As such, the town council has put in place precautions to keep the children safe and avoid exposing them to necromancy before they come of age.

For example, children are not usually permitted to be trained in the Craft until they reach the age of sixteen (give or take a few years), to give them time to properly develop before the magic stops their bodies from ageing. The coming of age ceremony is one of great celebration. Friends and family gather to take the honoured birthday child on their first salvaging trip — after gifting them with a gift both practical and sentimental. Their very first shovel.

~from *A History of Tombtown* by Emberlon the Disloyal

CHAPTER NINETEEN
RISKY RESEARCH

Power.

It had always been a foreign concept to Ree, something observed but not experienced. She had brushed up against the edges of it: a healing from Andomerys, a ritual from her parents, the *sense* for death and the Craft that came of being grown in the soil of necromancers. She'd been taught to focus and shield her mind, to know the feel of a curse or a mindsnare when she encountered it. But she'd never generated power herself. The reservoir of magic inside her had remained still and undisturbed.

But now ... now she could feel the magic shivering along her skin like beads of water. It prickled her veins, sending pins and needles through her limbs. Every note, every rise and fall of song sent a fresh burst of it; she felt like a cliff with waves of magic breaking against her. Her hair lifted from her neck and snaked free of its pins. Blue light gathered in her hands and flickered like firelight at the edges of her vision.

Pressure built; the pins and needles became painful jabs. But it was *real*; it was happening. Her heart swelled as she finished the song. *'Serasaph!'*

Magic exploded; Ree crashed into her bedroom wall, knocking over the small barrel she used as a bedside table. Groaning, she picked herself up from the floor. Her entire body ached like she'd been fleeing an undead horde. She examined her hands; the fire at the edges of her vision had left. There seemed to be no change to her sight. At a sniff, no change to smell, either.

She must have done something wrong. Perhaps it had been the wrong tune? She ran to collect her notes, rereading them and muttering under her breath. This was the closest she'd ever come to even a small taste of therianthropy. But there *had* been magic, however poorly cast — maybe even enough to lock her into the path of therianthropy.

'It's real,' she whispered, a warm glow spreading across her chest as she sorted through her notes. She just needed to find what she'd missed, correct the spell, and try again ...

The door creaked.

Ree spun from where she crouched over her notes. 'Oh! Pa, I was just —'

Ree's father swept whiteless eyes across the room, taking in the upturned barrel, the notes spread across the floor, and his daughter, clad only in a shift. 'We'll discuss this in the morning.'

Ree pressed her lips together, swallowing her protests. Her father radiated cold. His black eyes were flat, his mouth firm, expressionless. He closed the door without waiting for a response.

Ree stared at the door, then collected her notes, tucking them back into her journal with trembling hands. She put the journal under her pillow and climbed into bed.

Tired though she was, the memory of magic buzzing under her skin kept her awake. It was a long time before sleep claimed her. She dreamed of wings and darkness.

She awoke, fuzzy-mouthed and lead-limbed, to the sound of her parents talking in low voices.

She slid from bed and crept across the icy floor on bare feet. She cracked the door open, peering at her parents where they sat at the rickety table, a mug of something hot in her father's hands while her mother picked at a bowl of hot oats.

'I sensed something.' Her father drummed his fingers on the mug. 'There was magic in that room, I'm certain of it.'

'Perhaps she's practicing, for once,' said her mother. Even in her plain nightgown and lumpy woollen shawl, she still looked controlled and mysterious, dark eyes veiled by long lashes. 'Things are changing. She's almost eighteen. She'll be starting to feel the weight of her mortality: Morrin draws her to her destiny.'

Her father shook his head. 'It didn't feel like the Craft.'

'Healing, then.' But her mother sounded doubtful. Ree had never expressed the least interest in healer's work.

'No. It must have been the Craft — a curse, perhaps.' He lifted his mug up, then slammed it down without drinking. 'Morrin's teeth, Arthura! We're supposed to be raising her. But all she does is place herself in harm's way, with not the slightest bit of power to defend herself. We need to take her in hand.'

Ree went cold.

'We cannot force her to learn,' Arthura said.

'Can't we?'

Ree closed the door, taking long, steadying breaths. Her father had long threatened to curb her freedom, but in practice, neither of her parents had the time or inclination to watch her. But if her father had taken it into his head to *force* her to learn the Craft, to make it so that she didn't *need* watching ...

Ree's breathing hitched. The breaths came in gasps and gulps. What was she going to do about this? If her father saw her, he would demand to know what she'd been doing. She could tell him it had been therianthropy research, but without hard evidence that shapeshifting magic was real, he could take her notes — he could forbid her from researching —

Calm. Ree tried to get her breathing under control. She needed a plan — somewhere safe to practice. She was so close now, and once she'd mastered the spell, there was no way they could stop her. She'd be locked in for life.

Her first action was to gather up her notes, clothes, and gear and rush into the washroom. There was no way her parents would bother her in there, and she desperately needed both time to think and to clean herself.

After a teeth-chattering mountain-water bath, scrubbed teeth, and a fresh robe, she considered her options. Really, there was only one. Her father might be powerful, but they had a strict 'no minions in the house' policy. She buckled her belt, slung her satchel over her shoulder, and ran for the front door.

'Ree —' Her mother's fingers grazed her trailing robe. Ree didn't pause. She ran straight for the front door — and into the looming figure of her father.

'*REANIMA.*' He caught her eyes. Meeting her father's gaze was like staring into two pits of darkness. She tried to look away, but the lethargy was already setting in.

Mind snare, she thought. She built up her walls, tried to prise her control back from him, but she couldn't break his hold. His magic started to set into her bones; a desire to stop running, to stop trying, to give up and sleep ...

'*That's enough,*' he said, his voice gaining a death echo as he worked his spell. For a moment, she roused: he was working magic on her. On *her.* What made him think that was okay?

Rage and indignation did what pure willpower could not. She tore her gaze from his, energy flowing back into her limbs. She kicked him in the shins and hared off through the town square.

She could hear him calling her name, swearing all kinds of retribution, but if there was one thing even her father couldn't argue, it was that she was *fast.* Necromancers rarely did anything more physically strenuous than lifting a book, but Ree had jogged and climbed and crawled her way through the crypts nearly every day of her life.

It wasn't long before she was out of town. She didn't run far; there was a spidery tower spire with a hidden library in the attic. The noise of her passage was masked by the roaring underground river. After throwing a careful look over her shoulder to be certain her father didn't have line of sight, she vanished inside, climbing and leaping her way up the semi-collapsed staircase, and dragged on the rope that opened the attic.

There, surrounded by pillars of carefully stacked books, she slumped, panting.

She had no magic. She had no grimoire. And now she could not practice safely in her own home.

She got out her notes, smoothing them across her lap, her fingers tracing the song Smythe had advised in his flourished hand. It was the furthest she had ever come. If she closed her eyes, she could still remember the *feel* of the magic. Cold, like necromancy, but somehow different, too. If necromancy was an icy wind, therianthropy was a winter tide, fluid and changing.

And it might never have happened without Smythe's help. Sure, he had built entirely upon the research she had already done, but he'd been able to make new connections between information she'd been stalling with for the last year. She had never considered working collaboratively — necromancers rarely worked together, if ever — but then, she had never met anyone like Smythe.

Perhaps that was the key. Perhaps *he* was.

The next day, she crept back into town, skulking through shadows and keeping a wary eye out for her father.

She knocked softly on Emberlon's door, her gaze darting furtively left to right as she shrank into the doorway. When he opened it, she didn't wait for an invitation, half-pushing, half-falling through the entrance.

'Ree.' Emberlon acknowledged her with a solemn nod as she picked herself up from the floor. He closed the door behind her. 'Your father's been to call already.'

'I need to speak to Smythe,' she said breathlessly. She peered past him into his barren main room. The sarcophagus and its coating of dust seemed undisturbed, and everything seemed quiet.

Her eyebrows snapped together. 'Where is he?'

'Still sleeping.' Emberlon closed his eyes a moment in what Ree read as 'thank the gods.'

Ree hesitated a moment, her hand hovering on her parcel. 'I'll set up ready for him, then.' She hurried to the sarcophagus. She pressed two fingers to the stone cover, whispered, 'With your leave,' to the inhabitant, and started unpacking her notes onto it.

'Ree.'

She glanced up at him but continued to sort through her notes. 'If my father asks, I'm not here.'

'He did ask, and I told him as much then.' Emberlon put his hands on either side of the sarcophagus, studying her notes as she shuffled them around. At length, he looked up. 'There's a danger in seeking power, Ree.' He said the words quietly.

Ree shrugged. She dipped her quill in ink and started scribbling furiously on a page of previous notes. 'Everyone here wants power.'

Emberlon inclined his head. For a moment, his normally clear eyes were shadowed. 'But few are in actual danger of finding it.'

Ree paused, head raising. Where was this coming from? Why did *everyone* in this town think they knew better than she did how she should spend her life?

'I know what I'm doing.' Ree nearly snapped the words.

'I never questioned that.' He seemed to have worn himself out. His eyes grew tired, his face slack. He withdrew to the other end of his barren room, retrieving a book from the floor.

A yawning Smythe appeared in the doorway of one of the back rooms, glasses askew. 'Ree? You're up early.' He looked at Emberlon. 'It ... is early, isn't it?'

Ree seized him by the arm and dragged him over to the sarcophagus. 'Look at this,' she said. 'I almost cast it! The song, you were right about the song!"

'I was right?' He smiled fuzzily before his expression clouded over. 'It's — uh, what is happening?'

'Smythe! The spell! Your notes!' She wanted to shake him.

'Right! Of course, the — the notes. Um.' He ran a hand through his curls — his fingers got caught and he spent a few seconds disentangling himself. 'Which spell?'

'The one for wild senses — you translated it into a song.'

'Ah! That spell, the spell, the —' he snapped his fingers. 'Hold on —'

He flew to her research journal, flicking through several pages. 'You say it *almost* worked?' He thumped the page. 'Therianthropy is almost always referenced as a ritual — perhaps missing some component. You see, it might be easy to translate *shar* as spell, but when combined with *sira es* — '

'No.' Ree shook her head. 'We can't be missing components. I doubt it would have gotten as far as it did if we had. And if you look *here, serasaph* suggests a spiritual component, like many necromantic spells. Not all therianthropy is ritualistic. I think perhaps it was the wrong *tune.*' She scrubbed her face.

Emberlon stood up. 'I'll be in my room,' he said. He dusted off his book.

Ree waved at him absently, and when she heard the door snick closed behind him, she laid Smythe's sketch on top of the other notes. 'I think ... I think maybe it's time we visited the Lich.'

Smythe's eyebrows twitched. 'You —? Pardon?'

She tapped his sketch.. 'The Lich. This tableau you found? It's in the Lich's wing of the crypt — that's why it's uncharted.' She breathed out through her nose. 'I know it's dangerous but — what does the Lich *do* all day? I'm betting it's the same thing it did when it was properly alive. *Studying.* There'll be a library — a library with books related to *this* tableau. To a culture that revered therianthropes. Or *a* therianthrope, at least.'

'Sorry, I'm not quite following.' Smythe blinked at her blearily through the dusty lenses of his glasses. 'Only woke up a moment ago, you know. Usually, I'm quite sharp, and — nevermind.' He flushed. 'Are you suggesting we ask the Lich about therianthropy?'

The Lich couldn't see, not really. It was a pattern of behaviours: the most powerful necromancer in living memory, stuck on rails.

She was quick. She was sneaky. And this time, she would be prepared.

'Don't be ridiculous.' Ree locked her eyes to Smythe's. 'I'm suggesting we raid its library.'

'Oh.' Smythe opened his mouth, then closed it again. 'Well.'

I hate the way this kingdom has been carved up, each man willingly locking himself into his own cage. It seems everyone has their own suite of rooms, their own tower, their own little box to shit in.

It is better than the world above, of course. The King Below understands us far better than any of them ever could.

But a cage is still a cage, and all I want is to leap from the mountain and let my wings carry me into the sky.

My work for the King keeps me too busy for that of late.

~from the journal of Wylandriah Witch-feather

CHAPTER TWENTY

THE LIBRARY OF THE LICH

Ree approached the broad doors that led to the archive room. She glanced over her shoulder at Smythe, who was adjusting his glasses interestedly. 'Help me open this?'

'Certainly!'

Ree pulled the key from around her neck; it turned in the lock with a satisfying 'clunk' as the bolt slid free.

She started to push, and Smythe started talking. 'You know, even a leaner fellow like myself can move quite a bit of weight if correctly applied. The trick, you see, is to push with your shoulders, like so —'

Ree glared at him. With Smythe lecturing, most of the pushing had been left to her, and the door was barely moving.

'— and studies have found that strength is as much in technique as it is muscle mass, which is why the ancient —

the ancient, um —' He seemed to catch her look and quailed a bit. 'I'll just push, then, shall I?'

The door slid open just far enough for Ree to slip in. 'Wait here, don't let anyone in.'

'Oh. Certainly. The watchman! A most important role. Except — how exactly am I meant to stop someone? Ree?'

Ree took a moment to draw in a long, dusty breath. She loved it here in the cool, dry archive room. She'd spent hours here when she'd been training as Emberlon's assistant, sitting on the hard stone floor, encircled by record cards. The only disturbance for hours was Emberlon coming to check on her and nodding his approval as he looked over her work.

She hurried to the wall where her maps were scrolled and filed. She scanned down the rack for the correct sector and slid a map carefully into her satchel.

It had been here, in this dusty, airless room, that she had first discovered a love of order, of putting everything in its place. It had been that love of order that had first made her curious about the Lich's wing.

'What about the far eastern tunnels?' she'd asked.

Emberlon had set aside the borrower's record he'd been flicking through. *'You'll have to repeat that.'*

'The far eastern tunnels. We have records of the libraries in the eastern tunnels, but isn't there a whole wing beyond that? There must be libraries there. Why don't we have records?'

She remembered Emberlon's heavy sigh. *'Even necromancers know there are some things better left undisturbed. Whatever is there, it's not for us.'*

And she'd felt a burning desire to go, to see, to document. But it was the Lich, and with her parents' warnings ringing in her ears and a lifetime of cultivated fear, she had resisted. She had mapped nearly all of the crypt's sectors, towers, tunnels and tombs, but the Lich's wing beyond the eastern tunnels, she'd left well alone.

But she'd never had *cause* to go. Now she did. With Smythe's carefully sketched notes, she knew there was more to find there.

She was smart, she was careful, and she knew the Lich's behaviour. If she didn't get in its way, it would never know she was there. *Smythe* had managed to do it, after all.

When she got back outside, she was surprised to find Smythe quiet. He avoided her eyes, mostly staring at the floor.

'I got the map.' She said the words haltingly. It was weird to be filling the silence; silence never usually existed around Smythe. When he didn't react, she continued, 'I don't know how far in the library will be, or where, but it should take us two days to get to the other side of the tunnels, where the Lich's wing begins.'

Still nothing.

Ree cast around for something that might encourage him. 'I imagine it will be very old. It's about a day's travel from the embalming room where I found you. It might be —
'

'I've been thinking.' Smythe looked up, his lips pressed tightly, his eyes determined behind his glasses.

His expression did not bode well. '... Oh?'

He ran a hand through his curls. 'That Lich fellow almost killed us before, didn't he? Seems jolly rash to go knocking on his front door.'

Ree crossed her arms. 'Nobody's going to be knocking on anything. It'll be safe, Smythe. If we don't get in the Lich's way, then it won't hurt us.' It sounded like a hollow reassurance, even to her own ears. The Lich had almost killed them both already. 'You've already been there, and you were fine! While you were there, anyway ...'

Smythe scuffed his shoes in the dirt. 'I'm sorry to make a fuss — I understand the theory. It's just — that curse — it wasn't, um, pleasant.' He stared at the ground again, shoulders hunched. 'I'd rather — I mean, if at all possible — I'd rather not get cursed again. And — and it seems to me that this fellow must be exceptionally powerful. Everyone — even Andomerys, even your father — seems afraid of him.'

Ree's chest tightened at his words. She knew the risks. She'd barely gone a month in her life without being reminded of them, but this could be her only chance. She thought of her father, determined to force her onto his path. She thought of the feeling of magic prickling her skin — real, tangible power. She couldn't give it up.

'I'll go alone.' She adjusted the strap of her satchel to avoid meeting his eyes. 'Tell Emberlon to scry for me if I'm not back in a week.' She walked away.

'What? Festering rats!' He ran to intercept her, raising his hands. 'I never intended for you to go alone. I'm — it's just —' He rubbed his neck. 'I must admit to a certain amount of — well, fear.' His cheeks darkening. 'But I would never ask you to go alone. Not after everything you've done for me.'

Ree felt heat creeping up her neck. She wasn't used to being thanked. It made her more than a little uncomfortable. 'You saved me, I saved you. We're even.'

'Not even slightly.' There was a spark to his gaze. 'You helped — you're always so —' He shook his head, looking even more flushed than before. 'I'm going with you.'

Ree smiled and looked at the floor. 'Thank you.'

'Excellent.' Smythe clapped his hands together. 'Now that that's sorted, shall we collect Larry and head off?'

When Ree gave him a quizzical look, he explained, 'I don't like to think of the poor fellow, moping about town. He seems to rather enjoy excursions out into the tunnels, don't you think?'

As it happened, Larry was with Usther, who was thrilled to be rid of him and too absorbed in her own work to question where they were going with packed satchels and a borrowed minion.

'He's been ruining *everything,*' she said, eyeing Larry despairingly. 'Every time I chalk down a spell diagram he comes blundering over to muck it up. And I tried locking him outside, but he goes positively *wild,* howling and rattling the door like a great tantruming *infant.*' She glared at him. 'Take him.'

So Ree and Smythe set off with Larry in tow. Though they frequently had to help him up walls or along narrow paths, or right him when he lost his balance and toppled over, Ree was secretly glad to have him. She hadn't forgotten when she and Smythe had last faced the Lich. Useless though Larry might be, he'd distracted it for a crucial moment. And maybe he'd do so again, if they needed it. Given he appeared to be functionally immortal, she wasn't too concerned about what the Lich might do to him.

She and Smythe walked through rooms filled with sleeping dead. Ree showed Smythe how to calm them if disturbed, while Smythe studied the chambers with wide eyes and fingers that twitched to make notes. They spent the night locked in an embalming room, sleeping on thin bedrolls on the floor while Larry pounded on the door. He couldn't be counted on not to chew on them while they slept.

'I suppose tomorrow, it's the Lich's wing,' Smythe whispered. He hesitated, then: 'I hope you won't think less of me, but — I'm still scared.'

'We'll be ready,' Ree said, but what she wanted to say was: *I'm scared too.*

The next day, they stood at the edge of the eastern tunnels. Ree held a map in her hands. 'This is it,' she said. She hoped he couldn't hear the tremble in her voice. 'This is where the map ends. This passage should lead us right into the Lich's wing of the crypt.'

The passage was long, dark, cold. It seemed to Ree almost foggy; luminous lichen grew in this part of the crypt, lending the charred stone an eerie glow.

Ree took a long, steadying breath. 'Avoid its line of sight. Put out your torch at the first sign of trouble.'

Smythe hesitated. 'Actually — sorry, I'd quite forgotten — we shouldn't need to worry about that.' He put out his torch and after a moment, his eyes took on a familiar pale glow. 'I had Usther teach me the darksight ritual last week.' He shifted from one foot to the other. 'How, uh, how do I look?'

It took Ree a moment to gather her words. He looked, here in the darkness, with his eyes aglow and his face half-shadowed, like a practitioner. If not for the gleam of his glasses, she might not have recognised him.

Larry bumped into her shoulder. She found her voice. 'Like an undead creature,' she said, straight-faced. When he laughed, she smiled in return, though she wasn't quite sure what to think.

Together, they walked into the Lich's wing.

For a long time, there was nothing. Empty rooms, empty tombs. Rows and rows of shelves that had clearly once held bodies, now empty. It was like the crypt had been picked clean; everything of use had been taken away, everything else had been destroyed. They found little but splintered wood and shattered stone. Even Larry seemed subdued. He trailed a long way behind them, making hardly a groan.

'Hold on a moment ... I remember this!' Smythe pushed up his glasses, looking around at the bare brick walls and cobbled floor. He went to the wall and brushed away a layer of dirt and cobwebs. 'Not brown brick — red!'

Ree's hand went to her collarbone. She felt brittle with hope. 'The tableau?'

'Let's see, I came down here from ... and then there was the statue ... and then — this way!' In his excitement, he took her hand and towed her down the corridor and around the corner, and then down a narrow path with walls of rough-hewn stone speckled with luminous lichen like stars in the sky. Ree didn't pull away. The ease with which he took her hand shocked her, but not unpleasantly.

When he stopped, she bumped into his shoulder. He smelled of iron and mountain water and floral soap. Horrified to know that, she sprang back, releasing his hand.

'This is it,' he said, gazing up at the wall. And then Ree turned and all awkwardness slipped away, eclipsed by the biggest discovery of her life.

She was winded with awe. Smythe's sketch had seemed detailed to her at the time, but she had been utterly unprepared for the reality. The mage stared down at her with a wild gleam in her eyes. Blue stripes adorned her cheeks, shining lapis compared to the sparkling rubies of her hood and robe. Her eyes were hard with a cat-like gleam, bright against the jewel-brown of her skin. The animals around her were larger than life and so artfully depicted that they appeared almost to move as Ree watched. Bears with onyx claws, foxes with jade-red fur, and above her, a grey hawk with glittering hematite feathers and luminous eyes. A king looked down on her, his hands spread in a benevolent blessing, his eyes the inky black of a practitioner, his crown iron and twisted like thorns. But though the king's authority was clear in his positioning, he was a smaller figure, eclipsed by the power and presence of the sparkling mage and her many forms.

Ree rested her hand against the mage's open palm. Cold stone, and yet the touch invigorated her. This was it. This was *really* it. Definitive proof not only that therianthropes existed, but that they were venerated by the culture that built this wing of the crypt.

Her gaze fixed on the mage's hard stare. Confident and cold. Someone who never had to spend the night shivering in a tower attic. Someone nobody would dare cross.

'I'm going to be like you,' she whispered, hand against hand.

'What?'

She reluctantly withdrew her hand.

'Ree, what were you —'

'We should study it properly,' she said. 'Fill out your notes, make sure we haven't missed anything. This is not something to rush.'

'The discovery of the century!' Smythe pushed up his glasses then fumbled with his pack. 'And to think — likely, she's buried here. We know nothing of therianthrope culture or rituals — we could learn so much from how her body is entombed!'

Somehow, the words struck her with disappointment. Seeing this tableau had filled her with hope. Its discovery made therianthropy real and current, gave truth to her life's work. But it was still something locked in the past — this mage, like everything in her world, was dead and buried.

'Think — this doesn't have to be the end of her knowledge. Her story, as it were.' He spoke as if he'd read Ree's mind, his thoughts running along the same tracks. 'If we find her body, I can summon her soul. We can ask her — well, anything!'

'Anything,' Ree said, hope filling her. 'We could find out the therianskin creation ritual — could get her to sing the songs!'

'Everything you ever wanted to know!' Smythe beamed at her. 'You can have all the knowledge of a great therianthrope as if she'd taught it to you herself! We'll have to be careful how we time, it, of course, but ...'

As he continued, Ree's hopes fell. Soul summoning was a cruel school of necromancy — perhaps even crueller than curses. To be trapped in that body in excruciating agony, forced to answer questions ... the therianthrope would hate her. And it could damage her soul, even extinguish it.

She wasn't sure that was something she could do. Maybe it was the influence of her mother, or maybe it was the way the bone pits and mass graves had always discomfited her, but she was naturally repulsed by the idea.

Repulsed, and just a tiny bit tempted.

'Let's keep searching,' she said, trying to push away that line of thinking. 'If this is here, who knows what else we might find.'

But as they resumed their exploration, it was without any sparkling discoveries. A return to the frustration of barren walls and empty rooms.

'I don't understand,' Smythe said when they came to yet another empty room. It had clearly once held a sarcophagus, now empty. No treasures lined the shelves, no tapestries hung on the walls. 'How can everything just be — you know, gone? Poof!' He wiggled his fingers at the sarcophagus. 'As if nothing was ever there. As if it were just a stone crate someone left lying around.'

'Over-fishing,' said Ree, a little absently. She was trying to think about the construction in this part of the crypt. They were getting nowhere with this particular passage — they needed to branch off if they could. She carried the memory of the tableau in her heart like a torch. They would find something. They had to.

'Sorry — did you just say "fishing"?'

'It's what they call it when a necromancer uses up the natural resources of a tomb. You know, corpses, curses, that sort of thing.' She ran her hand down the wall and looked at the thick coating of dust. Surely not even the Lich had been here in a long time. 'It's been over-fished. It's usually applied to city practitioners who've tapped out the local graveyard. Resources aren't an issue in a crypt of this size.'

'But this Lich is a very old chap — old enough to have, what, used up all the bodies?'

Ree motioned him to follow her out of the room. 'Evidently.'

'Used them doing *what*, exactly?'

Ree flashed him a look. 'You're the necromancer.'

Smythe cleared his throat. 'Ah. Yes. So I am. Uh — let's just carry on then, shall we?'

More empty rooms. The torch in her heart dimmed; Ree started to despair of them finding anything at all. The Lich wasn't really human any more — what if it didn't really do anything? What if it just floated around these empty halls like a spectre? Disappointment was a tight fist in her belly. She'd been so certain that a necromancer so old and so powerful must have what they wanted, especially after the tableau.

She was about to tell Smythe to turn back when he waved frantically at her.

'Over here!' How anyone could whisper so loudly, Ree had no idea.

She padded to the other side of the door he was peering through. 'What is it?'

'*Him.*'

Ree took a steadying breath and peered through the doorway. A balcony over-looked a long room, stacked with shelves on every wall. The Lich drifted across the room, a thick tome in its hands.

It was the most normal thing she'd ever seen it do. Somehow, it only made it seem more dangerous. She was in the Lich's lair, its home territory. For all she'd assured Smythe that the Lich's behaviour was predictable, she began to doubt exactly how much she could predict.

They should leave. This wasn't skirting the edges of a fire; it was leaning forward and pressing her face into it. She glanced at Smythe. His skin was blanched and he clasped trembling hands in front of him. He looked barely a breath away from fleeing.

He'd never talked about the curse or what it had felt like. But it had nearly killed him, and she doubted it had been pleasant.

They needed to leave. Running into the Lich by accident was one thing; throwing themselves into its path was another. And Larry, who had been falling further and further behind the deeper into the Lich's wing they travelled, was nowhere to be seen. No counting on another rescue from the immortal minion, then.

But though a few quick steps would carry her out of danger, she found herself taking another step forward.

'Uh — Ree?'

The books she needed were *here,* she was certain of it. The Lich had been here for centuries longer than anyone could remember. It'd had its pick of the collected knowledge of several cultures and generations long past. Magic that had been forgotten. Magic like therianthropy.

This could be her *chance.* Maybe her only one.

'Stay here,' she whispered to Smythe.

'What? Why?' His voice spiked in panic. She half-ducked, but the Lich didn't look up from its tinkering at its desk.

'Because you're clumsy and I'm not. I'll be right back. I'm going to scout the room out.'

'Ree!'

Ree ignored his protests and slipped into the room on soft-soled boots. She'd crept past sleeping kings and the corpses of necromancers long past. She could be quiet, when she needed to. She skirted the bookshelves at the other end of the room, scanning the books with intermittent glances at the Lich. If she could just discern its classification system, she might get an idea of where to start looking.

As she edged further into the room, the Lich stiffened. *The Lich doesn't see, it doesn't hear,* Ree told herself, though her entire body clenched in terror. *It follows a set path. If I don't get in its way, then —*

Its robes swirled, tentacle-like, in the air as it began to turn.

Every few years, some hot-headed practitioner believes they have the power necessary to take on the Lich, and further that that would somehow be a sensible idea. The town has never yet been able to recover the bodies.

And yet none of this ever truly stirs it the way the council fears. It is known to kill adventurers, and any others that cross its path, but it doesn't do anything with them. Perhaps it is just too old and too removed from its humanity to think of vengeance any more. Perhaps it is too powerful to bother seeking more power.

But the council still fears it. Not because of its power, but because they do not know what it wants.

If the Lich no longer desires power, then why does it still wander the crypt every day? What is it searching for?

~from *A History of Tombtown* by Emberlon the Disloyal

CHAPTER TWENTY-ONE

WHAT NECROMANCERS FEAR

Ree dived to one side and tucked herself behind a bookcase as the Lich turned. It fixed its gaze at the spot where she'd been, the ragged ends of its robes swirling in slow-motion as if underwater.

Ree kept a hand over her mouth, fighting to keep her terrified breathing silent. She almost choked on the thick, humid feel of its power. The Lich was boney and withered, but its presence was enough to fill the library.

Ree peeked out from behind the bookcase, only to jerk back as the Lich's head snapped round. Her blood pounded in her ears as she pressed herself back against the wall. It must have seen her. Those white marble eyes ...

The Lich drifted past, gaze never flickering in her direction. Its shrivelled legs trailed bonelessly in the air behind it. For a moment, the pressure of its magic was so overpowering that Ree feared it would suffocate her, but then the pressure eased.

Ree gasped and lurched forward, one hand pressed to her chest. She risked a glance at the Lich, but it was leaving the room through a door beneath the balcony, heavy tome still held loosely in its too-long fingers.

Had it known she was there? It could have been a fluke, a coincidence. Must have been. The Lich wasn't aware of the world anymore. It had stopped being sentient, in the traditional sense, a long time ago.

She thought of the intensity of its gaze, the way its magic filled the room: cloying, suffocating.

Muffled footsteps. Ree had barely leaned out from her alcove before Smythe barreled into her. 'Ree!'

'I'm fine, everything's fine,' she said, because Smythe's eyes were wild behind his glasses.

'Ree, *it saw you*. It saw you — I'm certain of it! We *must* get out of here.'

Ree shook her head. Her heart-rate was slowing to a more manageable pace now, and she refused to leave empty-handed. 'There has to be something here, Smythe.'

Smythe's gaze wavered on her face, then he set his jaw and nodded curtly. 'Well,' he said. 'We'd best get started before that fellow returns and makes minions of us.' Larry, mysteriously returned, lumbered down the stairs after them and Smythe gave him a mock-bow that didn't quite hide his nerves. 'No offense, old chap!'

Ree knew she was asking a lot of Smythe. For once, he knew the danger they faced far better than she. But right now, they had access to texts no-one else in Tombtown had ever handled — or even knew existed. She and Smythe split up, Larry attaching himself to Smythe, to better cover the shelves.

Ree rushed along the bookcases, pulling off any likely books and thumbing frantically through the pages. She found books on strange rituals and ancient traditions, books on creatures long thought legendary, and books in languages so old that even she couldn't read them. She could hear Smythe muttering as he read and thought aloud, hear Larry's unusually quiet, high-pitched grunting. No matter how desperately she read or how absorbed she became in her task, her eyes always returned to the doorway the Lich had exited through. If he appeared there ... well. They needed to be ready.

To her relief, there were a few contenders. She shoved *Wynas Serasaphi* and *A Study of the Old Ways* into her pack with such roughness that it made her cringe, but she was in no position to waste time with careful treatment. Smythe, too, had added a few tomes to his pack, though whether they were on therianthropy or were just particularly interesting to him, she didn't know.

She pulled one more book — one with peeling leather and no title, but with various animals embossed on the spine — and looked to Smythe. Her stomach knotted as she saw him peering through the doorway, Larry drooling at his shoulder.

'Smythe!' She hurried and took him by the wrist. 'I've got the books, we need to go before —'

But Smythe resisted, his eyes on the other room. 'What was it you said the Lich does all day?' His voice sounded faint.

Ree's breath went short at the paleness in his cheeks. 'Nothing,' she said. 'It wanders, it reads. Nothing, if you don't get in its way.' Her nose wrinkled; there was a horrible, metallic smell growing on her.

'And — sorry but — how fresh would you say that is?' He nodded at something in the room.

Ree followed his gaze, hairs rising on the back of her neck. The other room was a further library, but the stone floor was a mess of blood and chunks of flesh and entrails, leading a gory path to the next door.

Ree's mouth went dry.

'I'm assuming — from your expression — that this isn't "nothing".' Smythe nodded to himself. 'All right, well, this has been a jolly adventure, but I think now we should —'

'There were no corpses.' Ree said the words quietly.

'Uh — pardon?'

Ree stared at the bloody smear. 'There were no corpses, no bodies, nothing. Empty tombs and empty rooms. What do you think he could do with that many bodies?'

'Uh?'

Ree looked at him. 'We can't leave. Not without knowing.'

Smythe ran a hand through his hair. 'You — but — you see, I'd really rather not.'

Ree breathed out through her nose, staring at him for a long moment, before following the trail. She didn't want to go either, but if the Lich was behaving strangely, that could be a danger to the town. After a moment, she heard Smythe follow. 'Keep an eye on Larry,' she whispered.

'Of course, I — uh, where is he exactly?'

Ree spun. The doorway was empty and Smythe was scratching his head. There was no sign of Larry.

Perhaps he had a self-preservation instinct after all. It didn't comfort her.

She came to the wooden door, so thickly smeared with gore that the handle dripped. She pulled her sleeve over her hand and carefully lifted the latch. The door creaked open, just a crack. The stench that rolled into her sent her reeling back, gagging. Smythe, behind her turned and wretched.

She pressed her arm to her nose and went to the door again. Bodies, ripped and dismembered, were mounded in front of her. She couldn't see the Lich, but she could hear its scratchy death echo as it chanted, could hear the meaty tear of flesh. It must be somewhere behind all that ... whatever it was building.

Something about the scene felt eerily familiar, but she found she couldn't place it.

'Ree?' Smythe wiped spittle from his mouth with a shaking hand. He was looking to her for direction, no — permission.

They could go now. The Lich was clearly practicing again, something she had been assured it did not do but had been raised to fear above all else. She could go back and tell the council, warn the town — but tell them what? That there were bodies and blood? Would they even take her seriously — she, being a non-practitioner, and Smythe only an acolyte. And it would take them another couple of days, even travelling fast, to make it back to the central mausoleum.

'We need to know what it's doing.' Ree tried to keep her voice even, tried to project a confidence that couldn't be further from what she felt.

Smythe blanched. 'I'd rather not,' he said. His voice was a little too high-pitched. 'You know, because he's — because before — what if he curses us?'

'Wait here.' She started through the door, but Smythe caught her wrist.

'No.' He cleared his throat. 'I'm — I won't let you go alone.' His entire body was trembling.

Ree pressed a finger to her lips, fixing her eyes with his, then squeezed through the cracked door and crept behind the mound of body parts.

Inside, the pressure of the Lich's magic had risen again. But now, instead of a suffocating blanket, it was bright and painful with ennervation, a magic that made her heart beat too fast and her muscles sting. Slowly, she peered around the mounded bodies.

The Lich had its back to the door. It faced an enormous pile of stitchwork flesh, with long tentacles curling out and a huge, fleshy head that blinked with too many eyes. As she watched, it twitched and jumped in response to the Lich's chanting, its many eyes rolling among the folds of flesh. Several books were laid in a spell diagram behind the Lich and annotated in bold letters inked with gore.

'Festering rats,' Smythe whispered. He swayed beside her; Ree gripped his shoulder and dug in hard with her fingers, praying he wouldn't faint. 'What — what do you think that is? That's not anything that Usther — I never realised that one could —'

Ree backed behind the mound and locked eyes with Smythe. 'Look at me,' she said, her voice urgent and low. Smythe's entire body was rigid. His eyes darted back and forth, as if seeking escape.

'It's very big, isn't it? I read about elephants in the northern lands, once — they were used as war animals in the third era, did you know? Very large and they always — and krakens, have you heard of them? Mythical creatures, not *real,* of course, but the tentacles —'

'Smythe.' Ree tried to force steadiness into her voice. She took Smythe's chin in her hands, forcing him to look at her.

'We shouldn't have come,' he said in a small voice. 'We should never —'

'Maybe not.' Ree kept her breathing slow and even. Gradually, Smythe's breath fell into sync with her own. 'But we can't leave now. Not when the Lich is doing *this*. Not when we don't know what it intends to use it for.'

There was a clarity in Smythe's eyes now, something that went beyond terror. 'It's because of us, isn't it?'

She didn't want to think about that. 'We need to stop this ritual,' Ree said. She released Smythe, now that the babbling had stopped. 'We can't let it use this on the town.'

What was she saying? She couldn't stop the Lich! She wasn't a necromancer or a mage of any kind — that was why she had come here in the first place. She was a coward, a creeper, a cartographer —

She was more than that. Whatever they thought of her, she was still more than that.

But she wasn't powerful enough to face the Lich.

She closed her eyes, thinking furiously. Maybe she didn't have to stop the Lich. She risked another peek at the ritual. The muscles all stitched together, the blood on the books ...

'Ghosts and gargoyles,' she whispered. She quickly withdrew. Veritas, in his isolated madness, had been *right*. Usther would be horrified.

Smythe watched her with an expression somewhere between wariness and hope.

'I know how to disrupt the ritual,' she said.

All magic is physical — by which I mean, of course, that it is tied to bodies. Healers repair and enhance living bodies. Necromancers animate and control dead bodies. Even magics of fairytale and legend, such as shapeshifting or mind-reading, rely on bodies.

What is interesting is the way in which magic also affects the soul. None can deny the link between soul and body — it has been seen and confirmed by necromancers and even healers time and again throughout history.

But the soul and body are also discreet, separate objects — or so necromancers claim. If the soul can be accessed due to its link to the body, what else, one wonders, could magic do if sufficient links were found?

~from *Envisioning the Future of Magic* by Elden Mannelyn

CHAPTER TWENTY-TWO

A GOOD DENIZEN

They were hiding behind a mound of gore in a room drenched in blood. The Lich's magic rolled over them in sickening waves. The tentacled flesh monster the Lich had constructed twitched and writhed with the sound of meat slapping against meat.

Standing in that room, choking on the stench while fear seized her lungs, Ree wondered why she thought she had any hope of stopping this.

At her side, Smythe looked at her with worry pulling at his eyes. 'Are you ... well, quite certain this is a good idea?'

Ree grimaced. 'Not at all. But we can't do nothing.'

Because the Lich was powerful enough to wake up the entire crypt and bring it down around the town. Because the Lich was only *doing anything at all* because she had foolishly leapt into its path and then, twice as foolish, she had stolen Smythe away from it when it had marked him for death.

This ritual, the stitchwork monster — it was all because of Ree and Smythe. And with the Lich so close to completing it, there was no time to find someone else to stop it.

The Lich took one of the monster's flesh tentacles in its withered hand and held it aloft, still chanting. It looked too frail to hold even so much as a book, but it hefted the meaty appendage as if it were weightless.

Ree nudged Smythe. They split up, Ree coming up behind the Lich, Smythe skirting the walls to sneak behind the monster.

Ree's heart thumped against her ribs. She could feel her blood pulsing, could hear it in her ears. How good was the Lich's hearing, now that it was awakened? Could it hear her muffled footsteps as she tread carefully toward the defaced books? Could it hear her frantic heartbeat?

She saw a flash of dark curls as Smythe ducked behind the tentacle beast, but the Lich did not let up in its chanting. Ree prayed to her mother's goddess that Smythe had taken as readily to shielding his mind as he had to summoning.

Ree looked at the books spread across the floor, a spell diagram webbed around them, blood smeared across the open pages. It was the central book, the heart of the ritual, that mattered most. She remembered Veritas's outrage when she had reclaimed *Astaravinarad.*

She didn't like to think what the Lich's fury would be like. She steeled herself and ripped the central book from the ritual; it tore away with the feeling of thread snapping.

In front of her, the Lich stiffened. Its chanting died. Ree dived for the mound of gore, only to freeze in her steps as the Lich spun and pointed at her.

The force of its regard drove the air from her lungs. Ree stood, transfixed, as it glared at her with white-marble eyes. She pulled her mental guards snugly around her, felt her father's magic flare in the amulet at her chest, but couldn't break free of its centuries-old gaze.

'*Akho rizha kun,*' the Lich intoned, its voice entirely consumed in the death echo of the Craft. Behind it, the flesh monster began to stir. Tentacles crawled across the floor toward Ree, trailing blood.

Now! Her thoughts were frantic. *It has to be now!*

Just as Smythe and then Larry had distracted the Lich before, so Smythe needed to distract the Lich now. He was better prepared, he would surely be able to —

Magic. The hairs on the back of Ree's neck rose as though in a chill wind. The Lich seemed to hesitate at this intrusion. Slowly, it turned to face the beast.

Ree went cold. Featureless figures, vaguely human in shape, oozed from every stitched piece of the tentacle beast, crying and howling in choked voices. Souls, somehow summoned from the assembled parts. Ree only had a glimpse of this horror before she rushed out of the room, gore-stained book clutched to her chest.

She heard the Lich chanting as she skidded through the blood trail and out into the library. She was almost through the next doorway when a clash of thunder shook the ground, knocking her from her feet.

She staggered into the doorframe as all around, books tumbled from shelves and dust rained from the ceiling. With bruises lining her arm, she pressed on for the balcony stairs — the only escape she could see.

When she got to the stairs, she turned, biting her lip. Where was Smythe?

He'd been meant to slip out of the room as soon as he got the Lich's attention. He should be climbing the stairs with her right now. Another *boom* shook the crypt.

Ree gripped the banister with white-knuckled hands, a hundred options running through her mind. Should she go back and help him, should she — but then he was tumbling into the library, blood on his hands and all down his linen shirt. For a terrible moment, Ree thought he'd been stabbed, but then he caught her eye and grinned.

He followed her out of the library and into one of the abandoned rooms down the corridor. Ree closed the door with trembling hands.

'What *happened* in there?' She didn't like the way her voice quavered, but Smythe seemed not to notice. If anything, he looked *pleased.*

Drenched in blood, he beamed at her. 'It was *quite* phenomenal. I wasn't sure that — but of course, it worked! I mean, there were a few variables that I couldn't ... but the theory was sound!'

'Smythe,' Ree said his name uncertainly. He looked very unlike himself — his cheeks too hollow, his eyes too shadowed, and blood smeared on his face, in his hair, and at the edges of his glasses.

Smythe stopped, blinked, and nodded, as if to himself. 'Oh, of course — silly of me, of course you wouldn't — I summoned the souls of the bodies he was using.'

A cold knot was forming in Ree's stomach. 'There must have been hundreds.'

'Oh, certainly, and of all ages, too. It was quite the piece of work and of course, I couldn't create my own spell diagram so I had to use what was already — it was not the most smooth of summonings. But, as you saw ... well.' He crossed his arms, looking smug.

He looked like a necromancer, she thought, but that wasn't true. A necromancer would be robed in sensible black, their hair pinned up and away from their face. Smythe in his blood-soaked linens with his tumble of curls, looked like something quite different. Like a butcher. Like a monster.

None of it made any *sense.* She tried, desperately, to understand. 'But how did you summon so many at once? I thought all necromancers have limits —'

'Oh, well souls are not *quite* so tiring, I'm told. And I am quite tired,' he said, but he didn't look tired. He looked happy. He looked ... invigorated.

Ree tried to think. How many minions could Usther hold at once? How many could her father?

'He must have a strong will indeed,' Andomerys had told her, when Smythe was lying cold and pale on her healer's table, fighting the Lich's death curse.

Ree thought of a hundred souls summoned to their dismembered, stitched-up flesh, and screaming.

Smythe's smile was faltering. 'Uh. Ree? Sorry but — did I say something wrong?'

His skin had a tinge of grey to it that would probably never leave. He was almost as grey as she was — the mark of necromancy. Of nearness to death.

Another *boom* shook the crypt. Ree's heart was a stone in her chest. 'Do you think it's looking for us?'

The smugness had left Smythe completely now. 'Hard to see how he wouldn't. We did ruin his ritual and run off with his favourite book, poor fellow.'

The fear that had gripped him when faced with the Lich was gone. That only made Ree more tense: now she would have to fear for both of them.

Ree pressed the heel of her palm to her forehead. 'It never used to be like this.'

'Sorry?'

Ree closed her eyes. 'The Lich. If it got stirred up — if an adventurer attacked it, or an upworlder acolyte confronted it, the whole crypt could feel it. But it would always settle down. It would always —' she cast about for a word '— forget. It would always forget.'

Smythe shrugged helplessly. 'Well, maybe it will! Pardon me for saying so, but we don't have all the information. Perhaps he does this all the time just to keep himself —'

But Ree shushed him with a look as the hairs on her arms rose. She seized Smythe's wrist and yanked him to her side, pressing against the wall just as the door swung open beside them. Ree struggled to breathe as the Lich glided in a few steps to observe the room. The door had opened in a way that eclipsed them from view. She couldn't help but stare in horror at the back of its head as one second passed, then another.

Don't go further in, she prayed. *Please Morrin, don't let it turn this way.*

Its power filled the room, rolling out from it in thick waves, filling Ree's body with lethargy. Beside her, Smythe barely stifled a yawn.

Please, Morrin.

The Lich turned away from them and glided back out of the room. The door creaked shut behind it.

Ree gasped in a breath.

Smythe blinked, mouth opening and closing.

Ree gathered her wits. 'It must have been working on this project for weeks — ever since it cursed you —'

'Sorry but — can we really know that?'

'Yes!' Ree pressed her hand to her forehead and started to pace the room. 'This is a big, big project. And the only thing that has changed in the last several weeks — the only thing that might have *woken it up* is when we crossed its path. The Lich doesn't *do* this, Smythe! It's followed the same pattern every day of my life, occasionally killing anyone foolish enough to get in its way.' She said 'foolish' bitterly. 'We need to get it back to its usual state. We need to know what was different about meeting us.'

Smythe's brow furrowed. 'But Ree —'

Ree stopped her pacing and threw her head back, hands clenching and unclenching in frustration. 'Ahh, what did we do? I walked into its path and —'

'Excuse me, Ree?'

'Then you walked in —'

Smythe touched her elbow and Ree jumped. 'I know what's different,' he said firmly.

'What?'

Smythe's eyes wavered as they locked with hers. 'Well, it's — it's quite obvious, isn't it? We lived.'

Ree spun away from him, her mind going numb as she tried to process his words. Another thought occurred to her. She went cold. 'Smythe — where's Larry?'

I wish I knew the future of my art. I wish I could prove that it will live on. The world will be duller and tamer without it.

~from the journal of Wylandriah Witch-feather

CHAPTER TWENTY-THREE

WHAT BELONGS TO THE DEAD

Ree pressed her hands to her temples, throwing her mind back. Larry had been trailing them at a distance for most of their time in the Lich's wing, but he'd been with them when they searched the library. Had they lost him? Had the Lich taken him?

The crypt shook with another pulse of the Lich's magic. Ree shivered at the feel of it. They'd interrupted the Lich's ritual in an attempt to keep to the town safe, but somehow it seemed more dangerous than ever.

Larry *had* been in the library, hadn't he? She had a strong memory of him grunting and almost *whimpering* during their time there. It wasn't like Larry to wander off — once he'd caught the scent of something living, he would follow until he latched on to something else.

'Uh — Ree?'

Ree turned to meet Smythe's worried look. He wrung his hands, his shoulders hunched. 'If this Lich fellow wants us — well, you know, *dead* — how can we possibly stop him?'

'I don't know if it does want us dead.' How had she not noticed Larry wandering off? And why had he done it? Or had something happened to him — had he fallen into a pit, perhaps, or been waylaid by other undead?

No, she remembered now. They'd followed the Lich through into the other room, and Larry had vanished.

'He didn't want to follow the Lich,' Ree said aloud.

'Uh — sorry?'

Ree chewed her lip as it all came together in her mind. 'Think about it — Larry's the oldest minion in living memory, but he's near perfectly preserved. He doesn't decay any more than he did before he was raised. Nobody knows who his master is, or why he's left to wander around. He can't be killed, not even with an arrow between his eyes — a magic more powerful than anyone's ever heard of.'

She could see realisation spark in his eyes. 'Larry is the Lich's minion,' he whispered.

'That's how we got away.' Ree held his gaze. 'Do you remember? The Lich was cursing you when Larry came into the room. It immediately left off to confront him.'

'I always thought — I don't know, that Larry had distracted him, perhaps?'

Ree shook her head. 'What's distracting about an undead to a Lich living in a crypt brimming with them? We were too slow and too preoccupied to think about it. It was *this particular* minion. *Its* minion.' She remembered again Larry sitting upright, a red glow in his eyes as the arrow wound between his eyes sealed. 'Maybe a special minion. Maybe a magic it hasn't been able to repeat.'

Smythe's eyes wavered on Ree's face. 'But ... oh, festering rats.' His voice was soft. 'The last time he saw Larry, he was with us. He must be jolly angry! It looks like — it must appear —'

'It looks like we stole its minion.' The words hovered in the air between them. Smythe looked even paler, under his grey-tinged skin. For herself, she hated to utter the words. The Lich had been a fixture of her world for as long as she could remember — a monster, yes, but also a protector. The most powerful, most dangerous, and most reliable aspect of life in the crypt. And now it considered her its enemy.

'And — and so he was creating that slimy fiend to take him back?'

In spite of the tension she felt, Ree's lips quirked at Smythe's description of the Lich's creature. 'We need to find Larry,' she said.

But finding one lonely minion in an unknown wing of the crypt was no small task, made worse by the Lich's agitation. Ree peered around every corner, her entire body tensed, certain that the Lich would swoop down on them at any moment.

The emptiness of the Lich's wing pressed on her. The wide, echoing corridors, the empty alcoves and shattered sarcophagi, the audible shush of her feet on dusty stone, with Smythe tapping after her. Ree had explored the crypt for years, and always there were hands trailing in her robes, eyes watching listlessly from corners, the creak and clack of ancient guardians standing with weapons ready. She might live in a crypt, but it was *alive,* or at least undead. It reacted to her presence, it moved and changed. But in the Lich's wing, there was only static, only silence, only emptiness. A true death, not the familiar undeath.

They peeked into destroyed rooms, roamed down long, cold corridors, and still found no sign of Larry. 'Perhaps he went back to town?' Smythe asked, pulling at his lips. Ree could see the hope in his eyes: return to the central mausoleum and forget about the Lich, its creature, its vengeance.

Ree thought about Larry's disappearance at the library — it must have been the moment he'd seen the Lich. 'If he's headed back to town, he can't have gotten far. You've seen how he shambles.'

Smythe nodded, shoulders hunched.

'We'll turn around. With any luck, we'll catch him before he makes it out of the wing.'

'Luck.' Smythe wrung his hands and Ree felt a pang.

I don't want this either, she wanted to say. *I want to go home and dive into my studies and forget all about this.*

But ignoring something didn't make it go away any more than shunning necromancers stopped the dead from rising. The world was what it was, and they needed to face that.

They made their way back toward town — or what Ree hoped was toward town. She was hopelessly lost without a map and had been turned around too many times during their flight to properly navigate. Every time Ree felt a prickle against her skin, every time she felt the air stir, she would pull Smythe aside and wait, breath caught in her throat, until she was certain the Lich had passed. As they walked down hallway after stone hallway, she began to doubt that they would find him. Larry had proven a mystery more than once now. Perhaps he was able to move much faster than they had ever seen. Perhaps he knew secret paths out of the Lich's wing. Or perhaps he had never headed back to town at all.

She could feel Smythe's eyes on her, though he hastily dropped his gaze whenever she looked around. Ever since she'd spied on him in the embalming room weeks ago, she'd always had a plan, always had all the answers. This was her crypt, her home, her world. She knew it better than anyone else. The first to be born here, the first to grow up here. The first to map it and document its secrets. But this trip had quickly shown up her weaknesses.

Maybe her father was right. Maybe learning necromancy was the only thing she could do to protect herself.

It had protected Smythe, back in the ritual room. But her heart railed against the idea. It was a silver bridle designed to tame her, to make her less when she had always known that she could be *more.*

When they heard panicked gargling, Ree's pulse leapt. She raced ahead of Smythe, only to skid to a stop at the edge of a wide crevasse.

Smythe caught up. He doubled over, panting and resting his elbows on his knees. 'Oh, poor chap! You really do have a hard time of it sometimes, don't you?'

Larry moaned and waved his arms at them from where he stood, neck-deep in the crevasse. His mouth sagged and his eyes rolled in what was clearly minion-ly panic.

Ree scrubbed at her face and looked around. The air was still; there were no lengthening shadows, no whisper of trailing robes. It appeared that they had beaten the Lich to Larry.

If it was even looking for him. But Ree tried not to think about what it would mean if she was wrong about this. 'Smythe, you take that arm, I'll take this one. On three.'

Together, they hauled Larry up, his legs kicking. She had her hood up, so all he could do was mouth at the thick cloth guarding her neck, but Smythe yelped a few times before they set him on his feet.

She took a moment to study the minion while he gawped at them. He looked no different than he had before the Lich — just as grey-green and putrid, his decay held in check only by the magic that animated him. There was no red spark in his eyes, as there had been when he'd revived from the arrow wound. He was … Larry. Slack-jawed and watery-eyed, swaying where he stood. A simple minion: masterless, purposeless.

'It's jolly good to see you.' Smythe clapped him on the shoulder. Larry started to teeter, but Smythe steadied him just in time. Smythe glanced at Ree. 'We've, um … well, let's just say it's good to see a friendly face.' He frowned. 'Although you've never really looked *friendly,* exactly, but I think that's —'

Larry swung around and tottered away from them.

'Larry!' Ree's voice was stern, but the minion was undeterred. He stumbled across the narrowest part of the crevasse, trapped his foot, and started howling.

'It's quite all right!' Smythe gave Larry's shoulder a squeeze, then grimaced and wiped the flaking skin off on his trousers. 'Hold still, there's a good chap, and I'll just —' The moment he pulled Larry's foot free the minion was off again, lurching as quickly as his spindly legs would carry him. Smythe hared after him, shouting, 'Jolly fast for a dead man, isn't he?'

Ree closed her eyes a moment, breathing in the musty smell of stone and earth. Eyes still closed, she pinned her hood to her hair. She ran her hands down the front of her robes, smoothing away the creases and dirt in its long skirt. She could hear Smythe shouting after Larry, and Larry's frantic gargling, hear their footsteps mingling in an off-beat mix of *shushing* and *tapping*.

Larry and the Lich were linked. With Larry's sudden desire to flee, she was more sure of it than ever. That meant they needed him.

And however frantic he might be, he wasn't fast. He could outrun Smythe, but he couldn't outrun her.

Ree streaked after Larry, her robes whipping about her legs, the air dragging at her hood. Her stride was long and easy, her feet light as she sprang from step to step. Smythe's head turned as she passed him, his mouth hanging open, and for a moment Ree felt a laugh well up inside her. In spite of the Lich, in spite of everything, she could still run. She could outrun every undead in the entire crypt if she had to.

Larry lurched frantically ahead of her, making wet panting sounds. She had never seen him move so fast, his torso bobbling atop his wildly pumping legs.

Ree passed him and then cut him off. She braced herself and he bowled into her. She gritted her teeth and shoved him back. He toppled.

'Larry.' She stood over him, wiping the sweat from her brow. He gargled and flopped around on the floor, eyes rolling in his head. 'Look, I'm sorry.' She gripped his arm and helped him to his feet, half-wondering, as she always did, why she bothered talking to a creature that surely couldn't understand.

Larry got to his feet and continued to gargle, eyes rolling here and there, resting everywhere but on Ree. She frowned.

'Here! I'm here.' Smythe stumbled to a stop and doubled over, panting as he leaned on his knees. 'You —' He paused, gasping for air. 'You're fast — faster than I thought.' His eyes flicked to Larry. He started to say something, then subsided into a flurry of coughs. 'Pardon me for asking, but — how did you get so fast? Was it like the darksight ritual?'

'Practice,' said Ree, who had been chased by greater undead every few days since she was old enough to leave the house on her own. Her attention was not on Smythe, but on Larry. The minion was twitching, eyes still looking everywhere but at Ree or Smythe. He didn't move to chew on them, as he did in moments of quiet, or lollop around them as he did when excited. He just quivered on the spot.

'You really do know it, don't you?' she whispered. 'The Lich.' Larry twitched away from her, oddly silent, but Ree could not have been more stunned if he'd spoken. Larry was the most empty-headed of minions: the least initiative, the slowest response time. She had always considered it part of his masterless existence, but now she had to wonder. He'd already proved himself more powerful than even the greatest undead, able to regenerate even a broken brain. And now, Ree asked herself: just how much did Wandering Larry, joke of Tombtown, actually understand?

'Are you quite all right, Larry?' Smythe touched the minion's arm; Larry jerked away from him as if burned. Smythe's mouth gaped. 'Oh — I'm so sorry! I never meant — there's no need to be afraid, old chap. We're all friends here, aren't we?'

'It's going to attack the town. And it's because of you, isn't it? Because it saw us together.'

If he understood, he didn't respond. Just continued to tremble.

'You can't blame that on him, it's unfair!' Smythe gave Larry's shoulder a squeeze, grimaced and wiped his hand on his trousers. 'If it's anyone's fault, it's the Lich's. And ... well,

I mean maybe not even his. He's undead, isn't he? Bit unfair to blame someone who's already dead.'

The Lich wasn't technically undead, although at its age and power, it was hard to tell the difference. She opened her mouth to tell Smythe as much — and that he really ought to know that, considering he had foolishly decided to follow in the Lich's footsteps — but the words died on her tongue. Larry stood, stiff as a cadaver, his eyes fixed above Ree's shoulder.

Ree's muscles tensed. Before she could turn, or run, or shout, a spectre smashed into her, pressing her into the wall. It was like being caught in a gale, or a between a tidal wave and a cliff. Gasping, she stared through its translucent body to see Smythe similarly pinned to the other side of the corridor.

'Not to worry — I can — I'll just —'

But the air was getting thinner and thinner, charged with an icy current. Larry still stood transfixed. Ree tried to wrench free of the spectre, but it held her fast. She felt like she was drowning. This spectre had so much more shape and force than the one Usther had used to pin her. 'Don't — '

'*Trzak trukoma* — ahh!' The magic Smythe gathered abruptly cut off. He screamed as the spectre pinning him darkened and snarled, shadows winding through the pale light that formed it.

And then the world seemed to go still. The Lich glided toward them down the corridor, somehow graceful in spite of its shrivelled limbs and long, ragged robes. It didn't spare a look for the denizens slammed against the walls. Its gaze was fixed on Larry as it spread its arms wide, fingers crooked in a gesture of welcome. '*Athenkryzta,*' it intoned, its voice like the crackle of old parchment. Larry walked stiltily toward it. The Lich's lips, so thin and withered that they barely scraped its teeth, widened in what might have been a smile. *'Atho athenkryzta. Kurat kwizzima.'*

Ree managed to wrench one arm free of the spectre pinning her. She reached for Smythe, muscles straining, then her stomach flipped as she tumbled to the floor. The spectres vanished in a cloud of grave mould. Smythe yelped as he hit the ground; Ree scrambled over to him.

'We need to leave,' Ree whispered. Her eyes were on the Lich, now embracing Larry as if welcoming home a long lost son. She seized Smythe's wrists and tried to tug him away, but he held firm.

'We can't just *leave* him!' He held Ree's gaze with his own, eyes bright with fear.

Ree could feel time getting away from her. At any moment, the Lich would remember them and finish what it started. She tugged at his wrists again, but he gripped her wrists with his own.

'He doesn't want this,' he said.

They had already lost Larry once and it had hurt as much as losing anyone could. He was more than the town's weird pet; he was her friend.

For a heartbeat, Ree could see it. She could see them seizing Larry and running for all they were worth. She had resisted the Lich's magic once, and Smythe had much more fine control of his will now. They could take Larry, and hide, and come up with a better plan.

But as her gaze swung toward the undead reunion, the Lich raised its marble eyes to meet her. Gently, like a father shepherding a child, it moved Larry aside. Then it happened all at once: the Lich pointed at them and cast a spell in an echoing whisper; Ree snatched at Smythe's arm to drag him behind her; Smythe shrugged away to plant himself between Ree and the Lich.

Bright light surrounded them and the world quaked. Everything seemed to peel, like the paint was being stripped from the world. And all Ree could see was Smythe, clutching her hands and mouthing 'I'm sorry.'

It was a curse like none she'd ever heard of. A maelstrom of wind and magic whipped around them, throwing them up, leeching the warmth from her skin, sucking the breath from her lungs. All the while, Smythe gripped her hands with icy fingers, eyes round and full.

Ree wondered if Morrin would greet them when this was over.

But then the spinning slowed; the wind died down. Colour and detail seeped back into the world, like ink spreading through water.

When they hit the ground, they hit it hard. Cold stone and a force that jarred through their limbs. The maelstrom was gone; they were in the corridor again.

'Where'd they go?' Smythe scrambled to his feet, straightening his glasses. 'Larry?'

Ree stared at the walls, a frown pulling at her mouth as a headache dawned. 'Does this look wrong to you?'

'Ree?'

'There's no moss on the walls …' Her gaze dropped. 'No cracks in the floor. I don't understand.' There was pressure building up in her chest, anxiety preceding understanding. Her stomach cramped as her meagre breakfast threatened a reappearance.

Smythe touched a wall, muttering to himself.

'What?'

He glanced at her, his eyebrows raised. 'It's fourth era stonework — see the tessellation of the bricks — but it's … unaged. Marvellous stuff; I rather wish I were a better artist, so that I could take a good image of it.' His hands twitched toward his threadbare satchel.

Ree got unsteadily to her feet. Was this some sort of illusion, or had the Lich transported them away?

'Jolly impressive spell, sending us away like that.'

Ree started to run down the corridor. 'Magic doesn't work like that.'

'Hold up!'

Necromancy, healing — even therianthropy. It was all about bodies, about life and death. This should not — could not — be real. She came to a door, not dry and knotted like she was used to, but smooth and polished. Heart in her throat, she pushed it open.

Two women in robes of lavish lace — one red, one black — were talking. As the door opened, they turned and caught Ree's eyes. Ree gasped and yanked the door shut, crashing into Smythe as she turned to run.

Smythe seized her shoulders, steadying her. 'Is something the matter?'

'They're speaking old Antherian,' Ree said. It was the language of necromancy, the oldest language ever spoken.

'They're necromancers, then?'

The door creaked open; Ree dragged Smythe aside, tucking him into an empty alcove. 'Nobody *speaks* Old Antherian,' she whispered. 'It's a dead language. *The* dead language.'

Smythe straightened his glasses. 'I'm not certain I understand. Are you suggesting —?'

'Halt!' The word was cried in Old Antherian, in an accent Ree had never heard spoken. The lace-robed women slid to a halt in front of them, their fingers crooked in spellcasting shapes. 'What business have you in the city of the King?'

Smythe's eyes were bright. Ree could practically see the questions queuing up at his tongue. But for Ree, there was another sickening twist in her gut and a cold prickle along her skin.

This was not something running away could solve.

The town hall of Tombtown is of particular significance, as it uses the largest tomb in the central mausoleum that makes up the heart of the town. Believed to be the final resting place of a king of old, it also depicts necromantic iconography on its columns and on the sarcophagus itself.

Though the name and origin of this king is unknown, he is a town favourite and much beloved. The name 'The Old King' is often invoked as a familiar, watchful figure, much like a local deity.

~from *A History of Tombtown* by Emberlon the Disloyal

CHAPTER TWENTY-FOUR

THE OLD KING

The lace-robed women stood before them, fingers crooked and ready to cast. The air stirred and shifted as if in a breeze. Echoes of their power hummed through Ree's body.

Ree frowned. She did not recognise either of these women, but the one in traditional black was clearly a practitioner, with her hollow cheeks and dull, ash-coloured hair. The one in red did not look like a practitioner, but neither did she have the rosy-cheeked, bright-eyed vitality of a healer. Her skin was the colour of baked clay, her eyes liquid amber. Blue paint lined her forehead down her nose, flicked across her eyes, and spotted her cheeks, giving her a faintly beaked, bird-like appearance.

Whoever they were — and wherever Ree and Smythe had ended up — their magic was making Ree's teeth ache. She held her hands out, palm up, to show she was unarmed and not casting, and Smythe followed her lead.

The women did not relax their stances, but the pressure of their magic eased. The red woman's gaze flicked from Smythe to Ree. 'You have not answered us. What is your business here?' The Old Antherian sounded so different in her mouth than it did when denizens cast spells in it; rich and rolling, more natural.

Ree scrambled for an answer in their tongue. She had read and written in the language since she was a child, but had never needed to be conversational in it. 'We were cursed here by a powerful Lich, the most ancient in our sprawling necropolis.' She glanced at the woman in black, trusting that whoever these people were, they were sympathetic to practitioners. 'We don't actually know where we are.'

The women exchanged a look, frowning. They looked like they might be about to say something when Smythe leapt in, 'Pardon me, but if you don't mind me asking — how do you keep the brick work in such excellent condition? We've dabbled in restoration techniques at the university, but little can be done to rectify the erosion. Also, where did you get your robes? They're very authentic, most convincing! I didn't —'

'No.' The woman in red held up a hand to silence Smythe. It looked like he was going to babble on, regardless, so Ree jabbed her elbow into his ribs. He yelped and rubbed his side, but finally stopped talking.

'They're funny, don't you think?' The woman in black tilted her head to one side. 'Their clothes. Their accents.'

'Who are you?' asked the red-robed woman.

'Chandrian Smythe, Third Rank historian at the Grand University and foremost burial scholar in the southern reaches.' He stuck out his hand to shake, which the women ignored with wrinkled noses. 'I'm quite delighted to meet you,' he continued, undeterred. 'And my companion here — she's really quite an extraordinary scholar and — well, I'm sure she can tell you —'

'Ree,' said Ree. When the women waited for something more, Ree offered, 'From Tombtown.' More waiting. 'A necromancer settlement.'

The women exchanged a look, and Ree resisted the urge to squirm. She didn't like talking about herself at the best of times, but even less when she had so little information. Giving these women knowledge was giving them power over her — and she had precious little power over them.

The woman in black tittered. 'Definitely funny. Can I play with them, do you think? I've been ever so good.' There was something about this woman's dark eyes; they seemed to smoulder in her face. Ree instantly brought her mental guards up, praying to Morrin that Smythe would do the same.

The red-robed woman gave her companion a hard look. 'The King will decide.'

The woman in black sighed. 'I'll tell him, shall I? Oh Frederick!' She summoned a spectre in a whisper of magic. Ree felt a jolt at the sight of a creature that had only moments before been crushing her, but this was not the Lich's spectre.

The woman in black smiled and stroked the spectre's cheek. 'Dear Frederick. Do Mummy a favour, would you?' She murmured something in the spectre's ear, and then it glided away in a gust of wind.

'I am Wylandriah,' said the woman in red.

Ree tried to draw breath and couldn't. Her eyes fixed on the woman in red. The paint ... the strange colour of her eyes ... she was the mirror image of the jewelled woman in the tableau.

'Wylandriah ... Witch-feather?' Ree managed to squeak the word.

Wylandriah's head turned, studying her with a hawk's precision. 'Indeed.'

She heard Smythe suck in a breath.

'And *I'm* Lizeria,' said the woman in black. She narrowed her smudgy eyes at them. 'I'm most pleased to meet you. And don't attempt any magic: it would be a shame to kill you, when we've not yet had a chance to get to know each other, don't you think?' Her power gathered, and before Ree could so much as cry out, she flung a long rope of intestine at them, which wriggled like a snake and cinched around their wrists. She started walking, yanking them after her. Ree tried to resist, but every pull of the gory rope burned like hot coals. Wylandriah brought up the rear, eyes gleaming under the stripe of blue paint.

'Aah!' Smythe stumbled after Lizeria, tears streaming from his eyes. 'Is this quite necessary? We've hardly been introduced!'

'Be silent.' Wylandriah shoved Ree into Smythe, and Smythe muttered an apology. He turned wide eyes on Ree, but Ree had more worries than unknown necromancers. More even than the sudden appearance of her hero.

Something about this place was *wrong*. These corridors were shockingly familiar, as if someone had put a new layer of paint over the crypt. Lizeria led them along a path that was seemingly step for step the way back to town from the Lich's wing. And behind them, Wylandriah, in her red robes and blue face paint, radiated an unknown magic that made Ree shiver.

Not entirely unknown. She had felt the brief kiss of it once. A magic like water that had rushed over her like the incoming tide.

The conflicting emotions around that threatened to crush her. She walked beside Wylandriah Witch-feather, the last therianthrope and figure from magical legend. But how could that be? How could *any* of this be?

They passed many rooms, nearly all occupied. The sound of shifting paper and murmuring voices was constant, if incongruous with the crypt that Ree knew. Every time she heard the sounds of life — voices, shuffling, footsteps — Ree's skin would crawl. She felt hemmed in by people, claustrophobic, suffocated. Worse, sometimes someone would come to a door and greet the women as they passed, their eyes following Ree and Smythe. She felt their gazes sliding down her spine like cold water.

But worse than the people was the sense of displacement. Everything here was wrong — brighter, cleaner, more alive. Ree lived in a world of dirt and shadow. She had memorised every crumbling stair, she'd explored every cold tomb. But this place made a mockery of that. It took her memories and painted over them, so that every glance was startling, every blink caused a headache.

She *knew* these paths and these rooms. This was home, but it also wasn't. How had the Lich trapped them in this paradoxical place? She had never heard of magic like this.

Smythe, by contrast, seemed energised by every change. 'Extraordinary,' he said, gazing up at the tiled ceiling or trailing his eyes along a bright-threaded tapestry on the wall. His excitement seemed even greater than his fear, or than his yelps of pain when Lizeria tightened the leash. 'Did you ever imagine that it looked like this?' She could see his hands twitching toward his satchel for his journal and pen, but the gory binds were too tight.

'Did you ever imagine that it looked like this?' With a growing dread, Ree was coming to terms with what kind of spell the Lich must have cast. And when Wylandriah and Lizeria led them up to the doors of the Old King's tomb, where she had attended every town meeting since she was a child, she knew that it was true.

'The King awaits you,' said Lizeria. 'Pray to the Undying One for his mercy.' Her smile grew wider. '*My* prayer is quite different.'

Lizeria and Wylandriah pushed open the doors of what in Ree's time was the grand tomb, and was now an opulent throne room. Many of the treasures that Ree had carefully catalogued and pushed to one side were now proudly displayed on stands and shelves, or lined the stairs up to the raised marble throne. The rest, she assumed, remained with their original owners, as they had before she had found them.

Ree, almost without thinking, started toward the throne, but Wylandriah held out a hand. 'Wait.' Her eyes were not on Ree, but on the throne.

Wylandriah. Ree tore her eyes away from the mage and followed her gaze.

A figure stepped around the throne. Velvet robes of midnight blue swirled about his legs, and a plain crown of thorny and blackened wood rested atop his brow. His dark skin was ashen with necromancy, but he didn't look as tired as most practitioners — his beard was perfectly curled and oiled, the hollowness of his eyes hidden by artful paints.

He lowered himself onto the throne and with a curt gesture, beckoned them over.

Wylandriah gave Ree a jab, and together, she and Smythe stumbled after Lizeria up the stairs. Smythe's eyes were full of stars, the treasure and candlelight reflecting constellations. Ree's fingers itched to raise her hood, to hide. She ached to disappear.

When they approached the last few steps, Smythe stopped and knelt. Ree looked around uncertainly until Lizeria yanked the rope. Ree hit her knees hard beside Smythe, biting back a cry.

'So these are the intruders,' the King mused. His voice was deep and calm. It reminded Ree of Emberlon, but there was an edge to it that Emberlon never had. 'Chandrian Smythe of the Grand University. Ree of Tombtown. Curious that I have never heard of any such place.'

Though Ree had already suspected as much, his words fell like stones in her stomach. Smythe, however, looked up with bright eyes.

'There is a strange energy about you,' said the King. He looked at them expectantly.

Ree answered him, his gaze seeming to pull the words from her. 'We were sent here by a powerful Lich.'

'From where?'

From when would be a better question, but Ree kept this to herself.

'From Tombtown,' said Smythe, stumbling over the Old Antherian words. 'In the Fourth year of the Seventh Era.'

Ree bit back a retort, wishing there was some way to take back those words. You couldn't just give a necromancer knowledge like that. You couldn't predict what they would do with it.

The King levelled his gaze at Smythe. Ree wondered that he could stand it — the King's gaze had a palpable power, as if he were mind-snaring without trying — but Smythe lifted his chin, excitement written into the tight line of his shoulders.

'It is a crime to lie to the King.' The King stood up, and as he stood a wave of power rolled over them, cold and tight. A necromancer beyond doubt. 'But if you tell the truth, there is much here to be learned. Wylandriah.'

Much to be learned here. Ree could feel the world crumbling around her. Much to be learned here — because the walls were newly bricked, the tomb was a throne room, and the Old King was alive and well.

Because this was a world where therianthropy was more than a fairytale.

'Sire.' She heard Wylandriah stand behind her.

'Bring Evanert before me. Persuade him if necessary.'

Ree tried to draw breath into thin lungs. This was Fourth Era Tombtown — before it was a crypt, before any of the dead she knew had ever died, let alone been buried.

It made sense of so much she had wondered in her time exploring the crypt. Why there were areas that looked more designed for the living than the dead. Stray accounts in old histories and journals that suggested a city here, a civilisation. When the founders of Tombtown had settled the crypt, it had been in the belief that they would *make* it into a civilisation. They'd had no notion that there were long lost precursors who'd done just the same.

'At your command, sire,' said Wylandriah.

Power gathered behind Ree, of an alien feel. It felt wild and fluid, with an electric crackle. As Ree turned, she watched blue light spiral around Wylandriah. She held a rune-marked hawkskin to the sky. Then Wylandriah was shrinking, *sucked* into the skin as if she were made of water and light, and then the light cleared and a hawk with blue-tipped feathers trod the air. Ree's heart seized to look at it, the magic that was everything she had ever hoped for, *real* and *here.* Then hawk-Wylandriah gave a high-pitched cry and flew out of the throne room with a few strokes of her long-feathered wings.

'You are surprised,' said the King.

Ree tried to swallow, but her mouth was suddenly dry. 'It was unexpected.' She didn't want to tell a man with so much power over her that Wylandriah held the key to her heart's desire.

The King's gaze bored into her. Ree kept her eyes lowered.

They waited in silence. Ree's thoughts raced. Smythe fidgeted beside her, clearly struggling to contain himself from asking questions.

He knew how to behave around royalty. Perhaps he had met Kings before, in the world above. Did historians garner those honours? Or was there more to Smythe than she knew? He was barely able to keep quiet under threat of death among necromancers, but before this King, he was a model of restraint. It seemed ingrained in him.

Then Wylandriah was back, landing behind them in a swirl of light and robes. She folded the hawkskin into her pocket. 'He comes, sire.' She knelt and bowed her head.

Footsteps echoed in the hall outside, and then two men entered the throne room. The first was an older necromancer in sanguine robes, his skin already stretched and pale from what could be a century of the Craft. He moved with an icy presence, chin raised and eyes flinty.

There was no give in him, not even for the king of this place. And behind him was a reedy man in simple clothes — a servant, perhaps, though there was a faint mark of the Craft in the hollowness of his cheeks and the grey tinge to his skin.

'For what do you disturb my studies, Your Majesty?' The necromancer wrinkled his nose as he considered them. His voice was nasally and thin, unpleasantly close to a whine.

Smythe gripped her arm, staring at the newcomers. 'Is that — does he —'

'Smythe?'

Smythe's nostrils flared as he breathed out. 'Does that man look familiar to you?'

Ree looked at the necromancer in his velvet robes. 'A necromancer from several centuries ago. How would I know him?'

'Not him. Ree — look at the man behind him.'

Ree frowned. The man behind him was reedy and thin, with sallow skin and a slightly wild look about his eyes. Why she would be any more likely to recognise him than the necromancer, she had no idea.

But now that she was looking, there was something about his face. Something she couldn't quite place. He was familiar, but ... off. Were his features sharper? Was his hair different? And as Smythe's grip on her arm tightened, she could visualise it. The same features, but on clammy, flaking skin. The same hair, but a patchy fuzz. The eyes yellow and rolling, the mouth hanging open.

'No.' She shook her head, then shook it again. She felt a strange lurch in her stomach, like someone had tugged out the rug beneath her feet.

'He's looking rather better, don't you think?' Smythe said weakly.

'Larry,' said Ree. Her eyes moved to the necromancer. 'Does that make him ...?'

'If this is true, I must study them!' said the necromancer. He looked right at Ree, and Ree could see it too, see the years and the magic withering him away. 'Lizeria. Wylandriah. Take them to my laboratory.' He stroked his chin. His eyes glinted. 'There is more than one way to determine the veracity of their claims.'

In spite of the mystery surrounding it and the danger it presents to denizens, the Lich has historically been seen as a protector or guardian. In 6E48, it ended a battle between rival necromancers that threatened to destroy the central mausoleum, killing both. In 6E70, it drove back invading witch hunters sent by the Semnian church. In 6E81, it ousted an enormous group of adventurers that had taken several practitioners prisoner.

The council continues to urge vigilance and caution, urging denizens to learn its routes and avoid it at all costs.

None of its 'rescues' were without denizen casualties.

~from *A History of Tombtown* by Emberlon the Disloyal

CHAPTER TWENTY-FIVE

WHAT DOES IT MATTER?

Evanert.

The most powerful necromancer of her time and probably of his. Ree stood with iron bones and icy skin, staring down the man that would become the Lich and wondering what she could do to stop him.

Smythe shifted beside her. She wondered if he, too, was testing the strength of Lizeria's terrible gut-bonds. He was a necromancer — new, but powerful. Maybe he would be able to disable Lizeria's spell.

She gritted her teeth. It was an idea too ridiculous for hope.

Evanert swept from the room, the man who would become Larry striding after him. Ree and Smythe were left alone with Lizeria, Wylandriah, and the King whose crypt Ree had grown up in.

'Sire?' Wylandriah's tone was questioning.

The King lifted a hand. 'As Evanert desires. This is too unique an opportunity to be missed.'

As one, the women rose. 'As you will,' said Wylandriah.

Lizeria yanked at the gut bonds; Ree gasped as the bonds burned against her skin. 'With pleasure, sire,' she said with a grin.

And then they were being dragged back out the doors, stumbling after Lizeria, too stung by her magic to resist. Wylandriah, eyes dark and gleaming under the blue paint, kept guard behind them.

Smythe leaned over to Ree. 'So, what's your plan?'

Ree hissed as Lizeria gave her rope a sharp tug. She glanced at Smythe, looking at her with expectant eyes, and felt the tight pinch of panic. 'There's no plan. I'm as trapped as you are.'

Lizeria almost skipped ahead of them, each sudden lunge forward sending an accompanying burst of pain.

'You mean you can't break the bonds?'

Ree wanted so badly to snap at him then. To say: '*Do you really think I would still be wearing them if I could?*' But she couldn't let her temper get the better of her — not in a situation as dire and strange as this. She narrowed her eyes and looked away, hoping that, intelligent as he was meant to be, he would read that as *'I'm not the necromancer here.'*

She wished Usther had gone with them. Usther might not be at the Lich's level of magic, but she was as sly and manipulative as any necromancer, and if she'd ever been foolish enough to let them get caught like this, she would surely be able to get them out again. When Veritas had set a rope like this around Ree's neck, Usther had not hesitated to break the spell.

She wished she had learned the Craft, or taught herself therianthropy, or learned anything useful in her life beyond the ability to run away. You couldn't run when you were already trapped.

Lizeria and Wylandriah led them back to the Lich's wing, across his library, to the room where, in the present day, he had built his flesh monster. Cold stone floors, sharp grey walls, and three stone slabs — beds? — regimented against the wall. One was stained brown with old blood.

Lizeria muttered a word and the intestines unwound from their wrists to coil neatly around her waist like a belt. 'This will be your little playroom.' She clapped her hands together and tilted her head to one side. 'Stone and blood and shades of dead past. Won't that be *delightful?* And then Evanert will join you for the *real* fun.'

'Miss Lizeria,' said Smythe. He spread trembling hands. 'I can't help but feel there's been some terrible mistake —'

'Ooh, I hope so. I love a good mistake. Such *tragedy* — most entertaining!'

'I'm sure there's something to be done,' Smythe ploughed on. 'And there must be a lot we could learn — we could teach each other, you see. If we just sat down and talked.'

Lizeria grinned. 'Oh, I'm sure Evanert will learn plenty from you. He's a talented practitioner — a bit dreary and pompous, but *inventive.*' Her eyes gleamed.

Smythe continued to petition the necromancer, but Ree's eyes were on Wylandriah, in her bright robes and her face paint. The therianthrope stood stiffly at the door, gazing not at them but at a wall, as if thinking hard.

Ree approached her and her head snapped up.

'Not a step further,' Wylandriah warned. Her mouth formed into a snarl; her canines seemed a little longer than was normal, her eyes a little wilder.

Ree raised her hands, palm-out. 'I'm not going to attack you.'

Wylandriah's eyes flashed behind the blue paint. 'It wouldn't go well for you if you did. But no ... you have little of a predator about you. What do you want?'

Ree's heart thumped in her chest. She wanted her to teach her. She wanted to sit down and hear everything about Wylandriah's life, from her own lips. She wanted to feel the strangely charged and liquid feel of her magic again. She wanted Wylandriah to touch her head and tell her that she'd been *right,* that she'd been right all along, and that she would be great one day.

But though Wylandriah was her hero, she was not her friend or her ally. She was the enemy, serving a King who sought to use them for his own gain. Though it caused her almost physical pain to turn that tumble of words away, there were more pressing concerns.

She licked her lips, choosing her words carefully. 'You need to get your King to speak to us before Evanert does.'

Wylandriah crossed her arms. Her nostrils flared. 'Oh? And what makes you think you can dictate to the King of the world below?'

Ree considered, knowing this might be her only chance to convince the therianthrope. From the moment they'd arrived, it was clear that they were powerless here. They had no allies and no real knowledge to help them. They didn't even understand the magic that had sent them here. But there was one key thing; something she'd been clinging to ever since these two women had brought them into what would become the Old King's Tomb. 'Because in my time, hundreds of years from now, your King is dead, but Evanert is still alive.'

Wylandriah's eyes narrowed, and Ree held her breath. It was her one hope, the tiniest scrap of a chance. Necromancers were competitive, were *always* competitive, even when voluntarily living together, like in Tombtown, or this strange civilisation in the past. There had been something in the King's voice when he'd summoned Evanert that made Ree think their relationship was less than certain — and Evanert had not been at all deferential, in contrast to the obsequiousness of Lizeria and Wylandriah.

Meanwhile, Smythe petitioned Lizeria. 'We have to — see here, we're separated by hundreds of years of history! Surely as a practitioner, as — as a scholar! Surely you can see the value in an exchange of ideas?'

Lizeria clapped. 'Wylandriah, look at this one — he just keeps talking! An inexhaustible source of words! And he goes a funny colour when you talk about him. Do you think Evanert will let me have him when he's done? I've always wanted a chatty minion.'

Wylandriah shrugged her sharp shoulders. Ree waited with bated breath for her to reply, to say *something,* but she only weighed Ree with her eyes for a moment before she turned and strode from the room.

Lizeria winked at a distinctly green-looking Smythe and flounced after her. The door swung shut behind her and there was the heavy thud of a bolt falling into place, followed by a pulse of icy air.

Smythe slumped, sinking onto one of the stone beds. 'I might be mistaken, but it appears she's cursed that door.' He took off his glasses and rubbed his eyes.

Ree's eyes flickered from him, to the door, and back. He looked very thin, his bony shoulders raised in tension, his cheeks hollow and shadowed. She closed her eyes, battling with herself. There was so much going on, so much she needed to *think* about. But when she opened her eyes, Smythe looked just as shrunken and fragile.

She breathed out through her nose. 'We'll find a way back.' She perched on the edge of the stone bed beside him. Though there was a human-sized gap between them, it still felt uncomfortably close.

Smythe shrugged, eyes on the floor. She thought for a moment he would say something — he was always saying something — but the silence stretched, thinner and thinner, echoing in the airless stone chamber until Ree felt compelled to speak.

'It's amazing magic,' she said. She gestured around the stone room. 'To be here, hundreds of years ago. I've never heard of anything like it, outside of stories.' She couldn't bring herself to mention Wylandriah. She watched him; he barely inclined his head, lips pressed thin. 'It must be especially exciting for you — to *see* history, to live in it. Isn't that a historian's dream?'

He stared at the floor. Ree started to feel his silence pressing down on her — like a physical presence, like a curse. How long had it been since she'd been alone without the sound of Smythe's amiable chatter? It had annoyed her, but in its absence was a vacuum, sucking the air from her lungs. She was trying to think of something else to say — anything to feed the hungry silence — when Smythe pulled his arms tight across his chest.

'What does it matter?'

Ree's eyebrows pinched. 'What?'

Smythe breathed out through his nose. 'I've been thinking about it and — what does it matter, to see all of this, to *learn* all of this, when no-one will ever know? I can't write a paper and send it to the Grand University. I can't show it to the Dean, I can't shove it under the noses of the historical society. I can't —' He cut himself off, jaw tightening. 'If we're trapped here, whatever we do, whatever we learn — it means nothing.'

Ree stared at him, torn between unease and sympathy. She couldn't remember him ever looking like this or speaking this way. She couldn't remember him bitter, but it fit him like a familiar cloak. She wondered how many times he had thought about the Dean of the Grand University, or the historical society, or any of those other scholars in the world above.

'I'm Chandrian Smythe, Third Rank historian and foremost burial scholar in the southern kingdoms.' He'd said it so many times, and all she'd seen was pride and a sort of belligerent formality. Now she wondered about those practiced words — the way he held up his achievements like a shield the moment he met someone.

'You can't think that way,' she said at length. 'Smythe — you can do things for yourself.'

He met her eyes. 'Would you? Would — would you bother with therianthropy, if your father didn't want to force you into necromancy? Would you bother, if he would never see it?'

Ree tried to respond, then found she didn't know what to say.

Smythe shook his head. 'It only matters if someone else knows about it.'

'I'll know about it.' She touched his hand with two fingertips, catching his eyes with hers. 'Smythe. I'm here, and *I'll* know.'

Smythe broke into a tired smile. 'Yes, but you're much cleverer than I am.' His hand curled almost imperceptibly around hers, and Ree froze. 'Much harder to impress.'

Were they closer than they'd been? She didn't see how they could be, but Smythe was taking up her entire field of vision and she couldn't look away. She almost asked, *'You want to impress me?'* but she couldn't seem to untangle her tongue.

The door opened. Ree sprang to her feet, Smythe a beat behind her. Wylandriah stepped to one side, eyes unreadable beneath the strip of blue paint. Ree gathered her scattered thoughts and drew air into her lungs. 'Wylandriah. Did you —'

'His Dark Majesty, King of the Undercity and the lands above.' Wylandriah's words were crisp, neatly cutting Ree's voice away.

I love my King. I owe him much. But I do not trust him.

~from the journal of Wylandriah Witch-feather

CHAPTER TWENTY-SIX

THE BLACK OATH

Smythe was already dragging Ree to her knees when the King swept in, velvet robes shushing around his legs, blackwood crown gleaming on his brow. 'My beastmage tells me you have proof Evanert is working against me.'

Ree and Smythe exchanged startled looks. Ree licked her lips. 'I don't know about that. But in our time, your Evanert is an immortal Lich, and ... well, we've seen your grave.'

The King studied her with flinty eyes. Again, Ree was aware of the almost suffocating presence of his power. She pulled her mental guards in tightly around herself and was careful not to meet his eyes for longer than a few seconds.

'You seemed familiar with my throne room. You know, then, that I intend to be entombed there, when my time comes.' He threaded his fingers together.

Ree hesitated, then inclined her head.

'Evanert outlives me,' he mused, gazing above their heads and into the distance. He stopped and turned to Smythe. 'And what of my legacy?'

'Uh — sorry, sire?' Smythe fidgeted with his glasses.

'My legacy. The kingdom I left behind. What of it?' His face went still. 'What do they say of me?'

Ree pressed her lips together and clasped trembling hands behind her back. There was something tight in his voice that sounded all too ready to snap. She didn't want to learn what that looked like in a King, or a necromancer of such obvious power.

Smythe wrung his hands. 'Well, I've actually been working on that. You see, it's very — it requires — well. Based on the age of the tomb and the relics left behind, I think I'll be able to narrow it down —'

'You don't know. You truly don't know.' The King's face went slack with shock. For a flicker of a moment, Ree could see past his regal demeanour to the man beneath — a man, like so many practitioners, who only wanted his name to be spoken in hushed tones long after his death.

'That's what power is all about,' her father had told her once. His tone had been wistful. *'Your deeds live on, the terrible awe of your creations holding sway in the nightmares of children for generations. We all of us want to be immortal, Ree — but the practitioners with* true *power, they can achieve it. A name that inspires fear, a legacy of darkness.'* He'd given her a look with shining eyes. *'I want that for you, too.'*

The King's shoulders went back. His guards snapped back in; he looked again powerful, inscrutable. 'So my greatest servant will live on while my name is forgotten. That, I cannot abide.' His chin rose.

'Have the Lich — Evanert. Have Evanert send us back.' Ree managed to keep her voice level, although she couldn't help the way her breath hitched. 'We'll go back, we'll make them remember your name — I swear it.' She watched the King for a reaction. His lip curled, but he said nothing. She pressed on, 'My companion is a renowned historian in the world above. And I was born here. My father is on the council of the largest —' and likely only '— necromancer community in the world. We can make sure your legacy lives on, if only you send us back.'

The King stroked his beard. A cool light grew in his eyes.

They needed to convince him. She elbowed Smythe.

'Ow! Uh — well, most certainly! I was immediately intrigued by your tomb and would be honoured to be the one to ah, as it were, to *resurrect* your memory, if you'll forgive the turn of phrase —'

'No.'

'I beg pardon, sire.' Smythe quickly bowed his head. It was such a knee-jerk reaction of servility that once again, Ree wondered what his experience of royalty was.

The King clasped his hands. 'It is not your words, spoken centuries too late, that will resurrect my memory. No — only deeds will do that.' He levelled his gaze at Ree. 'You say you were born in my tomb. You must know of the magic I speak of.'

Ree felt a chill finger run down her spine. Mutely, she shook her head, barely trusting herself to breathe.

Cobra-quick, the King grabbed her arm and yanked her close. He glared down at her, the icy blue of his eyes shifting like paint in water. 'You know.'

Ree gasped as his grip started to burn cold. 'I'm not a practitioner,' she said through gritted teeth. She kept her eyes low before he could try to mind snare her. 'I don't know anything about your Craft.'

'Release her!' The air shivered as Smythe gathered power. Ree barely had time to think *'fool!'* before Wylandriah leapt at him in a flash of light and claws, bowling him over in the form of a big cat.

'You're a liar,' said the King. He shoved her aside, sending her crashing into the wall. His shadow twitched and jumped as his lip curled in disgust. 'And you will do as I say or you will serve me from the afterlife. I am the *King.*'

Not mine, Ree thought. *Never mine.* But her arm was pitted and wrinkled a horrible blue-black and the pain of it was still shuddering through her body, and Smythe was talking very quickly while Wylandriah pressed enormous paws down on his shoulders, and *everything about this was wrong.* They shouldn't be here, at this time, with these people. They should be heading back to town with Larry in tow, with Usther waiting to scold them for being both careless and boring.

'Tell me.' The King's voice was dangerously soft. Behind her, Smythe cried out as Wylandriah dug curved claws into his flesh.

'There are rituals,' said Ree. Her eyes flicked from Smythe to the King. 'Human sacrifice. To bring back what was.'

'And you've seen the ritual I left, then. The tablet carved into my tomb.'

She'd been there when Emberlon found it. They'd been cataloguing the Old King's Tomb, trying to get everything archived and budgeted for when the trader caravans passed by. There were so many things Tombtown needed to trade for — so many things necromancers had no ability to grow or craft, and could not be salvaged from the dead. She remembered the gleam of polished gold as Emberlon prised the tablet from the wall and held it up to the light.

'We can never tell anyone about this, Ree. Do you understand?' He'd wrapped it in rags and slid it into his pack. 'Some things are better left unknown.'

Ree stared at the King's feet. 'I've seen it.'

'I am a generous King.' He lifted his hand; Wylandriah sprang from Smythe to back up against the wall as a woman once more. The King started to pace, staring down at Ree. 'If you swear the Black Oath that my ritual will be done, I will order my most powerful servant to send you back.'

'I'm sorry, but — what is this ritual?' Smythe got to his feet, wincing as he did. Red bloomed at his shoulders, speckling his linen shirt. Ree's lungs seized, but they must have been shallow wounds as his arms hung naturally at his sides.

Ree remembered the words carved carefully in Old Antherian. A city for a city... She said nothing, and the King did not answer Smythe, only staring hard at Ree.

She didn't want to make this oath. Didn't want anything to do with the King or the Lich or any of these terrible rituals, but it seemed she had little choice, when ranged against her was an entire civilisation of necromancers and not a friend to be found among them.

The Black Oath was a ritual so binding that none in Tombtown would agree to it. The council had banned its use. To break a Black Oath was to die — die, and your soul be bound as a greywraith, that most desirable and most rare of minions. It was said to be a pain more excruciating than any found in life, and after seeing the souls Smythe had summoned back into their bodies, she believed it.

Ree had avoided necromancy her whole life because she didn't want to end up like the Lich or any of the older practitioners — didn't want to become little better than a minion herself. As far as she knew, there was no way to break a Black Oath, but then she wasn't very knowledgeable in the Craft. If she went to Emberlon, or her father, or even Usther — there had to be some way of breaking the Oath.

'I'll swear it,' she said, and saying the words felt like a great loss. 'I'll swear it if you send us back.'

The King nodded his head toward Smythe. 'And him as well.'

Smythe's eyes flicked between Ree and the King, round with worry. 'Swear what? What's the ritual? Ree?'

Ree met his eyes. He must feel even more helpless than she did right now. Did it make him angry or afraid? Did it make him want to curl up in a ball, as she did? 'Smythe, I can't — I can't explain right now. But it means we'll get to go home.' She couldn't bear to ask him outright if he trusted her — not when she knew that trust would be so badly misplaced. But he must have, because he inclined his head to her. 'I'll swear.'

The King drew a goblet from within the folds of his robes — an artefact of scratched and blackened steel. He gestured with one hand toward Ree — she held out her arm. After a moment's hesitation, Smythe scrambled up beside her to do the same.

The King's eyes glowed with a banked blue fire. An icy breeze stirred in the room, tugging at robes and biting into skin. 'This is a promise older than any Craft. To keep it is salvation; to break it is damnation. Do you comprehend?'

'I do,' said Ree. His magic bit down; the first binding. She shuddered at the feel of it sinking into her flesh.

Smythe looked at Ree. 'I do.'

'Then this you must swear, on blood and death and soul: that you will undertake the Great Resurrection and thereby restore my legacy. Do you swear?'

'I swear.'

'I swear.'

Another bite, this time deeper. It was a magic more invasive than any she had come across, coarse under her skin. Instinctively, she began to panic.

The King lashed out twice with sharp fingernails, gouging a red line in Ree's and Smythe's bare arms. He caught the blood in the goblet, which immediately lit with black fire as the temperature in the room dropped to frosty levels. His eyes met Ree's. 'And so let it be done.'

The fire extinguished, and with it went the King's magic. The ritual was done, the spell wrought. Ree staggered slightly at the sudden release of pressure. Her arm burned; when she looked at the cut, still seeping blood, it was no longer a stripe of red but a harsh script. *And so let it be done,* it read.

Unless directly endangering the town, few necromantic practices are prohibited or even discouraged by the council. A notable exception is the Black Oath.

Necromancy is not inherently cruel, but the Oath is another matter entirely.

~from *A History of Tombtown* by Emberlon the Disloyal

CHAPTER TWENTY-SEVEN

CHIMARVIDIUM

Wylandriah shunted them back out into the Lich's library. 'Evanert is ready for you. He will attempt to duplicate the spell that sent you here.'

Ree didn't like the sound of 'attempt', but she kept her thoughts to herself. She would find some way to deal with the Lich if she had to.

'Well, I'm jolly ready to go back,' said Smythe. 'Not that you haven't been good hosts — although really you've been quite terrible, now that I think about it.' He paused. 'You know, with the making us swear some kind of blood oath, and locking us in prison, and binding us with guts and all that.'

Wylandriah gave him a sharp look. 'Be glad that Lizeria was not left to have her way with you.'

'I suppose apart from all that it wasn't an entirely unpleasant trip.'

Bookshelves just as towering and full as they were in Ree's time lined the walls, but they were more vibrant now — time had not yet faded and worn them. Evanert, who would become the Lich, whirled to face them as they entered, his robes billowing around his legs. Sitting in a leather chair with a book in his lap, the man who would become Larry looked up, thoroughly unfazed.

'Yes, yes into the cage with them. The keys are on that table, beastmage.' Evanert urged them toward a large, wide-meshed iron cage that stood to one side. Ree took it at first to be rusty, then realised it was merely covered in red-brown stains.

How reassuring.

'There's surely no need for a cage,' said Smythe. 'We're quite — we won't try any — I mean to say, that we have no *reason* not to cooperate. We want to go home after all.'

'Do not presume to interfere with my process,' said Evanert in his repulsive whine. His magic cracked like a whip at his words; Ree hissed at the spike of it. 'I am attempting magic that has been nothing more than speculation for centuries and I will not be interrupted by layman antics.'

Wylandriah waited beside the open cage, her hard expression making it clear that they would receive no help from this quarter.

Smythe moved first. 'Well, I suppose as long as we can watch, you know, it's not such an imposition.'

Ree bit her lip. It went against her nature to willingly submit to a cage. How could she have any control in a situation, any power for herself, if she could not flee? But Smythe was already hanging on the bars and speculating excitedly, 'Does it require summoning to work? Because the Fell Queen theorised that spirits exist outside of time —'

Ree followed him in; Wylandriah turned the key in the lock with a click and secreted the key away in the folds of her red robes.

'— Or maybe not *out of time* but certainly parallel to theorised timelines. And, of course, time travel in folklore usually involves meeting with a spirit or spirit-like figure — '

Evanert spun. 'Will he never cease his inane chatter? Lazerin, deal with it, would you?'

The man on the chair didn't lower his book but did raise his eyebrows. 'Must I?'

Judging by Smythe's sharp intake of breath, he had also noticed that Larry had been well-named. But Ree had no attention to spare for this particular subject. Wylandriah studied her, a question held in her eyes.

She was the closest thing Ree had right now to an ally. She didn't trust Evanert an inch: he seemed to hold no respect for the King and might attempt to undermine his plans. 'Why —' the word came out hoarse. She cleared her throat. 'Why are you looking at me like that?'

Wylandriah turned her head again in that sharp, bird-like way. 'It is no stranger than how you look at me,' she said softly. 'You say you come from a time that has forgotten our King's name. Yet you spoke mine almost with reverence.'

'Therianthropy is a dead magic in my time.'

Her eyebrows lowered minutely. 'But not to you?'

It seemed impossible that she was having this conversation right now. Emotion threatened to choke her as she agreed, 'But not to me.' She couldn't keep the bitterness from her voice as she added, 'I only wish it was something I could learn from a book.'

Wylandriah's eyes widened. Her face grew open, vulnerable with something that was either hope or pain. 'Maybe you could. If —' she hesitated. Her voice was thick with an emotion Ree couldn't name. 'If I were to write such a book, I would title it in the glyphs of my mastered shapes, given to me by the masters who taught me.' She rolled up her sleeve, baring an arm covered in rune-like animal tattoos. They looked almost familiar.

If Wylandiah wrote a book in the past as a result of this conversation, would Ree return to a future with that book? She had no notion of the workings of time, had never had cause to consider it.

But if she did, and Ree did ... then Ree could learn directly from Wylandriah. She could become the first therianthrope of a new era. It could really, truly happen.

'I hope you do,' said Ree.

'I hope so, too.'

'Beastmage! Are you quite finished with the subjects?'

Wylandriah faced Evanert in a swirl of robes.

'I am finished.' Her hands clenched at her sides.

Ree scrambled to pull herself back into the moment. They might need to escape. The cages were locked, and Wylandriah held the key.

She leaned forward, sweeping the therianthrope with her eyes. She could see the slight bulge in the shapeshifter's pocket where the key resided. If she was careful ...

'Do you require anything more of me?' Wylandriah's sudden words made Ree pull back, fearful of eyes moving to meet her. But Evanert didn't turn from the desk where he was sorting through vials of bubbling liquids.

Ree fit her hands through the wide struts of the cage. Her jaw ached from clenching as she slid her fingers into the beastmage's pocket.

'Need anything from you?' Evanert sneered the words and Ree froze, all too aware of her vulnerable position. 'Why should I need anything from *you*?'

'The King has advised me to assist you in any way you might need.' Wylandriah's words were stiffly formal. Her tone was cold, with none of the emotion or the flicker of vulnerability she had shown to Ree only a moment before.

Ree's fingertip hooked on a metal ring; she eased her hand free, praying to Morrin the Undying and any god who might be listening that the keys would not jingle. As soon as her hand was back in the cage, she clenched the keys tight and thrust them into the folds of her robes.

She glanced at Smythe, who was staring at her with undisguised shock. At her glare, he promptly closed his mouth.

Evanert gave a nasal bark of a laugh. 'Ha! I have no need of you and could have no need of you. If it's all the same to our *gracious* ruler, I'd rather you went and hunted mice or whatever it is he keeps you for.'

Wylandriah nodded curtly. 'As you wish.' She headed for the exit.

'Leave the keys.'

Ree's lungs seized. Her eyes fixed on Wylandriah as the therianthrope put her hand into her pocket, paused, and turned to look right at Ree. For one frozen moment, they studied each other, brown eyes to amber. *Please, Morrin. By all the undying souls, please ...*

Wylandriah's eyes narrowed. 'I shall.' She inclined her head ever so slightly and strode from the room with red robes swirling about her feet.

It took Ree a moment to get her lungs working again. Smythe flashed her a wide-eyed look and immediately ran to the front of the cage and started chatting to Evanert again. 'Did you know that I'm an apprentice summoner myself? I learned in a phenomenally short amount of time —'

The necromancer groaned.

'I'm a rather excellent scholar, you know — but I'm sure I have nothing on your level of experience. Would you, perhaps, consider explaining your working so that I might take notes? I have an ingenius system for notation —'

'Lazerin, *if you would.*'

The long-faced man in the chair set aside his books and strode languidly over to them. Smythe bumped into Ree as he backed hastily up.

Aside from physical features, there was nothing of Larry in this man. His movements were lazy with confidence, his expression a sneer rather than a vacant gawp.

Ree reminded herself that he *wasn't* Larry, not really. Larry was a body animated by magic. This same body stood before them, but now it was animated by a soul. And judging by the glitter in his dark eyes, not a kind one.

'I want to make this very clear,' he said. His voice was clipped, his accent upper class. 'If you interrupt my dear Evanert one more time, I will ensure that your death is as painful as possible.' He drew a small, curved knife from his belt. 'I am uniquely gifted in this regard.'

Ree suppressed a chill shudder at his words. She studied this cruel, confident man. She didn't like his carefully coiffed hair or his cold smile. Larry might be a centuries-old minion, but there was more to like in his inept, toothy grin than in anything this sharp-eyed man had to offer.

Smythe beside her, opened his mouth to speak, but Ree seized his arm and he fell silent. She forced herself to meet Lazerin's smug eyes. 'You say that like death is inevitable, and only the method is in question.'

Lazerin's smile widened. 'Death *is* inevitable,' he assured her. There was a honey to his voice that made Ree's hair stand on end. 'Sooner for some than others. Evanert! They don't realise, fools that they are. Shall we tell them together?'

Evanert turned on his heel, robes whirling, and stood close to Lazerin, his arm snaking around the other man's narrow waist. Ree barely had time to register this — and the tender smile Lazerin gave in return — before Evanert was speaking. 'We owe you, really. Though the King has chosen to hide it from me, it is clear why he is so eager that you return to your time. Our efforts to overthrow and outlast our *wise king* and his pathetic kingdom surely succeed, and he intends to return you to aid him in undoing that. Well.' He rested his chin on Lazerin's shoulder.

Lazerin bared his teeth. 'We'll tell him the magic was not possible, and that the attempt claimed your lives. He can hardly argue with us, since if such magic is possible, only one as powerful as Evanert could even attempt it. So you see,' and now Lazerin's eyes glinted with a strange red light 'death *is* inevitable, and quite soon.'

Ree kept a tight grip on the keys in her pocket, so hard that she felt the cuts bite into her palm. Warm blood trickled from her fist.

'Please — there's no need to make decisions in haste!' Smythe hurried to the fore of the cage. 'We're no threat to you — I'm a historian, and my companion a simple scholar. We're just eager to get home.'

'The blood on your arm speaks differently,' said Evanert.

'Been making promises you can't keep?' said Lazerin. 'It's almost merciful to kill you now.'

'No! I beg you to see sense. We're in an impossible position and —' Smythe argued on, but though his pleas never ceased, they fell on deaf ears. Evanert returned to his desk and Lazerin to his book.

Ree, for her part, crouched at the back of the cage, gripping the keys so tightly that her fingers cramped. She was glad Smythe was begging and bargaining — it would make their captors think they made no attempt to escape — but she needed time and space to think. They would likely only get one chance at this.

If Evanert intended to ritually sacrifice them — and really, there was no reason why he would pass up the opportunity — then it would take him hours to properly prepare. Sometime in that period, Ree was certain there would be an opportunity to escape. What they would do then ... well. They would have to find some way of making it back to their time. In a room surrounded by the world's most powerful necromancer's collected knowledge, she hoped they would find a way.

She gritted her teeth. Of course, if they realised the keys were missing, any hope of escape would be quickly crushed.

Lulled by Smythe's near constant fear-babble and the familiar sound of parchment sliding against parchment, Ree struggled to keep sharp. She had been scared and running for so long that her body sagged and her eyelids were heavy and drooping. Every time her head started to nod, she gripped the keys so tightly that they cut into her hand, the pain clearing her foggy brain.

At length, and with no signal to their prisoners beyond a quirked eyebrow from Lazerin, Evanert and Lazerin left the library, ascending the staircase and closing the door behind them.

Smythe's pleas died; he spun around, wide-eyed, as Ree sprang to her feet. 'You have a plan?'

Not much of one, Ree thought, but she flashed him a grim smile. 'Always.'

He frowned at her through his glasses, uncertain.

Ree worked at the lock, fumbling with the key ring as she tried key after key with shaking hands. The keys slipped in her blood-slicked grip and it was difficult to manoeuvre them into the lock from the other side. It required her full attention, and yet she couldn't stop her eyes from flickering back to the door their captors had vanished through.

'A little to the left, Ree — no, that was too left! Try again, but gently, gently ...'

Ree gritted her teeth and tried to shut Smythe out just as the key clicked into place. Heart-pounding, she turned it in the lock. The door swung open with a rusty creak.

'We did it! Oh, jolly well done!' Smythe pat her on the shoulder. Ree winced and started on an acid reply, but Smythe looked so grey and relieved that the words died in her mouth.

'There's a lot left to do,' she said instead.

'Well, you know, no reason not to be pleased about what we've already achieved,' said Smythe. 'We're one whole stage freer than we were ten minutes ago, and if they, uh.'

He gulped. 'If they come back and kill us, at least it won't be in a cage.'

Ree thought that was hollow comfort, but Smythe gave her a look of such determination that she could almost agree with him. Quietly, she took his hand in hers. His hands were colder now, from stone and damp and necromancy, but his touch gave her no less of a shock and her eyes leapt to his. There was a look in his face of growing clarity, as if clouds parted in his eyes. His other hand started to lift; Ree turned and pulled him toward the Lich's desk. She dropped his hand, lungs suddenly thin, and smoothed the pages of the open book on the reading stand on his desk. 'What do you make of this?' she asked, her voice much steadier than her pulse.

Smythe hovered at her shoulder. 'A ritual.' He peered closer, and now she could feel his warmth at her back. 'A sacrifice ritual, I think, as you theorised. Sorry, could I just —? If you don't mind ...' He eased past her and ran his finger along the lines of Old Antherian script, mouthing the words.

Ree mentally shook herself. They needed to find a book on temporal magic, something they might be able to use to get out of there. Now that she knew such magic was *possible*, there was surely a book or scroll somewhere discussing its practice or at least its theory. How else had the Lich discovered it?

She started toward the bookshelves, then stopped herself, thinking hard. If she were a rival to the king and two people claiming to be from the future appeared before him, she would learn everything she could about the magic that had brought them there. She went back to the desk and examined the books stacked to the side while Smythe continued to read and mutter to himself. She tried not to let him distract her; there was quite enough to deal with without her getting breathless over an upworlder.

She ran her fingertips across the spines. The books nearest the bottom of the pile were in a language she could not read: whether it was from another country or a version of Old Antherian too ancient for her understanding, she couldn't tell. The others ... *Kragvverak's Rituals, Chimarvidium, Immortal Soul* ... Her fingers hovered over *Chimarvidium*, since *Chimar* referered to the original practitioners of the Craft and *arvid* referred to an increment of time. She carefully extracted the book and studied the introduction and contents, trying not to let her tense grip damage the aged leather cover.

The link between soul and the aether planes ... in which case scrying can transcend temporal bounds ... displacement provides tethers for realignment ...

'Smythe?'

'Mm?' Smythe looked up from the book he'd been scanning.

She stepped aside and gestured at the book. 'Tell me what I'm reading here.' Her voice shook; she touched a hand to her throat, hope making her grotesquely vulnerable.

Smythe took over the book, his eyes flying across page after page as he flicked through it with impressive speed. 'Unless I am very much mistaken — and I *am* the youngest ever Third Rank historian at the Grand University — this is a book theorising rituals and spells to manipulate objects in time.'

'Objects,' Ree repeated. She needed to hear him say it; she could barely bring herself to ask.

He looked up, eyes bright behind the glare of his spectacles. 'Objects with souls. Objects like us,' he said. His gaze dropped to the book. 'Although, unless I am much mistaken, we're going to need help.'

An important aspect of scrying, for example, is the focus, or anchor. A lock of hair, a favoured brooch, an item of sentimental value, even a blood relative or close friend. This forms the connection required to scry and is rarely questioned further.

Many aspects of magic use this connection. Curses often require it. Healers can utilise it. Why has nobody asked what else could be done with this connection?

~from *Envisioning the Future of Magic* by Elden Mannelyn

CHAPTER TWENTY-EIGHT

THE SCRYWELL

'Ree?'

Ree tore her eyes from the stairwell to look at Smythe. He'd almost completed the set-up for the ritual: a ceramic bowl of water was in the middle of a pentagram of dried blood with various plants, herbs, and organs at the points, all procured from the Lich's collection.

Ree's gaze started to drift back to the stairwell.

'Ree, I know you're frightened but you must focus. I can't really — I don't have the connection to her that you do. And we're quite unlikely to manage this without her.'

Ree licked sandpaper lips. Though Smythe had worked quickly, it was hard to ignore that Evanert and Lazerin might return at any moment. It pecked at her, a painful, persistent reminder that they were not safe, and would never be safe until they made it back to their own time. But there was something else nagging at her, something she found it even harder to face. 'Smythe — I've never practiced the Craft. I don't know if I can do this.' *I don't know if I want to,* she thought. How proud her father would be if she returned home baptised by the touch of death? And when she was *so close* to finally achieving her dream of practicing therianthropy.

Smythe hesitated a moment, then touched her shoulder. 'You won't,' he said. 'It'll be my magic, passing through my body. It's only that, as Tymmeric Demonseed theorised in his treatise —' he stopped when he saw the look on Ree's face and dropped his hand, looking sheepish. 'Ah, well — I'll need a focus,' he said. 'And the best link we have here is you.' He rubbed his chin. 'Are you ready?'

Ree took a deep breath and nodded. They needed to get home, and quickly. This wasn't something she could run away from.

'All right. Would it be all right if I took your hand?' His grip was firm, professional. He was sure of himself, Ree realised. When it came to necromancy, no matter how obscure, he was confident.

Maybe he had been destined for the crypt. He certainly made a better necromancer than he did a historian.

Smythe took Ree to stand in the centre of the pentagram, before the ceramic bowl. 'It'll require blood,' he said.

Ree tensed and nodded. She wasn't sure why it made her so nervous; her mother had sacrificed Ree's blood for Morrin's favour for years when she was a child, but the difference between her mother's priestcraft and necromancy seemed suddenly vast.

Smythe lifted her hand, smoothing out her palm. 'Scars,' he murmured, eyes lifting to hers in surprise. 'Have you sacrificed before?'

Ree looked down and said nothing.

In Smythe's other hand was an ornate, sharp-edged knife. He put it gently against Ree's hand, giving her the chance to protest. Ree closed her eyes and turned her head. Then came the quick bite, the line of fire, and then Smythe was squeezing her hand in his and letting the blood drip into the ceramic bowl, the blood spreading and clouding in the water.

'You must focus,' he said, and he sounded excited now. He kept Ree's hand in his, but his eyes were on the bowl, and his other hand stretched toward it. He started to mutter an incantation; the air flexed with power. A mix of emotions flitted through Ree: relief that the magic was so clearly Smythe's, discomfort at being involved in what was surely experimental magic.

She needed to focus. She stared at the water, trying her best to call out with her mind — a strange sensation, the antithesis to the mind wards her father had taught her. The water clouded darker and darker, though she did not feed it any more blood. And then it rippled, and a familiar angular face appeared, surrounded by the sanguine clouds.

'I am really very *curious as to why you are scrying me right now. I'm in the middle of some* extremely *delicate experiments and do not appreciate whatever hedge-magic tricks you're playing. How did you even get through my wards?'* Her sneer barely hid the wild twitch of her eyes; she was surprised, and in Ree's experience, Usther didn't handle surprises well.

'Usther.' Ree's voice was tight. 'I need you to listen very carefully. We're desperately in need of your help.'

Usther rolled her eyes. *'Of course you are.'*

Ree haltingly explained what had happened: the Lich sending them back in time, the Old King, and meeting the Lich's past incarnation. Smythe interjected with technical explanations and theories whenever Usther got quizzical for specifics, but she mostly listened without comment.

'*So you're saying that I'm scrying to you across time.*'

Smythe nodded eagerly. 'Yes! As I said, it supports the theory that —'

Usther waved a hand, glaring severely. '*I'm scrying to you across time. Hundreds of years separate us.*'

Ree inclined her head, choosing to keep to herself that it was Smythe who was scrying, not Usther. She could see the older girl working herself up into a power frenzy — which was exactly what they needed right now.

Smythe leaned over the Scrywell. 'I've done our part of the ritual to bring us back — or at least, I certainly *hope* it will work, obviously nothing of this sort has ever been done before. Although Fthgorrgh the Putrid did attempt to anchor our plane to the spirit plane in what was arguably a very similar —'

'*Smythe. Shut up, would you? I'm thinking. What's the rest of the ritual?*'

'Well, Fthgorrgh —'

'*Not Fthgorrgh, buffoon! The ritual to bring you back!*'

Ree slid her hand from Smythe's. 'I'll keep watch.'

'Yes, of course! Excellent idea. Usther, the ritual, as written in Chimarvidium, requires first a circle of Qaranthian, modified as I will specify —'

Ree stepped carefully from the pentagram and spell diagram, knowing better than to scuff any of the lines. Smythe continued to chatter at Usther, whose usual ire seemed largely consumed in enthusiasm. In that moment, they were attempting a magic that had never been done before: Ree could hardly blame them for allowing themselves some excitement at that. But for Ree, there was only the growing pressure in her chest and a kind of sickly crackle in her head as she waited for Evanert to sweep into the room and kill them where they stood.

In their cages, they had been safe. They were sacrifices to be dealt with in the manner and time of Evanert's choosing. But now they were a real threat; not only free and unhindered but using Evanert's own resources to engineer their return to their timeline. While Evanert would surely prefer to ritually sacrifice them and use their bodies in his own craft, he would be foolish not to kill them quickly now.

A pulse of energy blasted Ree from her feet and rattled books from shelves. She hit the ground hard, the acrid smell of herbs and craft burning her nostrils. 'Smythe?' She rolled to face him.

'It worked!' Smythe picked himself off the floor, hair windswept and glasses askew. He laughed and punched the air. 'Yes! Now try the incantation, exactly as I read it to you —'

'I don't need you to handhold me through the process!' Usther's voice came through the Scrywell, louder now. Light spilled from it, but heavy, like a liquid; it flowed across the floor to lap at the edges of the spell circle.

Boom! Another pulse: this time Ree was braced for it and barely staggered. Books fell from the shelves; a mirror fell from the desk and shattered on the floor. Though the echoes faded, Ree's chest still vibrated with the force of it. She ran to the edge of the circle. 'You're going to bring them running back to us!'

Smythe didn't turn his head. 'And now the blood sacrifice —'

'*You don't need to tell me twice, fool, I heard you the first time!*'

'SMYTHE!' Ree hovered at the edge of the circle, wary of wading into a ritual this far in. She'd never seen anything like this; the air was so thick with magic that it felt like she was wading through mud.

Smythe glanced at her, then looked back and stared, his expression contorting in horror. 'Evanert!'

Ree whirled just as Evanert raised his arm and gave an echoing command; two greywraiths with withered hands and tattered cloaks swirled into being and bore down on her.

An arm crossed her waist; Smythe dragged her back into the spell circle. 'We have to jump now!'

The greywraiths smashed against the circle, stopped by an invisible barrier. They screeched in voices that sucked the warmth from the air and threw themselves at the circle again and again.

Smythe was still dragging her on, while the thick light lapped at her legs.

'*Quickly!*' A spectral Usther hovered above the opening, arms outstretched and an expression of concentration paining her face.

There was a crackle and clap as if of electricity as the greywraiths smashed through. Ree's gaze locked with the man who would become the Lich, and she felt her body seizing up as frozen mist curled through her mind.

'*TO ME,*' His voice was in her mind, made thick and rich by a hundred death echoes. '*YOU MUST COME TO ME.*'

Then Smythe was pulling her down, and Usther was screaming in Old Antherian, and she was plunging through light and then darkness.

For a while, there was only dancing shadows and the continual sickening lurch of nausea. She could feel Smythe's arm around her waist, but she couldn't speak and if he spoke, she couldn't hear.

Then, in a shock of sensation and colour, she hit the floor. Smythe bounced away from her. Arched ceilings, stone brick walls, hard floor. Usther stood over her, arms crossed, the shadows draining from her pale eyes along with her magic.

Ree's heart thumped against her ribs. She raised a shaking hand to touch her throat. Evanert had mind-snared her. She had felt his presence spreading in her mind, but now there was no trace of him.

Smythe groaned and sat up, curls tumbling. He rubbed the back of his head. 'We did it?'

Usther sniffed and smoothed her dark hair. '*I* did it. And I can't wait to see the look on the faces of those council fools when they learn I successfully pulled you from a different timeline.'

'*We* pulled us from a different timeline.' Smythe scowled and straightened his glasses. 'It would hardly have worked without the work on my end! Ree and I *were* the anchor!'

Usther rolled her eyes. 'Yes, yes, you were *very* instrumental in my success. Well done you for taking part.'

They were in Usther's house, with its garish tapestries depicting famous beheadings, and the black lace she had draped over every chair and chest of drawers. A converted lesser tomb, like Ree's home. Books were regimented against the back of her desk; the shelves were lined with vials of gory components.

Ree flopped back onto the hard floor. 'We're really back.' Evanert still loomed in her mind's eye, but he was gone, and the present Lich was hardly her most urgent problem now. Her arm throbbed as she thought of the oath.

'Yes, yes, it's wonderful that you're back. I feel positively *whelmed* with emotion.' She sniffed and offered Ree a hand, which Ree gratefully took. 'Which reminds me,' she continued, 'How exactly did you end up hundreds of years in the past?'

Smythe scrambled to his feet. 'Well, I'm not entirely certain yet,' he began eagerly. 'But I believe in theory that what the Lich attempted was a — I can't seem to remember the phrase, it was —'

'It's a long story.' Ree pulled up her sleeve, baring the still bleeding mark of the Black Oath. 'And it doesn't end well.'

To move away from the past for a moment, the growing families of Tombtown pose an interesting question. Necromancy has always been taboo, its practitioners hounded and mistreated. Now, with children being born and raised by necromancers in a society that reveres the Craft rather than reviling it, what might that mean for the future of necromancy? What will the next generation of Tombtown-raised necromancers look like, without the terrible weight of being outcast from society?

~from *A History of Tombtown* by Emberlon the Disloyal

CHAPTER TWENTY-NINE
WASTED OPPORTUNITIES

'We have to tell Igneus.' Usther was sprawled across her armchair, fanning herself with a translation scroll. She glared at Ree, as if expecting her to argue.

She was right to, because Ree was not so foolish as to ever let her father know one tenth of what had happened to her. 'We really don't,' she said evenly, as if she didn't want to punch Usther just for suggesting it. 'Pa is not any more likely to know how to break a Black Oath than you are.'

'*Ree.*' Usther rolled her eyes. 'I can't *believe* you're making me say this, but he *is* a much more experienced practitioner than I and may well have come across something in his studies.'

'He hasn't.'

'Well, how do you *know?*'

Ree's nostrils flared. 'Because the Oath is unbreakable!' Her voice echoed around the small stone house. Ree's face heated; she avoided Usther's gaze.

Usther clapped lazily. 'Excellent. Truly *beautiful* melodrama. Will you be writing *and* acting in the play?'

Ree clenched her jaw. *'Usther.'*

'Or perhaps you'd prefer to commit it to verse, like some maudlin bard?'

Smythe cleared his throat; both girls turned to glare at him. 'Terribly sorry to interrupt,' he said, 'but did I hear you say that this is an *unbreakable* oath? Not you know, just a very difficult oath, or perhaps a heavily inconvenient oath?'

Ree rubbed her eyes and nodded.

'Mm. Mm-hmm.' Smythe nodded, then nodded again. 'Yes. That's not very good, is it?'

'How have you not come across it?' Usther curled her lip. 'You consume books at a disgusting pace. It's like watching a pig at a trough, and frankly I had quite enough of that as a child.'

Smythe looked sheepish. 'I didn't see how it would be relevant.'

That hung in the air a moment. Ree closed her eyes, imagining a world where they had never angered the Lich and the Black Oath was still nothing more than an interesting piece of trivia. 'I'm not saying the situation is hopeless,' she said. 'Obviously, I'm going to try to find a way to break this. But my father is not at his most rational when it comes to me. We need to come at this with clear heads.'

'Well, can't we just sort of, fulfill the oath?' Smythe looked uncertainly between Ree and Usther. 'The ritual, or whatever it was?'

Usther rearranged her robes so that they draped more impressively. 'I assume whatever it is, it's not easily done, or else darling Ree wouldn't be so very *hysterical* over it.' She gave Ree a hooded look. 'What *is* this ritual that worries you so?'

Ree remembered long black nails gleaming in the dark. She rubbed her arm, feeling the ridges of the ugly scar of the Black Oath. *And so let it be done.*

She hadn't been able to study the tablet in the Old King's tomb, and she'd been outraged that Emberlon intended to hide an artefact. *'That tablet belongs to all of us,'* she'd said. She'd stood with shoulders tensed and fists clenched, surrounded by the glittering treasure of the long dead king. *'Why should you get to decide what people should and shouldn't read?'*

Emberlon had given her a long look and had let his gaze rest heavily on her for the full of it. But though Emberlon's stare could cause even council members to shift uncomfortably, Ree's anger and righteousness had held her head unbowed and her back straight.

Emberlon had set down his pack and carefully withdrawn the linen-wrapped tablet. *'This tablet belonged to a king, and kings are rarely good and never kind. It's a sacrifice ritual — to sacrifice one city to raise another.'* His blue eyes were steady. *'What do* you *think we should do with it?'*

Ree had shifted uncomfortably. She'd always known that there was dark magic out there — magic that could turn necromancers against each other, or bring the fury of the upworlders down on their heads — but that kind of magic was rare and hard to find. It wasn't banned in Tombtown — little magic was officially restricted, although much was unofficially policed — but she'd heard her father say that everyone just sort of *hoped* that nobody would come across it.

It had dawned on her how strange it was that, in a necromancer community of this size with the accumulated knowledge of centuries of practitioners, nobody had ever come across any of this dark magic.

Emberlon had waited for her answer.

Ree had licked suddenly dry lips. *'Even if someone tried to use it,'* she'd said. *'Even if they attempted it — resurrection magic doesn't exist. It's impossible.'*

'Hard to say anything is impossible,' Emberlon had said. *'Especially when you've lived here a few years. But let's say it doesn't work: what if someone made the attempt?'*

In the end, Ree had taken the tablet from him and hidden it back inside his pack.

Now, Ree said to Usther, 'It's the kind of ritual that could hurt a lot of people.'

Usther shrugged. 'Nobody cares about upworlders.'

Smythe cleared his throat. 'Um, actually—'

Usther glared at him and he blustered a bit, probably trying to wind up for what he thought was a cutting comeback.

'It probably poses more of a danger to the town,' said Ree. Usther's eyebrows shot up; Smythe's half-formed arguments died on his lips. And she knew that it did. *Sacrifice a city for a city,* Emberlon had said. Well, there was a city already here, living on the literal bones of the one that came before it. It could hardly be more convenient if people lined up to be sacrificed.

For a moment, nobody said anything. Usther pursed her lips and Smythe looked small and lost.

'And you agreed to it?'

Ree eyed Usther uncertainly. 'It was that or die.'

'*You* agreed to it. You, Reanima, precious first child of Tombtown. "Too good for the Craft" Ree agreed to sacrifice the town to save her life.'

Waves of bitterness rolled over Ree. She hated it when Usther got like this. 'I'm not planning on sacrificing anyone. And you weren't there — you don't know what we've gone through.'

Usther cocked her head to one side. 'I know you've tied yourself in knots and somehow dragged the whole *town* into it merely because you're too arrogant to use the advantages the gods gave you. Do you think *any* of this would have happened to you if you'd learned the Craft like *everyone* wanted you to? Do you think any of this would have happened to *me?*

Smythe's expression barely flickered at the raised voices; he seemed deep in thought. But Ree was quite willing to handle this argument herself. Why did everyone think she *had* to be a practitioner just because she'd been born here? Why did everyone act like her future had been decided at birth? She had aspirations of her own, she had the chance to do magic beyond the dreams of any of the denizens, and she was the only person in all the town who could survive the crypt — or even find her way around! — without magic. 'Smythe practices the Craft —'

'Smythe has been practicing the Craft for *five minutes,*' Usther practically spat the words. 'You could have been practicing from the cradle. You've had every privilege and every advantage and you've just *shit* all over it! You never had to struggle in the upworld, you were never —' She stopped, panting, eyes wide. Ree stared back, just as tense.

Ree had always known that it must have been hard for Usther in the upworld. She'd heard plenty of stories about growing up there from her father, and it sounded a terrible place, overwhelmed by sun and heat, with no dead but what you dug up yourself, and harsh judgement if you did.

Ree didn't take it for granted that she lived in the crypt. She loved the tombs, the town, the dead. She could hardly have dreamed a place with more to explore, or more to learn. But she could see how Usther might feel that she was squandering the chances she'd been given. If Usther had been raised in Ree's hometown, with Ree's parents, she'd never have had to run away at fourteen, which was how old Usther had been when she arrived five years ago.

Ree's stomach twisted sickly in a feeling Ree had not often felt for Usther: guilt. Usther, for her part, looked ashamed, her cheeks ashen and her eyes lowered. 'I think that's maybe not a topic for right now,' said Ree, twisting her hands in the skirts of her robe.

Usther took a shuddering breath. 'Quite.' She smoothed back a loose hair, looking sheepish. 'If we could just pretend I never said any of that?'

Ree nodded. 'So have you seen the Lich about? Or anything strange in the crypts since we left?'

'I've not seen or heard anything.' She sniffed. 'Bizarre to think it got all worked up over *Larry* of all things.'

Ree thought of Lazerin smiling tenderly at Evanert; of Evanert resting his chin on Lazerin's shoulder and wrapping his arms easily around his waist. 'I don't think it's about who Larry is now,' said Ree. 'I think it's about who he used to be.' And he'd done something to him. Tried to bring him back, tried to make him immortal. That's why Larry was the way he was. But you couldn't really bring back the dead. Only their bodies.

And whatever Larry had become, he held no love for his master.

She looked down at her arm where the words '*and so let it be done*' were carved in garish letters. She groaned and sank to the floor. 'What in all the worlds are we supposed to do?'

'I have an idea about that.'

Ree's gaze shot to Smythe. His thoughtful look was gone, replaced with the determination and zeal he got when discovering new books.

'Well, let's hear it then, apprentice, since you know so much about it.'

He looked at Ree, rather than Usther. 'I'll need to see the ritual, first. Am I right in thinking that you know where it is?'

Ree bit her lip. 'I know how to *find out* where it is.'

After some negotiation, they made their way to Emberlon's, but the senior archivist wasn't there, nor was he in the archives. Ree's chest pinched with early panic as they asked around town, but nobody was really sure where he'd gone.

'He must be doing a collection,' Ree said. She wrung her skirts in her hands. 'Or maybe an undead got into one of the libraries again — the masterless dead can be worse than Larry when left unsupervised.'

Usther eyed her. 'You're worried about the libraries, aren't you? You're marked for the most unpleasant death ever imagined by a practitioner, and you're actually worried that someone's messed up your alphabetising.'

Ree avoided her eyes. 'I can be worried about both.' The thought of the mark on her arm filled her with cold terror, but she was nonetheless queasy at the thought of some mindless cadaver chewing on priceless books. She'd been apprentice archivist for too long not to care if someone destroyed the collections under her charge.

They were standing in the market square, where Mazerin the Bold was currently trying to sell the fresh raven spleens he'd harvested on his last trip to the surface. There were a few denizens milling around and a few minions shuffling past, but it was otherwise quiet. It seemed wrong to Ree that they had all come so close to destruction at the hands of the Lich and yet they could act so normal. *They don't know anything about that,* she reminded herself. And it would be best if she never told them.

'Might I make a *small* suggestion?' Smythe looked at Ree very earnestly. 'It seems — forgive me, I know you don't want this, but — it seems that, without the ritual in-hand, we are going to need some expertise. If — if you won't go to your father and we can't speak to Emberlon, who should we go to for help?'

Ree looked down at her hands. The Oath burned in her mind as if it had been carved on her skull and not her arm. She had no idea how long they had before they were considered to have broken the Oath. She didn't want to think about what would happen when it did.

And she had dragged Smythe into this. He had only made the Oath because she had assured him that he should. He'd had no idea what he was getting into. And if she got him killed because she was afraid to face her father, she would have twice failed him.

But still. Her *father.*

She wrung her skirts in her hands. 'Well. There is *one* person I think we could go to.'

Smythe lit up. 'Jolly good! Is it someone I know? Nice chap?'

Ree headed up the crumbling stone stairs to the higher levels of town and motioned for Smythe to follow. 'I don't think anyone would call her that, no.'

I think I speak for everyone when I say that I don't like healers.

~from the journal of Wylandriah Witch-feather

CHAPTER THIRTY

NOBODY'S BUSINESS

Ree fidgeted on the doorstep, feet tapping and fingers twitching. She did her best not to meet Usther's too-close glare. She could feel the older girl's angry breath on her face.

'Andomerys.'

Ree sighed and cocked her head to one side noncommittally.

'You're asking *Andomerys* to help you break the Black Oath.'

Smythe beamed. 'I rather like Andomerys, you know. Great sense of humour.'

Ree resisted the urge to ask for an explanation. She was fairly certain Andomerys didn't even know how to smile.

Usther turned her glare on Smythe, giving Ree some much needed breathing space. 'Oh, well if you *like* her, then that's all right, isn't it? It doesn't matter that she's not *qualified* or that she's a bad-tempered *moose* as long as *you*, Smythe, find her funny.'

Ree said, 'Usther.'

Usther threw her hands in the air. 'Why don't we ask a cobbler for sailing advice? Or a bloody *donkey* to teach embroidery? I hear asses are rather good tempered, after all, so I can't think of a single person more *qualified* —'

The door swung open. Usther stopped mid-sentence as Andomerys scrutinised them. Her hair was tied in a curly knot atop her head and her warm brown cheeks were flushed with annoyance. As always, she was dressed in clothes so bright they made Ree's eyes water, in a long robe of red and orange with a blue chiffon sash across one shoulder, giving the impression that she was clothed in fire.

Her best and most fearsome accessory was, as usual, her scowl. She pierced Ree through with a sharp gaze; Smythe flinched as it moved to him, and Usther raised her chin and straightened her shoulders, as she always did when she was nervous.

Ree opened her mouth to speak. Andomerys sighed and closed the door in her face.

For a moment, nobody said anything. Then Smythe stepped up to the door, knocking smartly. 'Andomerys? It's me, your friend Smythe? I was a houseguest a couple weeks ago, do you remember?'

Usther rubbed her face. 'This is pointless.'

'Chan-DREE-an Smyyythe.'

Ree tugged her sleeves down, avoiding Usther's accusatory glare. 'Andomerys is one of the oldest and most powerful magic-users in town. And I *trust* her.'

Usther snorted. 'How old can she possibly be?'

'Well, she moved in a year after I was born, and she doesn't look any older now than she did then. So I really have *no idea* how old she is.' She held Usther's eyes this time.

Powerful healers were said to stop ageing, and Andomerys was the most powerful healer she'd ever heard of.

Usther's mouth twisted to one side. 'It would almost make it worth it to be a healer,' she muttered. 'But nobody properly *fears* healers.'

Ree barely restrained a smile. 'You do.'

'Andomerys?' Smythe pressed his ear to the door. 'You can hear me, can't you? Are you all right in there? Do you need —'

Andomerys yanked the door open and Smythe yelped and tumbled into her house. She looked at Ree and jerked her head to one side. 'Come in, then.'

They walked in and huddled in her small, brightly furnished sitting room. There was one chair, which Andomerys took. Once again, Ree was stricken by how differently Andomerys lived. She was part of the community, but she made no attempt to look like it. She wore her bright colours and lived in a shack, not a tomb, and out the back she kept a garden full of all the herbs and poisons needed in healer's work.

Andomerys levelled her gaze at them. 'Well?'

Smythe found one of her cushions, fluffed it up and offered it to Ree. 'Perhaps a cup of tea first? We have been through *quite* the ordeal and a spot of tea would not go amiss —'

'No.' Andomery's voice brooked no argument, but Smythe still looked like he was about to say something more. 'No tea. No chairs. No sitting. You aren't staying, so just tell me what this is all about and then get out of my house.'

It was impossible to forget that Andomerys had moved to Tombtown because she hated people. Apart from the town meetings, necromancers kept to themselves, and the dead didn't need healing. Frustration oozed from her, from the set of her shoulders to the set of her mouth.

Ree had already imposed on her patience too often in the last several weeks, but Ree liked Andomerys. She was smart and quick to cut through nonsense, and wise as a grey-hair (which Andomerys might in fact be).

'Maybe just a *small* pot of tea?' Smythe's eyes were wide with pleading.

Andomerys growled and waved her hand at her sparse kitchen. She kept it as clinical as her healer's room. 'Make it yourself.'

'Jolly good of you!' Smythe bustled into the kitchen and started clattering through the cupboards.

Ree set aside the cushion and clasped her hands behind her back. 'We … have been through some very strange things recently and could really use your advice.'

'*My* advice.' Andomerys sounded sceptical.

A clatter from the kitchen. Ree glanced up to see Smythe trying to balance several pots which had fallen out of the upper cupboard. 'Where do you keep the kettle?'

Usther made a disgusted noise.

Andomerys didn't look away from Ree. 'A hook beside the mantel.'

Ree cleared her throat. 'What do you know about the Black Oath?'

Andomerys's eyebrows raised. 'Don't. Tell me.'

Ree showed her the red scar on her arms. *And so let it be done.*

Andomerys sat up in her chair. 'Start from the beginning.'

And where was that? Did it start the day before with the Lich, or did it start weeks ago when she found Smythe in the embalming room?

There was a sense of inevitability about everything that had happened, somehow. It was all so connected, so tightly knotted, that it was hard for her to pull at one particular thread and say 'this wouldn't have happened if ...'

She didn't really *believe* in fate. Her father had always taught her that life was what you made it. Even her mother, who had a direct line to a higher power, said choices were what mattered.

But to Ree, looking at all that had happened and all that she feared was yet to come, could not go back to that moment in the embalming room and imagine that she would have chosen differently.

She decided to start with them raiding the Lich's library, and Andomerys visibly tensed when they described the flesh tentacle monster it had been creating. She left little out, telling of their journey into the past, their forced oath to the Old King, and their run-in with the man who would become the Lich. Occasionally, Smythe would chime in with a detail: *'The brickwork was pre-moneric'* or *'The King's throne was clearly designed to be converted into a sarcophagus — which is quite morbid, but also very forward thinking!'* And Usther interrupted when they described the ritual to return them to their own time: *'It was a magic unlike any that's been attempted before and surely would have failed without my expertise.'*

When they were done, Ree felt empty. A tension had been building inside her ever since the Lich had transported them into the past, and now that they had returned and told the story, she felt it leave her like steam escaping from a hot sponge.

Smythe, after poking around at the fire a bit and applauding when the kettle sang, brought them all cups of bitter black tea.

Andomerys took a long draft of the scalding hot liquid and thrust the cup back at Smythe. 'I'm calling a town meeting.'

Usther spluttered over her tea. 'What?'

'No!' Ree's spine straightened at the thought. 'It's nobody's business what's happened to us. We just need a little advice, we can't get the whole town involved —'

'The town is already involved, they just don't know it yet. This is too big for you young fools —'

'*Excuse me?*'

'— to deal with on your own. Now get my coat and follow me.'

Smythe found Andomerys' coat — a harlequin patchwork of different patterns and fabrics — and handed it over. 'I'd quite like to go to another town meeting,' he said.

Usther raised her eyebrow. 'Really? The last one almost ended in you being used as a blood sacrifice.'

Smythe nodded, eyes bright. 'Yes, it was all very exciting, but I think this one might be just as eventful, don't you?'

Ree rubbed her face. 'I certainly hope not.'

'Less chatting, more walking.' Andomerys nearly growled the words.

As they walked out, Usther said, 'Just because I'm going to this *poxy* meeting doesn't mean I'm going to tell them *anything* about the time warping ritual.'

'That's fine, Usther — if you don't want to speak, I can just explain it —'

'— and then I'll raise a greywraith to rip your tongue out.' Usther glared at Smythe.

Ree fidgeted uncomfortably, her satchel full of books bumping uncomfortably against her legs. She ached to open them. She'd had no opportunity to study them properly and she couldn't shake the hope that Wylandriah *had* written her book, and maybe one of them was in her pack right now.

But the meeting … her father would be running this meeting, and she still hadn't learned therianthropy yet.

She was fast. She wouldn't let him catch her. Besides, there were surely more pressing problems for him to deal with — not least the horrible curse on his daughter.

Nonetheless, she wasn't eager to flee her second town meeting in as many months.

There have been three true emergency town meetings in the history of the town. The first to strategise in response to the Semnian invaders in 6E70. The second to put down a roving horde of undead that adventurers had somehow disturbed. The third to plea for the life of a council member's daughter.

~from *A History of Tombtown* by Emberlon the Disloyal

CHAPTER THIRTY-ONE

EMERGENCY TOWN MEETING

To say that Ree was anxious about the town meeting would do a disservice to the vast, spreading vortex whirling inside of her. She clutched the edges of her rickety wooden seat, fingernails digging into the pitted wood.

Usther, Smythe, and Andomerys were sitting in her row, expressions ranging from disdainful (Usther), jittery (Smythe) to fuming (Andomerys). The seats behind them were gradually filling up, while denizens either complained loudly about the interruption to their work or speculated about what sort of enormous danger had led to the emergency meeting.

Ree's gaze flitted frequently to the black iron doors. She couldn't decide whether it would be better or worse when her father finally arrived. Surely anything was better than the spinning nausea and swimming head she had to deal with now — but then, her father was not best known for his patience and clemency.

Her mother arrived first, catching Ree's eyes and looking a question: *'Is this about you?'* To which Ree could only blanch and sit back in her chair. Emberlon did not arrive at all, and that was a worry all its own when it was possible the Lich was still riled. She tried to assure herself that he was on a collection, but to little effect. If somehow the Lich had gotten him, it would be entirely her fault.

When her father arrived, it was in full state with the rest of the council. His heavy brocade robes trailed his legs, and he clasped his staff before him. His eyes didn't seek her out, and neither did those of the council. They made their way to the dais, spreading out behind the sarcophagus and placing what books and notes they had brought with them upon it.

Usther leaned in to her. 'Always such a warm greeting from your father.'

Ree shrugged. 'Better than fury and mind-snares, I suppose.'

'You travelled through time and saw that therianthropy *does* exist.' Her voice was low. 'He'd be a fool to try and stop you now.'

She still couldn't do the magic. And it still wasn't what he wanted for her. She doubted something as trivial as time travel would derail her father's plan for her.

And then, just like that, the meeting was beginning in a room that was now familiar from two different incarnations. She could see at once the grandeur of the Old King's throne room and the age-worn town hall she had always known.

Smythe leaned in on Ree's other side. 'I don't suppose your father is feeling more kindly toward me? You know,

now that I'm a prodigiously talented summoner and no longer an interloping upworlder?'

'You'll always be an interloping upworlder.' She gave him a smile and an apologetic shrug as her eyes swept the crowd. She wondered if anyone other than the council knew why they'd been summoned today.

Smythe winced and Ree instantly regretted her joke.

'He's glaring at me,' Smythe said. 'He looks like he wishes someone had managed to curse me at the last meeting. He looks like he wants to curse me *now*. It's, um ... it's not very encouraging.' Smythe looked down at his hands. 'He must know, somehow, that I'm the reason you got into trouble.'

Ree blinked. 'In what way is it your fault?' She was the one who'd gone to the Lich's wing, knowing it was forbidden. And she was the one who'd agreed to the Black Oath. She was also the one who'd been so preoccupied by the boy in the crypt that she'd walked right into the Lich even though she knew his schedule. She might like to blame Smythe for all that, but if she was honest, she knew it was all on her. She had grown up here. Smythe was a recent immigrant and an apprentice practitioner. There was so much he didn't know — could hardly be expected to know.

Smythe glanced up at her face, then back down at his hands. 'Well. I ought to have protected you, of course. You know ... fisticuffs, black magic, er ... that sort of thing.'

His shoulders were high and hunched, his head hanging. Guilt written so clearly into the lines of his body. Ree almost reached out to comfort him but caught herself and stilled her hands. She had no desire to display any kind of affection, least of all in front of the whole town.

Her eyes flicked up to the dais. Her father frowned down at her.

'Smythe,' she said, and to her own surprise her tone was warm rather than irritated. 'I'm the one who knows this place. I should have done a better job of protecting *you*. I've been trying to protect you since I met you — and I've been doing a poor job of it.'

'But I'm the summoner. I have magic. That makes me the protector.' His eyes met hers, then skittered away.

Ree thought of the books in her satchel, waiting in Usther's tombhome. 'Maybe not for much longer.'

Andomerys leaned across Smythe. 'Will you two stop?'

Ree's cheeks heated, but before she could make a response, Usther leaned in. 'If you say the word "protect" one more time, I will eject my lunch. *And I'll make sure it lands on you!*

A resounding boom echoed from the dais. Ree looked up as her father set his staff aside. Kylath, the youngest council member, stepped forward with her lips pursed. Her red-rimmed eyes found Ree in the crowd; her lips twisted downwards.

Ree sat up straighter and raised her chin. She was asking for help and giving a warning; she was not on trial.

Kylath threaded her sharp-nailed fingers together. 'I call this emergency town meeting to order. I know many of you have questions. That is only natural, given the abrupt manner of this gathering.'

From the crowd, Mazerin the Bold yelled, 'Did a boar get into the crypt again? I've still got my trusty bone spear!' The reedy necromancer hoisted a yellow-white, serrated spear into the air.

'No ...'

'Have we decided to kill the upworlder after all?' This from Symphona, standing with her arms crossed. Her cloud of curly hair was pulled into a messy knot atop her head. Wings of draping black fabric fell from the shoulders of her robe.

Ree's eyes flicked to Usther, who was staring at the other girl like she was the secret to immortality.

'Not yet,' said Kylath.

Mortana, wyrdling innkeeper of the Bone & Brew, raised a clawed hand. 'Is it about the adventurers who entered the eastern tunnels a few days ago? Because I killed them and I have the right to their bodies. I'm going to make up a very nice broth from —'

Tarantur put one tattooed hand on Kylath's shoulder. 'I think that's enough guesswork, for now.' He smiled his thin-lipped smile. 'Do you mind if I step in, Kylath?'

Kylath looked like she minded very much, but Tarantur's smile only widened as he continued, 'Many lives are at risk. We wouldn't interrupt your craft for anything less.'

A murmur passed through the crowd. 'Our lives?' asked Mazerin.

'Your lives.' Tarantur spread his hands. 'The Lich has been disturbed in its wing. Thanks to the quick action of our denizens, it appears the initial danger has passed, but it is nonetheless possible that it will make an attempt on the town, or deviate from its usual paths. Be on your guard, and for safety it may be wise to travel in pairs or groups when going beyond the bounds of the town.'

Ree glanced around, catching many grimaces and wrinkled noses at the prospect of teamwork. Necromancers were rarely team players. Were the benefits of living together in the town not vastly superior to living separately, she doubted this town would ever have happened at all.

Tarantur's spidery smile returned as he surveyed the crowd. 'Yes, it is *quite* concerning, isn't it? To be so weak and *vulnerable* in the face of such a terrible power. Should any of you require —'

Ree's father cleared his throat. Tarantur's eyes flicked to him, and something hard and cold passed between them. Then Tarantur bowed his head and stepped back.

'If we are wise, there is nothing to fear.' Ree's father's voice was quiet, but still cut across the wide chamber. His long black hair flowed gently past his shoulders; his robes were a respectable black crusted with fresh blood. 'We are the most powerful town in all the world.' His eyes gleamed. 'We will endure and rise above.'

Something about his words struck Ree. She could feel the pride swelling in her chest. And she would join them soon — when she learned therianthropy, not even the Lich would be able to stand against her.

Usther's chin was raised; Smythe's eyes were shining. But Andomerys' lips were pressed into a flat line and she held her shorter arm in a tight-knuckled grip.

Her father went on to explain safety measures denizens should take until the danger with the Lich had passed, with interjections from the rest of the council. Ree worried her lip with her teeth.

'Lucky we went together, wouldn't you say?' Smythe murmured.

Ree looked at him sidelong: his eyes were on the stage, but there was a quirk to his lips that was only for her. She thought of Smythe using his magic to disrupt the Lich's ritual, of his terrible power and the blackness of his eyes when he called it. He was a more frightening person than she had ever imagined when she found him crouching over a shattered jar misidentifying organs.

But he was smiling at her, like he so often did, and it loosened something in her she hadn't known was tight. 'Lucky,' she agreed.

His fingertips brushed hers, and though he was no longer as warm as he had once been, her breath still caught at his touch. Their eyes met for a moment, then Smythe folded his hands in his lap and Ree looked back up at the dais.

Kylath nodded along with Ree's father's instructions, then folded her arms with a flourish of the trailing sleeves of her robes. 'There is also the matter of Reanima and Chandrian Smythe, which is possibly *more* pressing than finding a "safety buddy" when you want to harvest corpses.'

Her eyes found Ree in the crowd, and the hair on Ree's neck rose as all eyes turned toward her. Only Ree's father didn't try to catch her eye. He stared at Kylath, his lips twisted, and Ree wondered whether he had intended to mention the Black Oath at all.

Kylath ignored his hard stare and continued, 'What do any of you know about the Black —'

Boom! Dust shook free of the ceiling and showered the denizens. All eyes turned to the black iron doors.

Boom! They buckled and flung open; a lone, frizzy-haired minion lumbered in, jaw hanging.

Ree seized Smythe's hand, her entire body locking up.

Larry limped forward, his watery yellow eyes sweeping left to right across the room. His skin flaked in the air behind him and his feet slid over each other in an awkward shuffle.

Larry. Relief flooded her in a rush so powerful it almost hurt. She'd been certain the Lich would lock him up somewhere to keep him from them, but somehow the minion had gotten away.

Maybe this was bad. Maybe it would bring the Lich back down on them. But now, all she could think was that she was so happy to see the ridiculous minion.

Smythe squeezed her fingers, eyebrows un-pinching as his face eased into an open smile. He released her and got to his feet, scrambling over other denizens and into the aisle. He spread his arms wide. 'Good to see you again, old chap!'

Kylath cleared her throat and Ree's gaze returned to the dais.

'If you have any information regarding breaking the Black Oath, it is imperative that —'

'You come to speak with us privately after the meeting,' Ree's father interrupted. Kylath glared at him, her lips peeling back from her teeth. She thought for a moment that she might strike him — and Ree almost couldn't blame her. She was the youngest and least experienced council member, the only one who had to justify her place to the town, and she had been interrupted too many times already.

But Ree's father only gazed back impassively, his shoulders back and his jaw set, a statue that her rage could break against but could not shatter.

'The Black Oath?' This from one of the young acolytes, a boy with the sides of his head shaved and the rest falling in a greasy hank across his forehead. 'As in *the* Black Oath?'

'Yes, *the* Black Oath.' Symphona glared at him. *'Fool.'*

In the row behind, Ree heard someone murmur, 'Think I heard of someone who bathed in blood to break the Black Oath once?'

'We've all done that,' a woman whispered back. 'There's nothing magical about an old-fashioned blood bath. Works wonders on the skin, though.'

'Ack! Larry!' Smythe's strangled cry rose above the susurrus.

'Morrin's teeth,' Usther murmured. Her nose wrinkled.

Smythe and Larry struggled in the aisle, Smythe's hands on Larry's face while the minion put all his weight into leaning toward Smythe's neck with an open mouth. 'I'm happy to see you too, but this is a little over-enthusiastic!'

Ree climbed out into the aisle, muttering apologies as she went. Her fingers dipped into the pouch at her side. 'Larry,' she said wearily.

Larry and Smythe together froze. Larry's eyes rolled toward her, mouth still lolling wide.

'Stop it.'

Larry's eyes rolled back to Smythe. He struggled harder.

Ree sighed and sent a small pinch of herbs to cloud the minion's face. Larry's arms sagged and he released Smythe, blinking foolishly ahead.

Ree pat his shoulder, then pulled Smythe aside to the nearest seats.

'I could have handled it, you know. He just needs a firm hand — and I think I was rather getting the better of him!'

'Of course.' Ree's tone was flat. Smythe twiddled his fingers and stared into his lap. Ree felt briefly abashed that she'd upset him, but Kylath was still speaking.

'That concludes our official business. Any further matters can be postponed until the next town meeting at the end of the month. Those who have feuds to settle can submit their grievances through the usual channels. Please inform any denizens you meet who were unable to attend of the new safety measures.'

Ree and Smythe waited in their seats, with Larry lolling on a chair beside them, until all but a few of the denizens filtered through the black iron doors. Andomerys was the last to pass, nodding to Ree, her usual scowl tinged with concern.

'Not many staying behind.' Ree's eyes swept the handful of practitioners ascending the marble steps.

Usther moved to the row in front of them. She straddled a chair and rested her chin on the back of it so that she faced them. 'It *is* the Black Oath,' she said. 'If it were easy to break, nobody would bother using it.' Her tone was breezy, but her shoulders were sharp and there was a downwards tilt to her mouth that spoke of worry.

'Reanima!' Ree's mother swept down the aisle toward them.

Ree stood up in time and clasped her hands behind her back, not meeting her mother's eyes.

'Good to *see* you, Arthura,' Usther said silkily. 'Not *quite* too busy for an emergency town meeting regarding your daughter, I see.'

Ree's mother levelled a weighted gaze at Usther, but Usther shrugged it off. Her eyes returned to her daughter. 'Let me see it.'

'Seeing it won't change anything,' Ree said wearily.

Her mother seized her wrist. 'Let me *see* it. Oh!' She pulled up Ree's sleeve and gasped, taking a step back with her hand to her mouth, eyes wide and staring. The words *'and so let it be done'* glared, red and angry, against her pale skin. Her hands found Ree's and held them tightly, a startling affection.

'Your father was right.' Her dark eyes glistened. 'We were too lenient with you, let you travel too far unprotected. And now — I'm so sorry, Ree. I've failed you, and now —'

'We haven't failed yet.' Ree said. Her mother's words were too much an echo of her own thoughts. If she'd just committed to the Craft as a child, as her father had wanted, how powerful might she be now? Powerful enough to hold off the Lich? Powerful enough to reject the Old King and his cused Oath?

But Smythe had more raw power than any necromancer she'd yet encountered, and he'd not been able to stop any of this.

'You don't need to be afraid,' her mother said. 'Morrin will welcome you as one of her own. You are a child of her people. My Goddess is wise and powerful. She won't let —' she stopped and coughed, and for a moment Ree thought in terror that it might be hiding a sob. Ree's mother cleared her throat. 'She won't let the Oath take the soul of one of her faithful.'

'One of her faithful,' Usther repeated, and Ree could almost feel her exchange a look with Smythe. Because Smythe had certainly never worshipped Morrin, and as for Ree — well, her mother might be a priestess, but Ree was hardly devoted. She had once expressed to Emberlon a desire for a Goddess of Libraries, but the universe had failed to provide one.

But her mother was trying to comfort her, and that was something. 'We have a little time, I think,' said Ree. 'And maybe — I don't know, maybe the beginning of a plan. I'm not dead yet, mother.'

Her mother nodded and released Ree's hands. She stepped back and smoothed her long robes, her face sliding back into its impassive religious mask. 'Morrin let it be so.'

The last denizens descended from the dais. Ree's eyes scoured their faces for any clue, biting her lip. 'They're leaving. That seems like a bad sign.'

Smythe lifted his gaze to meet hers. 'It doesn't matter. We'll find Emberlon, find the tablet. We're a smart bunch and he seems like a resourceful chap. We'll find a way —'

Usther craned around in her seat. 'Is that *Veritas?*'

Ree looked up at the dais, her heart constricting in her chest. On the dais, encircled by attentive council members, Veritas talked and gesticulated animatedly. As his eyes met hers, his face split into a smug grin.

Ree fought to keep her breathing even. 'Do you think there's a chance that he's forgotten about the book?'

Grudges and feuds are common among necromancers, especially those living in such close quarters as in Tombtown. Denizens are expected to resolve their disputes privately and without disturbing their neighbours — or the Goddess of Undying, who seems to have a personal interest in the survival of the town.

If people occasionally disappear when in the midst of such a dispute, the council does not take issue, so long as they disappear quietly and with a minimum of mess.

~from *A History of Tombtown* by Emberlon the Disloyal

CHAPTER THIRTY-TWO

FAKING IT

Ree, Smythe, and Usther hovered awkwardly at the edge of the circle of practitioners crowded on the dais, Usther with her nose in the air, Ree with her eyes on the floor, and Smythe beaming around at the gathered faces. The council members stood proud and tall — apart from Bahamet the Eternal, who hunched blankly toward a wall. And in the centre, Veritas stood with a self-satisfied grin, his bald head crusty with blood, his mask and goggles hanging around his neck.

'I have done quite the research into curses and blood binding,' Veritas said. Leather squeaked as he crossed his heavy-gloved arms. 'Being, as I am, the *only* practitioner with the *vision* to explore the edges of experimental Craft, it is only natural that I have tested the limits of blood binding curses such as the Oath.'

'Such as the Oath,' Igneus echoed.

Ree raised her eyebrows. 'So ... not the actual Black Oath then.'

Veritas sniffed. 'Well *obviously* not the actual Black Oath since the cost of failure is quite high and it's said to be unbreakable —'

'What a *visionary* you are,' said Usther. 'Truly *groundbreaking* to shy away from any piece of magic that frightens you.'

'— but I *have* looked into the breaking of similar curses and the strategy is quite clear.' His beady eyes gleamed. 'Shall I tell you?'

Kylath pursed her lips. 'I find this all rather tedious. I trust you can handle the matter without assistance, Igneus?' She nodded to him and Ree's father inclined his head in response. She swept from the room — and, after a moment's hesitation, the rest of the council followed suit.

So now it was Ree, Usther, Smythe, and Ree's parents ranged around Veritas. The experimental necromancer rubbed his hands together with a squeaking of leather. His ratty gaze tracked the council members down the steps. He seemed deflated by their absence.

'Tedious?' he said quietly, then stood straighter. It did not quite level his hunched shoulders. 'So. The solution, then.' He sighed dramatically. 'It has come to me through years of careful research and experimentation. I don't expect you to grasp the finer details of such a subtle magic, but I shall do my best to distil my knowledge into a form more suited to your limited cognitive resources. You see —'

'On with it, Veritas.'

Ree glanced at her father; though his tone was mild, his eyes were anything but. He also managed to stand a lot straighter than Veritas — but then, while Veritas was hunched and craven, her father was tall and brittle. She'd inherited that brittleness — the poker-rod spine, the sharp, awkward movements. It was probably at least part of why Smythe had mistaken her for a walking corpse.

Veritas squeaked his gloves together again. 'Of course.' His tone was disgruntled. 'Well, then I shall say that all of my research led me to the conclusion that the Oath should be approached as a legal contract, in which the intent is significant but does not supersede the specific *language and structure* of the Oath. Ha! Do you see?'

Ree shook her head slightly. She looked around: Usther was pursing her lips in what Ree was certain was an expression of restrained violence; Ree's mother's eyes were closed in prayer; Ree's father's expression was hard but thoughtful; Smythe nodded enthusiastically.

'Yes, of course!' Smythe said at the same time that Usther said, 'Get to the *point*, you hideous buffoon.'

Veritas looked from one to the other. 'Well, I can hardly make it simpler. The way to avoid the consequences of a Black Oath is to comply with the specific, verbalised conditions of the Oath.'

Ree pinched her nose between her fingers. 'You're saying that the best way to break the Oath is to *keep* the Oath?'

Veritas flapped his hands. 'Exactly!' He lowered his hands. 'Wait ... not exactly. Or at least, exactly, but not in keeping with the intent.' His eyes gleamed. 'Ingenius, isn't it?'

'Quite!' Smythe leaned forward, face lit with interest. 'But how did you come to the conclusion?'

'With each of my subjects, I cast the same blood binding curse, with the same intent but different specific language.

In all cases, the subjects who broke the contract triggered the curse, as did those who failed to comply. But! On experimentation with later subjects, it became clear that the specific language could lead to different fulfilment criteria — in spite of the intent of each curse being the same. In *those* cases, the curse was triggered but not to full effect — which meant that the consequences could be avoided to a degree. My *final* subjects made it clear that the intent of the subject also affected the outcome of the results — and specifically, that, unless a failure condition was specified, intent could supersede failure. Also relevant is timeline. All curses take no more than seven days to take effect if the conditions are not met.'

At this point, Ree's head was spinning. She could almost grasp what Veritas was saying, but that there was too much information for her to easily parse. Not to mention, she was a little distracted by the thought of Veritas' subjects. Just how many people had he killed over the course of his research?

Seven days. And they had already used ... what? Three of them?

It was an awfully short time in which to break a curse. Even shorter in which to live a life.

Smythe started to speak, but Usther cut him off. 'I think you're being unnecessarily dense, but I'd like to put that aside a moment. Where could you *possibly* find so many living subjects?'

Veritas glanced at Ree's father. 'I didn't break any rules — I didn't go raiding the upworld, if that's what you're insinuating. I used wild caught adventurers, as is my right — I have plenty of traps about my tower, and I bait them well with treasure.' He sniffed and crossed his arms. 'It's all completely above board.'

'The curse,' said Ree's father. 'You're saying there's a way around it?'

'He's saying the exact opposite,' said Smythe.

Ree rubbed her eyes tiredly. 'He's saying that the only way to avoid the consequences of the curse is to comply with the curse.'

Veritas clenched his fists at his sides. 'Festering rats! Must you all be so obtuse? I'm *saying* you only need to fulfil the specifics of the curse. I'm *saying* you can fake it.'

'Fake it.' Usther's nostrils flared, like a bull about to charge. '*That's* your ingenius solution, which you wasted many perfectly useful living subjects to discover.'

'Yes!' Veritas squinted his eyes at her. 'Obviously! It's not like I could find a way to *break* the Black Oath, is it? It's *unbreakable.*'

'Mm.' Usther's lips were disappearing and her eyes started to flash. 'Mm-hmm.'

'You said that you had information on how to *break* the curse.' Ree's father seemed almost to grow in size as he looked down at the other necromancer.

'This is even *better* than breaking the curse!' Veritas insisted. Then his lips twisted and he cocked his head to one side. 'Well. Perhaps not. But I didn't see anyone *else* volunteering the information.' He sniffed. 'By rights, I should be demanding barter for this information.'

Ree's mother opened her eyes into narrow slits. 'Morrin will weigh the value of your contribution.'

'Yes, but I'm not very interested in a reward that can only be redeemed after I'm dead.'

'If there is any worth to your theory at all, *I* will be in your debt.' Ree's father crossed his arms.

Veritas looked, briefly, like he wasn't sure whether that was something he wanted after all.

There was a touch at Ree's elbow; she looked up into Smythe's face. His lips quirked in a half-smile and he drew her aside.

'Not a lot of help from that quarter.' Ree nodded toward Veritas, who stared churlishly at his boots while Ree's mother started a lecture on immortal rewards.

'On the contrary, Veritas has given us every advantage.' Smythe's stare was hot on her face. Ree wanted to hide from it, but found she couldn't look away. 'Do you remember the words of the Oath?'

Ree dipped her head. 'We swore to complete the ritual.'

Smythe's other hand came up, so that his touch was light on both of her forearms. 'Not what he wanted; the words he used.'

Ree breathed in and let the memory take her. It had been haunting her ever since she'd let the words slip from her mouth. She could remember the strange intensity of the Old King, the weight of his power and the mantle of authority that rested on him. She remembered Wylandriah in the background, eyes bleak under the stripe of blue paint. 'This you must swear,' she whispered, opening her eyes 'on blood and death and soul: that you will undertake the Great Resurrection,' Smythe's grip tightened on her arms 'and thereby restore my legacy.'

Smythe nodded, then nodded again. His hands slid from her arms to dangle at his sides. 'That's how I remember it as well — that's good, that means we have the wording right.'

But Ree could already feel the teeth of the trap closing in around her. 'But that's no good — it's too specific!'

Smythe ran a hand through his curls. 'We only swore that we would *undertake* the ritual — not that we would complete it.' He smiled to one side. 'That is, I believe, what men of law refer to as a "loophole".'

'We swore that we would "thereby restore his legacy".' Ree's chest was growing tight. Shadows danced at the edges of her vision. 'There's no way out.'

'There *is* a way out. That's less specific than you think, I think. And Veritas was very clear that intention plays a role.'

The Great Resurrection required an equivalent sacrifice — in this case, a city for a city. Ree tried to draw breath into thin lungs and shook her head. 'This is *not* going to work.'

The lightest touch at her chin; Ree's eyes leapt to meet Smythe's, whose mouth pinched in an expression of acute embarrassment. He hastily retracted his hand, leaving only the sparking memory of his touch.

'This *is* going to work,' he promised. His mouth dragged at one side. 'At least, I think it will. But first, we need to take a good look at this tablet you say the ritual is carved on. Are you certain there's no way of tracking down Emberlon?'

'Uhh.' She wrung the skirts of her robes in her hands. 'I suppose there will be a record card out in the archives. We usually make it clear to each other which account we're working on so that we don't get in each other's way.'

'More library work? How dull.' Ree startled as Usther appeared at her side, a brittle look to her expression. She met Ree's eyes, and Ree thought, for a moment, that Usther might be genuinely pained at Ree's situation. But then Usther bared her teeth. 'Well, I suppose he can hardly be more useless than that fool. The archives, was it?'

Ree nodded and went to make her goodbyes to her parents. Her father made it clear that she should come to him once they found Emberlon, and that he would continue his own research into the matter. Her mother said nothing but caught her sleeve as she turned to leave. 'Come and find me if the situation looks hopeless,' she said. Her eyes flashed with something fierce. 'You are my daughter. I will not let you walk into death alone and unprotected.'

A chill shivered down Ree's arms, but she nodded her thanks to her mother. That was as much love as she could ever hope to receive from her parents; threats and doomsaying.

But they did care.

As they headed out of the town hall, Larry shambling in their footsteps, Smythe leaned close to Ree. 'We'll find a way out of this.' His breath tickled her face. The hope in his smile held her captive a moment, her mouth dry. 'I'll make sure of it.'

I went to the surface again today, eager to feel the sun on my feathers, but the surface dwellers, frightened of all they do not understand, laid a trap for me.

My hawkskin destroyed and my other therianskins stolen, I was forced to march to a public execution, as city dwellers find entertainment in cruelty.

Faced with my death, I had no regrets. I have lived free and true to myself from the moment I ran from my village and I would change nothing.

But though I had no reason to hope for it, the King arrived in state and fury. He freed me by his own hand while his minions razed the village.

It was a horror greater than I would ever have inflicted and I hid my face from it. The King took my chin in his hands. 'If I must choose between my kingdom and any other, I will always choose mine,' he said.

~from the journal of Wylandriah Witch-feather

CHAPTER THIRTY-THREE

AFFAIRS IN ORDER

They shoved the heavy stone doors of the archive into a grinding admittance. Ree stood in the gap, wiping sweat from her forehead. 'Stay out here. Archivists only.'

Usther rolled her eyes and leaned against the door. 'Really? Is that *really* what's important right now?'

'Yes!' As if she would let Usther plunder the secrets of the town's libraries just because Ree's soul might be forfeit at any moment. She narrowed her eyes at Usther.

Usther sighed and flapped a hand at her. 'Yes, fine, keep your entirely dull secrets. Smythe and I will just stand out here like thoroughly mismatched bookends, shall we?'

Ree headed through the doors. 'That would be perfect, thank you.'

She heard Smythe ask, 'In what way are we mismatched?' before the heavy silence of the archives enfolded her.

She walked sedately to the cluttered desk on the right. This place was her nearest and dearest haven; a safe space for her to read and work and wonder, only a few dozen feet from her front door. It was saturated with memories: Emberlon patiently redoing her first attempt at filing; curling up in the corner with the first book she'd retrieved; walking in and finding Larry with his arm stuck in a filing cabinet. And always, the heavy quiet and the reassuring barrier of the stone doors.

The desk was scattered with loose sheaves of parchment and messily stacked books. She brushed aside the paper and carefully shifted the tallest stack of books, revealing a piece of wood with a note spiked onto it. *Berengar Request. 2 day trip.*

Ree replaced the books and worried her lip with her teeth. Berengar was another lone necromancer who'd taken up residence in the dungeons beneath the amphitheatre. While that wasn't so very far away, she didn't know when Emberlon had set out. He could arrive back at any minute, and if they set out for Berengar's to find him, there was no guarantee their paths would cross.

When Ree edged back out of the archives, she found Smythe speaking very earnestly to Larry.

'You don't have to hide it from us if you understand.' Smythe smiled encouragingly. 'We know all about you now, my good man. All the — you know, the business with *you-know-who* back in *you-know-when*.'

Usther sneered. Her arms were crossed, her back against the stone door. 'He can't understand you and he has *no memory* of any of that nonsense. Larry's an empty shell. Whatever soul resided in him has moved on to the ethereal planes.'

Larry's mouth lolled, jaw swinging loosely as his head turned from Smythe to Usther and back again.

'You can't really think that rule applies here! We already know Larry's ... you know.' He lowered his voice. '*Different*. Why shouldn't he be more knowing than a regular minion?'

'Because he's *Larry*,' Usther's nose wrinkled. 'He lost most of his teeth chewing on *rocks*. That's rather *less* knowing than the average minion.'

Ree cleared her throat and all eyes turned to her. 'He's on a trip. Two days' wait at most, but probably much less.'

Smythe's eyebrows pinched. 'Shall we go after him, then?'

Ree shook her head. 'All we can do is wait.'

Usther stared at her for a moment, then gave a bird-like shrug. 'Fine. You know where to find me.' She strode off, flicking a wave over her shoulder, the lace trim of her robes trailing dramatically.

Larry stumbled after her a moment, then stopped and shuffled back to Ree, bumping into her shoulder. She flinched a little at his closeness, remembering those eyes flashing with cruelty, the lips parting in a snarl, but there was nothing of Evanert's torturer in this wasted, drooping minion. 'It's good to see you, too, Larry,' she murmured. She did her best to meet his eyes; Larry had been like a pet to her since she was a little girl and had followed her on many of her furthest and most frightening journeys. He'd taken an arrow trying to save her; Lazerin couldn't take those memories from her.

She patted his clammy cheek and he gave her a gummy grin and started to shuffle into the archives. 'Hold on!' She caught him by the shoulder and hauled him back. In a flash of prescience, she could envision him overturning all their careful filing. 'Smythe, could you help me with this?'

Together, they got the doors closed and sank down to sit with their backs against the stone. Larry banged on the door a few times, howling his displeasure.

'So. Two days.' He bumped his head back against the stone.

'Maybe less,' Ree offered.

Smythe's lips quirked. 'Well, I'm sure that whenever he gets back, we can sort out all this "curse" business and return to what's important.'

Ree studied Smythe. He was sitting closer to her than they usually sat, his shoulder only a finger's width from hers. He was very still, as if worried she was a butterfly he might disturb.

'And what's important?'

Smythe's eyes flickered to her face, then away. 'I was making some rather good progress with my summoning into research on Third Era burial rites among the lower classes. It might be quite nice to take another look at my paper on it, once all of this is over.'

Once all of this is over. He said the words so casually, as if a happy ending was guaranteed. But while he seemed convinced that this was a problem with an easy solution, Veritas' revelation had only solidified Ree's belief that there was no way out of the Oath. There wasn't any wiggle room in the contract she'd made with the Old King. And at some point, when Ree failed to complete the Great Resurrection, the curse would trigger and Ree's soul would suffer a fate worse than death.

But it was hard to work herself up about that properly with Smythe's shoulder a scant inch from her own and when he projected relaxedness even through stillness.

Ree took a tight breath. 'What would you do? If you only had a few days to live. What would you do?'

'It's not going to be like that.'

Ree smiled tightly. 'Humour me.'

Smythe pushed his curls out from under his glasses. 'If I only had days to live?' He blinked and looked round at her — and now he seemed impossibly close, his eyes wide and dark behind his glasses, though his shoulder moved no closer. There was the faintest tickle of breath against her face, but Ree didn't pull away.

Smythe's mouth thinned. 'It's, um — it's not an easy question. What would you do?'

Sitting so close to him, with his dark eyes looking deep into hers, it was difficult for her to form a coherent thought. It wasn't just the thickness of his eyelashes or the small pull in the corner of his mouth, or the faint scent of him, which even after all of this was still parchment and ink and the cold tang of metal. It was that nobody had ever looked at her the way Smythe did. Like she was taking up all of his attention.

It wasn't like she wanted him. Not the way Usther wanted Symphona, or the way her parents wanted each other. Ree was certain by this point that she wasn't built that way. But she wanted to *matter* to him, in a way she had never wanted to matter to anyone else. To matter the most to him. The same way he had somehow become this central, shining figure in her life.

She wanted to be close to him. Sometimes, when he looked at her like this, like she was all there was to see, she wondered what it would be like to close the distance between them. She didn't want sex but she craved his intimacy. Would a kiss give her that?

But that was foolish, wasn't it? Even without the curse, even if everything was normal and they were just two scholars living in a town of necromancers, what if he asked her for something she was unwilling to give? What if the relationship she craved would necessarily be a disappointment to him? The thought of his rejection, or worse, his derision, was too much to bear.

Whatever happened, she was alone.

She lowered her eyes and turned away, breaking the connection that held her and gathering her scattered thoughts. Her hand went to her satchel, still heavy with stolen books, as she found a different truth to give him. 'I'd prove to everyone that therianthropy is real magic.' She closed her eyes and leaned her head back against the stone door. 'I'd fly.' She said the words quietly, barely daring to say them aloud.

'Well, that's settled then.'

She looked up as Smythe stood. He extended his hand. Not entirely sure what was happening, she took it, and he drew her to her feet.

'Nothing's settled, Smythe.' She tried to keep the bitterness from her voice, then wondered why she bothered. It was perfectly reasonable to be bitter about dying. 'Everything is still very much up in the air.'

'And soon you will be!' He was smiling now, the scholar's gleam back in his eyes. 'Between two such excellent scholars as ourselves, there can hardly be any way to stop us. Besides, we can't do anything about this curse until Emberlon returns. You've got the books; you've got the skill. It's time for you to fly.'

The priestess Arthura, said to have been possessed by Morrin the Undying herself at the foundation of the town, tended the Altar of Many Gods for decades, though few other priestfolk were in the town. Denizens requested shrines for their particular gods, and she would upkeep them alongside her own.

When asked why she had made the temple open to a pantheon, rather than dedicated only to her patron goddess — easily the most popular goddess in the town — she replied: 'People find the divine in many things. It is not for me to choose for them. Even I was not born a priestess of Undeath.'

As of the time of writing, eleven gods are represented at the Altar, cohabiting in a truce as uneasy as the town itself.

~from *A History of Tombtown* by Emberlon the Disloyal

CHAPTER THIRTY-FOUR
FLAYING AND FLYING

Her stolen books became the most precious treasures she had ever found. *A Study of the Old Ways* made relevant commentary on ancient therianthrope culture, although it made no comment on their magic. *Wynas Serasaphi* translated to 'music of the wild', providing notes on a musical notation very similar to those she had found with therianthropic spells.

And the last, the untitled book with the animal rune art, was the greatest treasure of all. Written in Old Antherian in a harsh, scratchy hand, it opened, *'My name is Wylandriah Witch-feather, the last therianthrope of my time, and here written is a guide to my art, that future generations may know its power.'*

Her voice shook as she read it aloud, looking up at Smythe with shining eyes. 'We found it.' She smoothed the open page with trembling hands. 'She wrote it and we found it.'

'You know — I think she could tell you would be the one to bring it back,' said Smythe. 'She risked a lot, leaving you with that key.'

Ree gazed down at the book, brimming with so many emotions that it was hard to identify them all. Again, she had that strange feeling of fate. Would Wylandriah have written this book if she hadn't met Ree? If not, then it was a coincidence of cosmic proportions that the Lich had sent them back.

Or was this what her mother had meant, every time she had promised her that Morrin watched her with all-knowing eyes, and had great plans for her?

They pored over the books together, checking each other's translations and writing up notes. Ree painstakingly copied it all into her journal, blotting away all the excess ink and keeping it concise and to the point. Her journal was the only modern study of therianthropy, and if she succeeded, it would hold pride of place in all the libraries of the crypt.

'Did you include the note about Wylandriah?' Smythe asked.

They were still sitting outside the archives, paper strewn around them in a semi-circle. Ree was cross-legged, her journal open in her lap; Smythe knelt with his hands flat on his legs, craning to get a look at her notes. She'd never done any of her research so publicly, but it no longer seemed wise to travel to one of the secret libraries when the Lich might still be holding a grudge against them. Besides, Smythe made it all seem so possible and admirable that it was difficult to be embarrassed.

A few feet away, Larry flapped her empty satchel, then scowled when nothing fell out. He flapped it a few more times, then started gumming the strap.

'I've included the note. It's only anecdotal,' she said, worrying her lip with her teeth.

'Some of the most important pieces of historical research are anecdotal,' he said warmly. 'And it's more than anyone else in our era has ever seen.'

Ree's cheeks heated and she looked down. Some of her hair had come unpinned, and fell into her face. 'I think I've got everything. Could we collect the specimen now?'

'Now?'

Ree nodded, avoiding his eyes. 'I know we've been at this a long time, but there's actually a tower not far from here which peaks above the surface. With any luck —'

Smythe stood up and stretched. 'Of course we'll go now. I was only surprised.' Again, he extended his hand.

Something had changed between them; Ree wasn't sure when. They had touched hardly ever before — and indeed, Ree had hardly touched *anyone* — but now it seemed that it was a thing that was meant to be normal — that Smythe could offer her a hand up, or touch her gently at the elbow, that Ree could brush her hand against his or squeeze his shoulder in support. It was happening more and more, with such regularity that Ree wondered if it felt natural to Smythe.

For her, it was still a breath-catching moment every time. She gathered her will and took his hand; he pulled her to her feet. For a moment, they just stood there, her hand in his, looking into each other's eyes.

Then Ree pulled her hand free, gathered her notes, and tugged her pack from Larry's grip. She shouldered it and headed off, Smythe falling into step with her. Behind them, Larry wordlessly — and loudly — lamented the loss of his chew toy.

She didn't talk much on the journey, focusing instead on getting them safely through the crypt. She guided Smythe across a crystal floor that held encased corpses, near perfectly preserved. She encouraged him across a rope bridge with missing slats, and up a crumbling ladder that was barely more than a series of deep gouges in a stone wall. Smythe, though, kept up a near constant conversation, speculating as to how their research would line up with the reality of shapeshifting, exclaiming loudly about every new room or chamber they passed, and coaxing Larry across the more difficult terrain.

They encountered some unbound undead; a trio of lesser dead, a skeleton awakening from an alcove. There was such a concentration of death and magic in the crypts that it wasn't uncommon for corpses to wake themselves up from time to time. Each time, Ree's hands found her belt pouch, but it was unneeded. Though Smythe was a summoner and dealt primarily with spirits, his Craft was plenty strong enough to lay the undead back to rest.

All the while, Ree's chest grew tighter at the thought of what awaited them. Daylight, which she hadn't been properly exposed to in months. Fresh air. Magic, she hoped. Failure, she feared.

They finally rounded a corner into a narrow stone doorway, the walls carved with sprawling constellations. The Lovers, the Paladin, the Gentle Beast. All images that she knew better from books than from the sky.

'This is it,' she said. She looked over her shoulder at Smythe, who had Larry's arm and was helping him up the step.

Larry tripped up onto the landing and Smythe dusted his hands. His eyebrows pinched as he took in the doorway. 'This is the tower, is it?' He walked over and ran his hands gently along the carvings, his fingers following the grooves. 'Ethian stonework,' he murmured. He raised an eyebrow at Ree. 'Was it a temple? Or — perhaps an observatory of some kind?'

Ree held in a smile. 'You're the historian.'

'I *AM* the historian, aren't I?' Smythe's smile held nothing back. Sometimes she wondered how he didn't *actually* light up whatever room he was in. His smiles could surely be harvested as an energy source. 'But *you're* the clever one. Well — the clever*er* one, obviously I'm rather impressive myself.' He chortled in a way that was only half self-deprecating.

Something loosened inside Ree. He was always saying things like that: that she was clever, that she probably knew better than he did. He was a highly qualified scholar (as he never failed to mention) but he still thought so highly of her. Nobody had ever had this level of confidence in her. It made her feel more confident in herself.

'Well, I don't really know,' she said. 'The furnishings were plundered years ago, and the upper levels have mostly crumbled. If I had to guess — observatory.'

'Because it must have been at least somewhat open to the sky to have crumbled in a few hundred years?'

Ree smiled. 'That, and I want it to be.'

Smythe laughed and straightened his glasses.

The interior of the tower was sparse. Some wood mulch that might have been from broken chairs and tables, bare stone floors, and a tight spiral staircase. 'Stay here, Larry.' She took the minion by the shoulders and stood him against the wall.

Larry grunted questioningly.

'There's daylight up there.' Maybe whatever strange magic the Lich had imbued Larry with would protect him from sunlight, but she'd seen too many minions stripped of their unlife under those harsh rays to take the risk. 'Just — stay here, all right?'

As she stepped away, Larry started to follow. She pushed him back. 'No. Stay.' She waved her finger, her expression stern.

Smythe clapped him on the shoulder. 'Cheer up, old chap! We'll be back before you know it. Hey! Enough of that!' He snatched his hand away before Larry could bite it.

And then they were up the staircase, following a tight, claustrophobic spiral. She could feel the air warm as they ascended. A bubble of anticipation popped in her chest. She didn't know how to feel. She only knew that it felt like something big was happening.

And then, she felt her darkvision fading. Colour seeped back into the world and she squinted her eyes against the brightness of it. Behind her, she heard Smythe heave a sigh.

The staircase ended on a wide platform. There were a few semi-destroyed columns of stacked stone; brightly coloured shards of glass littered the floor. But for Ree, her eyes immediately trended up, beyond the rocky mountainside, beyond the horizon and the distant hills, and up to a sky that was blue and cloudy and so bright it hurt.

Smythe stepped up beside her. She could hear his breath catch. He shaded his eyes, gazing at the long view of the upworld shrinking into the distance. 'Beautiful,' he murmured. Then he closed his eyes and turned up his face to the sky. His curls tumbled back from his face. 'I'd almost forgotten the feeling of sunlight. There's nothing quite like it.'

'No,' said Ree. Since he couldn't see, she set her smile free. They stood together a moment, just feeling the sunlight and studying the sky. It made Ree's eyes water, but she didn't much mind.

'I can see what you mean,' Smythe said. 'About wanting this to be an observatory. I mean — it's *terrible* scholarly method, but I see what you mean.'

Ree nodded and bit her lip in thought. She chased around for the words she needed. 'It's a place where the whole sky is cracked open. The perfect place to watch.'

Smythe glanced at her. 'And you've a natural bent to observation.'

'Do I?'

'Well, I *did* catch you spying on me, the first time we met.'

Ree shook her head. 'I'm pretty sure I caught *you* misidentifying organs.'

He smiled, then turned serious. 'I suppose I owe you an apology.'

Ree turned her head slightly. 'It's fine, I didn't really mind.'

'No — not for the organs. For calling you an undead creature.'

He was looking at her so earnestly now. Ree's cheeks were burning; she thanked the gods for the hundredth time that her blushes didn't show. How many times had she obsessed over him mistaking her for a minion?

'It's fine.'

'It's not. I was surprised and — well, more than a little scared. But even then I thought you seemed — I mean, you were much more, um, attractive than I thought an undead would —'

'Smythe.' Ree's face was actually on fire. Surely no amount of necromancy could hide this blush.

'Right, right.' He was blushing now, too, a faint pinkish-grey rising in his cheeks. 'That … didn't really come out right. I just felt I owed you an apology.'

Ree nodded, not sure whether it would be better or worse to meet his eyes. 'Well, thank you. Apology accepted.'

'Excellent.'

'Great.'

Ree smoothed her robes and looked up and around. 'So, according to our notes we need an animal.' And now, up here, they had the entire upworld to search for one.

Smythe cleared his throat. 'A bird.' He gave her a slightly embarrassed smile. 'You said you wanted to fly.'

She tried to keep her smile inside, but judging by the warmth in his eyes, she didn't think she managed it. 'You take the south east. I'll take the north west.'

And they began their watch. Ree had thought her eyes would adjust to the sunlight, but it was so much brighter than even a torchlit room that she found her eyes still watering an hour later. She saw many specks of movement — distant birds of prey circling, and scurrying animals among the rocky brush, but for a long time, nothing really came close.

But animals were skittish. In the crypt, the only animals she'd really encountered were rats, spiders, and sometimes fish, but stillness seemed to be key in getting them to approach. So, like she was trying to coax a rat with a handful of millet, she sat very still, let her breath come deep and slow, and waited

Surprisingly, Smythe didn't speak. Whether he, too, knew to wait in stillness or he was deep in thought, she didn't know. She resisted the urge to look over at him; staring at the back of his head would do very little to change the situation. But she wondered what he was thinking. She wondered if he was thinking of her.

'You were much more attractive than I thought an undead would be.'

The words still made her blush, though whether more from pleasure or horror, she found it hard to tell. Certainly, it had embarrassed her, and yet she couldn't stop reliving the conversation in her head.

Then: 'Ree!' The words were barely more than a whisper. He didn't look at her; his eyes were fixed on a point in the sky. Ree followed his gaze up to a bird with a long beak and sweeping black wings.

The crow circled above them. It appeared to be alone, though she'd thought crows usually flocked together. It was a beautiful creature, glossy-feathered and sleek in build with splayed wingtips. It dodged and played in the air, looking down at them with beady eyes, so at ease in its element that Ree's heart ached at the thought of killing it.

Not that she really knew *how* they might kill it, but before Ree could put that concern into words, the crow swooped in low to alight on one of the crumbling columns and Smythe threw out his arm. A flash of red-and-black magic arced from his hand to hit the crow in the chest. It immediately went limp and fell from its perch.

They both scrambled over to it. 'It's dead.' Smythe looked up at her with wide eyes.

Ree held in a sigh. 'Yes. *You* killed it.'

Smythe crouched down by the fallen bird. 'I mean, I *know* that but — well, I've never killed anything before.' He reached trembling fingers over to the fallen bird. 'Still warm.' He quickly retracted his hand. He looked greyer than usual, even as his power drained from him.

Ree hesitated, not sure what to say. He looked … smaller. Frailer, somehow. His shoulders sharp and pulled in, his eyes bleak as he studied the lifeless body of feather and bone on the ground. She settled for: 'Are you alright?' She studied him closely, anxiety pecking at her. 'It can be a harrowing thing, to take a life. Some necromancers never do, not even animals.'

'No, it's — look, I'm fine. Really.' He took a shuddering breath, meeting her eyes for the first time since the bird fell. 'I just didn't expect it, is all. Its life was sacrificed for a good cause.' He smoothed the feathers on its wing. 'What now?'

He didn't look fine. He looked … she wasn't sure. Shaken, perhaps. Alert. But if he wanted to move on, then they would move on. There was little enough time as it was.

'Now, we skin it,' she said. 'I think my mother has a skinning knife. We can start with that.'

I repaired my hawkskin again today. I know that it is old, and that it is inefficient to use it now, but I cannot bear to replace it. Every time I wear it, I remember that first time. The moment I became a therianthrope, with a song in my throat and a knife in my hand.

There is nothing in the world like that first moment. It is a unique act of worship.

~from the journal of Wylandriah Witch-feather

CHAPTER THIRTY-FIVE
STEALING FROM THE FUTURE

Ree had never known what it was like to practice the Craft, but she wondered if this was like it. This reverent feeling as she followed her mother's instructions, gently snicking the ties between the skin and the flesh, separating hide and feathers from fat and muscles.

'Keep it whole,' her mother warned. 'It won't do much good if you slice it full of holes.'

Her mother had been a hunter's daughter, long ago. Before Tombtown, before even Ree's father. She'd told Ree of it once, when she was a little girl. Of the feeling of goose feather fletching scratching her cheek, and hot, sticky flesh under her hands, and blood soaking the ground black. She hadn't known Morrin then, but she'd felt her priestess all the same, thanking nature itself for the life it provided that she might use its death.

Ree could see how her mother found this holy. Her hands found every part of the body, peeling away strings of fat, weighing the organs in her palm. The heart, as small and weighted as a lead pellet, she could just pinch between her fingers, and feel the strength that had been there once.

Smythe hovered anxiously as she worked, and she could practically see him biting his tongue every time her hand wavered, every time the tip of the small, curved knife threatened to puncture the skin. But he held himself in check; she wondered if he knew how important this was to her, how deeply she felt the quiet in her bones.

'Then we stretch it and dry it,' said her mother. 'Careful of the feathers.'

Ree picked up the skin, so loose and limp in her hands, the feathers like silk against her fingertips. Under her mother's instruction, they stretched and pegged the skin, careful not to stretch it far enough to dislodge the feathers. As she worked, Ree sang an incantation from the book written by Wylandriah herself. She could feel the power rising in her chest and curling around her tongue. As she passed her hand over the skin, the feathers straightened and steadied, cohering to the skin. An answering prickle ran across her arms and down her spine.

That would speed the drying process, but it would still be maybe eight hours before the skin was ready for the next stage. Ree looked around at her family home, now caked in blood and scattered eviscera, as it was before her father had been elected to the council and given access to his own workshop in the town. 'I need to stay with it,' she said, looking up at her mother. 'Is that all right?'

Her mother looked down at her, her eyes dark through her priestess paint, her hair a wiry storm cloud about her head. 'I'll tend the chapel. And I don't think your father will be back for some time. Morrin's eye upon your work; her hand in your success.'

'My heart in her hand,' Ree replied, finishing the blessing. Her mother straightened; her priestess' robes were splattered with gore, making her look as if she'd been savaged by some wild animal, but her poise was such that she appeared more like a queen in royal garb. She inclined her head to Ree, and swept from the house, gently clicking the door closed behind her.

'And now we wait,' Smythe said. The sound of his voice, after so long of silence, made her heart leap in her chest.

'And now we wait,' she agreed.

The hours passed, slow and stiff. She sat with her legs crossed and her hands flat on her thighs. Smythe came and went from her side, but never left the room, often touching her shoulder in silent solidarity.

She wondered if he could see her anxiety in the ramrod straightness of her back or in the tight lines of her shoulders. She wondered if he knew how afraid she was that this wouldn't work. That after all they had done and all they had sacrificed, therianthropy was really dead and she would never become anyone of note.

Maybe her father had instilled more necromantic principals in her than he'd realised. Ree was very afraid of dying unknown and unremembered. She wanted to be immortal. She wanted at least for her name to be immortal.

She knew the very moment the skin was ready. She could feel it like a hook in her gut, pulling her toward it.

Smythe stirred sleepily as she rose. At some point, he'd fallen asleep, propped against the wall. Her movements were stiff, her muscles screaming protest at this sudden and awkward use, but she took the skin gently in her hands. Cold radiated from it, as icy and sharp as any necromancer's Craft.

She took it and smoothed it and oiled it in a special concoction her mother had helped her make, following the directions of her notes. She sang as she oiled it and sang more still as she sewed it tight using her own hair as thread. Though no song was required, she continued to hum as she painted the ancient runes on it as instructed in Wylandriah's guide, her hands trembling from such slow and deliberate strokes. Where her physical skills failed, her magic took up the slack, sealing and smoothing and stitching. She could feel it seeping out of her, like blood squeezed from a cut. It left her skin chill and her lungs icy and at times almost faint. But it was magic, *her* magic. And if this didn't work, it might be the only magic she ever did.

When it was done, she held in her hands a small hollow crow, as if it had been made of cloth and never stuffed. She looked up and met Smythe's eyes. He pushed his hair out of his eyes and looked a question at her.

She took a deep breath. If her notes were correct, this was all she needed. Therianthropy was a sister to the Craft, the art of reshaping death into a new form. Necromancy was a chant, but therianthropy was a song, and she had sung it as well as she knew.

The memory of her failed attempts still weighed on her. She didn't know if she could face that kind of disappointment now, after all that she had learned and all she had gone through.

But the skin felt *right* in her hands. Surely this time it would work.

She drew her magic around her, closing her eyes against the whirlpool that closed in and cocooned her. The crow skin in her hands fluttered and filled. All the energy in her body focused into a cold pool in her chest. She could sense Smythe hovering, feel the awe rolling off him.

The door crashed open. Ree lost concentration; her magic fell in tatters around her, splashing onto the floor and dispersing. She stared as Usther lowered her boot and stepped smoothly into the room.

'I just saw Emberlon leaving the archives.' Her eyes swept from Ree to Smythe, taking in the gore and mess of the room, to settle on the small bundle of hide and feathers in Ree's hands. She sniffed. 'Am I interrupting something?'

Ree stared at the skin in her hands, no longer filled with magic, just a limp stretch of hide and feathers. For a moment, she struggled with herself. The pool in her chest was gone, as was the sense of her entire self being concentrated into one tight place. She had been on the very cusp of shifting. Or failing.

But every minute wasted sent her closer to her death.

She drew a shuddering breath. 'Nothing that can't wait until our lives aren't in danger.'

They found Emberlon at his house. It didn't take long to convince him of the danger they were in once they showed him their marks, but it did take a little longer to explain how it had all come about.

'Time travel,' he murmured, sitting back in his lone rickety chair while he digested all they had told him. He looked thinner than usual — his dark skin under a thicker sheen of grey, his eyes and cheeks more hollow. Likely, he'd had a fight on his hands during his travels, but he didn't seem to feel the need to bring it up. 'In all my time here, you'd think I'd have seen it all by now, but this town never ceases to surprise me.'

'It's rather urgent that we get a look at this tablet so we can decide how best to defuse this curse,' said Smythe. His eyes had the wild shine they got when he was summoning — he really did think he would find a way out of it for them.

Emberlon gave Smythe a long look. 'I swore when I found it that I would put it away where nobody would find it.'

'But it might be the only chance we have of breaking the curse,' said Ree.

Emberlon sighed and folded his hands in his lap. 'Then it's good that I didn't destroy it, much as I wanted to.' He shook his head. 'The Old King. What kind of king would sacrifice his kingdom?'

Usther gave Emberlon a strange look. 'His kingdom died centuries ago.'

'The kingdom is the land, and all who live upon it. To steal from the future to feed the past is the worst thing a ruler could do.'

'And you know so much about it?' Usther's tone was sharp, an eyebrow raised.

Emberlon went very still. 'No,' he said at last. 'No, I know nothing about it at all.'

Ree lowered herself to the floor and crossed her legs. She'd seen Emberlon get like this from time to time. Small things would trigger him.

'*Best not to upset him,*' her mother had told her once. '*He left a lot behind, coming here. More than most. And the truth is, you can never completely leave the past behind. Not until Morrin claims you.*'

Ree had heard whispers that he'd been a king. It struck her as strange that she needed to petition the new king to save her from the old one.

'Will it take long to recover it, this tablet?' Smythe's voice was strained.

Emberlon blinked and shook his head. 'No. Not long at all.' He stood up from his chair in one smooth motion. Ree was struck again by how Emberlon always managed to look so tired and yet stand so straight. He walked to the sarcophagus in the centre of the room, which he kept meticulously clean and uncluttered, and which he always complained at Ree for sitting on. She thought, for a moment, that he was going to push aside the heavy stone lid, that he'd been storing all the dangerous spells and rituals there all along, but he knelt at one side and eased aside a section of the stone base. He slipped his fingers in and pulled out something wide and flat, wrapped in old linen, then restored the base.

'Never far from my sight,' he said. Smythe's hands twitched out to accept the tablet, but Emberlon placed it in Ree's hands.

If they hate you, they will hurt you. If they fear you, they will flee from you.

~Tombtown proverb

CHAPTER THIRTY-SIX
A FATED DEATH

Ree brushed aside the linen wrappings, letting them hang rough across her hands. She stared down at the gleaming tablet now revealed. Heavy in her hands and gleaming in her sight. The Great Resurrection was a ritual engraved on a slate of pure gold, as if it were treasure or a trinket to display in some adventurer's grand hall.

Smythe and Usther crowded her on either side.

'The *Great* Resurrection.' Ree could practically hear Usther wrinkling her nose. 'Rather presumptuous, considering nobody has ever been resurrected.'

Ree bit her lip. 'Until recently, we thought nobody had ever traveled in time, and that therianthopy was only a legend.'

Usther sniffed but had no answer to that.

The tablet didn't *feel* evil or powerful. It didn't have the musky character of a book, which Veritas claimed had tangible souls. It felt like cold metal, weighty but dead.

'Let's set it down and look at it properly,' said Smythe. 'Your arms must be getting tired.'

Ree flashed him an annoyed look. She was an archivist; she'd carried plenty of heavier things than this, and more awkward too. But he didn't seem to mean anything by it, so she sat down and placed the tablet carefully on the floor.

For a moment, they all crowded around it on hands and knees. Emberlon stood in the corner, his eyes sad.

'This is older than Old Antherian,' Usther said. There was a crease between her brows, like she wasn't quite sure what she was looking at. 'I can read some of it —'

'I can read the first two lines —' Smythe cut in eagerly.

'It's Ancient Antherian,' said Ree calmly. She felt a weight in her chest. 'And I can read nearly all of it.' She looked up and met Emberlon's bleak grey stare. 'It's not good,' she said.

Smythe tapped his lips. 'An exchange of equal parts,' he said, running his hand along one of the lines.

Usther's gaze flicked at Ree, then back down at the tablet. 'A rift ... or maybe portal must be opened.'

Smythe, 'And there's a line at the end that reads —' he stopped and paled.

'And so let it be done.' Ree's words echoed around the stone tombhome. Wordlessly, she extended her arm and bared the mark carved there in flesh and blood.

'It's a sacrifice ritual,' she said. 'I can't translate the cadence properly, but it amounts to: "To raise one city, the other must be cast down. Cut a rift through the eighth plane and scry in a bowl of golden oil. The reagents are crysstone, blood, and fire. A hexapentath around the rift. Those spared must be marked on their brow with the same hexapentath. And the rift will pull inward that which lives, and push outward that which once lived, and that which once was will be restored, and that which is will be dust." The last two lines are the incantation. And then —-'

'And so let it be done,' Smythe said quietly.

'It would sacrifice the entire town,' Usther said. Her lip curled. 'And likely would fail in the attempt.'

'A dangerous ritual to have in the wrong hands,' said Ree quietly.

Emberlon spoke from the corner: 'Or any hands.'

Smythe had been following her hands as she translated, his eyebrows pinched together. 'And that which once was will be restored, and that which lives now will be dust,' he murmured.

Ree sat back and rubbed her hand on her chest. 'Still think this will be easy to circumvent?' Ree asked. She knew the bitterness in her voice was unfair — none of this was Smythe's fault — but she couldn't stop herself from doing it. Her chest was growing tight and her head faint.

'I know it looks bad.' Smythe spoke quietly, deliberately, with none of his usual quaver. 'But I remain optimistic. One way or another, we will deal with this.'

But Ree felt sick. 'We don't even have a proper translation,' she said bitterly. 'It's a language that was spoken hundreds of years before even the version of Antherian most of the Craft uses. A translation from me is worthless if we're looking for loopholes.'

Smythe shrugged. 'We have to try.'

Ree shook her head and scooted back into a corner. She huddled there, drawing her knees to her chest. It was not a time to be exposed, when she felt already that the universe had looked down at her and found her wanting.

Death, her mother had told her many times, was not to be feared. It was a transition, a lateral move between planes that necromancers merrily played between every day. But nothing changed the fact that death was final, nor that Ree had no idea what the deathly planes would be like. She closed her eyes against the sting of tears and wished she had managed to fly.

The crow skin was in a pouch hanging from her belt, folded with magic and careful fingers. Though the skin itself weighed less than a bird, it still felt heavy against her leg.

The day passed Ree by in a dull stupor. Usther and Smythe argued semantics of the translation and Emberlon brought them books in Ancient Antherian to test their translation against. Usther thought the key to finding a loophole in the Oath was in the ritual itself but Smythe insisted it was in the Oath.

'Intention matters,' he argued, as if it would make any difference at all. 'If we attempt the ritual — even if we don't complete it — it should prevent the full consequence of a broken Oath.'

But the conversation moved in circles, and every time Usther tried to clarify the translation, Smythe dismissed it, and every time Smythe suggested they start the ritual just to see what happened, Emberlon stepped in and said he couldn't allow it.

She wasn't sure how long she stayed like that, huddled in the corner while her friends argued against a fate impossible to prevent. But at some point, she felt a touch at her shoulder and blinked with bleary eyes up at Smythe. 'It's going to be okay,' he said quietly. Usther was nodding over a spread of open books; Emberlon slept flat and peaceful on his back, the tablet hugged to his chest.

'How can it?' She croaked the words. It was hard to keep her eyes open. 'Veritas said the Oath never takes more than seven days to resolve. We've already used almost six of them, and we're no closer to a solution.' Her eyelids fluttered. 'I want to go to the tower again, tomorrow.' Her words were breathy and slurred now with tiredness. 'I want to shift, just once. I want to be a mage.'

'Don't worry,' said Smythe. 'You will.'

The last thing Ree remembered was the sight of Smythe's dark eyes behind his glasses, and the curl of his hair, and the feel of his thumb sweeping across her palm. When sleep took her, she dreamed of the wind rippling across her feathers.

PLAY NICE

~Morrin the Undying, at the foundation of Tombtown

CHAPTER THIRTY-SEVEN

WHAT ONCE WAS

Ree awoke in fits and starts. First, she became aware of her shoulder and hip pressing against hard stone. Then her fingers twitched in the still air; her eyes fluttered against a crust of rheum and dried tears.

When she dragged herself upright and blinked blearily around at Emberlon's house, it took her a moment to place herself. She could see Usther curled around a pile of books and Emberlon flat on the floor.

She felt sick, though she didn't know why. There was a squirmy, roiling feeling in her stomach, as if she had swallowed a handful of worms.

The Oath on her arm burned as if on fire. It bled sluggishly, the wound reopened somehow in her sleep.

She rubbed the crust from her eyes, her gaze seeking Smythe. He was not here, in the main room, nor in the little side room where Emberlon slept.

She crept over to Emberlon and knelt beside him. 'Emberlon?'

Emberlon's eyelids fluttered. She touched his shoulder with one finger, then quickly withdrew. 'Emberlon?'

'Mm?' He blinked at her, then sat bolt upright. 'The tablet?' He felt around beside and under himself. 'I'm sure I had it when I dozed off.'

The squirmy feeling grew worse. Ree tried to play it off. 'I'm sure it's around here somewhere — perhaps Smythe put it back beneath the sarcophagus.'

Emberlon nodded. His eyes drifted up to her forehead. Ree touched it self-consciously; her fingertips away with black paint.

'Emberlon.' Her voice was tight. 'What's on my face?'

He still looked oddly bleary with sleep — unusual for him. 'A spell diagram. A hexapentath, maybe.'

Her stomach dropped. 'I have to go —'

'But the tablet —'

'I'll bring it back if I find it!' she called over her shoulder.

As she got out the door, a rumble shook the town. Dust shook free of the domed ceiling; a rock came loose and smashed onto the roof of a tombhome. She tripped into a tombhome wall as the ground rippled beneath her. Where once there had been faded, mud caked stone, there was now shiny slate paving.

'And that which once was will be restored,' Ree whispered. 'And that which lives now will be dust.'

Another rumble, a thunder of shifting stone. People were out in the streets now, shouting orders to their minions. A spectre glided straight through Ree, stealing her breath; a greywraith, all clammy hands and tattered robes, flew overhead.

Worse, everyone seemed to be ... fuzzy. Their edges bled into the air and their shadows shivered in their wake. She could feel the icy magic in the air like an oncoming blizzard. Her breath clouded in front of her; her skin felt sharp and hard as if rubbed with ice. But whatever was sucking and pulling at her neighbours did not trouble Ree. She was solid and wholly present. The paint mark on her forehead itched: the sigil of exclusion defined in the ritual.

She ran through the town square as the world shivered around her. She passed Mazerin the Bold clinging to his knuckle bone stall, his face pale and blurry; she passed Mortana and Kylath outside the Bone & Brew, using greywraiths to shore up the walls. Symphona lay across a doorstep, her breathing laboured, her usually carefully coiffed hair hanging limp and tangled around her shoulders.

Ree climbed over a collapsed beam, a heap of wood and stone, and nearly tripped over a minion's corpse, its connection to its master cut loose. Ree's heart seized as she saw Andomerys there, her hand aglow as she tried to heal Etherea's crushed leg.

Every step, she passed someone in need of help, and her heart stuttered every time, trying to pull her back, telling her to stop. But she knew where this magic had to be coming from and she knew there could only be one way of stopping it. It was surely only a matter of minutes before the rest of the town realised it as well.

She made it to the town hall just as a loud crack echoed overhead. On instinct, she dived aside as a hunk of rock plunged through the ground where she'd been standing. Panting, she gazed up at the black iron doors, now shining as if recently polished, the long-faded engravings brought into sharp relief.

She pushed, muscles heaving, and as the gap widened an icy wind whistled through, nearly knocking her to the ground. Green light flared, nearly blinding her. She shaded her eyes and ran low to the ground, slipping between the doors and ducking to the side of the archway.

As her darksight faded, she was able to take in the room. Smythe stood at the top of the dais. The sarcophagus of the Old King was gone, and in its place was a swirling green portal that sunk into the floor.

And so let it be done.

~the final words of the Black Oath ritual

CHAPTER THIRTY-EIGHT

A WORTHY SACRIFICE

The cold was overwhelming. Frost rimed Ree's hair and weighed the cloth of her robes. She watched Smythe standing above the portal, arms rising as he chanted. His curly hair was blown back by the force of the wind, swirling behind him like tentacles. His glasses shone. A long cut on his forearm bled angrily, beads lifting off into the air.

'Smythe!' She screamed his name but her voice was swallowed by the wind. Ice scalded her throat.

She dropped to the ground and used fallen debris as cover from the wind, but there would be no shelter on the stairs. She crawled up them, belly against the steps, muscles protesting every movement.

As she climbed, curses flew overhead. She looked back and saw denizens flooding through the black iron doors, some of them on their knees, others leaning on their staffs and minions for support. She saw her father, his eyes black with fury, his colours bleeding into the wind.

The curses shattered against a wall of screaming red spirits, all wrapped up in the wind. It was summoning like she'd never seen it. Smythe's eyes were more sunken than the Lich. Black veins crawled beneath his skin. He looked wholly alien from the boy in the crypt she'd found all those weeks ago. There was nothing bright or hesitant about him, no shine in his eyes, no quirk to his lips. But he couldn't mean to finish the ritual — he couldn't mean to kill the world Ree loved. This had to be about breaking the Oath. Hadn't he suggested just *starting* the ritual? Hadn't he insisted that intention would decide the severity of their punishment?

When she got to the dais, her hands touched the fringes of the green light, and suddenly the cold was gone. The roar was gone. The wind no longer dragged at her hair or chafed her skin.

'You can't do this,' she said across the silence. She got unsteadily to her feet, half-braced for the wind to sweep her away, but everything here was calm and still.

'Ree.' Smythe lowered his arms, but the storm still raged outside their small circle. 'I have no choice. The Oath will kill you for sure otherwise.' His eyes were blacked-out with the Craft and sunken into his face. He would never been mistaken for an upworlder now. He looked like an undead creature.

Ree eyed him uncertainly. He radiated power and was easily holding down a ritual on a grander scale than any she had ever seen. It was said that the Craft could turn your mind — that the constant contact with the deathly planes could make you something less than human. She'd always been wary of that — wary of Usther, when her voice took on the death echo, wary of her father, when he came home with grey skin and dead eyes. They were mad, in those moments. And none of them had ever held a power as great as Smythe wielded now.

'You said you didn't need to complete the ritual. You said just starting it would be enough.'

'Maybe it would be! But we can't take that chance, Ree.' He skirted the portal, his hands splayed. 'There's no other option.'

As he stepped toward her, Ree widened her stance. Her fingers slipped into the skin pouch, brushing the silken feathers.

'Besides — you saw it! You saw what it was like!' His eyes gleamed, as if lit from within by an arcane light. 'Can you imagine what it would be like to bring that back? Can you imagine what we would *learn*, what we could study!'

All at once, Ree remembered every time Smythe had spoken disparagingly of the scholars at his University — how they'd dismissed and belittled him. It was why he'd come to the crypt in the first place — to *make* them respect him.

'The past is *dead*, Smythe! We can't bring it back. We *shouldn't* bring it back! Not just so you can impress the Dean of your festering University!'

Smythe's mouth flattened. 'I *can* bring it back, Ree.' The death echo was back in his voice as he gathered the magic. 'And I'll do it save you.'

Ree's heart ached in her chest. 'I don't want this! I love this town, Smythe! This is my *family,* these are my *neighbours.*'

In two quick steps, he was in front of her. His hands hovered at her shoulders, his eyes, so alien and yet so familiar, gazed deep into hers. 'Greatness requires sacrifice,' he murmured. Something flashed in his eyes, a pinch of his eyebrows, a spark of vulnerability that Ree knew too well. 'I won't let you be one.' He shoved her, hard; Ree was thrown out of the circle to tumble down the stairs, the roar of the wind and the cacophony of curses crashing down on her as she tucked her head and tried to find footing.

The world was spinning chaos. She braced herself and her feet finally caught on a step midway up the stairs. She clung there a moment, fighting the wind.

'SMYTHE!' She screamed his name, but her voice was swallowed in the noise of the storm.

The denizens had tried. The stairs were thick with practitioners. Kylath lay a few steps down, her cheek pressed to a step. Tarantur sat up, his eyes hazy, among the corpses of three minions. She could see her father cradling her mother's limp form at the base of the steps.

Ree spotted black lace; she hurried to Usther's side. The older girl was collapsed in a half-crawl, panting, her eyes burning with determination even as the wind leeched the vitality from her. No minions supported her.

She looked up at Ree's touch and tried to say something, but her words were snatched by the wind. Ree thought she was saying, 'I'll kill him myself,' but the effort of it seemed to have drained the last of the rage that sustained her. She closed her eyes. Ree hugged her close; her body was like ice. Downstairs, she could see her father trying to get her mother out of the room, but he could barely stand himself.

Everyone that had ever mattered to Ree was dying in this room, or just beyond it in the streets. Ree's eyes burned at the unfairness of it all. She *loved* this town. Even when it hated her. Even when it tried to change her. This was *her* world. Nobody got to decide for her that she was worth more.

She turned her eyes to the dais, where the portal was growing, the green light spreading and spilling down the steps.

Then all the sound cut out. Her gaze swung to the black iron doors. The Lich glided in, faster than she had known it could move, its robes as gleaming and whole as they had been in the past. Larry followed it, still dead-eyed and awkward-limbed, but fleet now, animated by a greater power. They breezed past the denizens, past Ree where she cradled Usther against her chest, unfettered by the wind or by the orb of angry souls encasing the portal.

As the Lich crested the dais, magic gathered in its withered palms. It whipped a long tail of black energy at Smythe; Smythe twitched his hand and a spirit leapt from the portal to absorb the brunt of it. Larry stood at the edge of the portal, swaying, blackened teeth bared. A red light was in his eyes.

Smythe called more spirits from the portal, and more, a flood of screaming souls. They crashed into the Lich again and again in wave after wave of spirit fury. That he had the power to give them substance was boggling: a soul *needed* a body to have form. The Lich staggered back, then flung a dart of red light at Smythe's chest. Smythe tried to block it, but too slowly; it broke across his chest. His eyes went wide.

Ree laid Usther aside and hurried back up the steps, screaming unheard into the wind. She barely knew why she was running, whether it was to stop Smythe or to save him, but she couldn't watch him sway there, stunned, as if about to collapse. The Lich gathered red, steaming energy in its palms, but there were still too many steps between Ree and the dais.

Smythe's knees buckled. He swayed there a moment, just on the edge of consciousness. How he had resisted a direct curse from the Lich, Ree didn't know. The Lich drew its hands back, focusing its energy into another spear.

And Smythe flew forwards, arms outstretched, as all the wind and spirits suddenly tightened around the Lich in a spinning cocoon, tighter, tighter, suffocating its magic and then *squeezing*. Smythe lifted his hands and the spirits rejoined the whirling orb around the dais. The Lich hung frozen a moment, then crumbled into dust in the wind. A faint shade of red hovered in the air where it had been, then was sucked into Smythe's mouth.

Ree kept climbing, though her lungs felt withered and dry. The Lich was the most powerful necromancer in living memory. And Smythe had killed it.

How could anyone possibly stop someone with that kind of power?

As she crested the dais and into the eerie silence, Smythe shook his head at her. 'It's almost done.' His voice held a tinge of regret.

And then, almost in slow motion, Larry appeared behind him. The red light was gone from his eyes, but his teeth were bared in a feral snarl and his hands hooked into claws.

Ree barely had time to shout before Larry wrapped his arms around Smythe and tipped him, screaming, into the portal.

Ree's fingertips found feathers as she screamed the song; in a blur of wings and magic she was across the dais. The portal was closing even as Smythe disappeared below the surface, and then wingtips became hands and her arms wrapped around Larry's torso, and she was heaving with all her strength but it wasn't enough.

The portal closed with a crack of thunder and a pulse of energy. Ree rolled across the floor, her hands empty. Tears burned in her eyes. She choked, her lungs suddenly too thin to draw breath. She rolled onto hands and knees, her eyes sweeping the dais. The portal was gone, and in its place, the golden tablet lay small and steaming. The wind died. The spirits vanished. But her eyes snagged on the limp form of Wandering Larry, blown to the other side of the dais.

Ree scrambled over to him, turning his shoulders. 'Larry ...?'

He groaned and rolled aside, revealing a very rumpled scholar with glasses askew beneath him.

Ree's chest seized. The black veins were fading from his face and he was slowly returning to his normal colour. She reached for his face with trembling hands. He was utterly and completely still.

'Smythe ...' His name was barely more than a breath.

His eyelids twitched.

Hope lodged in her heart, jagged and hot. Her thumb swept across his icy cheekbone. She started to say something more when her arm caught fire. She screamed and fell back, clutching her arm to her chest as shadows streamed from the Oath's mark on her arm. It crawled under her skin, a pain more intimate than fire as her body seized and jerked, as if she could buck her way free of it. Dimly, she was aware of Smythe writhing beside her. The Oath had come to claim their lives in punishment for failing the ritual.

It was burning her away, she knew. Not her body, but her soul. The stuff that animated her, the life she would have had. And though she'd never wanted the ritual to work, never wanted to trade the lives of her neighbours for her own, she felt regret like ice beneath the consuming fire.

And then, like snapping thread, it ended. Ree gasped and lurched upright, rubbing her chest. The mark on her arm was healed, no longer a wound but a ropey white scar. *And so let it be done.* Her skin was greyer than she'd ever seen it. Across from her, Smythe stirred. His mark mirrored hers, his skin just as grey and strange, though fading even as she watched him.

Ree scrambled over to him on hands and knees, her entire body aching like she'd been pummelled with bricks. They reached for each other at the same time.

'We're not dead.' Smythe's eyes roved her face. His hands gripped hers tightly.

'We're not dead,' Ree agreed, and she didn't try to stop the smile that rose, warm and bubbling, to her lips. In spite of everything. In spite of Smythe. They were here and whole and everybody was alive.

Smythe reached a tentative hand to her face, tucking a strand of hair behind her ear. The brush of his touch made her shiver, but not unpleasantly.

Beside them, Larry dragged himself to his feet, gargling furiously. The movement broke Ree's daze. Worry and anger warred in her. 'Smythe,' she whispered, her eyes wide. His hand still hovered at the side of her face. 'That was wrong. That was so wrong.'

Shouts from below. Ree got up and ran to the stairs; denizens picked themselves off the ground and climbed to the dais. She spun and met Smythe's eyes. 'You have to *leave.'* The words came out forceful, rough with fear.

Smythe blinked, as if freed from a mind snare. He ran his tongue over cracked lips. 'I can explain —'

Ree's father charged up the stairs, Tarantur just behind him. Ree shoved Smythe to the other side of the dais. '*Run!*'

They looked at each other, and a thought hung suspended between them. Once, she would have run with him. Then Smythe disappeared over the other side of the dais.

Larry howled and lurched after him, but Ree remained rooted to the spot. She re-pinned her hood to her hair and flicked away the melting frost still rimed on the front of her robes. She wiped the flaking paint from her forehead, drew a shuddering breath, and turned to face her neighbours. 'He's gone,' she said as they charged toward her, curses in hand. Her voice was heavy with tiredness, a tiredness she felt deep in her bones. The ritual really had taken something from her. She felt simultaneously stretched thin and pressed under a weight, as if she would either snap or be crushed at any moment.

Her father's eyes were burning. He opened his mouth to demand something of her, but she raised a hand to silence him. 'He's gone,' she said again. She closed her eyes. 'Just let it go. Can we all just let it go?'

EPILOGUE

A warm breeze ruffled Ree's hair. She stood, wringing her hands, at the top of the observatory tower. She loved it out here, where the mountains touched the sky, but there was an absence about it now. 'Are you ready?' Her eyes nervously roved the gathered watchers, all blinking and squinting in the unfamiliar sunlight.

'Why would *we* have to be ready?' asked Ree's father. He held his staff with both hands and stood straight-backed and open-eyed in defiance of the sunlight. Every now and then his eyes twitched.

'Festering rats, this sunlight is *disgusting.*' Usther clutched her head with both hands. 'Urghh, I think I'm going to be sick.'

'I don't know about that,' said Ree's mother. She was wearing robes that had once been white and were now more of a cream, a special outfit in honour of the occasion. 'I don't regret the life Morrin has given me, but I do miss the sun at times.'

Andomerys heaved a long, frustrated sigh. 'Are you going to do the thing or not?'

'We're ready,' said Emberlon. He nodded in a way that was almost a bow.

There was definitely an absence. A hole in the conversation for an excitable word of encouragement, for something that would make everyone groan. Ree wondered when she would get used to it.

She lifted the crow skin from her pouch, letting it unfold across her palms. As she gathered her power about her, her eyes met each of her friends and family in turn. It had never been easy with any of them — would never *be* easy — but each of them had been a part of her journey. Become part of who she was.

The skin fluttered in her hands, filling with magic. She closed her eyes as she drew herself into a calm pool of magic and poured into the skin.

She opened her eyes and beat her wings. Her watchers were stunned — all but Usther, who put her hands to her mouth and whooped. Ree cawed a laugh and climbed up into the sky, each beat of her wings lifting her up, up. As she spread her feathers, she caught an updraft of air and spiralled higher, her gaze sweeping the ground below as her family pointed and cheered. She climbed and swooped and climbed again, then circled down and flew between the watchers, tweaking Usther's hair with her beak as she went.

She felt ... powerful. Like she'd always wanted to feel. She'd finally done what she'd always said she would, what everyone had told her was impossible. She was a true mage, and on a path she had chosen for herself. But more than that, she felt ... free.

Free, but not whole.

The failed Oath had taken much from her. Smythe was gone, and so, if the council was to be believed, was half her soul. Half a soul for half a curse. Andomerys had not yet found a way to put it back.

She cawed again and climbed high with three sweeps of her wings, only to plunge back down through the tower. She cupped her wings and took off along the roof of the passage, flying over the town with its shiny new cobbles and hive of minions working to rebuild, flying past the secret library where Usther had become a teacher.

She winged over the reaching hands of hungry undead and sailed past a skeleton sentinel that followed her progress with the creak of turning bones. She circled an embalming room with shattered jars and an overturned table, and with a strong beat soared down the long lonely tunnels where the Lich had once held sway.

She swooped low through the door into the library where she'd found her magic, only to land heavily atop a shelf, panting.

There was a boy in the crypt.

'No, not — the other one, man, the other one! Don't tell me he didn't teach you to read, old chap, not after all the magic he poured into you.' Smythe pulled a book from Larry's hands and nudged him back across the room. The smile faded from his face as his eyes met hers.

'Is it you?' His voice was hoarse. He looked rooted to the spot, like he was afraid he would startle her. His eyes were sorrowful with hope. 'Are you her?'

Ree spread her wings. She stepped from the shelf in a swirl of robes and feathers. 'Hello, Smythe.'

ACKNOWLEDGEMENTS

This book has been a long time in the making, in part because it is a Russian doll stuffed with all the other books I wrote learning to write.

I would not have made it this far without the encouragement, support, and feedback of so many people. Writing is hard, but friends make it easier.

First to Joh, my partner and companion, who stays up late to talk through thorny plot problems, who loves my characters as much as I do, and who challenged me to write a story about necromancers when I was certain I had no more story concepts left in me. Thank you.

I owe a debt to Kaitlin, whose keen eyes miss nothing. Your critiques always struck to the bone, and you somehow understood exactly what I wanted this novel to be. Every writer needs someone like Kaitlin reading their books.

Hannah Jones, you were the first cheerleader of this book back in its ungainly foal state. When I might have given up on this story, your words kept me going. There would never have been a BOOKS & BONE without your encouragement in the early days of TOMBTOWN.

Thank you to my beta readers Caroline Barnard-Smith and Angelica Fyfe, two savvy commenters who knew exactly when to praise and when to pick. You and Kaitlin all put up with my inconsistency and craziness as I tried to get a final draft together, and I'm so glad you did.

Thanks also to my family, who have encouraged me in the ridiculous endeavour of novel writing for so many years, who endured a complete cessation of contact every November as I willingly drowned myself in NaNoWriMo, and who I'm delighted can finally see my name in print.

Thank you to my Kickstarter supporters, who made publishing a reality and not just a dream.

And thank you, reader. I can hardly believe that you exist, and I am so, so grateful that you picked up my book, and that you made it here to the end.

SPECIAL THANKS

I could not have afforded to publish BOOKS & BONE without the support of these fine people, as well as many others. You heard my plea and you answered with messages of encouragement and pledges to fund.

So, without further ado and in no particular order, thank you to:

Eloísa Valdes, Jake, Doug, Twang Darkly, Lily ❀ V, Holly J, Sam R, Emma Maree Urquhart, J Tordiff, Scott V A Hunter, Rowan Sherwin, Dagmar Baumann, Jamie Bradway, Jasmine Lea Scanlon, Jack Corus, and Jonathon Miller.

Thanks also to The Selkie Delegation, Alex, Queen of Spoons, Paul Woolcock, Alyssa Alford, Caleb Karth, Jhaydun Dinan, Brian D Lambert, Heather Landon, Chimerae, D Moonfire, Corvus Robotica, and Nentuaby.

Thanks to Shelly Leonard, Robin Hill, @tayatrancends, Andrew Wooldridge, June Taylor, Krysta Banco, Michelle Yeargin, Unconventional Emma, Dzmitry Kushnarou, Paco Hope, and Sambience.

Thanks also to Algot Runeman, Kaitlyn Quach, Rob & Jenny Haines, Jade L Johnson, Alex Claman, Tessara Ahlin, Lyn Thorne-Alder, Mr Lee Phelan, Paige Kimble, Robin Sturgeon Abess, Sebastian Müller, and Mira Strengell.

And thanks to Justin Myers, Luke Challen, Sario, Victoria Johnsen, Kynerae, Elgen, Kat Armstrong, Toby Rodgers, Katre, Allison L, Hilary Hennell, Rev Ali Boulton, Neil Boulton, and Rebecca Fyfe & Robert Fyfe.

ABOUT THE AUTHOR

Veo Corva writes things and reads things and reads things out loud, and sometimes they get paid for that, which is nice because it means they can feed their cat.

They live in Wiltshire with their partner and their furry familiar and as many books as they could fit in their small flat.

They are anxious and autistic and doing just fine.

To find out more about them and read more of their work, visit https://veocorva.xyz

SIGN UP FOR PUBLISHING UPDATES!

If you'd like to receive an email every time a new Veo Corva book is announced or published, you can sign up to their newsletter here: https://tinyletter.com/witchkeyfiction

No spam, no extraneous updates; just letting you know when a new book is available.

Lightning Source UK Ltd.
Milton Keynes UK
UKHW011401150722
405908UK00002B/601